REcoil

Book Three of the "Rain Experience" Series

Thomas W. Everson

This is a work of fiction which takes place on another world. Names, characters, businesses, places, events, and incidents are the products of the author's imagination or used in a fictitious manner. Any resemblance to real persons, living or dead, is purely coincidental.

DEDICATION

My wife, Brandi, and my son, Thomas (Bubby), are my heart. They have come to know the life of an author can be hectic and crazy, and they accompany me to everything they can anyway.

CONTENTS

ACKNOWLEDGMENTS

I would like to thank fellow authors T.M. Franklin (The More Trilogy) and Elizabeth Guizzetti (Other Systems; The Light Side of the Moon) for allowing me to pick their brains for information, and for giving me some amazing opportunities to stand alongside them as we all pursue our dreams.

As usual my cover artist, Jake Murray, and my editor, Dean Fetzer get extreme kudos for their absolutely amazing work. On top of being great at what they do, they've had a big hand in bringing The Rain Experience into reality.

And my readers: Thank you for reading. To share this labor of love with people is really what it's all about. I do this for me, and for you.

1 EXPEDITION

Ami is beyond excited. The look of glee in her eyes is intoxicating.

"Looking for him is fine. But if we all agree this is the right era, we should discuss stopping the vortex here," Evalyn tells her.

"Auntie, in case the attempt fails, I want my father with us." Ami looks back. "I think right now finding him is important."

If there is a time we are supposed to stop in, it's here. I hope one of the artifacts will be able to help us.

Ami grips my hand firmly.

"Based on the development, we may be very close to when we were taken. We were here once after we left. Mother said she looked, but couldn't find him. I want to start right away!"

She runs inside, giving me no time to respond. Agatha comes and places her hand on my shoulder, and I smile weakly at her. I recall her description of his disconnection, but I know Ami won't be dissuaded.

"This is definitely several years after we left." Agatha's solemn whispering tickles my ear. "I didn't tell her so I could save her the disappointment."

"It's what I would have done. But she's going to try."

"I hope for her sake that seeing her will snap him back to reality. If he doesn't, if he can't be helped, she'll need you more than ever." She squeezes my shoulder a little.

"Rain, think smart. Let's not make finding the artifacts second." Evalyn takes over Agatha's body again. "If you want any hope of staying put in one place, now's the time."

"Don't worry, we'll look for them, but I need to help Ami first."

There's a sour look on her face, but before she can speak again Emma breaks my attention away.

"Can I help?" she asks.

I ruffle her hair affectionately. "Maybe later, but it's probably best if it was just Ami and me for now."

"I'm not letting you wander off with her alone." Eve retorts.

With a serious glance in her direction, I shake my head. "It's a lot to ask of you, but it's important that right now it *just* be me and her."

Eve huffs and crosses her arms, unhappy with my decision. Still, I am confident she will respect it. They stay in the yard as I head inside to find Ami. She's not in the kitchen. A loud rustling from the hallway directs me. The hall is empty, and the noise is now coming from Ami's room. At her door frame, I lean against the wood and watch her pack a bag.

I knock lightly and enter. Her face gleams with a brightness different than I've seen before. It's hope. She hurries around while I take a seat on her bed. Usually she's tidy, but now because of her fervor she's haphazardly throwing things in the bag. A spare change of clothes, a pouch full of gold coins. She comes to an abrupt stop, and hugs my head into her chest. Her fingers weave through my hair and I wrap my arms around her waist.

"I'll find him and finally bring him home," she says cheerfully.

"And I will help you look every step of the way." I pull her down on my lap, and soften my voice. "But you have to be prepared in case he doesn't understand right away."

"I know." She's either oblivious or unaffected by a possible negative outcome.

"If we find him, I'll be happy for you."

"Thank you, Rain." She kisses me on the cheek.

"You have been here for me every time I've needed it. It's only fair if I do the same for you. I do wonder though with all the things we've been through, how did you survive without me?" I chuckle.

"To be honest, we never got put in those crazy situations before. Maybe you should stop getting into trouble." She pokes me in the chest, smiling from ear to ear again.

Am I a trouble maker? Or some weird catalyst which changed the dynamic of the time traveling? I'll have to ask Evalyn. She'll be brutally honest with me.

"Were we planning on leaving right away? We haven't eaten breakfast, and I'd like a shower." I lift my arm and sniff. I make a disgusted face in jest and she laughs.

"I was, but I suppose you're right. You take a shower, and I'll make breakfast."

Tapping on her thigh, I signal for her to stand. We both stretch, and I head to the door.

She taunts me as I'm about to leave. "You better look out though."

"Why?" I quirk an eyebrow.

"Because I'm going to tell Eve that you were in here, with me, and we had a 'moment'." She's being impish.

I look her straight in the eyes and cross my arms. "You wouldn't."

"Why wouldn't I?" She winks.

"If you tell her, she'll follow me around wanting an opportunity to do the same – and to antagonize you. We won't be able to head off alone." I flash her a wide grin.

"You know those two. They might follow anyway," she retorts. "Then I'll be out the satisfaction of gloating."

"You're terrible." I waggle my finger at her. "You're a troublemaker."

"Mmhmm!" She walks over to me, and leans in closely as if she's coming for a kiss. She whispers, and her breath bouncing off of my lips causes me to blush. "But when you and Aunt Evalyn break the vortex, we can finally reveal our love for each other."

I desperately want to kiss her right now, but I've become flustered and can't even manage to stammer out a few words. Instead, I smile and hastily retreat into the hallway to retrieve towels from the closet.

In the bathroom, it doesn't take long to adjust the temperature to my liking. As the warm water flows over my skin, I can't help but miss the efficiency of the Vraditi purification chamber. Though it's not the same, my muscles still relax. I wash and shave quickly so I can enjoy the warmth before it turns cold.

The steam makes a sauna of the bathroom, and the heat enters my lungs as I breathe deep. In the middle of exhaling I hear the knob jiggle on the hallway door. Figuring they'll realize the bathroom is in use, I think nothing of it, until it swings open, and a cool breeze gusts in. Someone slips in and they shut it swiftly and quietly.

"Hey, the door was locked for a reason. Get out!" I protest.

"Shh!" Eve whispers. "You know I can't see you."

"That's not the point." I look over my shoulder making sure the curtain is in place. "What do you need?"

"Alone time with you. Ami's too prudish to come in here while you're showering, and that makes it perfect for me." She's smiling. I can hear it in her tone.

"Fine. Since you're here, I'm going to ask you questions." I poke at the shower curtain.

"Sure, but I can answer it before you ask. Yes, I will let you marry me." She snickers.

"Why did you hunt me down in your time?" I ask. "You could have had the mountain."

She speaks softly right next to the curtain. "Could have? I did have the mountain. But I couldn't let you escape. My reputation was on the line, but more importantly I hadn't won you over. That had never happened to me before."

"Why do you have to be so aggressive?"

"In my era there was no opportunity to be shy. You either acted, or you missed your chance. A person could be taken or killed in a raid." She's calm, despite the subject. "It's just my culture."

"I see."

"If it wasn't for Ami, and your wish to wait until you've found a way to stop this crazy situation, I'd be much more aggressive, and would have bedded you by now." Her confidence is almost overwhelming.

"In your dreams." I chuckle.

"You know I'm too stubborn to stop, right?" she says. "I don't care that you love her. I'll win your heart eventually."

I shiver. The water has grown cold.

"What if I am unable to love you how you love me?" I ask.

She's silent, and because I can't see her I'm unable to tell what she might be thinking by her expression. Not wanting to freeze in the cold shower, I turn the water off. Eve moves to the door.

"I don't have that answer."

She's careful not to draw attention when she exits. Pulling the shower curtain open an inch, I peek to be sure it's safe. She's gone. I dress in my dirty clothes, and climb the stairs to my room, thinking of Eve.

The vortex's power isn't the only thing I might have to break this month. If we succeed I'll have to be completely honest with Eve. It will be difficult because it will hurt her, but at least she'll be free to move on.

Grow a backbone.

I ignore Tiberius's intrusion, change into fresh clothes, and bring my full dirty laundry basket down with me. Ami's in the kitchen, and she smiles at me over her shoulder. I return the smile and head outside. Agatha is doing laundry, scrubbing clothes against the washboard. When she sees me coming she too smiles. The good mood is infectious.

"Need help?" I ask.

"No, but I would like it if you stayed and talked for a minute."

Setting my basket down, I crouch next to it and watch. Her sunny personality beams even without her saying a word – her joy lightens my heart. Still, with this long pause I wonder what she has on her mind.

"I may not talk about Evalyn much, but she's been diligently searching for a way to break the power of the vortex," she says. "She really thinks there might be an answer in these artifacts."

"I know."

"I'm hesitant though. This has been my life for so long."

"Life will continue on in a new way. We'll be stationary and I'll have to hunt a little harder for adventure." I laugh. "But if we figure out how to do it, do you want to stay here?"

"I can think of worse times just recently I'd rather never see again," she says, laughing.

We both become silent for a minute while she scrubs.

"I'm glad to have you around the house." Her smile weakens. There's a deep sadness in her eyes.

I place my hand on her shoulder, anticipating she's thinking of her estranged husband, whom she might have the opportunity to see.

I suppose I can't blame her for being sad, and maybe nervous. But if I had an opportunity to see my father again after many years I'd be doing the same thing Ami is. I suppose I will have to live vicariously through her. Chances of landing in a time where I could see my parents alive is probably small and I wouldn't be able to tell them who I am.

Finished with washing and rinsing, Agatha stands and hangs clothes. Not giving her the chance to deny me again, I grab some and help. She elbows me playfully, and we continue on in silence until all of the garments are hung and drying. I dump the basin at the edge of the property, and return it to Agatha. She starts refilling it for the next load, nodding at me in silent thanks. I nod and return to the kitchen.

Ami is stirring chopped potatoes with slices of sausage in one pan, and scrambled eggs and cheese in another. She dishes me up a plate in a hurry and shoves it at me. She's excited.

"Thank you."

"Of course." She rubs my arm affectionately as I pass.

With a fork from the drawer, I sit at the table and eat. The first bite of potato is too hot. My tongue wrestles with it, trying not to touch it too much while I breathe heavily to cool it. Ami plops a glass of juice in front of me. I smile. I wash the bite down with a swig, and take better care on the next bite.

"Mother, breakfast is ready!" she yells out the door and then joins me at the table with her plate.

Ami and I are well into breakfast when the others join. The meal is nice and quiet, despite knowing Eve isn't happy about me going out with Ami alone.

Maybe I can convince Emma to babysit Eve. She would at least weigh her down.

I finish eating, and begin cleaning the kitchen before we leave. But when I turn on the sink there's a rumble deep underground. The pipes shudder, and there is a faint grinding sound coming from the other side of the house. The clear water turns murky brown.

"Aggy, there's a problem with the water." I cringe, my mind bringing up that this could have happened while I was in the shower.

She joins me at the sink, and I hear her sigh deeply. Turning it off, she grabs a towel and wipes her hands.

"I'll have to hire help to figure out what happened," Agatha says, annoyed. "It's a good thing we landed here."

I think out loud. "I bet it's due to the earthquakes from the tribal time."

"I'm going into the city. Rain, please work on emptying the well,"

Agatha requests.

Agatha heads into the living room for a moment, and returns with a purse. I follow her outside while she makes her way to the stable. Working together, we gear the horse up, and I help her onto him.

"Thank you."

"No need to thank me, Aggy. Just stay out of trouble." I pat the horse on the rear lightly to start him moving.

I head to the well, set on a task which draws me away from both of my actual goals while we're in this time.

It's one day. We still have about twenty-nine.

Ami's already there, pulling up a bucket. She doesn't have to dump it to see it's the same brown 'water' as in the pipes.

"The well is tainted too, hmm?" I frown.

"I guess finding him will have to wait." She sighs sadly.

I wrap my arms around her from behind and nuzzle her hair. "Don't worry. We'll still look for him once we have this under control."

She nods and hauls the bucket out to the woods. Knowing there are more buckets we could use, I head for the basement. Eve is still in the kitchen, with her feet propped up on the table, relaxing. Below, in the storage, I load my arms with the extra buckets. On my way back I tap on Eve's foot. She's not quick to stand, but she follows me through the living room.

"Emma!" I bellow.

She comes bounding down the stairs and leaps onto my back, nearly knocking me over. I grunt, struggling to stay upright. I'm overburdened. My steps are smaller, but I make it outside and to the well without falling on my face. I drop her off, and then the buckets. Eve lazily walks over.

"Here's the plan. We'll create a chain to empty the well out and dump the buckets at the edge of the woods," I tell them.

"This might take a while," Ami adds.

"What will we do for fresh water?" Emma asks.

"I'll go search for some," Eve says, trying to shirk work.

"No." I point at her. "Nice try."

She blows me a kiss, and I ignore it. We begin, and several buckets in my arms are starting to burn from turning the handle. I push hard to ignore it. Bucket after bucket, I hand to Emma while she carries it to Ami, and Ami to Eve. Eve dumps them near the trees, and returns them up the chain. In the first dozen buckets I'm able to stay ahead of them, but they quickly catch up. They have to wait longer the deeper the bucket has to go.

Ami's 'a while' ends up being hours. Finally I lower a bucket and feel it hit the bottom; the rope goes limp. When I pull it back up the bucket has mud in it, and muck on the side. I wipe the sweat from my brow and show them it's empty. With no water to drink now, I feel more parched than I probably am.

So much for my shower. I suppose I'll take it one step further and climb in the well and see if I can find the damage.

Climbing onto the edge of the well, I dangle my feet inside. The light allowed to seep by the roof reveals precarious stone steps.

"Ami, will you get me a lantern please?"

"Why?"

"I'm going in."

Before she leaves, our attention is caught by the sound of the horse whinnying on the other side of the house. Agatha appears in time to stop me from descending into the dark well. A man dressed in thick clothing, and an orange dome hat follows behind her.

"I hired a contract service. You can let the foreman and his crew do the work now," Agatha tells me while dismounting.

I step down, and instead of diving into a dark well, I bring the horse to the stable, unsaddle him, and put the gear away. He steps into the stall at my lead and I stroke his mane.

"How about Hubert?" I ask him. No answer.

"Hubert?" Emma startles me from behind.

"Yeah, I've been trying to figure out a name for the horse."

"I think he looks like a Maximus," she suggests.

"Sure. He looks like he could be a Maximus."

I grab the horse brush from the shed. While I'm brushing him, Emma watches me, and I watch Agatha with the foreman. I can't hear their conversation, but she is pointing at the well, and then points off to a location on the other side of the house. They pass by, and I catch part of the conversation.

"…septic tank was serviced?" he asks.

"Several years ago, but we had the largest available installed."

"We'll want to dig it up also, and make sure it, and the pipes are okay."

"That's fine…" their voices trail off as they move out of earshot.

Finished with brushing the horse, Emma takes the brush while I close the door to the stable. I'm filthy with sweat, but without being able to take a shower, my only option is to change. Inside I head upstairs for my third pair of clothes today. I inventory what I've accumulated since I've been here.

I have clothes hung in the closet, including two cloaks; my sword rests against the headboard; on the nightstand is my necklace and a handful of gold coins in a pouch.

For this being my home, I don't have much.

Perhaps it's because you're not intending on staying. We have a world to mold.

I don't need much, though — I'm well cared for. Maybe while Ami and I are out I'll pick up a painting to hang on the wall.

Why make it harder to move on?

I sit on the bed and lean against the wall, but it's uncomfortable. I lie back on my pillow with the intent of resting for a couple minutes.

~~~~~~

My body jolts and my heart beats rapidly, but I don't know why. I can't remember dreaming. It's dark outside, and I've slept longer than I wanted to.

Well that's disappointing. I bet I missed lunch and dinner.

A light rapping on my door catches my attention and I stumble in the dark to open it. Ami is there, only illuminated by light coming from downstairs. I wave her in. Nervous, she looks to her left before entering, I assume to make sure Eve doesn't catch her. With the door closed behind her, I turn on the light and rub my eyes with the hope it will help them adjust faster.

She's dressed in a deep red, hooded cloak. Her beautiful wavy brown hair flows down from under the hood. In her hands is a plate of creamy white pasta with mushrooms.

"I brought you dinner," she says while sitting on the bed, and crossing her legs.

"Thank you…you're dressed for travel – we're leaving after I eat aren't we?"

"Of course. Get to it!" she demands, and shoves the plate at me with a smile.

I sit and eat. It's a little salty, a sign Eve helped cook, but it's not as bad as previous foods she's had a hand in. Ami leans on me while I devour it. The food and her presence bring a sense of serenity.

When the pasta is nearly gone she jumps up, grabs my white cloak, and taps her foot impatiently. I stand, and she drapes it over me. My white compliments her red, but I feel our colors should be reversed because of our characters.

"You know, if it wasn't important, I'd be telling you 'no' right now." I set my plate on the bed, and put my hands on her waist.

"You can't tell me no." She bats her eyelashes.

We laugh.

She's right. I would do anything for her.

"Isn't there a rule that says you can't sneak into my room at night?" I jest.

She looks to the ceiling. "I don't know what you're talking about."

"Oh, I think you do." I pull her closer. "What would Eve think if she knew you were in here? Maybe we should ask her!"

Ami turns her head, giggles, and then scolds me. "Don't!"

"Maybe I can entice you to tell me if I offer an exchange? A kiss maybe?" I bring my face close to hers, barely an inch apart.

The giggles keep her from catching her breath, and her face turns red. Trying to stifle her laughter, she covers her face with one hand while pushing me away with the other. It takes a moment, but she finally calms enough to talk.

"I can't tell you. I'd be violating the core of the rules…'Don't tell Rain.'"

"Aren't you already?" I brush a lock of her hair out of the way.

"We should go." She pats my chest and pulls away.

We exit stealthily. The house is quiet. We avoid the creaky stairs, slip past the swinging door, and head out from the kitchen to the yard. We're undetected. In the distance is our destination, lit up by lights of all kinds. But they're duller than Emma's Chas.

Work has started in the yard. The garden is half dug up, and the clotheslines are moved, resting upright against the house. There are large, lifeless machines not too far off with big, toothy scoops for digging.

How did I sleep through whatever was happening out here?

She pulls her cloak hood up, and jogs toward the city line, avoiding the obstacles in the yard. To keep up I do the same, sprinting when there's nothing in between us but distance. I near, and match her strides.

"Mother may not have been able to find him, but today she had several ideas of where to start. We'll follow her advice." With the threat of detection gone, she speaks at a normal volume. "I'm going to bring him home. Hopefully he will be able to accept what happened."

"Suppose he doesn't want to, or maybe can't?" I ask with a little hesitation.

"It's a chance I have to take. I haven't seen him since I was a child, and I want to know him — and for him to know me." Her cheer sets me straight.

"What information do we have on Chas for this time?" I ask.

"It's dangerous. Before I was born my father had the house built toward the forest to avoid the growing crime in the inner city," she says while pulling back her cloak to reveal the bag she packed earlier. She retrieves a piece of paper.

"I'd have brought my sword if I had known." I frown at her, but she isn't paying attention.

She looks at the paper while we walk, but due to the poor lighting I'm unable to read it.

"What's that?"

"Street names, and the address to a place my father lived at previously." She stares at it while somehow managing to keep a good stride.

We reach the streets. Rumbles fill the air as unfamiliar vehicles make their way along the ground. They are many different shapes and sizes, and vary in the number of wheels on them. They're horseless carriages.

"What are those?" I point at them while they pass near us.

"They're 'motorized vehicles', but most people use the shortened term 'MV', or 'MVs' as plural. It's the primary mode of transportation in this time."

"This time? Don't you mean your time?" I put my hand on her shoulder to gain her attention.

She smiles. "I do. Hopefully you and Aunt Evalyn can fix it so we stay, instead of taking my father with us."

Heading along the road, the MVs stop and go at intersections. They create an orchestra of movement, governed by rules I know nothing about. They deftly avoid one another. It's a peculiar and complex system I'm not sure I want to try and understand at the moment.

I suppose I will have to learn eventually.

Staying here would certainly provide opportunities. Clean up Chas, fight the injustices. But then what? What happens when there's no more adventure to be had?

We move up. We make this city ours. You can't deny the feeling of wanting to be in control. If we had control we could make it the place you want.

It's hard to argue with Tiberius's thoughts. Becoming a leader would allow me to better the city for the people. It rings more true with knowing how it eventually flourishes leading to Emma's time.

It must start somewhere, right?

Right!

She leads along the street and turns inward. We wait at a corner until the MVs stop for us. Without fear of being hit, she crosses the road into a new area.

Chas is noisy. The MVs emit hums and rumbles. People walk around, laughing and talking in animated manners, engrossed in conversation. There's clatter in the distance. A loud bang resounds further on. Ami looks around, and I'm left to soak it all in. Compared to Chas's future incarnation, and even to the Vraditi ship, this seems noisier. A headache starts.

While she leads, I observe the buildings. Here they're nowhere near the size of future Chas. Only in the far distance do I see lights higher in the sky. But the layout is clearly the precursor to the bustling metropolis I know, with numerous streets and side roads in between businesses. Most of the well-traveled areas are lit, but the ones which aren't seem to have groups of seedy looking people loitering.

It doesn't take long to pass the businesses and enter a residential area. The homes are single story, and packed tightly together. She leads me onto a new street. It's poorly lit, and there is minimal MV traffic. Ami hesitates and I place my hand on her shoulder.

"We should come back in the day."

"I don't want to waste any time," she answers firmly, though hidden underneath the confidence there's hesitation.

I place my hand on her back to let her know I'm here, guarding her. My hand presses in, hurrying her along. The shadows cast by the night give me an uncomfortable feeling. Footsteps behind us heighten my awareness of our surroundings, and when I look over my shoulder there are a few figures emerging from a dark alley. My attention returns to our front as another group emerges a few hundred feet away. A third set appears from the shadowy places to the right, and my heart thumps heavily against my ribs.

We're being surrounded.

We're fine.

"Hey!" a voice calls from behind us, and then a whistle follows.

Another whistle pierces the air in front of us. I snatch Ami's hand to pull her to the other side of the road, but we're intercepted. Five men and a woman, all unsavory looking characters, confront us. They're in ragged clothes. Their faces are tattooed with colors and images.

"Whatcha doin' out so late, honey?" The woman chews loudly on something.

"We don't want trouble," Ami tells them calmly. "We're just looking for someone."

"Well, surprise! You found someone!" A bald, muscular man laughs and slaps his buddy to get him to laugh too.

"We don't have valuables," she tries to reason.

"Stay near me," I whisper to her.

Stop hesitating. Act! Kill them!

"Is that so? What do you think we want?" a fat man grunts while they move to surround us. He grins and licks his lips sickeningly.

"Yeah, maybe we just wanna harass you!" says a greasy, gangly man.

The tension in the air rises.

"We're passing through. It would be prudent for you to let us go," I tell them, putting my arm around Ami.

"Prudent? What kinda word is that?"

"It means you'd be smart to let us walk away," I sneer. Tiberius is surfacing.

"Are you threatening me?" the woman protests. "I'm not sure you understand where you are, boy."

They prey on the weak! Kill them!

One of the men pulls off Ami's hood from behind. I turn, but he's out of my reach before I catch his shirt. Anger builds. A battle strategy forms, and I don't know if it's mine, or *his*. In anticipation of real danger I have to act. The biggest of the men launches into a shoving contest, and I'm pushed back and forth a few times.

Do it!

"We're gonna have to take this beauty with us, but he can't come," the woman tells the others.

The greasy man grabs at Ami.

KILL THEM!

I react faster than they can, grabbing the one locked onto Ami's arm. A little pressure into his wrist frees her. Yanking him toward me, I slam my palm on his sternum. The man exhales all of the air in his lungs, and collapses at my feet.

Sensing I'm the dangerous one, the others brandish weapons. The men wield knives, but the woman fits metal knuckles onto her fists. They lunge to overtake me, and I find an opening to push Ami out of the way. Dodging a knife from an attacker I step in and ram my shoulder into his, knocking him back. Spinning, I throw my hand out and let an uncontrolled shockwave tear through the night. It spreads, slamming the rest of them before they reach me.

While they are midair I bolt toward where they are coming down. I'm on them within seconds of their impact. Finding the largest man on the ground I pull him to his feet, while grabbing the knife lying next to him. By his jugular I hold him. He swats at my arm while I choke him. I head-butt and then drop him.

"I said we were passing through!" I yell and bend down to slam the knife into the guy's leg, digging it deep, and pulling.

Plunge it into his heart!

The man screams in pain. I spare his life because his anguish is pleasing to my ears. The woman leaps to her feet, and stumbles backward with her hands up in surrender. My thirst for violence isn't quenched. Tiberius urges me on. My drive for justice agrees. Grabbing her by the collar of her shirt, I bring her in close to my face. A guttural growl escapes my throat.

"Evil will meet its end!"

I lift her by her shirt. My hand comes up to her abdomen, and I build a shockwave to obliterate her. A hand grabs my shoulder. I turn to react.

"It's okay, Rain. It's okay," Ami's voice is soothing.

Ami is safe. I relax. Because of mine and Tiberius's instincts aligning, I nearly lost control. The rage is worse than when I killed the slavers. It's not a part of me Ami has seen, and I don't want her to. Because I clearly outmatch them, I let the woman go, and glare.

"Leave! If you attack again, I *will* kill you," I keep my tone even.

Her group is long gone, even the one whose leg I tore open. We're left alone. The other groups linger, then slink away. None dare to approach. I pull my hood up, and then help Ami with hers. My face is serious, but my expression softens when my eyes meet hers. Her gentleness draws me in.

"What came over you?" She's serious, but forces a smile. She puts her hand in mine and squeezes.

"I..." I don't want to talk about it with her.

"It's okay." She rests her head on my chest before pulling away and leading on.

My tension decreases at the warmth of her hand in mine, and our closeness. Now unhindered, she leads, searching several streets for the right one. She checks the list frequently, and finally puts it away, continuing without the paper. We stop in front of a run-down house sitting amongst others equally decrepit.

She looks up at me. "Even in the dark, I recognize this from mother's photos."

The shutters are heavily damaged, and the windows are smashed. The front door is hanging on by a single hinge, and the paint has all but peeled away from the entire building. There is a rickety chain link fence encompassing most of the yard, with a gap where a gate should be. I question her with a look. She nods, and leads on.

When we climb the stairs they creak heavily, and bow under our weight. At the door I knock hard. It falls off its hinge. I try to catch it, but it slips. Ami jumps out of the way, and it glances off me to clatter to the porch.

"What do you want? I have nothing! Leave me alone!" A hoarse voice pierces the air.

"Sorry!" I apologize for the door. "We're looking for a man who used to live here."

"Go away!" the man yells.

"Please. Give us a minute. We have travelled far, and were attacked on the way. I'd like for this trip to not have been made in vain," I tell him.

A face appears in the shadows, and I can barely make him out in the doorway. He steps forward. He's skinny to the point of starvation, and covered with dirt. The gray hair on his face is untrimmed and wild. Death looms over his head.

"What do you want?" His words are abrupt.

Ami clutches my back, so I speak for her.

"We're looking for someone."

"James," she whispers in my ear.

"His name is James," I repeat for the man.

He grumbles heavily, and scratches his beard. "What business do you have with him?"

Ami steps forward a little, and pulls her hood down. I copy, to hopefully disarm the man.

"My name is Ami. James is my father," she says nervously and squeezes my hand for support.

He huffs loudly. "He doesn't have a daughter."

I hope he isn't so far gone he doesn't recognize her.

"He does. I'm his daughter," she insists.

He steps into the eerie glow from a street lamp, and it makes him look worse. I feel terrible for him. He mutters under his breath, and leans in close to her. Reaching up, he takes her chin, turning her head from side to side.

"I suppose you do look a bit like him." The man sighs through his nose.

"I need to find him. Can you tell me where he is?" she pleads.

I'm relieved when I realize she wasn't expecting *this* man to be him.

"Even if I knew, it's best you don't know." He drops his hand, and reverts to being ornery. "The last time I saw him he was completely crazy. A raving loon. You should just go on home missy."

"What do you mean?" Ami asks.

"He showed up several years after he sold me this dump. I think he had escaped from a mental ward, because all he could do was babble about a house disappearing into thin air. Even drug me to the outskirts of town – t'weren't nothing there. Then he was gone, and didn't come back."

Ami sighs, and looks at me with sadness. I draw her to me, my arm around her waist. She buries her face in my neck. The man clears his throat to gain our attention.

"C'mon, I told you. Now get."

I look at him and beg for compassion without saying anything, something he likely hasn't received much of in the recent years of his life.

He sighs. "Look, I don't want to get yer hopes up, but when I visit the soup kitchen I hear stories." The sickly man tries to be sympathetic. "Heard a rumor of a babbling idiot who kind of fits James's description. Wanders the far side of the city, raving about a blue tornado and time travel."

My heart leaps a bit, and I hope for her sake it's true.

"Can you provide us directions?" I ask him.

"You got something to write with, 'cause I ain't pricking my finger to write you a note in blood." He scratches at sores.

Ami pulls out a pen, and the piece of paper she was using for directions to get here. The man leans against the doorframe and scribbles furiously. When he returns both to her, he gives her a weak and toothless smile.

"If he's still alive, I hope he's not too far gone," he grumbles and then turns to head back inside.

"Thank you!" Ami says, wiping tears away.

Turning, Ami steps down, and I follow. Back at the road, she stops and pulls out a photograph. It's a photo of a group of men standing in front of a large, unfinished building. There's a circle drawn around a man in the photo. He's clean cut, well-built, and looks happy. He's wearing clothes similar to the man I saw today with Agatha, that of a laborer.

Ami looks at the scrap of paper with a crudely drawn map on it. Barely legible street names are scrawled, and she looks for nearby signs. Pivoting on her heel a few times, I assume to regain her sense of direction, she finally turns toward the city. I stand behind her, and rest my hands on her shoulders, massaging gently.

"I know you're eager, but we have a lot of time left. We should rest and pick up tomorrow."

The reluctance to comply is obvious in her shoulders as they tense up. My thumbs knead at the muscles, and they relax. She turns and opens her mouth as if she might argue. Instead she lets out a large yawn. We aren't a block from the old man's house, and she starts to fall behind. I stop and crouch so she can piggyback. She climbs on, and I trudge forward.

I'm able to carry her for a few blocks, but my back begins to ache, and I tire. Back on her own feet, she seems to have regained enough energy to keep up. We walk hand-in-hand.

At home, and once inside, I fail to conceal my footsteps. The boards creek on the stairs, but I don't care if I'm heard.

Chas's light is pouring in my window and I draw the shades closed to rest. I throw my clothes to the floor, and climb into bed.

~~~~~~

The morning comes too soon. I want to sleep longer, but the light seeps in and there are heavy whirring and clanking noises coming from outside. I dress in a white t-shirt and heavy work pants before picking up my clothes from the night before. I stretch, and groan loudly.

Downstairs, Ami and Eve are sitting on opposite ends of the couch. They're quiet, and acting suspicious while looking at me. I wave half-heartedly and push into the kitchen. Agatha's there, busy with her morning already.

"Good morning, Rain!" Evalyn's voice comes out. Her verve startles me.

"You're awfully perky. Where's my cranky Evalyn?"

"Zip it. I don't want anyone thinking I'm in a good mood," she scolds me playfully with a glance and a pointed finger.

"Then you best stop using words like 'good' with 'morning'," I laugh.

Steam rises from the stove. In one pan eggs are being boiled, and in another there are sliced potatoes. Before I have time to be confused about where she got the water, I see a half empty jug on the floor around the corner of the stove.

Her attention is on the island countertop where she's preparing more food. I peek over her shoulder. She's cubing ham. Her elbow meets my ribs playfully.

"I'm going to be in Agatha's body for a while so we can research how to break the cycle," she says.

"We?" I rest my chin on her shoulder.

"You don't expect me to go tromping off into the woods to your old castle alone, do you?" She shrugs me off. "My hope is to not disappear into oblivion if we succeed."

"Agreed. It would be weird without you always taking over Aggy's body." I chuckle and she elbows me a little harder.

"It scares me…thinking about it," she says seriously.

"I understand. It's how I felt all those months ago. And it's how I felt when I was stuck in the despair on the Vraditi ship. Despite first impressions, you and I are a lot alike."

If Agatha is like my mother, then surely Evalyn is like my aunt.

She's silent for a moment and she tries to hide wiping away a tear. I want to comfort her, but she moves away. She takes the cutting board, and a frying pan from above, and heads to the stove. The pot of boiled eggs is pushed to a rear burner, and the frying pan with the ham is put on. While it cooks, Evalyn turns to me.

"Your castle ruins are where I first learned I had a latent power." She puts her hands on her hips and stares at me.

"You think the artifacts are still there?"

"Assuming nobody has been there and found the secret chamber." She turns slightly to stir the ham cubes with a spatula, and then continues. "I found them in my younger years. I could feel a sort of hum from certain items, but only one reacted when I touched it. Imagine my surprise when

I randomly jumped to a different time."

"Is there a version of you alive out there in time we might run into?"

"Theoretically, yes. But we don't ever meet my past self. Thankfully. Can you imagine the complications?"

I try to think of what 'secret' room she might know of that I don't, but even with the amnesia lifted, nothing comes to mind.

"We'll grab everything. Maybe we can make other pieces activate," she says.

We fall silent as she returns to cooking. I stare out the window at the heavy machinery digging up the yard. The kitchen door swings open behind me. Ami starts setting the table and, not wanting to feel unproductive, I prepare toast.

"Did you want to go out *today*?" Evalyn asks.

"Ami and I are trying to track down James." I look over at Ami, and wink. "But afterward, yes. I have a request though."

She pulls the pan off the stove and then glares at me.

"What request?"

"You show me where the secret room is, and I'll collect the artifacts. Then you can release Aggy for a break."

Evalyn huffs and dishes up each plate. Her stiff movements and downturned mouth tell me she doesn't want to give up her freedom.

When I shoot a stern glance at her, she sighs loudly.

"Fine," she replies with an annoyed tone.

"Don't worry. When we have the artifacts I'll make sure they're placed in your room, and then help you in whatever way you need."

Hearing Emma and Eve in the living room, quarreling over Eve using Emma's brush, I interrupt by poking my head in. I'm silent, letting the smell of breakfast do the talking. Eve breaks away, and sits in Emma's spot to antagonize her. I tap her shoulder and force her to move.

"Killjoy." She gets up and sits in her normal place.

The meal is mostly uneventful, and the food settles heavily on my stomach, but I'm satisfied. I slouch and stretch my legs until everyone is done. The dishes from last night are stacked at the sink, and I stack mine too. The women disperse while I clean.

In the living room I put on my shoes. Ami disappears into the hall for a few moments, and reappears dressed casually. I look at her, puzzled.

"I'm surprised you're not dressed fancier for meeting your father."

"I thought about what you said last night. We *do* have plenty of time left. If you and Evalyn succeed, I'll have all the time in the world," she says with a half-smile.

"Are you sure? I don't want to deprive you of any opportunity to find him."

"I'll be okay. Let's just make sure you succeed."

She hugs me. I wrap my arms around her and caress her hair. She smiles and pulls away to seek out Evalyn. With the stampede of footsteps I heard climbing the stairs after breakfast, I am positive she's hiding in her room. Leading the way, I remember the time she warned me never to come near her door, and I chuckle. I knock and she opens it. She's frowning. Her mood has shifted from happy to grumpy because of my request. A smile crosses my lips, and I hope to disarm her.

"Okay, previous plans are on hold. Let's head to the ruins," I tell her.

"Make up your mind!"

We glare at one another, but I won't let my smile fall. Evalyn huffs and slams the door.

"Eve, Emma!" I bellow.

Their doors swing open and, as if in sync with each other, both of them stick their heads out.

"We're going on a trip. Put on appropriate clothes for walking in the woods and getting dirty."

Emma jumps into the hall wearing a long sleeve shirt and her coveralls. "I'm ready!"

Eve closes her door and reemerges shortly, smirking. She's in a tank top, green and brown camouflage shorts, and knee-high leather boots. I cross my arms in disapproval. She strides over to me. Despite Ami's presence, she caresses my face.

"You should know by now, getting dirty with you isn't a problem for me." She's not even looking at me. Instead she's staring at Ami. "But I'd rather wear things like this and leave you speechless."

Ami swats Eve's hand away in disapproval, and they begin a staring match. Evalyn opens her door and walks directly in between them. She's dressed in heavy clothing, and a cloak. She huffs at Eve, glaring at her choice of clothes.

"Eve, save our eyes and put on real clothes. Or you can stay and clean the floors," Evalyn commands.

It's been a while since her snarky side has come out. It surprises all of us. Eve wants to punch her, indicated by her balled up fists. Evalyn grins smugly, and I anticipate it's because she knows Eve won't hit Agatha's body. Eve grunts and disappears into her room. When she returns, she's in cargo pants, a long sleeve shirt, and the same boots. The look on her face tells us she's clearly unhappy.

"How am I supposed to look good for Rain in this?" she protests.

Ami mumbles. "If looking good means being trashy, I hope I *never* look good."

Eve hears her, and stomps loudly all the way downstairs.

Because the shaded forest will be cold, I grab my white cloak hung by my bed. Though I don't anticipate a need for my sword, I grab it as a precaution.

At the bottom of the stairs, the women have gathered near the door, except for Eve. She's making a protest by sitting on the couch with both her arms and her legs crossed, staring angrily out the window.

"At least I'll be useful. I could carry Agatha, Ami, and Emma without breaking a sweat," Eve huffs.

"How many bags should we bring?" I ask.

"Several." Evalyn slips her shoes on. "In the basement there should be a tall wicker basket with bags. And grab some cord or rope too."

I nod. "I'll meet you by the horse. We should pack food."

In the basement, it takes me a few moments of rummaging to find the wicker basket she mentioned. I grab several bags, a few cords of rope, and head back up.

Outside the kitchen door, in the middle of the yard, is a hole several feet wide.

Aggy wanted to move the garden anyway.

Though I'm not near the hole, I am still cautious when I step down to the grass. Around the corner, Maximus makes an agitated whinny. I bring him out and calm him by stroking his neck and cheek. He allows me to harness him and sling the bags over his back.

Ready to go, I lead him from his stable toward the well, where men are working diligently. The well's cover has been removed, and they are lowering something in with a large pulley system.

I head to the steps leading up to the living room door, and where the women are. The bulging backpacks they have on make it seem like they're anticipating we'll be gone for days.

What did they pack?

I poke at Emma's bag and laugh. "Did you bring the kitchen sink?"

She grins in a way which makes me question whether she does have a sink in her bag.

"We're set." Evalyn is eager. "Let's not dawdle. I want to be back by dusk."

"Don't forget, you said you would relinquish her body once you show us where the secret room is."

Her response is to ignore me, and make quick strides to the forest. She leads us in, weaving through the bushes and trees. It's not long and we are deep in the forest, the house obscured behind us. The sound of the heavy equipment fades away, and the peaceful silence of nature and footsteps reign.

Evalyn stops a few times to look. Several hundreds of years have passed since our visit to Asta. The Forest of Hunger has consumed the land, and there are no landmarks to serve as a guide. Instinct and general direction are all we have. When I think we're heading the right way, obstacles force us to make several detours. It takes a few hours of walking steadily, and the silence becomes irritating. I speak up.

"We should stop and drink some water," I suggest.

Ami drops the bag from her shoulder and retrieves a couple bottles. She hands one to each of us, except Eve who pulls her own out. While we rest and drink, I feel a heavy tension between the two of them. They stand far apart, neither coming near me.

Emma is unaffected, I assume because she's not vying for my heart. She leans against the tree near me and whispers so the others can't hear. "You have to do something. Set Eve straight already."

"You think I haven't tried?" I return the whisper.

Evalyn surveys the land and walks away, calling out as an afterthought, "This way."

It has taken far longer to reach the castle than it did previously. Evalyn stops abruptly, and holds her hand up for us to stop too.

Eve opens her mouth, but before she can speak a word, Evalyn gives her a dirty look, and she stays silent. Evalyn points off to our right, and there is a clearing beyond a dozen more trees.

When we reach it, Asta is there, rotted, decayed, and overgrown to the point where it's almost indistinguishable from the surrounding terrain. My heart breaks to see it as a husk of its former glory. The farmland is gone, consumed by foliage. The walls surrounding the castle are demolished, barely one stone on another. But the outline is there.

Down in the valley, we stand on the outskirts of Asta's farmland. Hints of the cobblestone path exist under brush, ferns, and vines. I remember both the time we were here last, and when I was king. I had made it a powerful kingdom, but its beauty was offset by my corrupted soul.

Though the path is almost invisible, it doesn't take us long to enter the inner city. As we walk, I can see what destroyed most of it: fire.

It's scorched, likely from the rebellion against Drake, but I don't get the chance to examine the detail because Evalyn is pushing to get to the castle. The ruins cause me anguish.

Off in the distance, visible because much is demolished, is the shambles of my home when I was Tiberius. A mixture of feelings well up inside me. Anger for the outcome of my kingdom. Sorrow because I let myself become such a monster.

I was stupid to think I could control him. What a fool I was to meet him alone after I knew he wanted more.

It's done. Asta is finished and we are better off.

We pass what used to be the outer castle wall, which had a dozen watchtowers where my elite archers watched to protect me. Climbing the grand steps, we reach the doorway to the inner courtyard. Heavy wooden doors lie on the ground, eaten away by war, time, and insects. I kick the edge, and chunks crumble away. Despite my persistence in keeping control from Tiberius over my body and thoughts, I involuntarily shake my head at the condition of this once beautiful castle.

The inner courtyard is a large, open, square area. I recognize the different sections. A soldier's training area to the left, a stable to the right, a closet for precession instruments and flags toward the back left, now all gone. At the rear is the castle, its walls are damaged but the core building is still standing.

When we reach the area where the stables were, I tie Maximus off on the one remaining hitch ring still embedded in the stones.

Evalyn drops her bag at his feet, and heads to the archway with a lantern in hand. She places her hand on the stonework, and caresses it in a nostalgic manner. The girls follow, leaving their bags against the wall.

I grab the empty sacks and join them. At the doorway, stone lies strewn around. There are splintered remnants of one door still hanging, the other is missing altogether.

They must have brought siege weapons. Did they kill him?

He deserved this. Traitorous demon.

He is no more a demon than you. It was going to be you, eventually.

Evalyn heads into the shadowy doorway, having lit her lantern to light the way. The throne room greets us with a musty smell.

I immediately fixate on the throne. My chair lays on its side on the platform, stripped of its gold ornaments. Nothing remains on the once well-decorated walls. A few pillars stand in defiance of the attack, still holding a major section of the ceiling up. But there is a large boulder embedded in the marble, and light floods in where it tore a gaping hole during the attack.

Looking around brings back memories of the days I lived here. Not just overseeing, but plotting, scheming, assassinating. My chair wasn't my favorite place though. To the left are stairs leading up to a balcony overhanging the room. I recall a feeling of superiority over everyone while perched there. An overwhelming feeling of importance rushes over me.

Beyond the balcony on the second floor lie the hallways I'd play in as a child, in the time before Drake murdered our parents. The nooks and crannies were my playground, and I would sneak into places I shouldn't have been, including the guard barracks.

Ami snaps her fingers in front of my face. "Hey, are you okay?"

"I was remembering where it all started." I sigh. "Nothing to worry about."

We climb the stairs to the balcony, and enter a hallway on the right. I have a vague idea where Evalyn is headed, because the king's chambers are this way. The deeper we go, the darker it gets. Her lantern gives the castle a ghostly feel.

The hallway leads to the edge of the castle, turns ninety degrees, and heads toward the back.

Halfway between the front of the hall and the back, Evalyn turns inward at a junction and into new corridors toward the heart of the castle. We pass broken doors, torn paintings, and shattered statues.

Eve breaks the ominous silence. "How much farther?" she asks.

"Not much," I answer, sure we're headed for my old room.

"We might be out of luck. Everything seems plundered already." Eve sighs, disheartened.

"With all the evidence of siege and the revolt, I am surprised Evalyn found anything worthwhile."

"I'm hoping it's all still here," Evalyn adds. She leads us to the right, and we reach a large wooden door.

I push it open, revealing a massive bedroom: the king's private chambers. There lies my demolished bed, pillars collapsed on it. Bookshelves are toppled and destroyed, but there is not a book in sight. Everything remaining is in tatters, a few personal belongings of little value scattered here and there.

While Evalyn moves to the right wall, I move to the bed and stand over it, remembering the first time I slept in it. It was uncomfortable. As I grew, it was also lonely. In my world of power, I never sought to marry, or even lay with a woman. Power and control were my mistresses.

I'm distracted by Evalyn feeling her way along the wall toward the back right of the room, near a fallen shelf. She shoves on the stones hard, and a soft 'click' can be heard. A hidden stone door opens.

"Was this here the whole time?" I'm astonished.

"Inside," Evalyn says, motioning for us to follow.

The tunnel is narrow, and accommodates a single file procession into the darkness. At the end of a short passage we're forced to turn right, and descend a set of spiral stairs into the castle's belly.

Evalyn leads with confidence on the precariously narrow steps, spiraling down a few flights before reaching a hidden room.

The moment I enter, a hum of power pulses through the air.

Holding up her lantern, she leads to the left wall where a torch hangs. She lights it with a flint, then proceeds to light several others with it. With the room illuminated, we're able to see better, and she returns the torch to its sconce.

It's disheveled but intact, despite the siege. There is a collection of various items on shelves around the room. It doesn't appear there is any organization to the collection of potentially valuable items. At the back is a solid chair with a mummified body dressed in a black suit of armor. It's Drake.

"Eww!" Emma yells, clearly having seen the corpse.

"What do we take?" I ask abruptly. I want this over with, knowing his remains are here.

"Everything." Evalyn looks at Eve with a conniving smile.

"Now you're speaking my language, woman!" Eve hoots.

Eve grabs a bag from me, and tosses items in without caution. Her eyes glimmer with delight while she loots. Grabbing items of all sorts in her arms, I don't even see what half of it is.

"Okay, you showed us where it is. Time to head home Evalyn." I tell her.

"Let me help pack up and then I'll go." She's stalling.

I give her a hard stare, but she isn't paying attention. Sighing, I cave and hold a bag open for her. She is gentler in packing things in than Eve. A heavy book, a crystal ball and its stand, a pen and corked bottle of ink, a set of multi-colored beads, a goblet inset with four gems equally spaced.

Ami and Emma stand looking at the untouched items. The two of them grab a large silver shield from the wall and nearly drop it. Emma yelps, but they gain control by grabbing the straps on the back.

Next to where the shield was hung is a painting of Drake. His dark eyes unnerve me, and anger rises. Setting the bag on the floor, I rip the painting down. It clatters against the stone, and I stomp on the canvass. The women stop to look at me.

The painting was hiding a small safe. Its lock is simple, but the wood is brittle. I unsheathe my sword and press the tip into a seam. It pops open in a cloud of dust.

The air clears, and Eve gasps at the sparkle of jewelry inside. With my sword put away, I rifle through the contents. Emma and Eve shove past me to grab handfuls. They put on the rings, necklaces, and crowns.

They giggle hysterically while chattering. They parade, pretending to be royalty, forcing me to smile.

As I look again, there's a familiar necklace: a piece of amber, wrapped in gold and silver coils, hung on a gold chain. It was my coronation gift from my advisor, Ralig.

That viper!

It's a reminder of the evil we became, molded by his evil and selfish intentions. We should leave this behind.

For once, we agree.

I toss it to the back of the safe, and confiscate the rest.

"Take them off and put them in." I motion to them with a wave of my finger toward my bag.

Emma whines, and Eve sighs, but they do as I request.

The remainder of the room has been plundered by Evalyn and Ami.

Amongst the heap on the chair, a glimmer of silver catches my attention. Moving closer to it, an overwhelming sense of dread sets in, the hair on the back of my neck standing on end.

At Drake's hip is the infamous curved dagger. I remember how it felt when it pierced me. Tiberius's anger becomes my action. Rage floods me, as it had the previous night. I snatch it up, and I feel an evil power within it.

The blade sits comfortably in my hand, perfectly balanced for both swinging and stabbing. There's a hum in my head, as though the blade is singing to me.

I lean over the chair and plunge the dagger into Drake's skull, gritting my teeth. The anger burns like fire. Though I did not land the blow that killed him, I'm satisfied: I'm alive, and he is dead.

Ami's hand touches my shoulder, and I break free of the rage. The blade slides from his skull with ease. Anxiety replaces the rage. The room feels heavy, as if the walls are coming to crush me. With my eyes closed, I think of outside the castle, focusing on the house.

"I don't think he knew what he had in these artifacts. He died in this tomb, alone and probably scared," Evalyn says to comfort me.

He met his end. It's over.

We're free. He's dead.

It takes a few moments, but I control myself and push the dark feelings down. I turn to face my family.

They understand: there's compassion and understanding in their expressions.

I sigh and shake my head. "Let's finish and head home."

Ami leans forward and hugs me.

I throw the dagger in the bag, and we load up. With the sack pulled up to my shoulder I return to the entrance. Climbing the spiral staircase is slow due to the treasure. It takes twice the time to get out as it did going in.

The fresh air is invigorating, and I sigh, relieved. The warm rays from the sun wash away the dreadful feeling of the dead castle. Maximus has found a nice patch of grass growing in the cobblestones to nibble at. He takes little notice when Eve and I hoist the bags onto his back, and Emma ties them together.

"Let's have a picnic before we head home," Agatha says, her voice melodious in the silence of the ruins. She opens her bag and retrieves a large blanket. She lays it down, and Ami places plates and glasses in a circle.

Emma and Eve pull out the food sealed in plastic containers. Sandwiches, sliced carrots and beets, apples, and water.

Everyone dishes up while I dig through the bags for a treat for Maximus. There's some whole carrots, and I offer them to him. He practically inhales them, before I turn and sit down.

The silence is nice, having become less awkward. Ami leans on me while I eat. Seeing Ami's affection, Eve decides to do the same. They're not fighting and I stay silent to keep the peace. Even after our food is gone, we sit awhile until the sun peaks in the sky.

Standing up, dislodging them both, I stretch. I grab the rope and release Maximus from the hitching ring. When he moves, the bags swing, their contents clanking. Ami and Emma hoist the shield onto his back, and secure it with rope.

In the courtyard, the ruined city doesn't look as bad in this direction. My mind urges me to look at the castle again in what I hope is a final farewell.

I take too long reminiscing, and I'm reminded of the real world waiting for me, as Ami asks, "Hey! Are you coming or what?" She's already several feet away.

"Yeah, let's go, slowpoke," Emma adds playfully.

I'm quick to catch up, and it's not long before I've overtaken them. Asta disappears as the foliage obscures our view. My legs protest in soreness from all the walking and having to compensate for the uneven ground. I'm pleased when the house finally comes into view.

The yard is mostly quiet, no heavy machinery humming. A few men mill about the yard, including the foreman. He stops what he's doing and makes his way toward us.

Agatha stops to talk with him, while we continue on to the living room door. Eve opens it and I pull the knots to drop the sacks. Agatha joins us, but it's Evalyn who speaks.

"Move the stuff to my room," she remarks while pointing at me.

"All of it?!" Eve raises her voice in protest.

"Shut it." Evalyn smirks. "If I determine an item has no potential in breaking the vortex, *and* if you actually do some work, I might let you have a gem."

"You're a—" I elbow her to interrupt. Eve seethes. "If you were alive I'd give you a black eye and a fat lip!"

Eve grabs a bag, and stomps inside. All the way up the stairs and even into the hallway she can be heard. I sigh and follow. Upstairs, she waits by the door with the bag slung over her shoulder.

Evalyn opens her door and antagonizes her more, waving her hand in an arrogant manner. "Eve, you're dismissed."

Eve reaches her limit and throws the bag in the room. It slams to the floor, and items scatter from the opening.

"Have fun picking it up, wench!" Eve yells at her, and shoves past me. She hides away in her room and slams her door. The walls reverberate and

I flinch.

"Why are you purposely provoking her?" I whisper.

"Because I *want* to," she retorts, not holding back. "I'm releasing Agatha. You need to lay out the items."

Her face lightens. She's in a state of shock for a moment, but a sorrowful smile appears.

"What's wrong with her?"

"I don't know. She hasn't been this apprehensive since the first few months you were with us."

There's a moment of silence.

Is she in pain? Is she sad?

"When you're done, would you help me with dinner?" Her normal smile returns.

"Sure, Aggy. Can you have the girls bring the shield?"

She nods and heads downstairs. I turn the light on, and shut the door. It's clean, except for the mess Eve just made. I feel awful dumping items all over, but it's what I was told to do.

A large pile of treasure glimmers in the light, and I feel a rush of bliss looking at it. The feeling of greed rises, something which hasn't happened since I was Tiberius.

A knocking on the door breaks my lustful stare, and I open it. Ami and Emma have arrived with the shield.

I'm embarrassed to be found been thinking of the wealth. My face reddens and I try to hide it. "Thanks." I manage a single word while taking the shield from them.

Ami grabs my hand briefly and smiles.

Emma sees it and giggles, then pulls her away. "C'mon, he has work to do."

Emma closes the door behind them, winking before it's shut. Flustered by avarice, and now Ami, I try desperately to clear my mind.

I organize the jewelry, and come up with a dozen different necklaces and pendants, a couple crowns, and a ring for each finger of my hands. Each of them is adorned with various gems. The other treasure is a variety of items, which I organize by man-made or not.

The man-made objects I'd collected with Evalyn were my brother's dagger, the book, the goblet, the crystal ball, and the beads. The others had found a small wooden chest with two gold goblets in it, a crossbow, a silver platter, a few small metal urns, historical tomes, a knight's helm with scaly wings, and a wax seal. Oddly, there is also a painting of my parents he was keeping. Finally, to avoid tripping on the shield, I put it on the bed.

Next to the man-made, I lay out bear, rabbit, and wolf paws. There are a few pelts fashioned into wearable garments: deer and dire wolf.

The rest is unrefined materials: gold, silver, and uncut gemstones. There are several chunks of a lightweight metal in its natural formation. It's solid black, but it gives off an eerie shimmer in the light. It's the metal Drake made his armor from.

Once upon a time, I had a room of treasures like these. And what was my reward? Loneliness. It couldn't buy my way out of Drake's betrayal. It couldn't stop me nearly dying, or the amnesia.

With all of the items arranged, I turn to the desk and pick up a pen. Evalyn takes control of my hand and scribbles furiously.

"I'll be checking the items for special properties, but it's going to take time. Get out."

"What's wrong?" I ask out loud.

"None of your business! Get out!"

Evalyn acts as she has previously: angry. Controlling my hand, she slams it on the desk. I release the pen, and move to the door. Before I leave, I try to soothe her.

"If I did something, I am sorry. I will check in later."

Downstairs, Agatha is cooking dinner. In the window is the darkening sky and the illuminated city limits. I hover behind her, watching as she washes peeled potatoes.

"Would you cube these, and then throw them into the pot please?" she asks, and nods her head toward the pot on the stove.

A knife and cutting board are already set out on the island counter, and I do as she asks. I lose myself to thoughts of my brother.

Rather than die at the hands of the attackers, he decided to hide there. Starved to death no doubt. Coward. It's too bad neither of us were fit to rule and keep the kingdom alive.

He was a coward. But we can revive Asta in a different way. Our legacy can continue. We can—

Enough.

I drop the cubes into the pot of boiling water.

The others join us and help prepare for dinner.

Eve begrudgingly sets the table. She's scowling heavily, and muttering. I catch only part of what she's saying. "...stupid...work for my part...what does she think..."

I chuckle and receive a nasty glare in response. I shrug and she slams forks on the table.

The meal comes together, and we sit down to a pot roast, mashed potatoes and gravy, bread and butter. Ami and Emma chatter about new clothes patterns. Eve slouches and stares at the wall.

I admire each of them, but Ami gets most of my attention. She looks at me, and I flash her a smile. She smiles back and Emma elbows her. They giggle, gaining Eve's attention. Though she's upset, she says nothing.

If Evalyn succeeds, Eve can be free and move on. I'll tell her I want to be with Ami, and she won't have to endure the pain of watching us be happy.

All eyes are on me, as if I had been speaking my thoughts out loud. My appetite stalls, and I push the food in circles on the plate. I sigh and stand, taking my plate to the sink.

A nagging feeling causes the hairs to raise on the back of my neck, the despairing souls within me stirring. The collective has been mostly quiet since we've arrived, but it's beginning to voice itself.

"Are they bringing more fresh water tomorrow?" I ask without looking.

"Yes. Another ten gallons," Agatha replies. "Are you okay?"

"I'll be fine." I smile to disarm her, but her worry is apparent. "I'm tired, and I'll take care of these tomorrow."

After a quick retreat to the bathroom, I head upstairs. In my room a whisper nags at me. I can't tell what it's saying though.

Ignoring it as best I can, I turn the light off and slip into bed. It's an hour or two before I finally suppress the white noise whisper and fall asleep.

~~~~~~

A light rapping of knuckles on my door pulls me from sleep. It's so faint I hesitate, wondering if I actually heard it. But it becomes louder, and I pull my pillow over my head briefly. The door opens. Dressed to go out in her red cloak, Ami stands in the doorway. I know what she's about to ask, but I preempt her.

"Can we take tonight off? The trip wore me out." I yawn and rub my face.

"If we miss a day, we may miss him completely," she huffs, pouting. Her wide-eyed stare is imploring, and I can't deny her. Though I am tired, it's important because she's important to me.

Closing the door to change, I put on warm clothes and my white cloak.

A dark presence stirs and becomes heavier the moment I touch the doorknob. My heart pounds and I can't explain the sensation. I twist and pull.

Drake is in the hall, grinning evilly, poised to strike Ami. My stomach turns. I try to choke out words, but my throat closes.

She panics at my expression, and grabs my hands. "Rain? What's wrong?" she whispers.

I rip Ami into the room, shoving her at the bed. My sword is in reach, and I grab it. It is out of its sheath, and I'm ready for battle. But he's vanished.

"He's here!"

The sound of my own heartbeat thumps in my ears. My attention is locked on the doorway, waiting for him to lunge in and kill me.

Why is he here? He's dead!

Was it him?

What else could it be?

A nightmare?

I approach with caution, looking for his blazing red hair and dark, shimmering armor. My lungs labor to take in air when I flip the light switch. Ami grabs my arm.

"Drake...he was standing right behind you."

"Shh, it's okay." She pulls me into a hug, but I keep my sword at the ready. "It must have been a hallucination, or maybe a nightmare bleeding into reality."

Shaking my head, I can't forget his evil presence. It lingers like a rotten stench. But if he were here, she would have seen him. He would have attacked, or she would have heard him leave. Still, I'm unable to calm down.

Eve's door opens, and I shut mine quickly. The floor creeks and there's a knock on my door. I wave frantically at Ami. She hides behind the door, and I crack it open a couple inches. Eve is groggy. She rubs her eyes, and yawns.

"Hey," she says through her yawn. "You okay?"

"Yeah, I'm fine. I had a nightmare." It's impossible to remove the fear from my voice.

"Do you need me to hold you so you can go back to sleep? Y'know, like in the caves." She sticks her face close, her lips pursed lightly for a kiss.

Ami jabs me hard in the side. I can't look or even wince, lest Eve suspect I'm not alone. I smile and shake my head. "No, I'll manage."

Emma's door opens.

"Quick, let me in. That little brat is coming – I promise I'll be out by morning. I miss laying with you, wrapping my arms around your chest, and sharing our body heat."

My jaw drops. A storm brews right next to me, and it's unleashed before I can stop it. Ami shoves me out of the way and intervenes. The door is ripped open, and it slams against the wall. Emma yelps. Ami is ready to fight Eve, and Eve's eyes widen with a mixture of shock and anger. Both of their fists ball up.

"We were just leaving!" Ami is impetuous and assertive.

"What are you doing in there? And where do you think you're going?" Eve fires back.

Desperate to avoid the argument, I turn around and put my sword belt and shoes on.

"It's none of your business what Rain and I do behind closed doors." She goes right for the throat. "And I don't recall it being in the rules to inform you if we decide to go out."

"What about the *rules*, huh?!" Eve cries out.

"You don't get to invoke them when it's convenient for you! Forget the rules!"

Eve reaches to grab Ami's hair, and Emma jumps in between them. Her arms are too short, so she uses an arm and a leg to keep the two apart.

Eve knocks her leg away, so Emma shoves her shoulder into Eve's sternum to back her up.

With a glare, Ami stomps down the stairs.

There is a distinct look of betrayal on Eve's face.

"What was she doing in your room?" she growls.

"Waking me so we can go searching."

"Liar!" She hits me in the shoulder.

I become defensive at the accusation. "Do you see how I'm dressed? I'm not indecent, and this isn't sleepwear, Eve."

"Whatever. You heard her. 'Forget the rules'. I'm done playing."

Ami, what have you done?

Refusing to verbally acknowledge her, I leave without resolving her perception of the situation.

Ami is waiting for me outside the kitchen door.

I'm feel more at ease being away from Eve's tension, and because the dark image of Drake is fading.

We walk toward Chas. My head is swimming though, having only had a couple hours sleep. I nearly smack my head on the low hanging scoop of one of the machines, but dodge it at the last second.

"You were thinking of letting her in, weren't you?" she asks accusingly, hitting me on the arm. It's hard to tell if she's playing or serious.

"You better believe he was!" Eve barks from behind us.

We both jump, stopping suddenly.

"We spent all that time with each other below ground, and you don't think we became close?" She grins.

Because we're barely past the property line, it seems Eve dressed in haste to follow. Shots have been fired by both sides, and now I'm going to become a casualty of war.

Despite trying to avoid eye contact with Eve, I catch her wink at me. I shake my head.

"What are you doing, *Eve*?" Ami asks. "This is a private excursion."

"Oh, I wanted to see where you were taking *my* Rain."

"I'll take him wherever I want to because he's not yours. Go away. You're not welcome." Ami scowls.

"Your being in his room doesn't mean a thing." Eve makes a face right back at her.

"He pulled me in there for some alone time. He didn't want you to see…" Ami purposely trails off. The smile of arrogance on her face isn't attractive, and I grab her hand to calm her.

There's a fury in Eve's eyes like I haven't seen since we fought in the desert. She balls her fists, ready to ignore my original warning regarding my protection of Ami.

I seek to disarm the escalating situation. "Didn't want her to see you abusing me with that jab to the ribs?" I say, joking, and squeeze her hand.

Ami shoots me a glance, and then turns right back to Eve. "He and I are going to look for my father." She spins, grabs me by the arm, and pulls me away.

"Well then, time's wasting, and we're safer in numbers!" Eve interlocks her arm with my free one.

Ami is not amused, but she snubs Eve, and pulls out the piece of paper with the scribbled map. After looking at it for a few moments she heads in the opposite direction from the other night, leading with confidence. The nightlife of the city is bustling. MVs hum about, and people walk to and fro.

We head deep into Chas, where the buildings become taller as part of the expanding metropolis. There are a number of scattered shops around, but half are closed for the night.

Ami pulls the picture of James out, and enters a business. At the front counter, fruit is being grilled and put in bowls. My stomach growls, and my mouth waters at the sweet smell. A man in a plain white uniform and apron greets us.

"Welcome, what can I get for you?" He lacks enthusiasm.

"Nothing, thanks. We're just trying to find someone," Ami says, holding up the photograph. "Have you seen this man? He likely has gray hair now, maybe a beard. His name is James."

The man adjusts his wire frame glasses, and looks briefly before shrugging and shaking his head.

"Thank you." She's cheerful.

All along the strip, and down several streets we visit more businesses, and receive similar answers. When we reach the edge of the commercial strip, there's dark and unfriendly territory.

"We should come back in the day. You'll probably have an easier time recognizing him in the light. And I'd rather not get into trouble again," I tell her.

She's silent for a moment, looking from the map to the neighborhood.

"Please. I'm not ready to go home yet." She shows me the map.

Rubbing my hands together anxiously, I gauge the potential danger beyond the invisible border separating the lit commercial area, and another run-down residential zone. Eve is nearby, kicking rocks at a fence.

"I don't have a good feeling." I tell her.

"You'll protect me. I know it." She smiles sweetly.

"That's the problem…I'll protect you at any cost."

She's being naïve. Does she not understand our nature?

"I'll reward you with a dinner for just us, lovingly made. We'll eat and enjoy a bottle of wine under a starry sky far, *far* away from the house. No interruptions. And then, after a few drinks…" Ami giggles and bashfully covers her face.

Is this whole thing for Eve's sake? To get under her skin?

Eve stomps her feet in a battle stance, ready to start the fight again. Clearly the verbal slap has her attention, as if it were the challenge for a duel.

"Not on my watch, wench!" she yells.

"Oh really? We've snuck out without alerting you other times, and we'll do it again!" Ami yells back. "Tonight was a fluke."

"Hey! Shut up!" a voice yells from the dark residential area, and both of them quiet in a heartbeat.

"If we're doing this, we need to be quick," I whisper.

Eve stops and they both nod in agreement.

We step forward from the safe to the unsafe. A chill runs up my spine.

Through the streets crowded with hovels and dark alleyways, we take the direct path.

What number of delinquents infest this city waiting to pounce on those they think are easy prey? How many do it because they're impoverished? How does Chas change to its future incarnation?

They're calling to us. They're miserable. Despair is what they died in, but their true form is Misery. *They need someone to lead them to salvation. We can fix this.*

He's not wrong.

It will be a better place to live eventually. Does that start now? Am I the one to make the changes?

Yes!

The despair is hazy, but the deeper we go the clearer they become. I fight Misery's intrusion, fearing a blackout. No matter how hard I push it away, I can hear and feel their anguish in my head. The white noise clears, and I understand their plight. Poverty rules this era. They're distraught over not being able to feed themselves and their families, overlooked and forgotten by the people they elected. The despairs of the people cry out over the thieves and gangs taking what little they have. They are a multitude.

I fight to focus on following Ami. I watch her movements intently, matching her stride. Her body sways, and her arms hit her cloak as she swings them back and forth. I grab her hand. I'm drawn toward the darkness, but I'm on the edge of maintaining control. I am able to see and hear exactly what Misery is trying to tell me without being sucked into their black void.

"Why won't Law Enforcement do anything?"

"I'm hungry!"

"Please, let me get through the night."

"Stupid government. Can't do anything right."

"Why can't I find a job?"

The feeling is intense. Thousands are dying of starvation and gang violence. The ones who are lucky enough to be employed are victimized by the greedy local government eating their wages with steep taxes. The economy is collapsing, and trends in this time match what I had seen as a child, when my father sat on the throne.

By uprooting a large section of forest outside of Asta, Father funded several large farming areas, and allowed a group to manage it and farm for their survival. Does Chas have farmland right now?

I quell Misery with the promise and determination to find an answer later. I snap out of my daze. We've stopped.

"What's going on?" I ask.

In front of me is a park, but it's much smaller than the future one the house lands in. There are lights illuminating it, but it's eerie under the orange glow. There are odd structures spread throughout, but none of them seem to serve a purpose. Nearby is a bridge with a dark tunnel where MVs cross above, but not below. There is no one in sight though.

"This is it," Ami says.

"I'm sorry Ami, I don't see anyone."

"This is dumb. All that walking for nothing." Eve sighs.

"There's definitely someone here," a man's voice startles us. "Who ya looking for?"

We turn, to face a man cloaked with shadows. A gang appears from the houses and alleyways. The man steps into the light of a lamp; it's the greasy thug from the night before.

"Hey! It's the freak from the other night!" He turns his head and yells.

I stand between them and the girls, my hand on the hilt of my blade. My promise to protect Ami, no matter the cost, allows Tiberius's ego to surface.

"Looking for another fight?" I grin and goad him.

Their numbers grow, and they've come with heavier weapons this time. Chains, pipes, large tools. I have no fear for my own safety, confident in my ability to subdue them.

"You *are* looking for a fight."

"Nah. Revenge. And you brought me *two* pretty ladies tonight." He grins wide, showing us a mouth of gaps and rotted teeth.

"Good luck." I'm outnumbered ten to one, but my confidence is rooted in my shockwave power and Tiberius's arrogance.

"Whatever that was last night, it won't get me again." His ignorance of my power makes him bold.

My violent impulses take control. My sword is drawn, and I smile evilly.

I can't hold back. "Do you want another demonstration?"

"Stop!" I'm not sure if Ami's crying out to me or them. "Please don't!"

"Shut your pretty mouth, or I'll come over there and shut it for you." The greasy hooligan's face becomes serious.

Without warning I barrel full speed to him, sword drawn. There's no escape. I lance him with the sword. As it enters under his ribs, I push energy through the blade. His chest caves under the full force of a concentrated shockwave. His body flies back, colliding with the thugs behind him.

Ami screams. When I look, Eve is fending off attackers with punches and kicks flying in a flurry. I'm intoxicated by her ferocity, and I soak it in. She's pushing back a man and woman who had attempted to overtake them, and appears to have it handled. Her physical prowess delights me.

Stupidly, I've allowed myself to be caught off guard. A fist of iron connects with my jaw, then in my ribs. I stumble against a fence and feel my mouth fill with blood. I spit it at the mob swarming me. I'm hit in the back with something hard and heavy. I collapse, and they kick me repeatedly. Ami yells for me, and I can hear Eve still fighting.

I struggle and a new sensation surges. Rather than expelling a shockwave from my hands, it bursts from my body like a bubble. The assailants are thrown in every direction.

The shockwave has created a crater on the road. Everything around me is trashed. Fences and light posts lie on the road. Even Ami and Eve have been unintentionally caught by it.

My fury at the gang grows.

The street is now partially illuminated by the half moon. Shadows scurry in the night. Someone races across a yard, and I release a shockwave at them. It impacts hard, and they become airborne. Wood shatters in the distance.

"Ami! Eve! Where are you?" I yell.

"Here!" Ami responds from a nearby house.

"Are you okay?" I start moving toward the sound of her voice.

"I'm in a little pain, but I'm fine," she replies.

"Eve?" I yell but there's no response.

Another figure, not Eve, sprints toward Ami's location. Before they reach her, I'm on them and my pommel finds home in the soft tissue where their skull meets their neck. They stumble and hit the ground hard. I kick them in the ribs while they're down. The woman moans. I try to pull back a little but Tiberius's urges push me.

Ami's life supersedes hesitation of force. Kill her.

I kick the woman again to shatter her ribs.

"Stay hidden," I command Ami, who is hugging the porch of a nearby house.

"We have the other girl!" I hear a new voice echo through the neighborhood. "If you don't give yourself up now, I'll kill her."

"You're lying," I yell into the night.

I hear a sickening thump. Eve moans. With a short shockwave blast, I leap and land on the roof of a shack to scout the area. I can't see where they are hiding.

"I'm coming for you! You are a dead man!" I provoke them to hopefully lead me to wherever they are hiding.

"Give up or I cut her!" the thug taunts me.

"Eve, can you hear me? Are you okay?" I yell again.

"Rain! They have me tied up—" I hear them strike her again, then silence.

But they've given me a clue.

"How do I know you won't harm either of them if I submit?"

"It will be a trust exercise!" He grunts with laughter.

I pinpoint the area. The houses are close enough together I can jump from one to the next in that direction. I try to make zero noise. At the far edge of the second house, I turn and throw my voice to where I was previously.

Hopefully he believes I haven't moved.

"This would have been avoided if you'd left us alone."

"You had trouble when you entered our territory without permission."

A few houses away there is a larger alleyway, and the voice came from there. The hair on my neck stands on end as I carefully climb down. I press against the next house, slinking to the rear.

Sticking to the dark areas, I hug the building. I reach a smaller path between houses and peek around the corner.

Someone is coming, chains clinking with their strides. When they are in reach I thrust my hand over their mouth. They're caught off guard, and I muscle them into the wall. They struggle, hitting at my arm to free themselves, but I'm stronger. My blade meets their neck, and I draw it across, the body sagging instantly. Letting them down to the ground gently, I avoid detection of others I hear coming.

"What is your answer? Are you gonna surrender?" he yells from the alley another house over.

I avoid detection. The ones searching find the dead body. They whistle and call for me, as if I were some dog that would come running. I carefully poke my head out into the large alleyway. He has several more men and women on the lookout.

Eve is on her knees in the middle of them, bound. A knife pressed to her throat gleams in the dim light.

On alert, they wait for me to show myself.

Running in risks him flinching and killing her, but if I don't, he might anyway. I have to give myself up and wait for an opportunity to break her free.

My mind runs circles around the openings they're leaving. If Eve wasn't there, they wouldn't be standing. I'm conflicted by Tiberius's urge to take the risk, and my priority of ensuring Eve's life. When a trickle of blood runs down Eve's neck, I step from the darkness.

"I'm here. Don't kill her."

"Drop the sword," the man demands.

I do, and bring my hands up to a surrendered position. The other members of his gang rush and snatch my sword away. I'm kicked in the knees, sending me to the ground. My arms are twisted hard behind me. The man grins from underneath a hood. He leans down, puts his face right next to hers, and pulls the blade tighter against her neck. She flinches. The sight of actual fear in her expression begs me to act.

"It doesn't have to be this way. I know the government is treating the lower class poorly. I can do something about it."

He ignores me and licks his lips. He barks an order, "Go find the other girl."

A bald, tattooed woman heads off, obscured by the dark and a house.

"You don't want this," I tell him.

"Shut up! Don't tell me what I want." He sniffs Eve's hair.

"If you hurt either of them, I will not *just* kill you. I'll dismember you and feed you your appendages. I'll start with fingers and toes." I say things I wouldn't normally, Tiberius asserting his dominance once more.

"Give me that sword," he instructs a follower. They bring it to him and hand it off. "Tell me how this thing works and I'll let her go."

"It's a sword. You swing it."

I may as well call him a moron while I'm at it.

"There's more to it. Is there a chamber to load a shot shell or something? Those are illegal ya'know!" He laughs, but turns serious in an instant. "Tell me now, or she's dead, and then your other friend is next."

"*I* have the power. Maybe we can work together. You can run the show, and I'll be the muscle." I'm sarcastic with him.

He'd be stupid to believe that.

"Let one of my hands free, and I'll show you how it works."

He nods, to my surprise, and my left arm comes free.

What an idiot!

If I hit him with a shockwave, he might draw the blade across Eve's neck, even accidentally.

Eve will live. Blind him.

I'm sorry, Eve.

I bring my hand around front, point my palm at the loose earth, and unleash. Dirt and rock fly into his face. It hits Eve too, but I don't expect she'll be angry with me.

He tries to block it, and loosens his grip on her. It's the opening I've been waiting for.

I expel a shockwave from my core, knocking my captors away. Eve hops from her knees to her toes, springing up. Her head collides with his chin, causing his jaw to clatter shut. He grunts, and before he can recover I'm there.

I grip his wrist and pull his arm away. With the freedom, she leans forward, and then snaps her head back to smash his nose. The knife falls and she stands. Eve presents her bound hands, and I free her.

"Hurry!"

It feels as though I am floating, elated at what's about to happen. I pick the knife up, and plunge it into his ribcage. He struggles, trying to wield my own sword against me, but he's dying. He swings. It grazes me. I withdraw the knife, and stab again.

Those fallen by my shockwave recover and run at me. Death comes for them as Tiberius's murderous impulses compel me. I dance as if I'm on a stage, ducking swings and dodging blows. I wield the knife, and I'm as adept at killing as Drake was. My thoughts meld into Tiberius's.

How could I have lost to Drake? I was stupid. I let my guard down.

If I hadn't though, I wouldn't be here. He provided me an opportunity to protect people. The family I've been brought into.

And now I can start anew. I am powerful. I will protect what I hold dear.

But I must be careful with this power. Pull back!

I won't!

I can't stop. Eve and I work together as a killing machine. We use their own weapons to overtake them; she clubs them with a pipe, while the knife I hold finds home in half a dozen bodies. Attempts to stop us fail, and my rage burns at their evil.

A noise catches my attention and I spin. The bald woman has captured Ami. The thug woman's eyes widen with fright at the sight of the bodies. She panics and shoves Ami toward me. Fearing for her life she runs, disappearing into the night.

With both of them safe, my rage is suppressed.

But Eve's attention is drawn to the one who threatened her: he's still alive, and slowly crawling toward the street.

Eve grabs my sword and runs to him. A sharp kick to his ribs spins him onto his back. She points the sword at his throat, and roars in anger.

Ami hides her face with her hands to avoid seeing the killing blow.

Eve thrusts downward, easily decapitating him, his body now lifeless. Shadows move about the neighborhood. I glare maliciously, ready to defend again. The streets become motionless. Ami tugs on my arm.

"I want…to go home now." There's a hiccup in her voice, and tears streaming down her cheeks. Supporting her, we move to leave the carnage, Eve following.

I battle with Tiberius for control of my thoughts. Being the death-bringer has pleased me, and yet I'm remorseful because Ami has seen the side of me I hoped she never would. I am capable of killing ruthlessly.

It was done with the intention of keeping them safe.

Did I have to take it that far?

They were willing to kill all of us.

The guilt overrides Tiberius's presence, and I hide my face in her hair so neither of them see me cry. Ami pulls away and we walk in silence.

Leaving the bodies where they lie feels wrong, but I have no energy to clean up the mess.

We go back the way we came. I hold my arm out for Ami to take, but she shies away. Eve sees her opening, and swoops in to stand next to me.

She hates me now.

It doesn't matter. You're more like Eve than Ami. We're smart, vicious, and cunning people. She understands you. She won't judge you for what you had to do.

But I love Ami.

Eve will never forsake you.

The lines between Tiberius and I blur. Though it feels like a betrayal, I hold onto Eve for comfort. A battle rages in my soul. As much as I want to be Rain, and to be with Ami, it is becoming increasingly more difficult.

Is this destiny? Will I always be at the center of death and destruction?

By the time we return to the park, my feet are dragging. Sorrowful and depleted of energy, my motivation to keep moving wanes, but Eve pulls me along.

At home, I do my best to help tend to Eve's wounds, but Ami avoids me, and takes care of it. Her presence is cold and my heart aches.

Not wanting to make things worse, I head to my room. I peel away my shirt, and my arm throbs from the wound. But I ignore it.

I sink onto the mattress, my heart dropping into my gut. I'm queasy. The thought of ruining Ami's feelings toward me, because of my violent tendencies, eats at my mind.

Tiberius mocks me.

We need a title. 'Rain the Violent' or 'Violent Rain'?

~~~~~~

My limbs jerk and I'm snapped awake. A heavy and dark presence lingers over me, worsened by the headache pounding at my skull. The headache could be from last night, or the heavy machinery clanking outside my window. It's painful, and it reminds me of a time when I was king where I drank far too much and woke up sick.

I dress, and when I open my door Eve is propped against the sewing room doorframe, waiting for me. The swelling in her face is down significantly since last night, and the small slice on her neck has scabbed. She saunters over and leans on my doorframe.

"Hey." She shies away from direct eye contact – she's being bashful. "What you did for me last night…"

"I would do it for anyone in this house," I tell her.

"Yes." She reaches out and grabs my hand. "But you did it for *me*. I saw how Ami wouldn't look at you for the rest of the night, and how much it hurt you."

"Eve, it—"

She puts her hand on my mouth for a moment. "I don't blame you. You had to take lives. It's a tough thing to do, but you have to admit we're alike. You and I are warriors. We belong together."

"Stop." Though my mouth says stop, my voice projects hesitation.

I'm afraid of her winning me over, but her words ring true. The thought of wanting to be with Ami hurts worse because I'm recognizing my true self now. I don't know if Ami will ever accept what I've done to protect her. Eve understands.

"Rain, you make my heart flutter." She puts my open palm over her heart. It thumps hard and fast. Mine begins to race.

Embarrassed, I try to pull my hand away, but she keeps me pinned there. She leans in. Her lips come close to mine, and the closer she gets, the more I want it. But the sound of Emma's door opening startles me, and I struggle to free myself. It's too late. She's emerging from the room and spots the tryst.

"What are you doing?" she yells. "You let him go right now!"

For the sake of previous appearances, I attempt to pull away even more. Eve uses the doorframe to overpower me, and pulls me into her bosom while smothering me with her arms.

"He didn't have a problem with what was happening until you came out, *little girl*," Eve spits at her. "Go back to your room."

Emma attacks, hitting Eve's arm. She must have hit a soft or sore spot, because Eve's grip weakens. Emma pries Eve's arms away, rips us apart, and stands in front of me defensively.

"He's Ami's! You won't get anything from him."

Footsteps echo in the stairway. Ami comes up to see what the commotion is. She assesses the situation with a stern look on her face, but won't look at me.

"She was forcing herself on him again!" Emma guards me. "I intervened before she could kiss him."

"Like I said, he was fine until you came out," Eve says calmly.

"Enough!" Ami interjects. "He's a grown man and can defend himself…if that's what he wants. Grow up."

Her words are a shock to all of us. Eve is smug in her triumph. Emma turns away to face me, looking as if she's about to cry. Coming from Eve, it's nothing for her to shrug it off, but Ami's scorn has hurt her deeply. I hug her to be comforting. Ami crosses her arms and looks away, ashamed.

"I have a right to thank him for saving me last night," Eve breaks the silence.

"Whatever," Ami huffs.

She heads into her sewing room, and slams the door.

Agatha appears at the top of the stairs. "We will have fresh water shortly." Her worried look makes me feel worse. "They've patched the hole in the well, replaced our water pump, and repaired a few pipes. As soon as the replacement septic tank is hooked up, they'll put water back into the well and test the whole system."

I nod. Letting go of Emma, I knock on the sewing room door.

"Ami, when they're done I'll take a shower and then we can head out to look for James."

I want to mend the situation, but there's no acknowledgement. Confused by a mixture of thoughts and feelings, I head to the kitchen to gorge myself; sadness wins and I do my best to drown it by eating.

When I'm finished trying to kill my sorrows with food, I look out the window and watch the men work. Their busyness distracts me for a moment. A large MV carries a tank away, and I assume it's the old one. Several men climb from the hole in the yard, and no more enter. The foreman comes to the door and knocks. When I open it he hesitates, likely because I'm not who he's used to talking to.

"We're finished, and water is being pumped in the well now. Turn on a faucet and keep it going until it runs clear."

I turn the faucet on full, and watch it intently. After a few minutes the murky brown turns clear. Hope exists within this water.

Can my soul ever become clean like this?

You are who you are.

I nod at the foreman, and he leaves.

I head to the bathroom to clean up. In the mirror, I see myself caked with blood. Disrobing, I force myself to face my violent reality, judging who I want to be versus who I am. My eyes are dark because of Misery, and it eats at me to know I caused part of them.

Who am I?

The line between Tiberius and I blurs more. I am trying to resist it, but I keep coming back to a phrase.

You are who you are.

I am who I am.

Is this Tiberius's thought? Or mine?

Unsure of what to think, I climb into a cold shower, denying myself comfort as self-punishment. The water bites, and my wound stings, but I endure it. A few moments into lathering up, Ami's door slams shut, and the walls shudder. There is muffled yelling and then it becomes quiet. There's a light click of a latch moving beyond a strike plate. When I look out of the curtain, Ami's coming in.

"I'm in here," I tell her.

"Shh!" Ami demands while stepping in.

"I'm showering," I protest.

What in the world is she doing?

"I know." She frowns, moving closer. "I won't pretend to understand what came over you last night. I'll chalk it up to the person you used to be, and we can move past it."

I can't hide it from her any longer. I can't be dishonest. I have to tell her I am not the innocent person she wants me to be.

It's for the best. If you...I...push her away now, she can't be angry later when I move on. My presence will inflict tragedy and pain on her life.

"Ami, the truth is—"

"Do you love Eve?" she cuts me off.

"I—"

She cuts me off again. "If throwing myself at you like she does is what it takes, then I will!"

In anger she starts to take off her shirt. I pull the curtain closed, embarrassed and confused.

"Ami, stop. I have a secret you need to know. I can't allow it to fester any longer."

"I don't want to hear it. I won't let Eve steal your heart from me!"

"It's not about Eve…This isn't the first time I've killed someone. I've killed many."

"Stop! I don't want to hear this!"

"I *killed,* and I *liked* the power I felt while doing it. I'm not as brutal as Tiberius, who killed in cold blood, but I've killed people to affect an outcome. Inside me, I'm fighting a battle I might lose. I feel like I'm both Rain and Tiberius right now."

"Why are you telling me this? Are you trying to push me away so you can be with Eve?"

I peek out the side of the curtain. Her arms are crossed over her white bra, but I stay focused on her eyes.

"I excel at violence. I'm not ashamed because of what I've done, but because you've seen my true self. I never wanted that."

"If you're ashamed because I know now, then don't do it anymore."

She doesn't understand. She's too…good.

"I can't promise that, because it's part of me. The future is uncertain, and I might have to protect you again."

"Please…try. I was shocked last night, and I'm sad and upset this morning. But Tiberius is who you were, not who you are. Don't let your past define you."

She steps forward and uncrosses her arms. I pull the curtain tight so she can see only my face. I blush.

There's a loud commotion outside the bathroom. We both jump, fearing being caught.

Ami grabs her shirt, and runs for her bedroom. Her door to the bathroom clicks shut, and I'm alone. Even now, she has my mind and heart racing.

Done with my shower, I dry off, dress, and pursue her. I rap lightly on the adjoining door to her room. She opens it, dressed in a new, flowery shirt. We exchange weak smiles.

With no one to interfere, and no reason to hide, I bring my hand to her face and stroke her cheek.

Ami pushes hard into my palm with her face and closes her eyes. My hand moves to the back of her neck, and I pull her in gently. She starts to follow my motions, but stops mid-way and opens her eyes.

"Rain..." she hesitates. "I want this more than you know, but I can't...I don't think my heart can take it if you're not serious. Do you love me or Eve?"

Both, but that's not fair to either of them. I've tried almost everything to push Eve away gently and she's slowly breaking me down. Maybe she'll quit if I confess my love for Ami to her.

It's a mistake. You're going to hurt Ami. One day, you will hurt her, and she'll never recover. Save Ami, and confess your love for Eve.

I'm done listening to Tiberius and my doubts. Pulling her in, I press my lips to hers. It starts as a soft kiss, but an emotional dam bursts. Passion leads me, and I lead her. Her hands wrap around my back, and pull me in hard. I can't get enough, and grab her by her hips. My hand slides up to the bottom of her shirt, and I caress her skin. We nearly lose ourselves in the moment, but she pulls away. My whole being aches for her. I've made my choice.

"Does that answer your question?"

She blushes.

"Why did you pull away?" Our noses are touching, and I stare into her brilliant blue eyes.

"The shower is off. Everyone is going to realize you haven't come out." She smiles brazenly.

Should I care? Even knowing my dark secret, she's here. I don't want her to change her mind once we're outside this room.

"One more?" I ask.

Leaning in, she presses her lips to mine. It's quick, and not what I hoped for, but it will suffice. She steps back in her room, and I close the door.

I finish up and head to the kitchen.

Ami has beat me there, and is preparing a day bag of essentials. We exchange coy glances and deviant smiles while I throw my dirty towel in a basket of laundry near the wall.

I slip on my shoes and step outside. Dirt is being dumped on top of the new tank, and Agatha is speaking with the foreman. The emptiness of this side of the yard, even devoid of grass, is weird to see. Ami passes me, brushing her hand over mine. I follow, and stop by Agatha.

"The pipes are fine, and with the repairs to the well and replacement of the tank, you should be solid for the next fifteen years," the foreman explains.

"Thank you for your quick work." She hands him a pouch, likely filled with gold coins from previous spoils.

He leaves and I step up.

"We're heading out."

"Rain…please be careful…and protect my daughter." Agatha's serious now. "It's a dangerous city."

She knows I will. Is she saying it for Ami's sake?

Protection comes in many forms, but sometimes there's no other choice but violence.

"With my life," I promise and look over my shoulder at Ami.

"That doesn't mean you can get hurt either. You need to stay safe too." She smiles. "We need our protector."

"Thanks, Aggy, I will." I lean in and kiss her cheek.

Ami tugs on my hand and leads me away. Pulling the map and picture from her pocket, she looks at them before we head off into the city. I stop her near the apple tree.

"Ami…" my voice fails. "I don't want you to be disappointed with me. I will try to resolve problems differently, but I can't promise I won't take every precaution and action to ensure safety for those I care for."

If we…I refuse to kill, would I die to protect her?

I would!

"Last night the despair cried out. I can't undo what I've done, but maybe we can change the fate of others. Give them hope."

"We already have a lot to do. Can we add any more?" she asks.

"I want to at least talk with the local government. We know Chas will grow and prosper. It has to start somewhere." I shrug. "What if it's us?"

She purses her lips. I've put a thought in her head, but she doesn't answer. Instead she pulls me along.

MVs pass by, and we take an opening between them to cross the street, following the same path from last night. What surprises me is that even with the night life being lively, there are at least double the people awake during the day. However, in the daylight the devastating poverty is much clearer. The buildings are worn. The paint on the MVs is faded or chipped; rust can be seen on the bodies. The people are dirty, sickly, and skinny.

"What if you're wrong?" she asks while observing the same things I am. "What if they are supposed to do it by themselves?"

"Look around." I shake my head.

Admitting I was a poor leader as king is hard, but I have to acknowledge my failures to make advances.

"I recognize this type of people. It's similar to my kingdom when I was king of Asta. It took an outside force to finally spur those people to rise up to fight Drake, and take control of their lives."

"What if it's not supposed to be *you* then? What happens to Emma? She could end up not existing." Ami looks down, saddened. "She's like a little sister to me."

I assume she's feeling bad because she snapped at Emma.

"Did you talk to her after what happened upstairs?"

"Yeah…I apologized. She said it was okay, but I still feel awful."

What happens if we affect something that causes Emma or Eve not to exist? Is it possible? How would that affect us?

"I suppose we should ask Emma if she knows what happens." I scratch my chin.

"Ask me about what?" Emma unexpectedly chimes in.

My heart leaps, and we both turn to look. I laugh nervously and realize we've been tailed.

Emma's matching blue shirt and jeans, and blond ponytail stand out in the dreary backdrop of the city. Eve's just as colorful, but for different reasons. Her fiery red hair is a mess, and she seems to have thrown on random suggestive clothing.

"We were discussing making Chas better. I was nearly drawn into the despair of the people last night. The local government is corrupt, crime is rampant, and people have no means to make a living. The city needs a change." I have started a speech without meaning to. "I might be able to make it better, but we were discussing whether it was my place, and if it would have an effect on the future and your existence."

"Well, I'm still here, aren't I?" A sly smile crosses Emma's lips. "I'm sure whatever it is won't change a thing."

Does she know something?

"Thanks. But nothing has been decided. We are trying to find James right now."

"Where do we start?" she asks cheerfully.

"I was hoping for alone time with Rain." Ami smiles weakly at her.

"It's okay. I understand!" She winks. "Get him, lover-girl!"

I blush. Eve laughs sarcastically. Emma tries to leave, but Eve grabs her by the arm and pulls her in.

"We're going wherever he's going," Eve insists obstinately.

We walk two by two. I put my hands in my pockets, but I really want to be holding Ami's hand right now.

Ami stops in at a few shops, asking about James, showing the picture. Though there are no positive identifications, she is not discouraged, and we keep moving as the day rolls on.

She changes direction, and instead of heading deeper into the residential area, leads us along the boundary separating the multi-story buildings and single story houses. She walks with purpose.

"Where are we going?" I ask after a few minutes.

"To City Hall. We might be able to accomplish both of our goals at the same time." Ami smiles.

"I don't want your time to go to waste."

"It won't. City Hall might be able to help me." Her mood is a total shift from this morning; she's cheerful.

Ami leads our journey into the big city. The change of buildings is sudden as we pass out of residential neighborhoods and surround ourselves with skyscrapers.

These aren't decaying like everywhere else: they're well maintained. The MVs humming around here are nicer. The people are well groomed. There are far fewer of them per square foot, and their movements are with purpose. The difference is as if we had walked into an entirely different city altogether.

Ami points to an area far off. "That should be it."

There is a large park around a single imposing building. It's significantly different. Its base is wide, and as it rises it comes to a point at the top, making an elongated pyramid. Its faces are glass windows, held together by metal framing. The sun hits it just right, blinding me, and I have to shield myself.

Beacon of light. Fitting for a City Hall. Too bad its reputation is poor.

You could govern them. You could lead the people of Chas to salvation.

Let's not jump ahead. We don't even know if Evalyn will succeed.

Ami leads us fearlessly into the concentration of well-dressed men and women moving around the establishment. People stop to stare at us as we approach. She's unfazed, and motions for the other two to move up. Ami stops short of the stairs leading to the doors.

"What's your plan?" Emma asks with a slight giggle.

Yes, what is our plan?

I draw from my past, remembering the things my father did. I'm filled with confidence, and I don't know if it's me or my past personality empowering me.

"We need a solution for the economy. A city this size should have some sort of product for export. Export will create jobs and begin to lessen the poverty. The revenue can then be used to improve Chas," I say with authority.

"What export?" Eve asks.

"Trees and lumber first, then agriculture. Farmland built outside of the city."

Emma titters again.

"In my time, my father uprooted large sections of the forest and created farmland, and then employed the people to tend it so they could make a living. Since he was paying them, he didn't tax them on their wages. I plan on presenting this idea to the city's leaders."

Emma's in a fit of giggles at this point. I arch an eyebrow at her.

"What is so funny?"

"Nothing," her voice is almost sing-song.

She's holding something back. She must know what's going on.

At the top of the steps, a large arched entryway eclipses normal doorways in size by at least three times. Glass doors are recessed into the pyramid-like tower. Two tall guards are posted on either side, dark glasses covering their eyes.

People come and go freely, unrestricted, but when I take the lead the guards shift to intercept. One steps forward and raises an open hand.

"What is your business here?" his voice is deep, but not intimidating.

"We need to speak to the governor of Chas," I reply.

"Do you have an appointment?"

"No—" I start, but he cuts me off.

"That's what I thought. It's unusual for you people to travel in from the outskirts. Your ignorance of how your own government works says you didn't even know you needed one."

His arrogant attitude puts me on defense. "Then schedule me one for today."

"You can fill out paperwork. They'll get to you when they get to you, maybe in a few weeks."

How infuriating. And yet I did the same thing to people seeking me when I was king.

"That's unacceptable." Despite the irritation, I am unwavering.

He points aggressively at me. "If you want the papers, I'll grab them. But then you and your party will vacate the area."

"I'm sorry." I sigh. "You're just doing your job, but I can't take no for an answer. I'm entering this building today."

He moves to grab something from his waist. I can't tell if it's a firearm. I point my finger at the ground off to the side where there are no people. Looking at Ami, I wait for approval. Despite our conversation, she nods. The girls move out of the way, and using restraint I expel a small shockwave.

The thundering noise causes a panic. Cries and screams come from everywhere, and people scatter like insects. Even the other guard lets out a yelp.

The one in front of us pulls a black box from his hip and speaks into it frantically. "Domestic terror situation at ground level. I need backup!"

I snatch it from his hand. As it sits in my palm, it reminds me of the communication devices used by Denis and his gang, except there's no holographic image to talk to.

He looks at me fearfully when I hold it up.

"How do I use it?" I glare.

"You push the button and talk."

Pushing the button, I speak, "Cancel the request. No need for backup. This man has decided to allow me in."

I head toward the doors. The other guard steps aside, and even opens the door for me. I'm stopped by a voice from the box.

"Who are you?" a woman's voice.

"Someone who wants a meeting," I answer while stepping inside.

The interior is decorated with marble. The floor is polished to a bright shine. Large desks and counters make patterns around the lobby, and in the middle is a pillar with elevator doors. The people inside the lobby stop moving around. They tear their attention away from bulky screens to stare.

"You aren't authorized. Vacate immediately," the woman's voice comes again.

I press the button and look for whomever might respond. "You don't have a say. Confront me, or show me to the person in charge."

An older woman dressed in the same uniform as the guards appears, followed by several other guards. They close in, holding firearms trained directly on me. I sigh loudly and put my hands out.

"Leave. Now."

"Contact the governor and tell them I'm not leaving until I get a meeting," I demand.

They hesitate to use their firearms, and I'm glad. The woman backs away slowly, her attention still trained on me. Leaning over a counter she presses a button and speaks. Though I cannot hear what she says, her lips are moving fast. She returns and holsters her firearm.

"Follow," she says reluctantly, backing up to the elevator. She presses the button to call it.

Looking over my shoulder, her guards are still there, their weapons trained on me.

A ding signals the doors opening. We enter, and she presses the button for the twenty-fifth floor. While the doors close, she keeps her eyes on us. The elevator climbs rapidly, and we're in it for a minute before it dings at our destination. The new room is spacious, with no one else here.

We are not at the top of the building, but I suspect we're close. The carpet is deep red. There are a few tables with dozens of chairs tucked in on all sides. Clear of the elevator, the doors shut, and it comes to life.

"Sit," the woman orders.

We head to a table near the windows, but I'm distracted and take the opportunity to get a better look of the land from a unique perspective. I can see the forest boundary where the house is, in the far distance.

Chas is small right now. There's lots of forest out there.

Does this area develop in the same type of cycle over and over? Terrible leadership, people in poverty, gangs. It wouldn't surprise me if there was another earthquake and another incursion of Tarak.

A ding resounds, and the elevator doors open. Two men and a woman emerge. The first man is hefty, his pinstripe suit is two sizes too small, and the single button which holds the coat closed threatens to pop as he walks. He runs a hand over his slicked back, blond hair.

The second man is tall. His pale skin is nearly albino, and is in contrast to his black hair. A stern look is plastered on his face, his lips spread in a long frown.

He looks like he could be Chase's ancestor. Does he have the same speed?

The woman is slender. She has curly black hair that bounces when she tilts her head to peer over a pair of glasses. Her scowl and rigid body movements tell me she's in a foul mood.

The three sit on the opposite side of the table. The heavyset man sits in the middle of the other two, and places his elbows on the table. His hands are clenched together, and press against his chin. He grins and shows deep yellow teeth. His position and his demeanor mean he's in charge.

"I'm Renaldo," he starts and then points to his accomplices. "This is Terrance and Vicky. You have caught my interest, and that is the singular reason I'm feeling generous enough to give a few moments. Why are you here?"

"I have a proposition – an opportunity – for this run down, crime filled city of Chas. It's about time for Chas to prosper."

"My city is in great order." His grin doesn't fade.

Misery cries out in me. They call him a liar.

"You're wrong," I bark harshly.

"Exactly who are you?" he asks sternly, his attitude changing to match mine.

"A concerned person with a vested interest. My name is irrelevant, but what I can offer isn't."

He studies me for a few moments before his smile returns.

"You've got a lot of nerve kid, but I like it. It's not something I see frequently, and it intrigues me." He leans back in his chair. "But seriously, I want to know who I am dealing with."

"I'm a traveler with a unique set of abilities. But I'm not here to cause more trouble than necessary."

"What is your proposition?" He looks left and right to his own people, who have to this point been watching silently.

"The far sides of the city have fallen to poverty. Food is scarce, and the means to support one's self is even more so. Chas's economy is in disarray," I begin.

"Were you elected as a representative to come to me?"

"No. You could call me an expert, of sorts, and Chas needs help." I sit up straight and cross my arms. "What I propose is an initiative to create jobs through agricultural means, and improve the economy. By creating city-owned farmland beyond the borders, you can maintain a renewable resource as well as create an export. Or you can keep importing on loans and drown in debt."

Renaldo strokes his moustache, and studies me, appearing to be deep in thought. Vicky writes on her pad, looking up every once in a while.

"You seem smart, kid. Smart enough to know how things work," Renaldo says earnestly. "Your idea is lofty. It would take a significant amount of money and manpower. Tell me why you care."

"I like Chas, and want to help it grow."

"Help? I'm not sure the people will want help from the monster who destroyed a street and killed people last night." His grin turns malicious.

My eyes open wide in surprise.

"That's right. Rumors make it back to me quickly. I heard a whisper of a 'monster' demolishing part of my city while fighting a few rats. Your demonstration outside implicates you as the culprit."

"It wouldn't have happened if *you* had been taking care of the real problems. They attacked me. I had to defend my friends." My tone becomes sharp, intending to cut at his ego.

Renaldo seems to accept the answer as he nods and continues our previous conversation. "What do I get out of this deal?"

"Chas will be a better place. I'll even help you start."

"That's pretty low incentive," he replies. "The definition of 'a better place' is...relative to the person. For example, I see Chas as a great place."

"Your economy will recover, and you'll be pulling in money from exports."

"I'd have to delegate and have someone develop a scenario to see if this is feasible. Then we'd have to have a committee. And a vote. We'd be tying people up when they could be focused on other things." He stands. "It has been surreal, but we have other matters to attend to."

"Wait," Ami speaks. "I need help finding someone."

"I'm sorry, I really don't have any more time to talk. If you'd like to schedule an appointment, I'm sure Terrance or Vicky would be able to accommodate you." He frowns.

The four of us stand as well, and I extend my hand across the table for him, just to be cordial. He contemplates and hesitates, but finally reaches his hand across and shakes mine weakly. Renaldo, Vicky, and Terrance enter the elevator, and disappear behind the double doors. After a minute of whirring, the elevator returns, and the guard waves us in.

We're returned to the bottom level, and in the lobby we're met with uncomfortable stares until we exit the building.

When we're outside, the sunlight relaxes me, and I sigh. It's apparent that talking with Renaldo was a waste, but I put in the effort.

We walk in silence for several hundred yards.

"A waste of time and breath," I mutter.

"Renaldo gave me a bad vibe," Ami blurts.

"I agree. I can be pretty conniving, but he's just slimy," Eve adds.

Looking at Emma, I expect her to chime in. Instead she smiles silently, keeping her secret.

Rather than ask, I pay attention to walking. When we reach the street separating the big city from the residential, it appears there is still a fair amount of daylight left to search for James.

"Eve, do you remember the way home?" I ask.

"I have a great directional sense. I can lead us," she says proudly.

"Good, you two head home. We'll be there later." I'm polite but firm.

"Where are you two going?" Emma laughs. "On a date?!"

"Absolutely not!" Eve barks, straightens her back, and puffs out her chest.

"To look for James, and because of the gangs, it will be safer to protect one instead of three." I cross my arms.

Emma winks and then playfully punches me in the arm. "Mmhmm. Sure."

Eve sighs and spins around with attitude. She grabs Emma's arm and drags her away.

"Don't stay out *too* late!" Emma calls to us playfully.

As they head back to the house, Eve's stomping away fast and angrily.

When they're nearly out of sight, I grab Ami by her hand, and she looks at me bashfully. She overcomes her shyness and turns toward where we need to be looking.

~~~~~~

After hours of wandering and searching with nothing to show for our efforts, we head back to the house. The sun is setting on another day of not finding James.

Ami's disappointed, so I distract her by squeezing her hand and smiling when she looks over. Her smile makes me think of her lips, and I want to kiss her right now.

The moment we enter the door to the kitchen, Agatha practically leaps on me. But it's not her. Evalyn's facial expressions give her away, and she's worked up with excitement.

"Where have you been? I was expecting you back hours ago!" Evalyn protests, though she isn't mad.

"We have been looking for James."

Ami breaks away, and heads to the refrigerator.

"Well, eat quickly and head to my room," she demands.

I nod and watch the physical change in facial expressions when Agatha is returned control of her body. She titters, and I give her a confused look.

"I haven't seen Evalyn this excited in a very long time. She has so much positive energy right now, it's...refreshing," she says while helping Ami pull food from the refrigerator.

"What's going on?" I ask.

"I'll let her tell you." Her smile widens.

Did Evalyn do it? Did she find a way?

I hope so. We need to usurp Renaldo.

There's no plan for dinner tonight, so I'm content with making a sandwich.

Ami and Agatha sit at the table chatting about our search for James, while I head upstairs.

With no sign of Eve or Emma I tiptoe across the wood floor. Eve's snoring permeates the hallway. I sigh, relieved because she's unlikely to wake.

At Evalyn's door, a strange orange light seeps out from the cracks.

I don't knock, knowing she wouldn't be able to answer me. But when I enter the room I'm startled. There's a woman in Evalyn's room. She shrieks, and I slam the door shut, severely confused. Emma pokes her head out as I stand there. Waving her back into her room fervently, she nods and disappears.

"Are you coming in or what?" Evalyn calls after me, though she sounds much younger.

I push the door open and I'm confused and amazed. She's visible, though in a ghostly form and with a slight tinge of orange. She appears young, likely the way she looked when she died. Her hair is short, cut above her ears, and her dark blue eyes match Agatha's. She is the same height, but a little more slender than her sister. She's wearing things Eve would be jealous of. Her collared shirt is nothing more than white cloth flowing down over her collarbone and chest, tied around her back midway up. The shirt ends at a tight fitting belt at her waist holding a pair of black shorts. She has on solid black stockings to match, but no shoes. I blush heavily and am forced to look away.

"That's right. Quit ogling my body and close the door," she says harshly, but the smile on her face indicates she's playing with me.

I do as she says and fix my gaze on the second new thing in the room. Swirling upward is a small vortex as thick as my wrist. This one is orange. It's being emitted from one of the salvaged objects: an urn.

Squatting, I examine the simple urn. It's painted white and there are red symbols. Upon closer examination, the markings look almost identical to the Vraditi alphabet.

Were they here again? Or did someone discover remnants of the cylinders?

"Okay." I look up at her, avoiding staring. "How? And what does this mean for us?"

"I don't know how. I was thinking, and it hit me. What if I tried to possess the items I could feel power coming from? As I was doing so, this happened with the urn."

Standing up I reach for her arm, and when I touch where it would be, my hand passes through.

"Stop! It tingles!" she scolds.

"Sorry!" I pull my hand back.

"I feel the energy. It's like it's trying to counter time. It could be in direct relation to the power in the house. If we can amplify it we might be able to use it against our vortex." Evalyn crosses her arms, and her face turns sour. "Of course, there's a second possibility, based on what you can see of me now: these are my death clothes. This orange vortex might lead back to the original point in time that I died."

"It would be nice if we could use it to go back and stop you from using your power," I state as a passing thought.

"If that were possible, none of this would have ever happened, resulting in the person never having gone back to stop me. I have no idea what kind of strange paradox it might cause."

"I understand at least that much, but what happens if we succeed in cancelling the vortex?"

"My hope is that the orange vortex cancels out the blue, and we stay put right where we are."

"So, how do we amplify it?" I ask the obvious question.

The mischievous smile on Evalyn's face tells me the answer, and I'm not sure I am comfortable with it. "You, Rain. I want to combine our power."

"You're going to possess me? You're really going out on a limb aren't you?" I smile back.

"I don't know if I can, but we have to try. When it's time, I'll occupy the same space as you, and combine our energies. It's the best shot we have." She pauses for a moment.

"We don't want to miss our window. You'll have to take the urn to your room. I'll just be there...hovering over you...while you sleep. Waiting for the perfect moment..."

"That's terrifying!" I laugh.

"Yes, yes it is." She laughs with me.

I step close to observe the orange vortex. My foot bumps an item. It's Drake's dagger. Kneeling, I pick it up. As soon as my hand clasps the handle I shudder. An ominous, dark feeling rolls over me and floods my senses. I'm unable to drop it.

Springing to my feet, I stare at the blade, and it takes on an evil glow in the orange light. An arc of electricity shoots forth from the dagger to the vortex. My hand shakes violently, but it's not me. It's pulsing, vibrating in resonance with the swirling. It pulls like a magnet and every fiber of my being tells me to run. But I can't break free. It's pulling me in. It becomes unstable and violent.

"Get it out of here!" Evalyn yells.

"I'm trying!" I plant my feet and fight the pull.

Electricity continues to connect the dagger to the vortex. I do what I can to keep them from meeting, but I fail. It connects and explodes outward. I'm thrown across the room. My back meets the wall, all breath violently pushed from my lungs.

Everything has gone dark. When my eyes readjust, the vortex and

Evalyn are gone.

There's running in the hall. The door swings open quickly, and hits me square in the face. I can't react. My body is frozen, my jaw clenched.

"Rain?! Are you okay?" Ami asks frantically.

My gaze is locked straight ahead, to where the vortex was. My muscles are unresponsive. I have no control.

Ami kneels next to me and snaps her fingers in an attempt to gain my attention, but I'm paralyzed.

What…was that?

You can feel it.

My soul feels like it's being crushed.

You feel him!

Emma jumps in. "Can you hear me?"

It takes me a moment, but I realize I'm not breathing.

"Why won't he respond?" Eve asks.

Ami is stricken with concern, and drops to put her ear to my nose. "He's not breathing!"

They lay me on my back and tilt my head. Ami puts her mouth to mine. She breathes in.

My muscles are locked. Though I can't move, I still feel pain and everything aches.

Her hands move to my chest, and she pumps up and down, then returns to breathing into my lungs.

"Don't die!" Emma cries out.

The paralysis begins to subside. Control returns, and I cough, gasping for air. My body starts breathing again, my heart pumping hard. The beat is loud in my ears. My eyes water and I shut them. The pain dissipates, replaced by tingling in my extremities.

"Rain? Can you hear me?" Ami asks.

"Snap out of it!" Eve calls.

What was that…?

You know! He is here!

Alarmed, I open my eyes. Drake is hovering over the girls. His eyes glow with an eerie power. His red bushy eyebrows are turned downward in a scowl, and an evil grin is plastered across his face.

Though everything is returning to normal, I'm still finding it hard to move.

He reaches for Ami's head.

I struggle to intercept.

Ami sees my fright. "What is it?"

"You're okay! We're here," Emma chimes in, caressing my shoulder.

I grunt and groan. My arms aren't willing to support my efforts to push myself up. When his hand reaches her, I regain control of my body once more.

"No! Don't touch her!" I yell. "Drake is here! Get out!"

They look over their shoulders, and then return perplexed stares to me.

"You must be hallucinating," Eve says.

His hand passes through her. He's trying to reach me, and though I can't hear him, he's laughing. His lips move, but I can't make out the words. His hand touches me. I leap to my feet.

"Don't touch me!"

They can't see him.

He's a spirit possessing the dagger!

Is Evalyn safe? Can he possess me like Evalyn can possess Agatha?

Why are we waiting to find out?

"Get out!" I yell.

The girls protest while I shove them. When we're in the hall, I slam the door behind us, and move them toward the stairs. Looking back to see if he's following reveals an empty hall, but I'm positive I can still feel him.

Down in the living room I shake with fear of my brother. Sitting on the couch, I put my face in my hands and lean on my knees.

"What's wrong?" Emma asks. "You're freaking me out!"

"Drake has found a way to reach me. He must be inside the dagger," I tell them.

"I'll throw it outside," Emma offers.

"Don't touch it! He might be able to possess you."

"You should rest. I'll sit with you if it makes you feel safe," Eve says earnestly.

"We'll take shifts," Ami adds. "And we'll be there in case you have an episode with 'the darkness'."

"I don't want to go back up there," I tell them.

"You don't have to." Emma rubs my back. "Just lay down and rest."

Following instructions, I lay on the couch. Closing my eyes makes me anxious. It feels as though Drake's going to reach me without my touching the dagger. Even with minimal shadows for his figure to lurk in, his evil presence haunts me. Ami brings a chair in and sets it near the couch.

"We'll rotate in two hour increments," she says. "I'll take the first shift."

Eve grabs the chair and Ami resists. They struggle over it before Ami wins.

"I'm not leaving," Eve says, defiant.

"I'll stay too." Emma smiles at me gently.

With my back to the couch, I face Ami. Her light blue eyes are calming me. Every time I close my eyes, his image appears, and I use Ami as a focus to distract myself. She runs her fingers through my hair.

Still, I can stay focused for only so long. I glance around the room. There is no sign of him.

An hour or more passes while I try to convince myself that because Drake hasn't possessed anyone yet, he can't possess anyone not holding the dagger. Or even better, that it might have been a hallucination after all.

Exhaustion sets in and I close my eyes. He still haunts me, but finally his evil recedes.

~~~~~~

A change in Misery causes me to wake. The weight on my soul has lightened, though I don't know why, or by how much. But there is a difference, and I wonder what caused it.

It's better, isn't it? Has something changed within the city?

Eve is on the floor next to the couch, her face propped on the cushion near my head. She's close enough for me to feel her breath. Rolling over I stare at the ceiling. It's daytime, and outside is gloomy, but I can't tell if it's raining.

Eve stirs, and I close my eyes, not feeling up to talking yet. She inhales deeply and lets out a groan. She runs her fingers across my forehead, causing me to shiver. Pressure on the cushion indicates she's coming closer. Her breath hits my lips, and I feel her presence.

I get the urge to pull away. Thoughts of Ami circle my head, my lips wanting to know only hers.

Ami intervenes. "I leave for five seconds and you're trying to steal a kiss?" she yells, and something hits the wall, making me jump. Ami's shoe lands by my head.

"Are you kidding? You had your mouth all over him, and you're yelling about me?" Eve yells back at her. "Besides, if I want to kiss him, I'll kiss him. I don't need your permission!" She stands to confront Ami.

"That was mouth-to-mouth! He was dying, you imp!"

"I'm awake now, so let's forget it." I sit up and laugh halfheartedly. I wink at Ami.

"Can I kiss you now you're awake then?" Eve asks, looking at me with a cheeky grin.

"Absolutely not!" Ami protests reaching for her other shoe.

I give her a curt shake of my head and a sigh. "No."

"Well then I should'a kissed you when I had the chance," Eve mutters under her breath.

Ami points furiously for Eve to go into the kitchen.

With a loud huff she complies, but not without stomping the whole way out. When she's gone, Ami stares at me.

"Did she kiss you?" she demands.

I yawn and stretch while answering, "You stopped her."

"Okay." She's convinced and her mood changes. She heads into the hallway and I'm alone.

As I stand, my muscles ache. It hurts to walk to the window. At the edge of the forest is the spot where I should have died, where I was reborn. Drake's image is in my mind's eye, but I don't feel his evil presence.

Was it all a hallucination, or did I actually see his apparition?

We've spent too much time in his presence to deny it was him.

He was there after we brought the dagger back. But he's not here now, and I'm not possessed.

As long as it exists, it's not over. He will come for us.

The smell of bacon fills the air, and it draws me to the kitchen. Emma's at the stove, and Agatha is whipping up batter. Eve is outside, grunting and yelling. She is violently throwing Ami's clothing into the wash basin, one garment at a time.

"Anything I can do to help?" I ask Agatha.

"Sure. Toast some bread for me, please," Agatha says, smiling.

The task is too easy. Not too long ago, these things were alien to me. Technological marvels such as the refrigerator and toaster had astounded me, but now they're commonplace.

Once, I was a barbarian.

Now I'm better. I'm smarter and more experienced in diplomacy.

Everything was different then. I didn't think about what it took to make breakfast. I was the king. I didn't have to know.

The kitchen staff probably slaved in a hot kitchen all day fixing my meals. It's too bad they didn't have these marvels.

With my delegated task done, I stop at the stove where Agatha has left Emma in charge. She's pouring batter over a couple strips of bacon. My first response is to cringe at pancakes with bacon in them. She hums a tune cheerfully, like this is a normal idea, and I watch intently.

"Where did you come up with this?" I ask.

"I played around with a lot of different combinations when I was trying to start a restaurant. This one sort of stuck in my head, and I always seem to hum a specific tune when I'm making them."

"Rain, would you get Eve please?" Agatha says and sets the table.

I poke my head out the door and whistle sharply to catch Eve's attention. When she looks, I wave for her to come in. She huffs and throws one last piece of clothing into the washbasin. The water splashes up and hits her in the face, causing her further aggravation. I have to stifle a laugh.

Leaving the door open for her, I sit at the table. Eve slams it shut on her way in. She and Emma have a near miss, and a plate of a dozen bacon-pancakes nearly end up on the floor.

Breakfast is silent, and when we're finished I wash the dishes.

I love this family feeling, even when they're at odds with each other.

We ate at the table when I was young, but it was enormous. Most times it felt like I was alone at it.

"Breakfast was delicious," I commend Emma.

"Thank you!"

When I'm done I head to the stairs. Climbing them scares me. Though I don't want to go up there, I have to ready myself for another day out. Sword, cloak, necklace, shoes.

Downstairs and outside, Ami is waiting patiently for me with the horse readied. She's unfazed by our lack of success, her cheery smile contagious.

A smile crosses my face, but it soon fades when I see someone coming, heading right for us. I recognize her.

Vicky strolls awkwardly across the grass, her high heel shoes not the best choice across the undeveloped land. Disgust is plastered on her face. She nears, looks me in the eyes, and frowns even more.

"You offered to help if we took on your idea, correct?" she says sharply, with not even a 'good morning.' "While Renaldo doesn't think it a worthwhile investment, I do."

That's it. It makes sense. The despair must be less because I've affected time. But how much can I change it? When does an irreparable problem occur? Will it be possible to change enough so Misery is never created?

"How did you find me?"

"We've been tracking and watching you. Preparations to clear have already begun, and I wanted to know what assistance you could provide."

"What about Renaldo?" I ask.

"He doesn't have say in my pet projects. How can you help?"

"I can't demonstrate here. I do however need help in return."

"If you're looking for a cut of profit or taxes, I can't accommodate." Her bluntness is almost offensive.

"Nothing quite so easy." I look at Ami, and she smiles at me. "I'm looking for a man, and searching the streets one by one has been tedious and dangerous. I want assistance in searching."

Vicky crosses her arms. "Unlike tracking you because of your... uniqueness, scouring the city for an unknown would take too much man power. However, if you're willing to put in the work there is a possible solution."

"I'll take a partial solution over none."

I hop up on Maximus.

"Ami, lend me the photo of James to show while I'm out."

Reluctantly she pulls the photo from her back pocket, and hands it up to me.

"Don't lose it." Her tone is firm and she points her finger at me, but her smile tells me she's playing. "I expect you to find him."

Vicky grumbles impatiently. The picture slips easily into the inner pocket of my cloak, and I hold my hand out for Vicky. She looks at me confused.

"Do you want to walk back across the grass?" I ask.

"Not particularly."

Ami helps her up, and though she is pressed to my back she refuses to hold onto me.

Pressing my feet against his flanks, Maximus walks across the grass toward the way Vicky came.

At the street she speaks, "Let me down. I'll take my MV and you can follow," her tone clipped and precise.

I pull the reins and slow Maximus. She drops to the ground and marches to a matte black MV idling a dozen feet away. A door opens vertically as Vicky comes within a foot of it. She climbs in, and it closes. The lack of traffic allows her to merge onto the street easily and she creates a gap between us.

Putting my heels into Maximus's flanks signals him to trot. Despite the MV technology, I'm able to close the gap without pushing him too hard. Vicky leads us in a straight path through the city. A distant forest line appears beyond the broken houses.

At this boundary of the city there is an open area before reaching the Forest of Hunger. A small section is already being cleared, dug up by large machines similar to the ones the contractors used in the yard.

Terrance steps into view, and when he sees me he scowls. But he continues about his business, talking to several workers.

Vicky stops her MV along the side of the road.

I stop Maximus near the MV, and dismount. The remains of a chain link fence nearby allow me to tie him up, and there's an overgrowth of grass for him to graze on.

Vicky waits patiently for me. We cross the street to where some men stand, just watching me. Their attitude makes me grin.

Terrance glares before laying into Vicky. "This is why you left? What's he going to do, cut them down with the antique on his waist?" he says, pointing to my sword, but never taking his attention off Vicky.

"He offered to help, he's here to help," Vicky barks back.

"Terrance, it's so nice to see you," I greet him with sarcasm.

"This is ludicrous!" he snaps.

"Keep the workers out of my way." I draw my sword from its home and ready it.

Terrance rolls his eyes and scoffs, but when I shoot him a serious look he grumbles and has the men halt their machinery. When everyone is clear I head toward the trees.

I can do things without being violent. I can use my power for a greater good.

We can be the greatest good the world has ever known. We can bring prosperity through our powerful influence.

It sounds stupid when you say it like that.

Passing the machines, an idea forms. I plunge my sword into the dirt at an angle, pointing toward the trees. Breathing deeply, I collect myself and place both hands on the hilt. The tingling starts, and I gather an enormous amount of energy. When it feels like I've reached my limit, I expel it through my hands into the sword.

The result is as I had hoped. There is a small earthquake, the shockwave sending the ground rolling toward the tree line. There are bursts of dirt and rock as it barrels toward the forest. When it hits, trees collapse by the dozen.

It's loud, as the trees fall in on each other. One tree collapses into the next, knocking it over also. The Forest of Hunger now has a wide arc of leveled trees.

Confident of myself, I don't even look back. I know they're watching me, and I revel in it. Part of this feeling is me proving myself to them, and the other part is Tiberius who loves the attention.

Several yards farther down, I continue. It feels amazing to unleash such devastation, and because no one is being hurt I have no guilt. Sneaking a glance at Terrance, I smile smugly at his dismay and unleash the force again. When it has done its work, there is nothing but destruction in sight.

I hold in my giddiness, fighting back laughter as I return to Terrance and Vicky.

Before I get to them, the machinery moves in. The workers have started toward the wrecked section of the forest to clean up. Vicky writes fervently on a pad while Terrance avoids meeting my eye.

"Here's the deal: I continue helping, you help me with resources to find someone," I tell them.

"Help? You've made a mess of things! The men are going to have a hard time untangling those piles of trees," Terrance scolds me.

"How long would it have taken them to cut them individually? And pulling the trunks out of the forest? It may be work to separate them, but it's *less* work than you would have had to do," I reply contemptuously.

"Enough, both of you." Vicky's voice is calm as she peers over her glasses. "You have a photo, correct?"

"Yes," I reply.

"I'll direct you to a copy shop where you can print off copies. Make copies and we will assist, but we have only the manpower to spread here in the labor community, not neighborhoods."

She flips to a new page on her writing pad and scribbles. Ripping the page from it, she hands it to me.

The directions will mean more to Ami than I.

Shoving it in the pocket with the photo, I nod and return to tearing down the forest.

~~~~~~

I spend the day contributing to their efforts, providing the workers several days of work.

It's dusk by the time I head home. The lunch Vicky and Terrance provided for the workers was tiny, and my stomach growls in protest.

Approaching the house, I dismount and lead Maximus to his stable, and remove his riding gear. Once his needs are met, I enter the kitchen. Soup is simmering on the stove, but there's no one in sight.

Curious, I bend over and sniff at the soup. It smells like beef. A poke to my side startles me and I jump to stand straight up.

When I turn, Agatha's there, but the stern facial expression tells me it's

Evalyn. Though she clearly doesn't look happy with me, she doesn't look angry either.

"Where did you go?" she asks.

"Go?"

"You were in my room, and then you weren't, and everything is a mess."

"You don't remember?"

"Strangely, there's a lapse in my memory. I blacked out, which hasn't *ever* happened while being a disembodied soul. I remember yelling at you to get out with the dagger, and then nothing," she explains.

"I had the blade, and a force was pulling it to the vortex. When they touched it caused an explosion of energy. You and it were gone, and I saw Drake instead of you."

"That explains the potent presence I've been feeling." Her expression turns gloomy.

"You felt him? Then where is he now?" I ask. My heart races.

"He's inside the dagger, possessing it." She shakes her head. "It doesn't seem he understands yet how possession works."

What I hoped might be a hallucination has been confirmed as reality.

"We can't have it here. I'll bury it or destroy it." I breathe hard. Anxiety wells up.

He's not gone.

"Okay. But it has to be you. The others are too weak to handle a presence like that." She puts her hand on my shoulder. "You at least have a shot at resisting him if he figures possession out."

"I don't even know if *I'm* strong enough. If he catches me off guard, I may not be able to resist him." I cross my arms, staring at nothing.

"Whenever you are ready." She smiles weakly and relinquishes control to Agatha.

"Shall we sit for dinner?" Agatha asks, flustered.

"Sure, I'll fetch the girls."

~~~~~~

After dinner, I lay in bed with my arms behind my head, and I relax after my exhausting day to reflect. Today, I imagine, is what it must have been like for the laborers in my time: a working man goes to work, comes back to his loved ones and eats a hearty meal.

My family listened intently as I told them about my endeavors, and Ami became excited when I told her about Vicky's suggestion for copying the photo.

Though the vortex coming to steal us away to another time is still a ways off, there's a sense of urgency to find James sooner rather than later.

The thought of having another man in the house seems like a good idea, at least to balance things out.

Unless he's insane.

Agatha and Evalyn might not be sure how to handle having him here, but I'm confident we can all adapt. If he's lost his mind, then we will have to help him find his sanity.

If we fail to stop the vortex, at least his presence will be a comfort to Ami. If we succeed, I'll have a place here as the 'Monster of Chas,' and perhaps be able to settle from my adventuring.

Those who perpetuate injustice would come to fear us, Violent Rain.

I won't be a king or a governor again. But maybe I can positively influence the outcome of time, make things better for everyone from this point forward.

My eyes become heavy. I shut the light off and return to my bed.

~~~~~~

I wake with harsh feelings from a dream I can't remember.

I wonder if it's because of the past, the present, or the future. Or maybe the feelings are because Drake still exists.

Sunlight falls through the window, and I let the warmth energize me.

My task for the day is to help Ami make copies and distribute them. It seems as if it's not enough. It's too simple. And yet it's a reprieve from action and danger.

I dress in clean clothes, which Eve so 'graciously' washed and dried yesterday. Throwing my stained white cloak over my back, it hangs like a cape. After lingering for a few minutes, I head to my door. When I pull it open, Ami falls forward, appearing to have been listening.

I try to catch her, but she knocks me back into the bed. Trying to stay upright, I grab her hand. But it's futile. I fall and pull her with me. We both laugh. She hovers over me with her arms propped on the bed.

"How long were you out there?" I push up with my elbows. Our faces become closer.

"I was about to knock. I was listening to see if you were awake." She blushes and turns her head.

Her hair brushes my face, tickling me. The beauty of her smooth skin forces me to reach up and caress her cheek. She looks at me, and I could lose myself in her eyes, feeling our connection, our closeness. Because she's near, I lean in for a kiss, but we're interrupted by a battle cry at the doorway.

Eve slams her fist through my door, and wrenches Ami off of me before either of us can react.

I jump up to intercede, as Eve is ready to punch her.

"Who's the hussy now?" Eve yells, pulling Ami's wrist around mercilessly.

I reach for Eve's hand, but she pulls away.

Ami's not content to let her do what she wants. She slams her whole body into Eve, pushing her back into the doorknob. Eve's grip loosens, and Ami pulls her arm free. As she brushes her shirt off, she has a smug look on her face.

Eve retaliates by shoving her backward. Without missing a beat Ami slaps her in the face. The impact is heavy, and the sound echoes through the hall.

This can't go on.

I step between them to stop Eve from throwing the punch I know she's gearing up for.

"Stop!" I tell the both of them.

"What's going on?" Emma appears, rubbing her eyes.

"I don't care how much Rain says he'll kill me if I hurt you. I won't hold back from now on! The next time you hit me, you better knock me out because I will hit you so hard…" Eve's face has turned completely red.

"Maybe if you stopped throwing *other* things around, like your voice, your ego and your body, you might realize Rain and I are a couple!" Ami shoots back and scowls in defiance.

"After the way you treated him the other night? Scorning him after he *saved your life*?! I'm surprised he wants anything to do with you!"

"What happened between us is none of your business. We're together, get used to it."

Emma's eyes are wide with shock.

"Until he's married, he's fair game!" Eve yells.

"Married? What a great idea!" Ami yells back. "I'll make sure you get the invitation!"

It's not too late. When the time comes to leave, we should leave with Eve. Ami is going to get hurt.

We settled this, Ami.

There is silence for a few moments, my stomach interrupting with a loud growl. I point them downstairs, but hold Ami back.

Eve looks at me, and I stare at her coldly.

Eve and Emma reach the living room, and when I'm sure they're out of earshot, I whisper, "She's not going to let this go. It might be safer if you stayed near me as much as possible."

"Is that an invitation?" she smirks.

"You're becoming bold, but we still have to live with her for now."

"For now…"

I make sure I'm the first in the kitchen door, in case Eve has any surprises. Neither she nor Emma are there. We eat, and Ami prepares a bag for the day.

"So, we *are* going looking for my father today right?" She jabs me in the ribs.

"Yes." I laugh. "Bring some coins. I'm sure they're not going to copy the photo out of the goodness of their hearts."

"Already done," she replies and pats the bag.

"If we find him, is he coming with us?" I ask, leaning on the counter.

"Let's find him first and go from there. It's going to be difficult to convince him of what's happened." Her face becomes worried. "I want him to, but I'm not sure how Mother will react."

"Are you ready?"

"Almost. I'll meet you outside."

I step into the bright sun and Emma ambushes me. "Horsey-ride!" she yells, jumping on my back. Her arms go around me, but her grip slips and tightens around my neck instead.

Choking, I instinctively lean to try and alleviate it. All I manage to do is lose my balance, and we both arch backward. We fall, and I land on her. Slightly annoyed, I cough and struggle to get back on my feet. She laughs uncontrollably and it's contagious.

"What were you thinking?" I ask and help her up.

"I was thinking you could haul me on your back."

"You know we have an *actual* horse for that, right?" I tap her lightly on the forehead.

Eve laughs from the side of the house. Ami steps out and sighs, I assume because she didn't want them tagging along.

"You two are coming with us today. We need extra hands." I tell them.

They nod, and I provide Ami with the directions given by Vicky.

"Lead and we shall follow," I say, flashing her a smile.

Ami studies the paper and leads us toward the upper class area. With my familiarity of Chas in this time growing, I become more confident in staying in stride with Ami instead of letting her lead. Several streets in, we take a new turn toward the tallest buildings. It's not long before we enter a shopping district.

There's a wide variety of indoor and outdoor shopping opportunities. Stalls are lined up as a bazaar in the middle of a concrete platform, where people bustle about, buying, trading, and peddling.

Ami stops for a moment to regain her sense of direction, before diving into the fray. Beyond the bazaar there is another row of buildings. One of them has a sign which say "Copies" in the windows.

Inside, gray boxes line the walls, leading to a counter with a couple people standing behind it.

Ami steps confidently forward to the counter to be greeted by a dull, dreary woman. The apathetic look and reluctant sigh the woman gives tells me we're an inconvenience to her. Ami reaches in my pocket without warning, takes the photo, and sets it on the counter.

"We need to make copies," she says.

"It's six bits per copy, or we're having a special of one hundred copies for ten credits. Just follow the instructions on the placard," the woman replies in a monotone voice.

Ami looks at me, and I shrug. Pulling out a single gold coin from her bag, Ami sets it on the counter in front of the woman, and her dreary attitude changes to gold lust. Her eyes open wide, and while there is no outward sign, her reaction tells me she is thinking of stealing it.

"How much will this coin get me?" she asks.

"Uhh…I…let me ask my manager."

She turns and moves to a back room, the door closing behind her. The other workers eyeball the gold piece. Gold lust comes over them too.

With the economy as it is, I can't blame them; I'd be thinking the same thing if I were in their position.

I lean against the counter and give each of them a warning glance. It takes a few moments for the woman to return with a well-dressed, tall, dark-skinned man. Picking up the gold he holds it in the light and examines it through thick glasses. After a moment he looks at us, then back to the coin. Despite the other's reactions, there's no gold lust in his eyes.

"I'm certain with this you could purchase one of our machines, and a case of paper, miss." He sets the coin down. "This is worth a lot, so why don't you tell me what you really need."

"I need enough to put up fliers across the city with this picture on it, preferably customized with directions for people to follow, and something to tack them up with," she replies while placing her hand on the picture.

"We can help you with that," he says politely, and heads around the end of the counter and over to our side.

He moves to one of the gray boxes, motioning for Ami to follow. She takes the photo and coin with her. The man instructs her how to operate the box. I'm curious, but I don't want to crowd them. It takes them a little time, but finally she hands the man the coin, and puts her photograph in her pocket. He nods and she returns to me.

"It's going to take a while for the fliers to print. He's getting staplers to hang these up," Ami says with delight, clapping her hands.

"We should split up to cover more ground," I tell her. "You three should stick to the safer areas. I'll take the area heading toward Vicky's worksite."

"I'll go with you, Rain." Eve winks. "We can watch each other's backs."

"If you go, you might be at risk. It will be easier for me to dump the stuff and leave if I need to," I say firmly.

"You'd run knowing we'd take down any challenger?" Eve laughs.

"Yes. I'm trying to save the city, not kill it." I look at Ami. "I let my rage control me the other night, and I don't want to put myself in a position where that will happen again."

"*I* respect your decision," Ami replies, more for Eve's sake than mine. Eve rolls her eyes.

Watching the clock on the wall, it's fifteen minutes before the copying machine stops producing.

Ami pulls a page up for inspection. Over her shoulder, I see the flier. It has Ami's photo of her father, as well as the words 'Missing: James Mason (circled). If found, Ami and Agatha are looking for him. Reward offered,' and then gives a brief description of how to get to the house.

"Your surname is 'Mason'?" I ask. "How has this never come up?"

"I suppose because it wasn't important." Ami shrugs. "What about you?"

"My family didn't have one. We were royalty and so the 'King' or 'Queen' titles denoted who we were. I was 'King Tiberius'. And now I'm just 'Rain'."

Just?

"Mine's 'Pureheart'," Emma offers excitedly.

I laugh because it's extremely fitting. Eve ignores our conversation, and I surmise she doesn't want to join in because she's still angry at the earlier events.

The manager returns and sets several unfamiliar items on the counter.

"Here are some staplers and boxes of staples."

"Thank you." Ami nods at him before divvying up the fliers into four approximately equal piles on the counter. She then places a 'stapler' and a box of 'Standard Staples' on each pile.

"Okay, everyone grab a pile and let's get to work," she says, smiling broadly.

We load our arms up and head outside. Before we can split, I hold the stapler up. "Care to demonstrate?"

"Oh, yeah!"

Ami leads me to a wooden pole, holds up a flyer, and presses the stapler over it. It clicks, and when she pulls away, the flyer is held in place by a tiny metal bracket. She uses it to secure the bottom of the page also.

"I guess there's still significant things for me to learn, isn't there?" I frown.

"I wouldn't say significant, but there are still things." She winks. "Don't worry though. We have plenty of time. Let me show you how to reload the stapler too."

She's quick in her demonstration, but I understand. I survey the area. The number of people moving around are prime recipients of the fliers.

"Stay safe. I'll meet you at home when I'm done," I tell them.

They nod and I turn away.

Along this street I stop at every other wooden pole methodically to post a flier. The chore is tedious at best, trying to manage a thick stack of paper, the stapler, and posting. I march toward the work camp, hoping Vicky might take these fliers off my hands as she said she would.

At the invisible border separating the commercial district from the residential, I collect myself for a moment.

I hope I don't run into trouble.

Ami would never know though.

Unfortunately, the impoverished community is where response is more likely to come from.

The neighborhoods aren't as deserted as I originally thought, because I know where to look to find people hiding in plain sight. Their clothes are worn and dirty, and they appear malnourished.

When did they last eat?

Lackluster movements tell me the motivation to make changes is in short supply. The people are crying out for help through Misery, but I fear that even if we stay, it will take longer than my lifespan for Chas to make its strides toward a better place for all.

Unless we succeed, the best I can do is what I've already put in motion.

But if we do stay, I can do great things.

I move through the streets, posting fliers to whatever I can. A few people randomly look, but continue on their way. A couple times I detour to avoid gang-like groups.

The day wears on, the stack thinning. I finally reach the work site. There are hundreds of people working to clear fallen trees. The noise of the rumbling MVs and machinery is loud after the relative silence of the city.

Neither Vicky nor Terrance are in sight, so I approach a few men who appear to be taking a break. "Is Vicky here?" I ask.

"Naw. She left."

"What about Terrance?"

"Him too."

I sigh. I still have fliers left and I don't want to go home without having given every last one of them away.

"Thank you. I have an agreement with Vicky. She said I could bring these fliers, and they would be passed out. I'm looking for this man right here." I point at his face on the picture. "Can you please help me by passing these around?"

"Eh, sure." The man shrugs and takes the papers from me. He starts immediately by handing them to the men next to him.

"Thank you." I stretch my hand to shake his. He responds, and shakes my hand vigorously.

Now I can go home. The sun has reached the other side of the sky, and will be below the horizon by the time I get there. I'm tired from lack of food and hours of walking.

~~~~~~

It's dusk when I arrive.

Agatha's in the kitchen at the stove, preparing dinner. She gives me a smile when I step in and kick my shoes off. My hunger is great, and my sense of smell is sensitive enough to pick up beef, potatoes and carrots. I salivate.

"Hey, Aggy, have the girls returned yet?"

"Yes, they came home a while ago. They've been worried about you, but I told them you'd be fine," she says handing me plates.

I set the table before I go to find them. I don't have to travel far, because they're sprawled on the couch. None of them stir, even at Eve's saw-like snoring.

Many times they've let me sleep when I needed it. I won't wake them yet.

Sitting on the arm of the couch, I watch as they sleep. I chuckle at a thought.

They're peaceful. How long do I have to savor this moment?

~~~~~~

Days pass like blinks. I feel restless.

How is it that I can't savor the downtime? Is it because my work isn't truly done?

There's been no news from Vicky, and Evalyn hasn't made any progress reestablishing the orange vortex. Time not spent looking for James is spent tidying up a number of things around the house and yard.

It's mostly peaceful and I'm drawn to do more than chores. Agatha is appreciative of what I accomplish, but I feel empty.

Thoughts of higher satisfaction through helping and governing the city pester me. The despair within is a constant reminder that things could be better, despite the foundations laid for the agricultural growth and creation of jobs. But I'm limiting myself on more meaningful interactions until we can confirm whether we'll be staying or not.

"Rain." Agatha catches my attention while I'm bringing up a bucket of water from the well. "Would you help me plow a new section of the yard later so we can start the new garden?"

"Sure, Aggy." I nod at her and dump water in the horse's trough.

She heads around the house, and I brush Maximus's mane while debating whether I should check on Vicky and Terrance. I pull the horse's gear from the shed and hang them on the side of the stable.

Cautious about anyone seeing me preparing to leave, I slip quietly inside to grab my sword and prepare a small day bag. Dried fruits, half a loaf of bread, and a bottle of water.

Outside, and around the corner, Eve greets me with a grin while brushing Maximus. "You weren't thinking of taking off and leaving me here, were you?" She asks, batting her eyelashes.

"No, certainly not!" I play along.

"Good." She sighs and grunts in an exaggerated manner. "Because I'm bored, and tired of doing manual labor."

She puts the reins on Maximus and pulls him out.

"What I'll be doing is boring too."

"Nothing is boring with you, baby." She winks.

Eve saddles Maximus. When she finishes cinching the straps she stands straight up and smiles. She intends the smile to be innocent, but I know her well enough to see she's up to no good.

"What are you doing?" I ask, slowly moving closer.

"Nothing," she says sweetly.

I point my finger at her, and inch closer, but that provokes her and she puts her hand on the saddle's horn. Shaking my head, I keep eye contact. The innocence fades, and she lets her impishness show. Racing towards the horse is futile.

Eve jumps into the saddle and trots out of my grasp. Several feet away, she spins the horse around.

I cross my arms, provoking her to taunt me with her cheeky smile.

"Where are *we* headed?" she asks.

"'We'?" I reply.

"You know, I figured you'd enjoy company." She walks Maximus around, flaunting him.

"It's easier and better if I go alone."

"Well, then you better start walking, because I'm using the horse. Or if you want the horse to get there, he comes with a gorgeous companion." She winks at me and spins him again.

Get on the horse. She'll follow anyway.

I concede defeat and drop my arms.

"Okay, fine. You can go." I start walking toward her.

"I thought you'd see it my way." She leads him to meet me. "But I'm in front."

"Why?" I hesitate.

"Come on!" Eve grabs my arm and pulls.

In the saddle behind her, I'm caught by my wrists. It's too late to get away. She pulls my arms around her, clasping them tightly to her chest. The fear of Ami seeing causes me to struggle to free myself.

"Eve! Cut it out!" I tell her, nearly falling from the saddle pulling away.

Eve leans back and whispers in a seductive manner, "You must hold me tightly. I wouldn't want you to fall and injure yourself." She has no choice but to let one of my arms free in order to take the reins.

While she's directing Maximus toward the city line, I try to pry her grip from my other arm. But I'm too late, and my fear comes true. Our struggle has drawn the attention of Ami, Emma, and Agatha who are near the replanted clothing lines.

To save my skin, I yell, "Help! I'm being kidnapped!"

"Eve! What are you doing? Get his hand off of your chest!" Ami yells.

"What?" she says coyly and looks down, continuing to grip my arm. "Oh my! Rain, you're making me blush!"

Ami runs toward us, but Eve trots Maximus away, laughing. Emma tries to run in front, and Eve spins around to trot away from all of them.

"If you don't let him go, so help me I'll…" Ami barks at her.

"You'll what? Cry?" Eve jabs.

"You let him go right now!" Emma yells louder than I've ever heard her. "If you make her cry, I'll smother you in your sleep!"

"In your dreams, twerp. Don't be mad because he doesn't even see you as an interest."

"Enough is enough," I tell her. "You've taunted them, which is what you no doubt wanted all along."

With a loud sigh, she releases my hand and stops. Ami finally catches up and punches Eve's leg hard, causing Eve to yelp. Eve tries to kick her, but misses because she has little room to swing.

"You little whelp!" Eve snaps, starting to dismount. I'm the one doing the holding now, to keep her from attacking Ami as she'd promised to do.

"Stop," I tell them both, but Ami keeps at it.

"If you stopped pushing yourself on him we'd get along better!" Ami berates Eve.

"Who said I'm pushing?" Eve grins. "He got up in the saddle willingly."

"He's a gentleman!" Emma tells her voraciously.

"And we know better. You have *no* modesty!" Ami keeps digging at her.

"I should go with. *She* needs supervision!" Emma adds.

"They're right. You should know by now this isn't okay," I scold.

She huffs loudly, aggravated because she's been ganged up on. Though it's her own fault for taunting them, she crosses her arms and acts hurt.

"I'm heading across town to check up on Vicky's progress. It might be best if I go alone," I say aloud, for Eve's benefit.

Agatha steps forward. "When will you be back?"

"I'm not sure. It depends on how much there is to do."

"Okay. We kind of need you and the horse for plowing." She smiles.

"I'll do my best to make it back with daylight to spare," I promise.

"Thanks, dear."

"You heard him, Eve. He wants to go alone," Ami insists.

"I'm not getting down. I'm bored and tired of sitting here."

"Then walk. I don't trust you to not pull another stunt." Ami grabs Maximus's harness.

Eve dismounts and stands next to the horse with her hands at her sides. "I should still follow."

Emma glares at Eve.

"I'll be fine. Thank you," I tell her.

I grab the reins and lead Maximus. As Eve and I head away, I wave goodbye to them.

Toward the edge of the park, a man veers onto the grass. He stumbles when his feet sink. His footsteps are unsure, and there's a fogginess in his sunken eyes. Tattered clothing, skinny, and dirty, it doesn't look like he's eaten recently. His facial hair is matted and gray. He looks at me as we pass each other, and with his attention on me instead of where he's walking, he trips and falls.

I jump down to help him. "Sir, are you okay?" I ask.

He pulls himself up on my arm, and I examine him for injuries. The blank look on his face tells me he is unaware of his surroundings – I wonder if he even knows he's being helped.

Looking harder, I realize who it is. It's James. "Hey. James, right?"

He looks at me, and I can tell the name stirs something in his mind.

"You need to head over there." I point toward the distant house. "There are people waiting for you. Hurry home, because you're almost there."

A sense of joy washes over me, and the hair on the back of my neck stands on end. I have the urge to turn around and escort him, but the thought of being an intrusion on their reunion decides me against it. He grunts and I let him go. Shuffling along, he heads for the house. I'm happy for Ami.

Back in the saddle, I watch him to make sure he'll make it

When he's half way there I pull the reins and start Maximus trotting. It's not too long before we've reached the ragged residential area. Though danger lurks on every street, we are unhindered.

"You could let me up now. I'll behave." Eve sounds remorseful.

I don't respond.

"They're not here now. Let me up. We'll get there faster."

"Fine, but you're riding behind me."

I stop so she can mount.

Eve turns seductive once more. "I'll hold you so I don't fall off," she says wrapping her arms around me, and massages my chest.

I swat her hands. "Restrain yourself."

"What if I can't?" She moves her hands down my body, and I become flustered.

As her hands reach my hips I jerk and plant an elbow into her ribcage.

She grunts and backs off, putting her arms at abdomen level. We both wobble and have to focus on not falling off.

"You need to stop. You must realize by now my feelings for Ami are genuine. By doing what you do, you're hurting Ami and yourself."

You're pushing away the one person who knows you. The one who will never judge you for your actions. You are more than a conquest for her. Eve loves you.

I know. But I love Ami.

Eve's quiet for a moment.

"Do you think you and Evalyn will be able to break this curse?" she asks.

"We're certainly going to try, but there are no guarantees." I shrug.

There's silence between us again and I take the opportunity to gain my bearings. It only takes a moment to see the large area of missing trees in the distance. I alter my course to put us on track.

"Do you love me?" she asks as though she were reading my mind.

"You ask difficult questions. I don't like this game," I dodge.

"I'm being serious right now. Despite your pushback, I can feel it between us."

You do love her.

I choose Ami.

"My answer isn't what you want to hear. Yes, but I love all of you. You're my family," I explain.

If I let her think she has hope for a relationship, it will complicate things further.

She doesn't pursue it further, but I know she hasn't fully dropped it, and it *will* come up again later.

Thankfully, the progress on the tree removal provides a distraction. The deforested area has grown significantly since I last saw it, and it will soon be able to start accommodating farmland.

The size of the crew appears to have tripled. There is a greater amount of machinery cutting, lifting, moving, and loading trees onto long beds hooked up to massive MVs.

Stopping on the side of the road, I look for Vicky or Terrance.

A new two-story building stands as a hub in the deforested area, several hundred yards away, and it seems to be a good place to start.

Nearing, I slow Maximus so as not to run over the workers coming and going around it. We dismount into the freshly overturned dirt, and I tie our horse to a nearby bench.

At the door, I hold it open for Eve and follow her in. The large outside is misleading compared to the small office we've entered. There are doors to our left and right, and a desk directly ahead with a woman behind it. She's paying attention to screens similar to the ones in City Hall, glancing up only to look at us for a moment. When we approach, she's furiously pounding her fingers on buttons with letters.

I clear my throat and look at her expectantly.

"If you're here for labor, you'll need to fill these forms out." She sets a stack of papers on the desk.

"Can I speak with Vicky or Terrance, please?" I say, pushing them back at her.

She looks at me hesitantly, but reaches for one of the portable communication devices, and puts it up to her mouth.

"Terrance, there's a couple looking to speak to you," she says with an inconvenienced tone.

She sets the device down and we hear him through it.

"I'll be right there," he says.

As I turn, the door to our left opens and closes at an incredible speed, and the room is filled with a gust of air.

"What can I help you with?" Terrance says abruptly.

"I wanted some fresh air, and came to see if I could assist. How long have you been able to move with that speed?"

"A while. I've hidden it until recently. When you showed up with your destructive power I figured my ability wasn't nearly as bad," he grins for the first time since we met him.

"I am glad I could be of service," I jest and bow.

"If you want to tear up more trees, I won't stop you. But do it away from the workers so no one gets hurt."

"Do you have a place in mind?"

"Yes. Follow me."

He motions and heads for the door. Exiting, he points off to our right and leads. We talk along the way.

"Where are the trees being shipped?"

"We're keeping half stored away for future construction, and we've found a city across the ocean to export the other half to," he tells us.

"Good. Hopefully it will be the start of trade lines for agriculture too."

"Agreed. I may not have been on board at first, but I've come to acknowledge that Renaldo cares only of himself. Vicky cares about our city, and I care about Vicky."

He stops. We are far from the city line, and beyond the area which the workers are hauling downed trees away. Terrance leaves me to head toward the tree line.

Eve follows, but I motion for her to stay back while I draw my sword. I breathe deeply. She stops following, and I proceed to work.

Looking at Eve I smirk. "You watching?" I ask, knowing she is a glutton for destruction.

She nods and her smile widens. I put both hands on my sword, plant it into the ground, and unleash a shockwave.

~~~~~~

I should feel bad for destroying a forest a couple thousand years in the making.

It doesn't matter.
I'm helping people make a living and creating hope for the future.
We have done something good for the people.

The house comes into sight and I'm relieved to be home. Ami and James are sitting on the stairs outside the kitchen. He is eating ravenously while she watches.

Maximus recognizes home and heads toward the stable.

As we pass, I smile at Ami and she smiles weakly back. I dismount and lead Maximus by his harness. When Eve dismounts, I hand her the reins.

"Be a dear and put him and his gear away." I poke her in the side.

"What? Not fair!" she protests.

"That's life." I walk away looking over my shoulder with a smile.

She huffs, but she's smiling.

Maybe this has softened the blow. Can she see that we are just friends?

I round the corner to where Ami and James sit.

He looks at me with his sunken face, but there's a spark of renewed life in his eyes. He's not too far gone, and musters a weak smile. I extend my hand for him to shake. He brings his hand up to mine; the taut skin over bones causes my heart to ache. My grip is gentle.

Hello James, my name is Tiberius.

"Hello James, my name is Rain," I kneel and introduce myself. "Ami had a great deal of faith we would find you."

"I...thought...I thought it was a dream. My family...my home," he starts slow. "It's hard. I'm waiting to wake up. Please, don't let this be a dream," he begs me as if this is a fantasy, and he will come crashing back to reality – alone.

"You aren't dreaming, I promise." I try to be as encouraging as possible. "I'm glad you came."

"Thank you...for keeping Agatha and Ami safe," his voice is raspy.

He coughs and covers his mouth. Ami rubs his back, and I wait for him to recover before I respond.

"They saved me first. I've been trying to repay them ever since." I turn my attention to Ami. "Have you explained everything?"

"Only the basics, but we have the rest of our lives for stories." She smiles.

"If it were anyone else, I wouldn't believe. Time travel..." He scratches his head.

"If all goes well, that will be over soon," I tell him. "I've been working with Evalyn to stop it."

"She's still alive?" He looks puzzled. "She was so sick."

"It's a long story. Ami can tell you, but for now don't worry yourself," I tell him. "Where's Aggy?"

"She's reading in her room," Ami responds and frowns.

She must be hiding away from James. It must be weird for her after all these years. Maybe I should leave her be and ask about plowing later.

I run my hand across Ami's hair as I pass.

Once upstairs, I see a familiar orange glow seeping through the crack under the door. Hesitation overwhelms me, because Drake's dagger is in there. It's difficult to take steps, but when I reach Evalyn's room I push the fear down, for now.

I have to get rid of it. If we're unsuccessful in stopping the blue vortex, it can't come with.

I knock lightly and wait for Evalyn's response.

"Come in, Rain."

The door squeaks, the vortex whirs, and Evalyn hums. She has become visible in her incorporeal form again, the same as she had appeared the other day. She practically dances around the room, a smile plastered on her face, and motions for me to close the door. The latch is barely heard over the vortex.

She's in a good mood, despite James being here.

"Hey, isn't that the same outfit? You should really wash it," I joke.

"Yes. Hilarious." She rolls her eyes and puts her hands on her hips, still smiling. "Unfortunately, I'm stuck like this. I assume it's because it's what I was wearing when I died."

"You dressed provocatively to die?"

"You're lucky I didn't die in my underwear...or worse!" she laughs.

"Don't put that image in my head!" I laugh nervously.

"Don't insult me. I'm beautiful!" She tries to hit me, but her hand passes right through.

I throw my hands up and open my eyes wide in exclamation. "You don't understand. You and Aggy are twins, and she's the mother of Ami, whom—"

"You love."

I blush, and her smile grows wider.

"Anyway, I mustered enough energy to reinitialize the orange vortex, as you can see. It's stable for now as long as nothing interferes with it."

"I came to take the dagger and dispose of it." I look for it.

"Take the urn to your room first. I don't want to risk another reaction." She points at the little urn. "Remember, we have to spend a lot of time together as we near the end of the month. No more of your outings."

"You can't hang out in there while I'm sleeping or changing," I joke, pointing at her accusingly.

"It's not like I haven't seen you..." she cackles.

I shake my head and shiver at the thought of her watching me when she's invisible. Kneeling, I'm careful when I pick up the urn. I keep it as level as possible. My movements are calm and calculated. Opening the door allows the orange light to flood the hall. In my room I'm all too glad to set the urn on the dresser at the far side near the closet.

"Why there?" she asks.

"If I keep it on my nightstand I might knock it over in my sleep."

"Good point. You wrestle your blanket and pillow at night." She hovers around, grinning.

"I'm heading back to grab the dagger." I wipe the sweat from my hands. "I need to get rid of it."

"By the wall, near the window," she says while I walk past her.

In her room I look for the weapon. It glimmers in the light and when I touch it I can immediately feel his presence. My hand clasps the handle and his evil image appears. Shocked, our eyes meet. His malicious glare causes me to shudder.

"Tiberius, brother. How do you live?" his voice is audible, his deep and ominous tone clear.

Vile creature!

"Be concerned for yourself and what is about to happen," I tell him and exit Evalyn's room with haste.

"Oh, I am. I see you are holding my blade! Did you miss it that much?

And what am I, a spirit?" He laughs. "Oh the irony that you would live and I would die."

What I wouldn't give for you to be alive so I could kill you!

"True irony would be killing you with the blade you tried to kill me with." My voice raises and I spin to shove the tip into his ghostly form. "Don't worry. Your current existence won't last long."

"You are completely wrong." His confident and snide tone grates on me. "Now that you have somehow brought me back, we have much catching up to do."

I will destroy you!

"There will be no catching up. I'll destroy your soul!" I head to the stairs.

Emma's door opens. "Rain? Who are you talking to?" She tries to come close, but I hold my empty hand up and show her the dagger in my other.

"What is this brother? Are these your limbs I feel moving?" Drake asks.

His heavy presence pulls and tugs at my soul. I can feel him trying to assert his will over me. Remembering Agatha's description of her possession, she was able to initially fight Evalyn off. But it reached a point where fighting was useless. This drives me to rid myself of the cursed item as soon as I can.

As I grit my teeth, fighting him, Emma sees there's something wrong. "Are you okay?" she asks.

"Who is this sweet little girl, Tiberius? A lover?"

I want to stab him. To kill him!

"Shut your mouth!" I stare behind Emma at him while he hovers over her.

"You're scaring me! Is it Tiberius?"

She can't hear him.

I shake my head and grab at her roughly. She flinches. Placing her hand on the hilt of the blade, I pull her close. When I spin her, she sees him.

"Hello, little one." He reaches for her.

She screams and wrenches away.

"Drake, my brother. He tried to kill me, and now I have a chance to repay the favor by removing his stain from the world once and for all."

"How noble you are now, brother. You make me sick. Going by

another name, does it make you feel better? Does it ease a guilty conscience for the people *we* killed?" he sneers.

I...

I was out of control.

But I can fix it. I can be better.

I can't drop the dagger. I try, but my fingers won't let go. Prying on them with my other hand does no good and Drake laughs.

I turn to leave, and I'm stopped by Evalyn floating out into the hallway. Emma screams again. Agatha and Eve bound up the stairs.

"I don't know what will happen when you destroy the dagger." Evalyn frowns and crosses her arms.

His presence pulls at my soul, trying to replace it. It's painful, and I've never felt anything like it. It's not like Misery overwhelming my senses, or the alternate personality of Tiberius speaking in my mind. Drake seeks to replace me, and I can feel my essence, my soul tearing apart.

"Rain?" Agatha questions.

"Things just became more complicated." I tell them. "I need to destroy this."

"Evalyn?! What was that nonsense about dressing appropriately?" Eve asks half angry, half excited. "You've been holding out on me! Where is that outfit, because I need it for Rain."

"It's gone. Buried in another time."

"Tiberius, you took concubines?" He laughs and intrudes. "I cannot wait for them to be mine!"

"They won't be, because I won't allow you to reenter this world. I'll die before that!"

"You will die, but your body will live on. Your heart beats, and I feel it."

"Rain?" Agatha puts her hand on my shoulder.

"Too much. There's too much to explain. Drake...he's in here." I wave the dagger menacingly.

"Let go of the stupid thing!" Eve commands.

"It's stuck!"

"Your soul is weak." He reaches his hand into me. "I shall end your misery by snuffing it out."

"Shut up, Drake!" I snap.

You will not win, brother!

He can't have our power. The world would be destroyed.

He tugs harder. Tiberius's thoughts fight for control. I am being lost, torn away. Drake pushes harder, and I leap away as if it will do any good, knocking Agatha down in my attempt to escape his grasp.

Eve grabs my hand and pries at my fingers. It takes all the strength she can muster to move them. She's able to open them enough for the dagger to slip from my hand.

He disappears, and his presence is no longer intruding.

"Destroy it. Make sure it's gone," Evalyn instructs.

"Are you sure destroying it will work?" Agatha counters. "What if it releases him and allows him to return somehow? Or what if he still possesses the pieces and can infect the world?"

"What else can we do with it?" My hands won't stop shaking.

"Take it back to the castle and dump it next to his corpse," Eve suggests. "Then collapse the castle in on itself and no one will find it."

"Destroy it," Evalyn pleads. She's desperate. "I need to know what happens when I'm no longer bound by the power holding me! If you destroy it and he no longer exists, then…maybe I can be at peace."

My attention is focused on her existence for a moment, and her request makes sense. I understand the anxiety she's feeling because of my own struggle to continue to exist in the midst of Drake, Tiberius, and Misery.

Would she roam free or cease to exist? Would she be pulled into Misery's collective since she died without hope?

"I understand, but the risk is too great. If I destroy it, and Agatha's right, we'll be in a lot more danger." I look to Emma. "If I bury it in the castle and cave it in, will it be safely hidden away there?"

"Chas will expand, and the area will be excavated. You have to bury it where no one is going to dig," she offers.

Stepping is heard on the stairs. Ami appears looking confused. "Is everything okay up here?" she asks.

My voice is shaky as I explain it all as quickly as I can. She hugs me, but the comfort can't undo the anxiety.

Agatha is right. If we destroy it, he might be released.

He can't be released. Even if his soul was sent somewhere else, I can't take the chance it will be into Misery. If he found his way there, he would take control of it, and me.

He must be buried, forever.

"I'm going to bury it," I decide, to Evalyn's dismay. "He doesn't deserve mercy, but it's smarter to keep him imprisoned."

"Can't we keep it safe?" Ami asks.

"One day, when we're gone, it will still remain. It has to go." I shake my head. "Sorry Aggy, I'll plow tomorrow, I promise."

"Do what you need to do. We have time."

I want to taunt him; to show him I have the power and control. Picking it up, he materializes in my vision.

"Brother! We have our differences but do not act rashly."

He heard us without anyone holding the dagger.

Refusing to respond, I head to the stairs. Looking back I see my true family standing there in support of me. And then there's my brother, standing amongst them. I give a swift nod and leave. Drake has no choice but to be dragged along against his will. He's focused more on talking now than on trying to possess me.

"Let us discuss what you are going to do," he says, trying to soothe my agitations, trying to placate me.

"You have no place in this world."

The grass cushions me as I run across the yard, elated because I'll have some revenge on him. The woods are ominous under the darkening sky, but the invisible monster I was once afraid of isn't in there. I have *him* in my hand, and he will face punishment. Trudging through the thick bushes and ferns overtaking the forest floor, I glance at him with an evil smile.

"You are making a mistake," he growls, returning to his normal arrogant demeanor.

"The mistake was when you turned on me. When you stabbed me! I would have given you everything had you asked!" I yell, my memories of being Tiberius flooding in.

"We can still have everything!" he shouts back. "It is not too late! This world can be ours!"

"It *is* too late. Tiberius is dead—"

I'm still here. I've always been here because I am you.

"I am a new man and my name is Rain. I should probably thank you for nearly killing me. I have a deep understanding of the evil you intend to bring into the world, because I was once like you." I can't control the volume of my voice and it spikes higher. "I'm going to bury you forever."

"When I reenter the physical plain, I shall bring with me your worst nightmares," he starkly responds. "I will rip those people away and have you beg for their lives. And then I will kill them while you watch."

"You're going to be buried so deep you'll never get the chance."

The air has become chilly. I pull my cloak over my shoulders and put the hood up. The sunlight is almost gone, and I can barely see the forest floor. I head in the direction I think the castle is in. Determination to rid myself of Drake drives me.

In the dark, making my own path is difficult. I'm forced to combat bushes, holes, and fallen trees. My legs tire, and I take a moment to rest. His dark form hovers and I feel his pull again.

"What became of my castle?"

"*My* castle is in ruins thanks to you." I laugh at him. "It ended well didn't it? You cowered in a hidden room until you died."

"Tiberius, see reason. Together this world could not stop us. We could rule together with me in your body…" He is confident, but his words stink of self-preservation. "Let me in! I promise I will care for your concubines."

"Stop calling them that! They are family. More family than you ever were. They are guiding me to atonement by restoring hope to people."

And he will destroy what we're building. Bury him now.

We're not far enough yet. I want to make sure it's never found.

"Pathetic," he screams at the top of his lungs. "You are weaker now than you were then!"

"If I'm so weak then why am I alive and you are the one who's about to disappear forever?" I do my best to check my emotions, but it's difficult.

I resume my walk, but not for much longer. Emma's warning about the excavation of the castle makes me positive it's not the right place for it. The one place I can think of is down, as deep as I can bury it. A flat patch of land ahead appears to be a suitable burial site. Drawing my sword, I focus on it and the hope I'll bring to people in spite of my past and my brother.

He can't defeat light. Good will destroy evil.

That's an endless fight. Can good ever truly defeat evil?

"You are making a mistake, brother."

He tries to overpower me, but I fight him. I push his presence away and he's unable to take hold.

As he has no power over me, I throw the dagger to the ground. He disappears and I'm left with a headache.

One handed, I point my sword at an area several feet in front of me. I let loose a concentrated shockwave, and the forest echoes with the thunderous clap. There's an explosion of dirt and shrubs. When it settles I examine the area. It isn't very deep.

Create a chasm.

My step nearly falters as I walk onto the soft dirt of the small crater. I jam the sword in the middle and kneel. Both hands grip the leather of the hilt tightly. Building my energy, I force everything into my fingertips. I expect the amount of force expelled to send me skyward. Instead the earth beneath me starts to collapse. A sinkhole forms.

Not wanting to be buried alive, I sheathe my sword and struggle to get away. A blast with both hands which should pull me free, doesn't. I am stuck, and continuing downward. My heart races as I fear being buried, or worse, encountering the Tarak, if they still exist.

Bending down, I work my feet free of my shoes. Using them as a fast disappearing platform, I launch myself upward and collide with a branch. I have enough presence of mind to grab on, but the tree is collapsing under the sinkhole.

From one branch to the next, I work around to the other side while it topples. It arcs and descends. I ride it, bracing myself with my feet and gripping onto branches for my life. I'm nearly sent back into the sinkhole when the tree collides with another.

It stops moving. I spring up and run to the trunk. It begins to succumb to the widening hole and I leap off and onto solid land. The dagger is waiting for me. Picking it up, Drake's form appears for me. I grin.

"This is your prison." I laugh harshly. "Your sad life is over."

"Tiberius, our fight is not done."

"It is. You have no power over me." I end the conversation and throw the blade to the heart of the sinking dirt.

It lands near the 'eye of the storm', catching the moonlight to be illuminated for a moment, and then it's swallowed. Watching for a while at a safe distance, the dirt finally slows to a trickle. All that remains is a crater and fallen trees.

Rid of him, I am satisfied and set out for home.

This chapter is closed. Now, maybe it's time to close another. Like me, Evalyn isn't who she used to be. She deserves consideration for the fear she's feeling, and the loneliness.

The journey home seems longer, because I'm without shoes. Stones, branches, and thistles aggravate the bottoms of my feet as I walk, but I make it without major injury.

The light is on in the living room, and Emma's face is peeking out from the curtains in the window. She squeals with delight, "He's back!" her words muffled by the window.

She flings the door open and pulls me inside.

"What in the world did you do? Roll in the dirt? Where are your shoes?" She pulls at my dirt and sap-covered cloak.

I smile, but the chance to answer is interrupted as Agatha pokes her head in from the kitchen and greets me warmly.

"Welcome home. You're just in time for dinner."

"I'm dirty. Is that okay?" I ruffle my dusty hair, and Emma jumps away laughing.

"It'll be fine dear. You might want to wash your hands though." Her loving, motherly tone makes me feel warm inside.

Ami and Eve are shocked at my dirtiness when I enter the kitchen. I laugh at their surprised faces.

I wash in the kitchen sink, scrubbing up to my elbows. Using the hand towel by the sink, I dry off and head to the table. Despite James returning to the home, the head of the table is still open as my spot.

It's awkward, but I sit.

Ami serves me smoked fish, brown rice, and a delicious array of sautéed vegetables. She puts large helpings on my plate and smiles.

"Thank you." I smile back.

"We're here for you if you want to talk." Emma isn't dancing around the issue, and I understand she wants me to be okay.

Everyone looks at me with curiosity. I smile, triumphantly. The demon which has haunted me is defeated. It's safe now, for all of them. Even though his evil weighs on my mind, I allow myself to feel relieved.

"He tried to possess me, but it's over. He's lost." I take a bite and chew while talking. "I won't be looking over my shoulder for him anymore, and if we stay, I can focus on fixing Chas."

"Do you think you'll be successful?" Agatha asks.

"I have no idea, but I promised I'd find a way. We have to take a chance on this."

"I think so too," Emma chimes in with enthusiasm. "How weird will it be though if I live in Chas a hundred years before I'm even born?"

"Weird indeed," Eve says with her mouth full. "What if you are your own great-grandmother?"

"I'm fairly sure that is impossible," Ami giggles.

They're managing another rare moment of calm. Finally a change for the better in our circumstances. There's hope yet.

As I look at each of them, I admire my surrogate family. They laugh and converse, sharing stories of our travels with James.

One more responsibility to finish, and then I can start my adventure with Ami.

~~~~~~

After dinner, and a long hot shower, I climb the stairs to my room. Evalyn is there, looking at the city. She looks at me but returns her attention to the cityscape.

"Hey," I greet her.

"Hey." She's quiet.

"What's wrong?"

As she looks back at me, I see a great sadness is in her eyes. She begs to speak with me privately, without speaking a word.

I close the door and I drop my dirty laundry in the basket. Sitting on the bed, I patiently wait. I understand her hesitation.

Evalyn sighs loudly a couple times before turning fully to me. "Every day is a day closer, either to the end of our time here or when we finally stay put. If we break my power over the house, it might be the end for me," her voice quivers.

"It will be okay. I'm here, and I won't go anywhere for the rest of the month," I say, trying to reassure her.

"Thanks for caring. I was such a brute in the past. So bitter. You were a catalyst for my change." She smiles sadly. "I'm not sure anyone else will miss me if I do disappear."

"I understand because I've felt that way too. But it's a lie. If you do move on, you'll be missed by all of us."

She 'sits' on the bed next to me. I place my palm up on the bed for her. It takes her a moment, but she places her hand within mine. Though I can't feel it, I want her to have the comfort of knowing she's not alone.

"I can't see the future, but I do know one thing. You're not in the collective inside me. If the end of this month is goodbye for us, there is something better waiting for you."

"You know exactly what to say to an old woman." Her smile is genuine and I find myself empathizing with her fears even more.

I match her smile to keep her mind off upcoming events.

"I'm fairly tired," I break the silence. "Tomorrow let's discuss your plan to stop the vortex."

"Sleep well." She turns away.

The light being off doesn't change the lighting in the room much. The orange permeates even my eyelids. I roll away and cover my face with the blanket.

~~~~~~

I stay busy around the house. The garden, Maximus, cooking, and spending more time with Evalyn than anyone else.

James is still timid and shy, but I make it a point to talk to him and include him whenever I can. It makes me happy to be able to share information and stories about his family with him. He in turn shares things he remembers with them from before.

Our time slips by, and the end of the month creeps up.

Evalyn tells me she can feel the power growing every day, but she can't pinpoint the moment it will happen.

Heading to the kitchen for a quick bite, I find Ami and James sitting at the table discussing the nuances of traveling in time. Today, his alertness has increased, and he doesn't look as tired.

Getting a glass of orange juice, I sit next to Ami. She smiles at me and I think of our secret kiss. I smile back.

"Where are the others?" I ask.

"They went off to the market for food. They'll be back soon," she replies.

"Rain," James speaks softly. "Is it okay if I stay?"

"It's not my decision."

"I was hoping for your opinion." There's hesitation, and I'm unsure what he wants me to say.

"I won't lie. Time travel is dangerous. We've encountered things you couldn't dream of. But we worked hard so Ami could have you in her life."

He strokes his graying beard and nods silently. Ami reaches over and holds his free hand, but her smile is directed at me. Though I've helped people in the past, this time is more personal: seeing direct results brings a greater sense of accomplishment.

Standing, I take my empty glass to the sink and wash it. Looking over the changes in the back yard, I watch clothes waft in a slight breeze. The freshly plowed dirt toward the apple tree has been planted with seeds, and though they're too small to see from here, sprouts have started already.

Everything is changing, for the better. Ami's family is whole, Drake is gone, and soon we may no longer be forced into time traveling.

"I'm not sure if Vicky plans to plant this season, because they're still clearing an area, but I anticipate a small harvest for us before the cold season," I say, still looking at the garden.

"It will be okay. Even if we don't get the garden back this season, we'll have access to stores," she replies.

After a long pause, Ami speaks in a cautious tone.

"How is she?"

"Well, I've been able to keep her in a lighter mood, but her spirits have been up and down. You should come up and see her."

I kiss her on the cheek as I pass to go upstairs and spend more time with Evalyn. The time is close, and her fate is uncertain, making her eager to see me. Her eyes light up when I walk into the room.

"We should practice what we're going to do," she states.

"What's our plan?"

"Alone, I don't have enough energy to do what we need. It took a lot out of me to establish the orange vortex. I feel it though. It's trying to counter time, and if we can use it against the blue, I'm sure they should cancel each other out."

"You realize this sounds insane, right? We're hoping it will do what we want, but we won't be sure until we try."

"Yes, but what other option do we have?"

"None, really," I sigh sitting on my bed.

"I'll focus my power into you and you'll funnel into the vortex."

The thought of her possessing me is slightly terrifying due to my encounter with Drake. Feeling my entire essence being torn at while he tried to replace me has left an invisible scar. But this is our chance; a chance at peace and safety – I won't rob Agatha and Ami of a permanent solution by hesitating.

I have to uphold my promise.

"Do you want to try and possess me?" I ask after a long pause.

"I didn't think you were for sale," she jokes, and we both burst into laughter.

"No, I'm not! Remember, we've been through that. Not very fun under Duchess Tamiell!"

"Did you mean under her…or *under* her?" she laughs harder. "You had to beat her away with a stick!"

"It was embarrassing for me, and I felt embarrassed for *her!*"

We're roaring with laughter. Whenever we look at one another, it fuels the fire. Tears are streaming down my face and I can't see clearly. A once upsetting situation has become humorous. Our time together there was meaningful and it was then she became different. She opened up and her bitterness started to ebb away.

Please, don't let this be goodbye.

"Okay, stand up. We're going to try." She stops laughing suddenly and commands me.

I stand and try to stop laughing, but she can't keep a straight face for more than a moment. It feels good to laugh this hard, and we're completely unable to focus. Instead of practicing, the night is spent reminiscing.

~~~~~~

"Rain! Get up *right now!*" Evalyn yells in my ear.

My eyes spring open and I throw myself out of bed.

"Hurry! It's coming! The pressure is at its peak and it's about to burst!" she continues to bark.

It's dark and it could be late night or early morning. Leaping to the small urn, I snatch it up and rush downstairs, keeping a firm grip on it.

"Let's go! Let's go!" she yells again, floating behind me.

When I reach the living room door, I fling it open with one hand. It slams against the wall with a massive thud. But I don't have time to care about not waking the house.

Out in the yard I set the urn in the grass, and hold it steady with my feet. The orange vortex beams high into the sky, lighting everything up in the nearby area as if it were daytime. The ground quakes, and the blue vortex begins to swirl around. It builds in magnitude and speed as usual, and Evalyn has to yell over it to instruct me.

"Put your hands into the orange vortex and start building power, but don't release it!" she orders.

"We didn't practice!"

"It's too late! Do it now!"

Doing as she commands, I let my inner power build, and it courses through me like rapids. Every ounce of my will is put into drawing the energy to my fingertips. It's similar to when it first manifested. I'm on the verge of seizing.

Unlike with Drake, there's no tearing at my soul when she inhabits me. Her presence is aligned with mine. She controls my arms and points my hands at one another. I understand what she's doing. Instead of expelling the energy outward, we're focusing it inward. My palms are an inch apart from each other. Channeling, my vision fades, but Evalyn keeps me upright. She doesn't assert full control, but assists me in controlling the energy buildup for just a little longer. A new sensation fills me, and I feel her dumping her power into me.

She yells, but it's my voice, "This is our only shot!"

The swirling blue vortex threatens to tear us to another time. My energy is at its maximum, and I can tell Evalyn has mustered all she's able to control.

"Now!" we yell.

In a big push I expel the entire pent up power. The orange vortex wavers, and rapidly expands outward. In a surprise effect, I'm caught with it.

As the orange expands to meet the blue, I'm pushed away from the urn and the house. Evalyn is left in the spot I was standing, and the house is engulfed.

I become pinned in between the two, the forces crushing my body.

She appears to be yelling and trying to reach me, but I can't hear what she is saying over the noise of both vortexes raging in my ears. Her movements are hindered by an unseen force, and she slows down. Like the strange effects in the white void, her movements become sluggish.

A line of people come barreling out of the house. The horror in my family's eyes is apparent. Though they attempt to reach me, they too are held back by the same slowing force which has bound Evalyn mid-stride.

My lungs feel like they're collapsing. It's becoming hard to breathe. My limbs are pinned and contorted in ways they shouldn't be, but I pull enough energy for one last burst. Releasing a shockwave, I watch a ripple effect shimmer across the orange vortex.

And then...nothingness.

~~~~~~

My back itches. I become uncomfortable and stir from a deep sleep. When I roll over my face isn't met with a pillow. It's not even met with grass. I breathe in, and sand gets up my nose. I sneeze several times, and I jump up to brush myself off.

I scan my surroundings, confused. I'm on a beach, the house nowhere to be seen. Instead, in front of me is a motionless ocean. A wave a couple hundred feet out is in the middle of its crest, unmoving, as if time has stopped dead in its tracks.

"Oh," is all I can manage to say. The sound of my voice is hollow, dissipating moments after it's left my lips.

Nothing is moving. Nothing is breathing. Nothing is making any sort of sound, save for me.

My heart beats fast, and fear sets in. We've stopped time, and I appear to be the only thing unaffected.

I panic.

What did we do? How is this possible?

~~~~~~

2 SEPARATION

There are countless people out on a sunny day, taking strolls, sunbathing, and enjoying themselves. Birds litter the sandy beach, pecking away at morsels of food. The beautiful blue ocean is a few steps away. But it's an illusion. They're unmoving, stopped by an anomaly I can't see or feel. Something not affecting me.

I run over to a man lying face up on a towel.

"Sir, excuse me!" The deadened syllables don't stop me from trying to get his attention. I don't want to believe I am alone. "Hey, I'm talking to you!"

When he doesn't answer, I kneel and lean the man up to shake him, but his eyes do not open. Moved from his position, a black shadowy mass is left in place of where he was, in the shape of his body. It's not the same as Misery's dark form, which consumed everything, and nothing could be seen beyond it. It's a void of light, a shadow existing in three dimensions, but behind it the edges of the towel he was lying on are visible. It appears as though there is something wrong with my vision. What I'm seeing is bizarre and it terrifies me.

I try to drop him but my heart nearly stops when he stays in the exact same place after I've let go.

I jump up to run away, but stumble and land on my back. Blips of black shadow play with my vision. I grab at the sand under my palms for leverage. There's an embankment and I scramble to climb it. Toward the top, my vision returns. There is a city in the distance. Looking toward the ocean perpetuates my fear of the unknown. The blob of dark has followed me, aiming directly for my face.

I run on unstable ground toward the city. The shadow follows, stalking me.

What is it? Is it alive?

My arms flail, and my feet carry me away from the beach. With every movement I leave a three dimensional shadow.

Is this Misery? Are they leaking out? I can't hear them.

Like everything else, the air is frozen. There is no breeze, and while I run my skin heats up. The sensation is similar to standing in the noonday sun in the summer. The fear of *it* following me fades a little, and I slow to a fast walk. I huff for air, but it's stagnant: it becomes thinner the more I breathe.

Calm down. Think it through. You still have knowledge from the Vraditi, use it. Breathe. Think. What is this? Misery is silent, so it can't be them, right? It's something else.

Turning in circles, arms extended, leaves shadow-voids in the air, but I can still see beyond them. It grows larger when I swat at it. I turn to my left and walk five paces. The air is temporarily restored, and I can breathe normally for a moment. When I turn back, it matches my movements everywhere I've been. The phenomenon is an echo of my presence, an emptiness wherever I've walked. Anxiety still keeps my heart from slowing though.

I talk to myself. "It's not alive, it's not moving, so I'm not in danger. Because it's an echo of me, it's not another entity, right?"

The sky catches my attention, and I have to squint. Despite nothing moving on the planet's surface, I am sure the sky has become a little brighter. It has the appearance of an aura, and a white mark traces the ocean's horizon line.

"Light?"

Sitting on a sandy bank to think, I put my hand into an area I've already passed through, into the shadow-void. It's cold. With an idea in mind, I stand and step in the shadowy echo. The temperature on my skin drops, and it becomes hard to breathe. Stepping through a new area, the rays from the sun hit my skin, and I'm warmed. The space I'm occupying stays warm until I move my arm out of and back into the void area.

Is time frozen? Or am I moving so fast it seems that way? Evalyn said she could feel the orange vortex trying to counter time. It didn't counter the blue, it put into place a different problem.

When I move into new areas, I absorb the sun's rays and displace the air which was occupying that space. Pushing things out with no movement to fill it back in creates empty space. If I stay still, the heat coming off me shouldn't move, and I should be protected from freezing.

The thought of time being halted is as terrifying as thinking the shadow-void was alive and stalking me. I'm also worried that my family is also here, just as stunned as I.

Are they safe? They're probably scared too.

I need to think of survival. There will be provisions in the city. They'll figure that too and head there. Maybe I can meet up with them.

It isn't far, maybe twenty miles to its limits, but because time is stopped I have no way to tell how long it will take to get there. Off the sand and onto a paved lot, there are wheel-less MVs in the area. The ones on the ground would confuse me if there weren't ones in flight overhead.

Too bad I can't use one of these to fly to the city.

Curious, I stop and look at one of the vehicles. It's sleek and easy on the eyes. Inside there are two seats side by side, and a short black stick between them.

How far ahead is this in the timeline? They're clearly more advanced.

Despite these MV's ability to fly, I take note of their strict pattern of staying above the lot and the roads. A road leads out to a highway, which leads directly to the city. Even from here it's apparent it isn't like Chas. It's more elaborate, and beautifully symmetrical. The buildings are short along the boundary, but the deeper into the city, the higher they reach to the sky. It makes it look like stairs leading up to a massive tower at the center.

Closer, the buildings' pink hue makes me wonder about them. They remind me of images of from Quva's world.

The crystal has powerful properties. Did humanity discover their usefulness?

The city may be one big resonator for our shockwaves.

The road follows parallel to the ocean. Trying to gauge how long I've been walking is impossible. My body is my guide, and it's telling me I'm already tired and hungry. Nearing the closest group of buildings, they're almost identical to one another. They're spaced equally apart, highlighted only by minor differences such as window tinting. None of them are under three stories tall.

Are any of these homes? It's wrong to steal but—

It doesn't matter if I steal. I need to survive long enough to fix this.

I can only hope it's temporary. And if it is, I should take care not to disturb too much.

Drake was right. I've grown weak.

No, I've grown a conscience.

I am –

Who I am.

At the intersection of the highway and the street bordering the city, buildings stretch for as far as I can see. MVs hover mid-air. People are out for a stroll. Their lives are unaffected, except for being frozen.

Inside the building to my left, beyond a large, light-pink door, are multiple desks in neat groupings of fours. People are scattered all across the huge room. People who were sitting, talking, moving, carrying papers. I hold my breath and wait for anyone to move. Nothing. Not a sound.

The technology is nearly identical to the Vraditi. Small slim screens are mounted to perfectly white desks with larger ones hanging on the walls. Electronic tablets are scattered on many of the desks. And each person has eyepieces strapped across their heads, just like Quva. On the screens are multitudes of images, faces, and blueprints.

Is this a communication hub? They're extremely busy.

They must have tapped into what the Vraditi left behind. Will humanity spread from this world to others?

The artificial light doesn't give the same warming sensation as the sunlight. Wandering, everyone appears to be content in what they were doing, collaborating in the construction of something massive by the looks of it. Curiously, they're all dressed alike in light pink shirts and pants, despite their diversity otherwise.

Subjected to my own hollow sounds and with no one to talk to, the quiet agitates me. I speak out loud to keep myself focused and calm.

"What did those vortexes do?" I ask myself, unnerved by the hollowness of my own voice. "Is it even possible to stop time? And if it is, how far does it reach? The whole universe?"

In another section, there are more people doing the same thing; everything and nothing. Busy and standing still.

"Ami and Agatha have been traveling for so long, they must have seen this age, or sometime close to it."

"Where are they? Where am I? This isn't Chas. The house wouldn't be here would it? Could it be?"

Weaving between desks, while looking for food, I observe the lives interrupted. Beyond the technology are photos of families, books, papers, and other personal items in their work areas.

"I saw the orange vortex envelop the house and the girls. Did we accomplish our goal? Are they in Chas, and in that time?"

While I try to stay away from the darker thoughts, they creep in on me.

"If I was pinned between the vortexes, then maybe I'll continue traveling through time. Am I alone now? If I time travel now, will everything still be frozen?"

Sighing loudly does nothing to make it sound less hollow.

At the back of the building is a kitchen, with several refrigerators. The first one has dozens of different dishes at my disposal, and different colored drinks. Thirsty, I pick up a clear bottle of what appears to be water with the name 'Tarsha' handwritten on it.

"Sorry, Tarsha."

I twist the cap and attempt to pour the liquid in my mouth, but nothing happens. It sits in the bottle upside down, appearing to defy gravity. I shake it over my mouth, but the liquid barely moves. Frustrated, I squeeze the bottle. Water comes out of it, now floating above my head in a blob. I'm no longer frustrated, but amused. Standing on my toes, I do what I can to sip it.

Inside my mouth, it's still liquid and I can swish it like normal. It's regular water. With the bottle at mouth level, I squeeze it more, displacing a line in the air. I walk along, slurping and gulping. On my last bit, I swish it and then spit. Instead of staying put in the air, it drops to the floor.

"What...? That doesn't make sense..."

Trying it again yields the same result, and I'm severely confused as to why. But more pressing matters interrupt my curiosity in the form of my stomach grumbling.

Finished playing, I open the refrigerator and rummage for a meal. A white container with the name 'Anatol' draws my attention, and when I open the lid there are several rolls of rice. In the middle of the rice is a mixture of different things; some are apparently vegetables while others have fish or meat.

"Food is food. Right?"

I pick one out and shovel it in my mouth. The texture and taste is extremely odd. The cold and sticky rice combined with the sliminess of whatever ingredients are in the middle is bizarre. Chewing vigorously, I force myself to finish the bite. The rest go back in the refrigerator where I found them.

"Anatol, you have a weird sense of taste."

Trying again, I grab a brown sack labeled 'Gris'. Inside is food I'm much happier with; a sandwich and packaged cookies. My stomach grumbles in delight at the sight of it.

I should be nervous sitting at a table of strangers, to eat food that doesn't belong to me. But it doesn't bother me, because if time ever restarts, their inconvenience will only last for a few hours. Meanwhile I'll have survived for a while in an impossible situation.

Despite the simplicity of sliced cheese and processed meat, the sandwich is the most delicious thing I've ever tasted. My hunger plays a big role, and I've devoured it in a few bites. The package of cookies is next.

What happens to the world at this point? Does it stay frozen?
I can't mold the world into a utopia if it does.

Can I unfreeze it? How would I even attempt such a thing?
If we had the urn we might be able to harness its power. We might undo this situation.

If it still exists — and if we can find it.

Crumpling up the trash, I throw it away in a nearby waste bin. The shadow-void I've left in my wake directs me out of the room, and helps me avoid the areas where I've already been. Though finding Ami and the others is a concern, I don't want to venture too far until I process and plan.

There's no lack of time for me to think while I seek to keep myself busy. My options are limited because everything is at a standstill. Yet there are things I can do now that I never could if all was right.

The people are there, and while they were busy, they don't look as though they're having fun. It doesn't take more than a few moments before repositioning them comes to mind. I play with the people, and set them up in various positions. It starts off harmless enough with repositioning their hands, feet, and desks, but becomes mischief as I move whole bodies to create elaborate works of art.

In one area I create a kingdom with a "queen" presiding over her subjects. Setting her on top of a desk, she stands there with a paper crown, and a pencil in her hand as a scepter. I gather people around her with their hands in the air in worship. In another section I form a large line of people appearing to dance, holding onto each other while they each kick one leg up.

Is it right for me to make such a mess?
It's entertaining. When would we ever have another chance at this?
It's not like I'm hurting them.

Each of them receives an attempt at a smile, but because it's not natural, they come out looking awkward. I can't make them look right. When I look back on my work, it's a strange sight to see voids of light and my strategically placed cast of people, but it has amused me for a while. I laugh when I place a short woman into the arms of a tall man, and give them ridiculous looking grins. The sculpture was supposed to be the appearance of a man carrying his 'new wife' across the threshold, but it looks more like he's holding an awkward mannequin.

If time unfreezes, their reactions will be priceless.
There's so much more we can do.
We have the city. And infinite time.

The amusement doesn't last though. I feel hungry again and wonder if it's already been long enough for my stomach to digest. After a quick stop in a bathroom, I head to the kitchen once more for food. Grabbing containers from the refrigerators, I decide it's time to take food with me and move on. Before leaving, I satisfy my hunger by eating someone's lasagna.

A bag lying on a nearby table is the perfect container to carry the food.

A nagging sense of morality pecks at me while I empty the contents of the bag on the table, and pack it with stolen food. But I justify their loss of a single meal for my continued survival while I try to find answers. The container with the rolls of rice goes in, despite my dissatisfaction with it.

I can't afford to be picky. Even if I don't like it, I'll have to choke it down if I run out of other things to eat. I'm sure there will be more food, but why take a chance?

Heading out, the rest of the city becomes my playground, with no one to play with. Misery is still utterly silent within me. The idea of not having to worry about it because of frozen time is pleasing. They were like a constant buzzing in my head, even when it was completely silent. To not hear them gives me relief.

Fatigue sets in, even though I feel I haven't been awake long enough to be this tired. Attempts to keep walking and shrug it off are futile. It overwhelms me and I have to sit. I've only made it three blocks farther. With my back against a building. I close my eyes.

~~~~~~

Feeling suffocated and warm wakes me. I jump to my feet, hoping it was a bad dream. But I'm still where I sat down: alone in an unknown city.

Everything is the same as I had left it, with the exception of the sky looking brighter. My vision adjusts to the blurriness caused by the shadow-void, but the brightness stays. I don't know how long I've been asleep, but it wasn't restful.

"This is awful," I say out loud, trying to keep myself sane. "Okay. What are my options? There are many buildings."

"Are there people to help? It seems to be paradise here. The buildings are immaculate, the people are clean and healthy."

"Maybe I could find a library. Do some research."

My stomach grumbles and interrupts my thoughts. I'm confused by the frequent need to eat. It's impossible to ignore. I close my fist and tap my stomach.

"Fine!" I tell it, annoyed. "We'll eat first."

On the top inside the bag is a brown paper sack. My next meal is assorted fruit. Slinging the food bag over my shoulder, I pick out some sliced apples for a snack.

Still on the outskirts of the city, I wonder which way I might go to find a library. Common sense tells me it likely wouldn't be this far out, but rather located centrally somewhere.

Devouring the apple slices while I walk deeper in, I pass people and flying MVs. While Chas had an active nightlife, this city is busy during the day.

Observing the people, there isn't a single unhappy face. Everyone is smiling. This future, however distant from my last stop in Chas, gives me hope we can achieve a fairly utopian society.

I should observe everything and find out how things progressed. It should help me integrate if I can ever get time to start again.

Though there are many people all around me, I couldn't feel lonelier. In the silence, I almost miss the collective souls wailing at me from Misery's dark world to fix some injustice. But even if time was unfrozen, I'm not sure they would be vocal in this peaceful era.

What do I do when food runs low? Or out?

Save some and move on.

I'll look for maps too.

Even though there are directional signs for streets and landmarks, I'm not finding one for a library. My curiosity has me looking into a random building with glass panels as its front wall. Inside are people in a stranger position than what I did in molding people at the last location. There appears to be an instructor in the middle of assisting one of his students on how to achieve what they're all doing.

Eating a banana from the sack, and people watching, I wonder about their experience. Each of them is dressed in form-fitting clothing, all set up on blue mats in an awkward position. They're on their hands and knees, with one arm, and the opposite leg, off the floor and stretched out, precariously balanced. Looking further, toward the front of the room there is a screen illustrating the pose.

With all the time in the world, I suppose I could give it a try.

We need to focus on hunting artifacts which might undo this.

We have eternity.

That's not the point. There might be a way out.

A thought occurs when I pull open the door. Neither these doors, nor the last, have locks on them. While it could be due to it being a public space, it seems more likely this might be a time where locks are unneeded.

Inside, I discard my trash in a waste bin, having to push it down because it won't fall on its own. There are a few unoccupied mats. I leave my bag hanging midair, and kneel.

On my hands and knees, looking up at the screen, I attempt to duplicate the pose. One arm out in front, and its opposite leg up and stretched backward. But as soon as I have my hand and leg off the floor I lose balance and put them back down.

"It doesn't *look* hard…"

I try again, extending my arm first, but the moment I try to extend my leg, I have to stop and rebalance. Grunting in frustration, I put my arm and leg up hastily, and fall onto a woman next to me, squishing her to the floor.

"Hah! Whoops."

I stand and try to place her back in the same position she was, but I'm unsuccessful. No matter how much I adjust her arms and legs, it still looks unnatural. I laugh.

There is another glass wall at the back, and another door. Inside are metal cabinets, and I hope to find anything useful to surviving my current situation. When I open the drawer, a new, strange effect is noticed. There is nothing but solid black inside. I'm reminded of the white void time when Ami and I hallucinated entering Emma's shop, and the darkness lunged out from the back room.

Because Misery is silent, and this can't be them, I'm driven to put my hand in it. There is immediate resistance. Fumbling my hand across the objects, they feel like books.

I grab one and move to an area untouched by the shadow-void. Light hits the book as I walk, and slowly reveals it. On the cover it's titled "The Art of Stretch Exercise," but when I open it the same issue arises; darkness.

"So, I need to pass through light to see the pages. How much light is needed for a page to become readable?"

Out on the main floor, I flip to the middle of the book and test.
One. Two.

Three steps into the light a page becomes readable. I'm not surprised to find it's filled with instructions and illustrations for stretching techniques. The image portrays a strange pose of a person lying on their back. They're stretching their hamstring with a long piece of cloth around their foot.

"This might be useful to stay fit while I'm stuck."

I close the book, shove it into my backpack and leave. The shadow-void makes it easy for me to ensure I don't get lost and double back on myself. Inward to the heart of the city, I leisurely stroll. Seeing the people's joy makes me wish I could be a part of their generation.

A peaceful world is one I never imagined, but here they are living in it.

We wouldn't fit in. Our abilities, our knowledge and presence. We'd be an affront to this society.

If we restart time, what then? We'll be here and have to adapt. Do we fade into the background?

These people would treat us as an outsider.

True.

I walk, and we're both silent for a while. I try to talk to Tiberius again.

If we could shockwave-jump to the roof of these buildings we might see better, but there's no telling what effects might occur if they are made out of the same crystals.

Do it anyway. Make it a small one to get to a ladder, and then climb to the top.

We might find stairs up one of these and not need to.

After a long trek, I reach a park. It's fairly open, with patterns of trees and beautiful flower arrangements. A cobblestone path mazes around inside. People are sitting in grassy patches, or on benches, taking in the sun. A few steps into the park I become tired again.

"What is happening? I can't be tired already."

I fight it, keeping one foot moving in front of the other, but I fail. My body winds down. I can't even reach the next open bench ten feet away.

There's grass. It will be soft.

~~~~~~

My skin is tingling with warmth. I'm overheating. I'm suffocating. A bubble of heat and exhaled air have surrounded me and I have to move now. I jump up and move into fresh air.

"Time is frozen," I remind myself. "The heat given off from my body will collect around me. My air will stagnate."

My face itches. I scratch, and my facial hair has rapidly grown out. I'm intrigued and unnerved at the same time.

"What is this doing to me? I've eaten and slept multiple times in a short span since I first woke up here. Hair growth is faster. Is time really frozen, or am I moving faster than everything? If I was accelerated it might explain my hunger and tiredness, maybe even fast aging."

My stomach replies with a heavy gurgle. Pulling the bag around, I retrieve the container with the rolls of rice. Despite my dislike of the taste and texture previously, it's appetizing now that I'm hungry.

It's devoured in a matter of moments. I set the container in the grass and move on. With everything to see, I focus on a single story building out of place amongst the rest, where a large number of people are coming and going from. Though it doesn't look like a library, it does gain my interest.

Instead of following the path, I cut across the park, taking care to avoid damaging the flowers when I step over them. A particular patch catches my attention. Orange chrysanthemums. I pick one and smile while thinking of Ami. Tucking it behind my ear, I hold onto it as a reminder of the family waiting for me somewhere. Or sometime.

When I reach the crowd heading into the building, a dark form flashes between two people, just visible in my peripheral vision. It's not the same as the shadow-void. It was there, but it's gone. My heart races.

"I'm sure I saw something…"

I wait with caution, keeping my attention focused on my sides. Whatever I saw doesn't reappear, making me think I'm seeing things.

"I'm becoming insane already. Maybe my eyes can't keep up, or my mind is having difficulty interpreting what's happening."

The staircase leading up is large, and the establishment is enormous; much larger than I had originally perceived. Its length is enough to make me arc my head from one shoulder to another.

At the entrance, there are half a dozen glass doors in a row. Due to the amount of people, I have to move some of them out of my way. Inside, I understand the reason for the volume of traffic. It's an enormous buffet.

My mouth salivates.

"A cafeteria!"

Smells frozen in time permeate the air, and they're fantastic. Numerous lines of people getting food exist in this first area alone, and there are more all across the premises. Because of the abundance, I conclude this will be my return point from any excursions.

As if my stomach has obtained control over my legs, I'm led to a line where people are serving themselves with a wide variety of dishes. My mind races with anticipation as I grab a plate and silverware from their tidy stacks. Because of the selection, I have a hard time choosing what I eat first. That changes when I find the meat. Sliced and neatly placed, I load up on ham, brisket, and chicken, followed by carrots, peas, and mashed potatoes with gravy.

With my plate full, I examine the tables. Though there are empty ones, I sit at one nearby where there are people.

They are unaware of my presence, but it feels wrong sitting alone. I can at least keep myself somewhat company.

Looking at each of them, there's a curiosity about their eyes I hadn't noticed until now. They all have orange rings around their irises. Thinking back, the others had it too.

"What's with the orange ring in your eyes?" I ask, knowing there won't be a response.

When I take a bite of the food I'm distracted from my imaginary conversation for a moment because it's as warm as it would be if everything wasn't frozen. Savoring my first bite of ham, I chew it thoroughly. I sigh in satisfaction and continue to devour my food.

"Oh, that's interesting!" I pretend to have received an answer. "What's to know? Anything fascinating besides orange rings?"

Their complexion is darker than mine; my skin is pale compared to everyone else. "You must get a lot of sun, hmm? Be careful, too much sun will turn your skin leathery."

I shovel food in, my stomach growling as if I'm starving. "The food here is excellent. They have such a way of keeping it fresh, freezing it in time and all." I laugh at my own terrible joke, and wave my arm in the air to leave a black void. "New slogan: never gets old, never goes moldy, always hot and fresh!"

I am going insane.

Was I ever sane?

I'm talking to myself in my head.

Once I'm finished with my food my body tells me it's time to use the restroom again. A big sign depicting the image of a man points me in the right direction, and I wash my hands with a bottle of water after. Done eating, for now, I head to the doors.

Tiberius asserts enough control to speak audibly.

"How do you think the population would react if we set up a monument of me?"

"It would disturb their peacefulness and be an affront to this society."

"There's no such thing as true peace. These people need us to remind them they're human. It might do them good to feel a little strife."

"Let's try to be more constructive. Find a library, stay busy, and maybe research how to fix this."

"Fine, Rain."

~~~~~~

Day log: Slept 5 times.

This is the first of my entries, should anyone ever find them. Because time is seemingly frozen I don't know what else to do. I can't keep track of time, so instead I'm keeping a log of how much I sleep, and my personal thoughts. It seemed like a useful way to stay busy and keep myself sane. Or maybe from going more insane.

I'm calling each time I go to sleep and wake up a "new day," and since waking up I've eaten twice already. My hair is growing at a quick rate, and though I can't tell the exact amount on top of my head, my facial hair is at least half an inch long now. I think my body's aging is accelerated, but I'm thinking and acting at the same speed I normally would. It's such a strange feeling knowing everyone around you is frozen and you're still aging.

I sought out a library and found one, of sorts. It has a large amount of books on every different topic I can possibly think of. But this place is like a school. There are people sitting in rows of desks, staring at screens. It makes me wonder what this society is really like.

My goal for the day is to read. Though the choices are numerous, I'll focus on history books, and hopefully stumble upon information about the house and my family. Or look for record of people with special abilities, and track down potential artifacts. I might go for a walk to places of the city I haven't been.

Setting the pencil on the paper, I stand from the desk I've taken as my own. Moving to the balcony nearby I stretch and groan. Looking up to upper levels of the library, I observe the people.

It's odd. The thought of no worries. Of harmony. How does harmony happen?

A nearby wide-arced staircase connects the floors. Up two flights, to the fourth level, I head over to a section for historical stories and events.

Coming across several books on Chas, I pick one and walk around while flipping the pages. Due to the unfortunate problem of having to flip to a page, and then walk forward so it absorbs light, it takes me a great deal of time to read the book. My effort to read is labored, but I make progress. I keep to a set pattern, overlapping my movements with the shadow-void and holding the book out to catch the light first to avoid creating excessive voids.

The book talks about the founding of Chas, and its original founders. The Forest of Hunger was untouched, but the outskirts of it were settled as a community of separationists from their oppressive government. Over time they expanded into the forest, using the trees as an export to facilitate growth. Two hundred years passed and it developed into a major hub.

I search for their economic-agricultural growth era to see what happened. But the section is small, giving no information on the park or the house, and the person named as having started the agricultural program is Vicky. We're not mentioned. No record of the sighting of the blue or orange vortexes. Not even information on the places I had fought, or the use of my ability to tear up trees. It talks about the food grown, the jobs created, and their beginning of prosperity.

Well, I know how it turned out. Denis.

Regardless of being a wealth of information on Chas, there's oddly not a single mention of the vortex.

Surely someone must have seen it. Was its existence hidden?

Done with this book, I place it on a table, and move back to the shelf. Though it's cold, and hard to breathe, I keep my movements within the shadow-voids to leave enough light to absorb for the next book. I find several other books with Chas mentioned, and continue on the same pattern.

In between naps and eating, I eliminate them from the list of ones which might help me. None of the books on Chas mention the house, and it dawns on me it might not be included as fact.

I wonder if there's a book on folklore or myths regarding the area. But where would I start looking if not in the history section? Fiction?

Sitting and looking over the fourth floor balcony I see the shadow-void left when I entered the building. The loneliness is setting in, and my heart aches for anyone at all to walk through the doors. After spacing out for a while, and creating shadow-void butterflies by blinking, my stomach calls me to reality with a long grumble.

I head to where I stored the bag on the second level. My stomach grumbles harder, and I devour a few rolls while pulling out a container of turkey. It's gone in a few bites, and I guzzle a bottle of water to wash it down. But my food has run out, and I need to return to the buffet for a refill. I zip the bag up, sling it on my shoulders, and follow my shadow-void back to the entrance.

Without solid sleep, stepping outside hurts my eyes. The sky *is* becoming brighter, but I have no explanation as to why.

It could be an optical illusion. Or maybe it's part of the effect of time being frozen.

At the buffet, I've shifted people back a few feet so it's easier for me to get where I want to go. No plate this time, I pick at the food, using the utensils stuck in each dish as my personal silverware. Because the food underneath the top layers haven't been exposed to light, I'm careful to leave spots untouched so I can see what is what.

Pretending to exchange pleasantries with the locals did nothing for my loneliness before, so I sit alone and eat quietly.

I miss dinner with my family. The loud nights, the quiet nights. I'd give anything to be with them now.

I hope they're okay. I wish I could find some information about them.

After my hunger is sated, I pack more food to take to the library. The containers I've kept are helpful, allowing me to stay there and research longer. I make sure each one is completely packed, and put them back in the bag. Loosely thrown in are more rolls, and a few bottles of water and juice.

Looking at all of the people waiting to resume their lives, I sigh and wish I was a part of it, even if it meant being frozen.

After using the restroom and washing my hands, I head to the exit.

I catch movement out of the corner of my eye. Something dark and the size of a short person. A sound similar to growling hits my ears for a brief second, despite that sound doesn't appear to be moving normally.

My heart jumps and I turn to look. Whatever it was, it's gone, and there's no shadow-void left by it.

"Hello?!" I yell out. "Who's there?"

There's no response, but I keep my gaze pinned to the far end of the building, waiting for movement. I stare for a long time, but fail to see it again.

"Could it be the lack of a full sleep cycle? I guess I knew I'd hallucinate at some point, but I didn't think it would be this fast," I say to calm myself. Looking all around, I'm still antsy because of the movement.

"There is no shadow-void. It couldn't be real, right?"

To try and shrug it off, I leave. The feeling of eyes watching me, combined with the eerie silence, unnerves me even more. Humming does nothing to alleviate the tension.

Moving down the steps to street level I look back to check for movement. Everything is still.

In case I'm being trailed, I decide to go anywhere besides the library. Taking a new route, I look for somewhere to conceal myself. A metal staircase attached to a building seems like it might be a good place to hide from something I'm not sure even exists. The staircase in the alleyway ascends to the roof, but neither it, nor the attached ladder, come to the ground.

"What's the purpose? To keep people off the roof?"

There comes another growl for a brief moment, but it seems distant. My options to reach the ladder are to use objects as stepping stones, or shockwave-jump.

There are people I could use as a stepping ladder, but it would take too much time trying to pull them in and position them.

Meanwhile, whatever is making the noise will find us. Jump.

I jump and push off with a small burst. My hands clasp the bottom rung, and I pull myself up to the safety of the platform. The view below is intriguing: the shockwave didn't expand outward. Instead there are two streams bound where I pushed off, not even making it to the pavement.

Strange.

The noise has ceased, but I'm in a hurry to climb to the top and out of its view. At the top, I walk to the edge closest to the street I came from. The shadow-void is there, but no movement. There's still no evidence I'm not hallucinating.

The shadow-void is where I've been. But where are you?

It's gone.

Was it there?

Along the edges, I observe and wait for it. The motionless people below are a reminder of my aloneness.

Having made a full perimeter sweep, I look at the buildings which climb to the center of the city. The tallest one, in the middle, is unique with a glass sphere at the top. It's too far away to make out what is in it.

"I'll have to make a trip there and see if I can get in it," I promise myself. "I bet the view is breathtaking."

With no sign of the creature stalking me, I feel safe enough to try to make it back to the library. Before I reach the staircase I run out of energy.

Lying down on the roof, I set my bag beside me. The smooth but hard surface isn't comfortable, but that doesn't stop me from curling into a fetal position and letting sleep overtake me.

~~~~~~

Day log: Slept 11 times.

No explanation for the need to sleep so much. I'm getting tired faster and faster. I should have energy. My hair has grown even more, and I now have at least an inch of beard. My fingernails are getting long too, but I have no way to cut them at the moment. I could chew them off.

I'm losing my mind. My reprieve is reading. I'm being stalked by...I don't know. It doesn't leave a trail, but it makes a 'grrrrr' sound. I think it's in the shape of a man. It flickered and then appeared to duck behind a man in the lobby. It's stalking me, but I don't know why. It might intend me harm, or might be curious. It hasn't approached me.

I have to go outside and walk down the street to read anymore. It's going to keep getting farther. There's enough light left in the library to still see untouched book spines, but I've traveled every walking path in the building. It's mostly dark and cold now. Harder to breathe too. I'll have to move on soon.

It's a strange sight when half the room, the half you travel in, is dark, while the upper half of each level is still lit. I've left enough light for me to navigate safely, and pockets of air, but it's strange as I look against a wall and I'm in this bubble which keeps everything out. I can see the light there at the end, but it never encroaches to where I am.

I've found nothing about the vortex, or artifacts. I've read several books on the history of this world. They unlocked technology from unearthed Vraditi cylinders. Humans moved beyond petty squabbles. No one seems to have higher status than any other. They're reaching for the stars and each person has an essential duty to perform for success of their society. No one person has a say in change. No one person controls them. Driesen set things in motion. In the middle of the reform a reconstruction project commenced and there they found it. Driesen. An interesting turn. Somehow I contributed to this new society.

Was I ever there? My past doesn't seem real. None of it. I've slept 11 times but it feels like I've never been outside of this. Whatever this is. It's like nothing is real, and I'm a ghost of a man who wanted to exist.

The goal today is to read more folklore and legend books. There has to be something about the house somewhere. Maybe, if I can find it, the nagging doubt of my existence will go away.

Loading my bag with items on the table in front of me, I pack several books, the pencil, and personal log, and somehow fit the food and water on top. With a single book left over, I pick it up and then sling the bag on my back while heading to the entrance. Reaching the bottom, the open doors are in front of me. The tunnel effect with light at the end plays tricks with my vision.

My legs are jelly, trying to ignore my commands to walk through the shadow-void near where I last saw the creature. I sprint, despite the fear. The hair rises on my neck as if an attack is imminent. Outside there are areas not yet consumed by the shadow-void I can use as shelter from the unknown creature. Looking back, nothing is chasing me.

"Idiot. You're hallucinating."

"It's not a hallucination. It was there. It's lurking, stalking us."

"You're paranoid and talking to yourself."

"Says you…me…I…"

I stare at the doors for a few moments longer, searching for a direction I haven't taken yet. While I want to eventually make it to the tallest tower, I don't know if I'm ready to give up the security I have being in walking distance to my food source.

I open the book in my hand titled 'Mythos Examined' and begin reading. As I stroll I read a number of different myths from around the world. Half creatures, sea monsters, massive birds, spirits, and the dead walking. All of which, by the tone in the book, seem to have been debunked in the writer's mind.

"It's not true, at least in part. Evalyn's a spirit, right? And what of the souls inside us?"

"I remember things, but were they real? Is our life all *just* remembering things from books? Or our love with Ami *just* the idea of love with someone who loves us completely?"

"I refuse to give up and believe we are nothing more than an echo of life."

Doubt consumes me as I flip through the book. There's a section in it about people who could supposedly exhibit unique abilities on command, and even a few names. None I recognize though. Further into this particular legend lists other sightings of strange happenings around places or people, and there's a listing for a blue tornado.

"Finally, something!"

"Have we read this before? Are we inserting ourselves into history?"

"No. I was there. I…"

I read the passage.

The blue tornado is a rarely seen phenomenon. There has been one known location for its supposed occurrence: located in Chas's 'Central Park'. It was discovered through several fragments of passed down stories; it may have even appeared when the land was known to be Astid or the Forest of Hunger.

The blue tornado's height varies from story to story, with speculation it might be a beam from beyond our world, actually extraterrestrial in origin. This idea was disproven with the advancement of our communications and technology finding nothing in space that could have caused this phenomenon.

Several of the stories which originally fueled the idea it was extraterrestrial was the addition of people coming and going into the blue tornado, disappearing with no trace. One such instance is during Chas's reform. It became part of the legend that men and women came from it to incite riots, or become saviors, or both, but due to Chas's heavily edited history books it's impossible to verify if there is any truth in those claims. It could be that the people who helped start the movement were attributed to the legend, possibly for anonymity, or maybe to create the lore behind the need for reform. It's impossible to tell because the 'official' history books make no mention of saviors or the blue tornado. The history books give credit to Driesen and a city council for the efforts.

Local legends claim there are witnesses to the blue tornado, but if there were, they did not take the time or make the effort to record it. The stories have been passed from one to another verbally, and therefore are likely distorted and reimagined. There is no evidence the event or events of the blue tornado has occurred.

"We don't exist. We must have learned of the legend and imposed ourselves into it."

"They were protecting us from being exposed."

"We are an echo of life."

"We are not."

To my disappointment, there is no information about them, my family. My love, Ami. My struggle to prove my existence is growing, but I refuse to claim insanity, yet. Chas existed, and may still exist.

"If we are to determine our existence, we need to find Chas. There might also be hidden or buried information about us there."

"And artifacts. If we can find artifacts..."

I am still unsure of which city I'm in, or how to locate Chas. I can't help but wonder if they'll be there waiting for me, or if they're frozen in time and I'm doomed to die alone.

When I look up, I've traveled further than I had intended. The shadow-void extends far behind me. My stomach growls violently, and I pull fruit salad out and shovel it in my mouth. It's deliciously sweet, but even if it weren't, I've decided taste is not a concern – if it's food, I'll eat it.

The fruit salad doesn't satisfy, and I rummage again. Smothered ribs become my next victim, and I gnaw on them like a wild animal. The mess doesn't even concern me. I'm still hungry and want more.

With sticky fingers I shove everything in the bag. When I stand, I suddenly feel insecure.

Beginning back toward the library, and the food, I feel eyes on me again. In a window a shadow streaks across my peripheral vision, not in a running motion, but more of a visual echo jumping back and forth. It growls, and I scream. It bounces between a few locations, flickering in and out of my vision.

Once, I would have stood my ground. But I'm tired and losing my mind. Whether it's a hallucination or a creature, I can't tell, but I choose not to find out. In the nearest alleyway with a staircase to climb, I boost myself with a shockwave without a second thought to the repercussions. When I'm on the stairs I don't stop to look back.

On the roof I huff and wheeze. My mind races and I look for any movement whatsoever. Turning in circles several times, I stop, facing the area where the stairs are, waiting to see if I've been followed.

Watching the top of the stairs, I try not to blink often. They water and become heavy. My movements become sluggish. I fight it, determined to stay focused so I might leap to the next rooftop.

I lose momentum. The edge is out of reach.

~~~~~~

Day log: Slept 17 times

I grow wearier. Wearier. Is that even a word? More weary? I'm the weariest of them all? I'm tired. I can't sleep for too long. It, or they, are watching me. Waiting patiently. Taunting me. Maybe they will kill me and end this.

I found maps. Found Chas on a map. I bet there are no shadow creatures there. I found one hovering over me when I woke up. Maybe. I don't know where I am. Still looking. If I knew, then I could make my way to Chas.

They are appearing more frequently. They're waiting for the right opportunity. Why haven't they taken me in my sleep? Sleep. My eyes are always heavy now, but I need to eat. I need to eat. I bet there's a cart in the food court. If there is, I could load it with food and take it on the road with me, and head toward Chas, if I knew which direction to head. I need to find out where I am. Where am I? My beard is longer.

My goal is to refill my food supplies and find out where I am. Maybe go to the tower with the ball on top. It's pretty.

Sitting in the library, I glance around, watching for movement. There's none. Between the lack of solid rest, and the paranoia, I can barely focus.

My thoughts are becoming more disconnected. I don't know if I'm Rain or Tiberius. Or both. Or neither. My ability to express the thoughts outwardly is becoming diluted.

Shoving the paper and pencil in the bag, next to a stack of folded maps, I zip it up. Its weight on my shoulders is heavy. Despite my thoughts being scattered, I still have the sense to know when to flee.

There are eyes on me.

There are always eyes on me.

Without slowing I leave the library for the last time. I've tried to overlap my previous shadow-voids as much as I can, but it has become increasingly difficult. There's not much left between here and the cafeteria. The street is dim from where I've walked, but there's enough light and air left to get there.

My steps are quick as I push toward the buffet. My shadow-voids have overtaken the building. The way in and out is through it.

"I'll have to hold my breath. There's no air left up to the entrance."

"Be quick."

"They're coming! Run!"

I nearly trip over my own feet, stumbling, but I recover. There's a pocket of air and light I've kept to the right. I take it. Shallow breathing is impossible, and I gulp at the air while finding my next pocket.

Heading into the kitchen door at the back wall, there are men and women dressed in long white jackets, their hair covered with white caps. There are cooking stations, all manned and in process of cooking more food. It makes a king's kitchen pale in comparison.

It doesn't take me long to spot what I'm looking for. A large cart. It has three tiers, big enough to carry a substantial amount of food. Not wanting to return unless I absolutely have to, I load up food ready to consume. I'm able to fit three full size, and two half size deep-well pans of assorted foods on the bottom tier of the cart.

One after another, I stack more on, and finally the cart is filled with enough to last me at least a dozen meals; two dozen if I'm conservative. I leave a pan empty for bottles of water. Out on the line, I grab as many bottles as possible.

The remaining air pockets in the cafeteria are scarce. I zig-zag around the people, toward the door. Observing my left and right for movement, I anticipate seeing *it,* or *them,* sometime soon.

Outside, I have to run to the side of the building to breathe. When I catch my breath, I head to my cart. There's a ramp to roll it down, and I take it, despite it being crowded with people. Weaving, I'm certain it's taking longer to descend the ramp than if I tried the stairs. But even though time is stopped, I'm sure I don't want to test if it's possible to dump my food.

At street level, I stop for a moment to shovel ham in my mouth.

Deep into the city, I ignore the signs and look for the tower with the glass ball at the top. I enter areas I've never been to, and wonder how these people were living such perfect lives. While some seem to be working, there are a large number of people who don't appear to be occupied.

"If this is a utopian society, and everyone contributes, what do these people do?" I ask while passing a man and woman walking arm in arm. "I should look for books on social development."

Every inch of me is weary. Drinking a bottle of water revives me for a while. Then I resort to slapping my face. I'm too tired, though.

With the creature no doubt lurking and watching me, I feel unsafe on the ground. An external staircase lies in an alley, and I run to it.

I leave the cart at the alley entrance and boost myself with a shockwave. I grab the ladder, and pull myself to the security of the walkway.

I have no energy left. Instead of climbing to the top, I lay on the uncomfortable metal grate, and close my eyes.

~~~~~~

I awake staring straight up at the next level of the staircase. My heart jumps, fearing the cart and my food might be gone, but when I sit up and look, it's still there. My food is safe. I sigh in relief.

"Slept eighteen times. Slept eighteen times. Slept eighteen times," I chant to myself to remember it.

Up the staircase and onto the roof, I count the building as fifteen stories high. Though I have no proof the creatures are unable to reach me here, I feel secure.

In front of me, toward the glass ball tower, are more skyscrapers taller than the one I'm standing on. To both sides they're the same height, and shorter behind me. From this vantage point, the ocean is partially visible.

Having figured out my direction, I return to my cart and set off to the heart of the city.

Along the way, I stop and look in a few doors to see what's in them. One interests me much more than the others.

When I pull a solid metal door open, what's inside is a massive dark metal object suspended in the air by thick cables. Scaffolding is wrapped all around it. It's too wide for me to see all at once, but I note its similarities to the Vraditi ship, except on a smaller scale. I'm intrigued. Leaving the cart, I head inside. The floor is being showered with falling sparks as frozen people work on the underbelly.

Men and women are spread in and around the building and along the scaffolding leading to the Vraditi-like ship. It appears to be in the middle of construction. Tools, cranes, and parts litter the area around it.

Interested in the object which could be a scaled down starship, I look for a way up. There aren't any stairs to the scaffolding, only elevators. Attached to each floor are elevator stops on the walkways leading to the ship-like object. But without power, the elevators are useless.

I could boost myself, but a shockwave might cause significant damage if time ever restarts.

Underneath the behemoth, I run my hand along its warm metal, admiring its sleek and smooth design. There are men and women underneath welding together the panels. I take a moment to play in the sparks falling to the floor, swiping my arms through them. In wonder, I walk in the shower of fire.

My amusement is brief and I resume looking for stairs. There's a set at the far end, and I climb them to the third level. When I reach the ship, I can see inside. It's deep and long. There are workers performing various tasks, but it must be early in the construction process. It's the beginning of the frame. I'm disappointed and I lose interest. Short on meaningful rest, I'm actually irritated they're not farther along.

"Don't they know I have better things to do?" I grumble.

I realize what I've said and laugh at myself.

"Better things to do. As if they're slow to finish their job."

"We have nothing better to do."

"Walk, eat, sleep, and fear the Shadow Goblin."

My stomach growls loudly. I make a hasty retreat back to my cart, and by the time I arrive I feel like I'm starving. I devour a roll, using a bottle of water to speed the process. I leave my trash hanging in mid-air, not wanting to pull excess weight, and continue on.

When I finally reach the tower with the glass bubble at the top, I marvel at it. Surrounded by a garden of bushes and beautiful flowers similar to those in the park, the building has a wide base and grows thinner as it nears the top. It reminds me of the City Hall of Chas, in that it's the center of attention. The design is different though. It's conical, and sitting precariously at the top is the jewel I've been seeking.

The long, sloped walkway up to it is packed with people. A challenge lies ahead of me, and I wonder if it's worth it to try and maneuver the cart through, or if I should move them out of the way.

"I don't know how long I'll be in there. I shouldn't leave the cart."

I pull the cart as far as I can, but I finally reach an impasse and start moving people. This leaves large shadow-voids, hindering my route in and out, but I have no choice and keep moving forward. By the time I've reached the large glass doors I'm sure I've moved at least fifty people.

The interior is even more awe inspiring. Smooth, white spiral columns rise from the floor to support a ceiling fifty or so feet in the air. In the center is a much larger column. On every wall, on stands, and hanging from the ceiling, are wonderful works of art. Paintings, drawings, and statues of all materials, subjects, and era appear to range widely.

My taste for fine artwork when I was Tiberius kicks in, and I forget for a moment that I'm tired. Leaving the cart, I admire the works. Each piece has a date and a name listed under it. A few vibrant pieces gain my favor as I browse, and one in particular keeps my gaze for more than a few moments.

In front of me, along the left side of the round building, is a painting of a vibrant green grassy field with patches of magnificent blue flowers, a flower I don't recognize. Beyond the grassy field lies a forest, and the colors used in the painting make it seem realistic, as if I were looking out a window.

Moving closer, I examine the textures on the canvas by running my fingers over them. It's remarkably soft, unlike paintings I can recall from my own time where the paint was rough and unrefined.

My heart is lightened looking at the works of art. I give each piece a great deal of attention, studying the intricacies and taking in the details. Half way around the center column, a black and white photograph in large print catches my attention. I'm stunned; it's so beautiful I have to choke back tears.

There, in the photo, are three women.

The first is tall with long, light, wavy hair. Her complexion is darker than the other two, and her numerous freckles accentuate her tone. She's running her fingers through her hair to pull it back. Her loose, light colored t-shirt is lifting, exposing her stomach partially. Her smile is coy and devious as she flirts with the camera.

The second is shorter than the first, with darker hair pulled into a high ponytail. Tied neatly on her head, off to the left, is a multicolored ribbon, indicated by the different shades. It matches the form fitting, V-neck top she has on. She's smiling sweetly. Her arms are wrapped around the first and the third women in a pose which tells me they're friends.

The third girl's long, light hair is done up in a braid with large twists. It hangs down over a spotted tank top and unbuttoned overalls. She hugs the middle woman tightly. Her eyes are as bright as the cheeky smile she's giving the photographer.

Ami, Eve, and Emma pose for a photo in our yard. Though the whole house isn't in the picture, they stand next to the clotheslines, and I know exactly where in the yard they are. Behind them is the house, and beyond that is the Forest of Hunger.

They never left the last timeline of Chas, where we found James.

It's impossible to hold back. My eyes well up as I notice differences about them in the photo: they're more mature, and years have passed for them. They appear happy to be together, maybe even to the point of genuine friendship in my absence.

"Have they moved past fighting with each other?"

"They've moved past me."

They aren't stuck like me. They aren't here. They lived out their lives.

A mixture of happiness and sadness overwhelms me. I'm torn between loneliness, and being happy they got to move on. I slump to the floor and, as much as I try to fight it, I weep.

Despair sets in. Lying on the floor, I curl up and sob. My tears pool on the floor, and air runs out in this location, forcing me to move. Even when no more tears flow, my chest heaves.

I will die here, alone.

If only Drake had killed me.

This is my punishment for my evil deeds.

Time fails to move, and yet an eternity passes for me while I shift from one spot to another. My mind bounces between anguish and relief, as the photograph serves as a testament to my success – they got to live normal lives. But I'll never see them again and it hurts.

Is my journey over?

Ami and Agatha have been repaid for saving me.

Even though my promise is fulfilled, I need to find some kind of new meaning for my life. Feeling sorry for myself is getting me nowhere, and the air grows thin near the floor where I'm lying.

On my feet once more, I examine the center column. There's an elevator, and the doors are partially open, but there is no other option to reach the top.

"Can I climb in the shaft somehow?"

I think about it while I head to the cart, distracted briefly by the food on it. Exhausted, I'm famished and I scarf down handfuls of food. I'm disgusting in the way I eat, uncaring about how I would look if time were advancing. Nothing goes to waste as I lick my fingers for the oils and salts.

Back at the partially open elevator doors, I pry them open. They're tough to move. I wedge my body in between them, and use my back and feet to press them open completely. It's crowded inside, but I shove people to one side to make room for myself. On the ceiling is a hatch.

The railing around the inside provides me a place to put my feet and climb. The hatch pops open with little effort, and leads to a dark shaft, lit by a few lights all the way to the top. Though I fear the possibility of being trapped by the Shadow Goblin, I want to see the city from the globe.

"It'll be worth it."

I pull myself into the shaft. What little light is being shed reveals the mechanical workings of the elevator, as well as a ladder in an alcove on the wall. I grab the rungs and pull myself upward. Hand over hand, foot after foot, I climb.

Halfway between the top and bottom my energy wanes. Fatigue hits hard and a sense of urgency to reach a safe place hits me. But neither up nor down would be faster at this point. I struggle hard to get to the bottom, swearing to rest when I'm safe. Consciousness is slipping away from me. My eyelids become heavier. My hands slip and there's nothing I can do about it.

~~~~~~

I snap awake and yell frantically.

As I flail, it occurs to me that I'm upside down, my feet caught in between two rungs of the ladder. My heart races and I panic. I try to gain control, but dangling precariously several hundred feet above the roof of the elevator heightens my fear.

Swinging back and forth, I see movement inside the elevator, unmistakably this time.

"RAAAAA…" It growls at me.

The Shadow Goblin is looking up at me, or I assume it is because it has no eyes. Its arm is outstretched trying to reach me but it can't maintain its presence.

Flickering in and out of sight, it still leaves no shadow-void, but the reality that the Shadow Goblin isn't a hallucination hits hard. A feeling of horror sends me clambering to reach the top. In one big swing, I catch a rung of the ladder. Without looking down, my hands grab, and my feet push in a flurry. The doors are closed when I reach the top, and I'm forced to hang on and claw at the seam between the doors.

It's coming for you! It followed you!

I don't know if it's entered the shaft. Thoughts of what it might do causes me to struggle against the two door halves with as much strength as I can muster, all the while balancing precariously on my heels.

The doors start to cooperate, and I stick a foot and forearm in to pry them open. They move enough for me to squeeze in. Once inside, I turn with my palm toward the door, ready to fire a shockwave at whatever might follow.

"Come on!" I yell at it. "What are you waiting for?"

Nothing emerges from the shadows of the elevator shaft. It takes me until I'm out of air in this spot to feel comfortable moving away from the opening. Even then I back away cautiously, my eyes fixed on the elevator doors.

After a great deal of "time" passing, the fact it hasn't followed me allows me to relax and investigate my location.

At the top of the tower, I am among many more people. I'm at the bottom of the glass bubble. Steps lead up from the elevator area to a platform wrapping around the sphere. On the platform are more stairs, which lead to another level made of glass a few feet thick. There's no art in this section of the building, but when I reach the glass wall I understand why. The world outside is the art.

I can see in every direction for miles. Struck with amazement, my heart hurts when my first thought is wishing my family could be here with me.

I walk the circumference on the first level. The city is even larger than I thought, and the tower is the actual center. Beyond the borders, there are only roads which lead in several directions; no other human-made structures can be seen. The landscape ranges wildly from the beach and ocean on one side, while on the opposite side are plains, a forest, and mountains. When I approach the stairs to climb to the next level there's a sign. 'Caution: Do not wear a dress or skirt beyond this point.' I snort and look up out of curiosity. No one above dared to break the rule.

On the next level, I mingle with frozen people. There's an open space I claim as my own to set down my bag. I set my maps in a stack. Next to them I lay out paper and my pencil. Then I bring out water and food.

"What point is there, knowing they won't be there waiting for me?" I ask. "I could travel the world until I die. Might not take long. I would need a lot of food and water."

Unfolding each map, I move them into the light to illuminate them and meticulously arrange them in two rows of four. The first map's title is 'Salvoa: A Map of the World'. While I've seen the world from above, and real life versions of the things depicted on the map, I never knew there were names for all of the seas, continents, and mountain ranges. There are four large, abstract continents connected by land bridges. Each has its own clusters of islands, big and small.

There is so much I haven't seen.

And so much I never will.

The subsequent seven maps are of Salvoa's regions.

Where am I?

Content with my current set up with all my maps readable, I sit and pull the pencil and paper to me. Looking into the sky for a few moments, I sigh from a mixture of emotions rolling around. I lean forward and write.

Day log: Slept 19 times...if you can call the 19th time sleep. I passed out and nearly fell to my death.

While I can still feel my mind drifting, and my thoughts becoming hazy, I am having a moment of clarity right now. I figure I should write a few things I can read later on, or perhaps someone else will. If I'm dead, assume I've fallen to my death or that the Shadow Goblin has caught me. There's certainly no fear of starving, at least for a while. I might head out on the road. I might run out of food then, but I have time to plan for that.

As much as I had hoped to reach my home with my family – and my love – waiting for me, it won't happen. They continued their lives without me. Ami and Eve even appear to have become friends without my presence there to pit them against each other. It makes me happy they were able to go on, but I'm sad too. I'll have to get used to life without them. My existence is going to be lonely, and I'm not sure I'm ready to come to terms with that. Talking out loud does no good, other than to hear my own voice. But who is there to talk to, but me?

I could stay here forever, though the concept of time is a joke since everything is frozen, and I am aging rapidly. My beard is at least two inches long now, and when I eat my moustache gets in the way. I could shave, but it gives me an illusion of time. I'll leave it.

With the Shadow Goblin lurking, stalking me, I don't feel safe. I have my maps. And if I made a train of food carts, I could see more of the world before I die.

The ocean might help me decide.

~~~~~~

I'm filled with some energy after sleep and food.

Running along the rooftops, I make my way across the city. Despite my mental faculties slipping, I try to keep myself in shape. I use shockwave-jumps to leap across gaps, and land on the next rooftop in line. I try not to put too much power into it because I don't know how it will affect the buildings. Traveling has become an insignificant task without having to worry about using the streets and keeping my direction straight.

I've reached the last row, where I first entered the city. My original shadow-void from the beach is there to greet me. I look at the ocean, close my eyes, and imagine the sounds I would hear: the wind, waves crashing, birds cawing, people talking. When I open my eyes though, it's all the same as it was. Still and silent.

From the top, I leap down and pad my landing with a couple small bursts. Back on the road, I walk toward the beach. Where the pavement ends I sit and take my shoes and socks off to walk out onto the fine, soft sand.

I walk toward the smaller waves suspended breaking on the beach. The sand gives way underfoot. It's warm. I bend over and snatch up a handful, pushing it between my fingers while I walk. When my feet hit the water, it's cool, but I press forward. My solid form displaces it, like the air and the light, to leave a shadow-void. It amuses me and I play with the effect, stomping and splashing the water. It moves only enough to part for my solid mass.

I wonder what it looks like under the ocean's surface. I bet there's much to see. Too bad I couldn't reach the air above.

After leaving a knee high shadow-void in the ocean for a mile, I finally emerge and head to dry sand. There's an empty towel in between a couple people sunbathing, and I lay on it. Putting my arms behind my head for support I stare at the sky. It's become so bright I can barely see the outline of where the sun is. I have to shield my eyes to find it.

If we travel, where will be go? What will we do?
We'll walk until we can't walk anymore.
We'll walk until we die. Maybe then the world can move on.
What lies beyond this life?
Will I join Misery's collective?

Because it's such a strange thing to look at, I can't keep my eyes closed long enough for a nap. Reaching to my neighbor's stuff I grab a large straw hat, and plop it on my face.

~~~~~~

Day log: Slept 30 times.

I haven't been writing. My clarity is not clarity. It's hazy. Everything is a blur. I can't last. It's time. I'm leaving from this city, Gowar. My destination is Chas. I've decided to let death take me when I get there. I have no hope. I'm tired. I want to be in my home when I die. Maybe I won't feel so alone there.

Though I am alone, I'm not. The Shadow Goblins are following me around. There's a couple of them I think. They've been so close we have practically touched. Always with their roaring and growling. I'm not sleeping well. I tried chasing one. It disappeared before I got there.

I'm not sleeping well. Wait, I already wrote that. I'm tired all the time. Even though I eat and eat, nothing helps. I feel slow. It's a long way to Chas, but I'll get there. I found maps...oh yeah, you already know. I know where I am and how to get there.

From here I'll head to the center of the...what's that word? The middle of the land. I'll have to stop in a couple towns and cities along the way to replenish. I can only pull so much. My face itches, and I often have to scratch it. How will I pull the food and scratch my beard?

Time to go. Goodbye.

Packing my bag, I gather a few books, my maps, and my writing utensils from their scattered places on the glass floor. Hoisting it over my shoulders, I move to the edge of the glass sphere and look out over the land in which I'm going to travel.

Beyond the fields and the trees lies a mountain range waiting for me. Mapping the terrain visually, I can see the road I'll follow. It's littered with small dots I know are flying MVs. I sigh.

I make my way down the several hundred feet of the elevator shaft, and into the elevator through the hatch.

In the art gallery, I head to the photograph of the women and pull it off its stand. I want to preserve it, but I don't want to carry it in my hands either. Carefully I fold it so no crease falls on their faces, and place it in the front pouch of the bag.

Outside on the street, I left two carts tied together, stolen from another buffet a couple blocks over. I took as much food and water as I could pile on, and a few other supplies.

Stuffing a roll in my mouth for a snack, I grab a rope harness attached to the cart's handle and wrap it around my chest. It takes effort to pull it, but with every step, I forge a shadow-void path toward my eventual destination. Gowar's design makes it easy to find the highway into the mountains. I only have to travel in one direction until I reach the edge of the city, and then the highway will be apparent.

On the open road, quite a way from the city, I look back at Gowar for one last time, admiring the design of it all. But when I turn toward the wild, the simplicity of the grassy plains between me and the mountains is equally as appealing.

No people to not talk to.

I am, and always have been, alone.

No shadow-voids exist here giving me clear vision heading out. The deep green hues relax my mind, reminding me of the grass at the house.

With my resolve to die in peace in my homeland, I keep moving forward. I stop as my body requires, and no more.

My thoughts are scattered and I'm easily distracted. I think about my time as the king of Asta, the women and the house, the people I've saved and the people I've hurt. But none of it detracts from the long voyage ahead of me. The forest and mountains grow closer, but I have to take frequent breaks to recover energy.

After having rested half a dozen times, I stop and eat, then leave the carts to lie in the grass. The grass makes me itch. After squirming and scratching, I close my eyes.

~~~~~~

Day log: Slept 62 times.

This road is long. I just follow it. It's all I can do. I'm nearing the gradual incline to the mountain range, and cannot see the road beyond a certain point. Though light exists along the road, looking off into the forest I find it is an eerie place. Maybe it's because I'm used to the ambient noise of a place like that, but its silence gives me the *chills.*

The next city over the mountains is still far away. It could become miserable as there are clouds over the mountains. Dark ones. There might be rain. There will be Rain. Hah.

As much as I want to forget the life I had before, my mind keeps bringing me back to it. I took it for granted. I love them all and I didn't get to express how much they meant to me. I thought for sure I had more time with them. But it's for the best. They lived.

After packing, I stand in the middle of the road shoveling handfuls of chopped dried fruit and nuts into my mouth. The sloping highway isn't steep, but I still feel a burn in my calves and heels. I don't let it hinder me.

With the change in altitude comes a change in temperature. Unlike the warm beach air, the heat I am generating now bleeds off as I walk.

I should have taken a coat.

The flying MVs are out of my reach. Their need for roads confuses me because their vehicles fly. They stay above the road, so my guess is that they're still used for navigating and ensuring people don't crash into one another.

I wonder how fast I could reach my destination in one. A week? Time is difficult enough without being trapped in a moment. I suppose in literal terms it won't be long now.

Before I begin the hardest part of the climb, I eat and drink to keep my energy levels up. The forest continues into the mountains, but the trees thin along the highway. The road turns, heading between two high peaks. Down below, there's a valley filled with green, a sea of plants. Within the shaded thicket is a world which will continue again, eventually.

My life will be a blip. A millisecond. Though I'll have left a mark, it will be forgotten quickly. A speck in the universe, forced to choke down its limited existence.

The road follows a natural pass between the two large mountains. The trees thin even more, leaving patches of white visible, scattered across the mountainsides. At the pinnacle of the road there are low hanging clouds directly in my path.

As I had anticipated, getting wet is in my future. It puts a damper on the pace I set, but I trudge forward.

They start as little drops, scattered and infrequent. Farther into the pass, I reach a wall of water droplets. Breathing was already a strain, but now the air I struggle to take in has water mixed with it. I cough and do my best to find gaps in the rain to breathe in. There are areas big enough for me to put my nose, but not much more.

After a long struggle to the top and over the pass, the road slopes downward again into a range of hills. The road levels out at the bottom, cutting a swath right through the middle of them, and I'm thankful. Several miles farther along, the air clears and I can breathe easier.

Fatigue is overtaking me. I've already pushed past as much as I'm able to stand so I didn't drown in my sleep. My feet protest, and I can barely keep my eyes open. But I ignore both while shuffling along, pulling the carts.

When I reach the point where the suspended droplets become infrequent, I quicken my pace to break free of it. My heels drag as I shuffle. I look back and realize I'm well past the mountain, and deep into the lower hills.

Even though I'm soaked, I'm too tired to care. Throwing the tow rope off, I lie down in the middle of the road. The clouds above block most of the growing brightness in the sky.

~~~~~~

Having exited the hills and forested areas, I've entered a large plain.

I'm approaching what I thought would be a large city, only to be surprised when the buildings aren't taller than two stories. The highway leads around the small town, then turns into an area of houses and stores mixed together.

With my clothes soaked, my food and water supply dwindling, and my feet needing a rest, I'm delighted to reach civilization. The highway merges with the main street.

Unsure which direction to go, a more immediate need comes to mind: fresh clothes. I'm soaked through, and my underwear is chafing my inner thighs.

I could steal someone's.

And leave them naked?

I push the idea aside.

There will be clothes in a shop.

Hunting doesn't take long. Several blocks into town I find a large building that looks promising. Pulling the carts into an area where numerous MVs are parked in neatly marked spaces, I head toward some glass doors.

Leaving my possessions outside, I enter the store. Despite a fair number of people, it doesn't feel crowded because of a wide and open interior. There are plenty of supplies, and I'll be able to stock up enough to make it to my next destination. But beyond the food, there is a whole section filled with clothing.

Even though no one can see me, I feel self-conscious taking off my clothes and leaving them in a heap.

I find the men's section and pick out new underwear, pants, and a shirt. I keep it simple, picking a long sleeved red and white plaid shirt, and black jeans. When I look at my old clothes they *look* old, as if I'd been wearing them for a long time. My hand catches my beard when I pull my shirt over my head. I play with the coarse hair, now three or four inches long.

Refreshed, I hunt for new shoes. After trying several pairs on I opt for some light weight ones to keep my walk as easy as possible. It's nice to feel clean, but I'm going to get dirty again and, in the end, it won't matter as I'll sleep eternally when I reach my final destination.

Not yet.

Peace. In my homeland.

In the store there are many things for me to eat right away, mostly within the fresh section, but my feast is interrupted by the call of nature, then the need to sleep.

The store which seems to carry everything also has furniture. There are beds, couches, and chairs, all ready and waiting for me to lie down on. I bury myself in the fluffy comforter of a bed and swim in a half dozen pillows.

My eyes close and my muscles relax.

~~~~~~

Miles outside of the town, and many more still from reaching Chas, I have a hard time picking my feet up.

There was enough in the store for me to live out the rest of my days comfortably, but I couldn't stay there and ignore my last quest.

Farmland exists as far as I can see, full of what I think is wheat. The dull scenery makes my eyelids droop. Several times I'm positive I've fallen asleep while walking, marked by seemingly instantaneous scenery changes.

Soon. Soon you can sleep forever.

Find the park. Find home.

Looking into the sky I can barely differentiate between the fluffy clouds and the clear sky. It is blindingly bright. Even shielding my eyes doesn't help because the horizon is equally as bright.

A nagging feeling creeps up the back of my neck, and my hair stands on end. I feel eyes on me. It's been a while, since I left Gowar, that I noticed one of *them*.

I look over my shoulder, and in the shadow-void I've left is a Shadow Goblin following along at a much slower pace. It doesn't jump or phase in and out like before. It's more real now. I'm unnerved.

I'm faster. It can't catch me. I'm faster!

Shockwave.

I can't.

Wait for it to come closer.

Maybe I can catch it. Strangle it.

Now you're thinking.

I'm not paying attention, and I trip off the road, having missed a subtle right turn. After regaining my bearings, I look back and the Shadow Goblin is gone.

Monotony returns as I focus on my destination, and the rest I will get when I arrive. My solace is the peace I'll find in death, because I saved Ami.

Those who die in despair. A sick and twisted world awaits them.
When the end comes for me, I will keep you in my mind.
I'll keep our love in my heart. I won't become part of Misery.
I could never die hopeless knowing they loved me and I saved them.

My pace has slowed to a few inches with each step. Try as I might, my legs won't move any faster. My muscles ache and my feet protest.

Forced to sit and rest, I hang my feet off the side of the road and lie down on the pavement. The sky is too bright to look at. I close my eyes but I don't want to sleep. I struggle to pull enough energy to keep moving. I'm startled to find the silhouette of a Shadow Goblin hovering over me. I scream in fright.

I roll away and scramble to stand. Unleashing a shockwave does nothing because it stops mere inches from my hand. The creature doesn't fade or blink in and out, and it isn't running away.

Leaping up, I try to break away.

It follows me with an outstretched shadowy hand.

I trip and fall hard onto my back. It gets nearer. "Get away from me!" I yell at it.

"Raaazzzrrtt…drzrt mzrrst…"

There's a squeal and it sounds like it's trying to form a sentence. I turn, leaving my carts, and run away.

"Razzzrrttt. Rrrrain!" it yells my name and I'm terrified.

I can't shake it.

"Rain!"

It has kept up with me. Fear and anger overwhelm me, and I stop. I spin on my heels and yell at the top of my lungs, "What? What do you want?"

"Rrrrrra-a-a-in. Rain-n-n-n. Cccannzzzztt…"

I'm not sure what to think. It's the only contact I've had since arriving in the frozen time. I want to run from it, strangle it, listen to it, ignore it.

Fight it!

"Rain." A deep voice comes in clearer. "C-c-can youuuuu unders-s-stand?" Its speech is choppy.

"Who are you?" I demand.

"We a-are cleaning u-u-up the c-c-onnection. Please be patient."

Connection? Have they reached out from another realm?

Strangle it now!

I reach my hands for its neck.

The Shadow Goblin disappears in a flicker. It doesn't return, and I'm baffled.

Alone again, I'm left with no answers. I wait for what feels like an eternity, and my patience fades. I run back to the carts, pull the rope over my shoulders and walk briskly away

The energy I was hoping to find found me. Whether the Shadow Goblin was a construct of my mind to keep me moving or not, my pace has improved.

At the end of the farmlands are more hills, but they're different than the rolling ones. The highway leads me into a rocky area with cliff edges. From my path, I can see down into a beautifully colored canyon. Hues of blue, red, and purple create a waving pattern lining the cliffs.

I don't wish they were here, but I wish they could see this.

There are many things I missed in both of my lives.

Even if there was a way to fix time being frozen, I'm a long way from them.

Onward to Chas.

~~~~~~

Day log: Slept 122 times.

I'm wearing down. Thoughts run together. I keep moving. Toward Chas. It's not far now. Another set of hills.

The Shadow Goblin hasn't come back. It was fake, made up to keep me going. I had hope. But it's gone. Dashed. Rest is coming in Chas. No more walking. No more hallucinations. Lonely rest. I'll go to sleep. When I wake, I'll sleep again until I don't wake again.

What happens when I die? Will I be able to see them again? Evalyn hung around, and so did Drake. Maybe I could imbue my essence into an artifact. I guess I'd have to die in despair like they did though. This log of papers perhaps. What happens to the collective of souls inside me? Will they be embedded too?

It will be better to let it all go. Find peace and let it go.

Restful sleep is elusive; it feels like the literal blink of an eye. At the beginning of this, I had more energy after sleeping, but that's long gone.

When I stand and pull my bag onto my shoulders it nearly topples me. I regain my balance and return to my carts on the highway. I'm running out of resources and the previous city is too far away to get back to.

Shuffling things around, I realize there are enough empty pans that I can leave a cart behind. I rearrange, keeping everything still useful on one cart, and untie the ropes to leave the other.

I open a bottle of water and guzzle it, leaving it midair while I go around a bend of trees lining the highway. Their leaves gleam vibrant green in the frozen light. I lose my thoughts to admiring them. The pavement snakes gently upward into the hills.

My muscles protest even now just pulling one cart uphill. Breaks come frequently. I relieve myself and eat, then rest on the slope of a nearby hill.

I close my eyes. It's not helpful. I'm stuck suffering a form of rest which is not regenerative, aware that when I move on I'll be no better off than when I laid down. A few moments or an eternity, it would feel the same. When I do open my eyes, the Shadow Goblin is on the road near my cart.

The…audacity…!

"R-r-rain. You c-c-cannot continue. You sh-should go no further," it communicates hastily, in a broken and buzzing manner.

"Mmmuh!" I grunt in anger. "Be gone figment!"

"We ar-ar-are not a figment. It is imperative that-that you go no further."

"Go away!" I shout.

"There is an…-m-maly causing…problem…are trying to fix. It will become impossible to-to-to…break you-you free."

"I'm not listening, Shadow Goblin! I'm going home! End of story!"

"We n-n-need more time. We-we are working on a solut-t-t-t-tio-n…" The sound breaks up and the being is gone.

"GAH!"

Is the Shadow Goblin really a hallucination?

Yes. You're insane.

Why doesn't it want me to move forward then?

Heading to the road, I look for traces. There's still no shadow-void left by it. Pulling the cart once more I continue up along the hillside.

What anomaly?

Break free?

Is the Shadow Goblin actually Misery wanting me to survive for their selfish whims?

The road becomes steeper. I struggle to climb, wishing I could leave the cart. Instead of pulling, I switch to pushing. My energy is waning but I push on, because beyond these hills is my destination. The desperate need for this all to be over drives me on.

The peak comes into view as I round a bend. A curiosity catches my attention. Though it's difficult to make out due to the brightness of the sky I'm positive there's an unnatural orange color high in the atmosphere. It has gained my interest, and I pull faster. The road levels, and the orange becomes a line reaching from the ground into the sky.

My heart skips a beat and I know what it is. I run. Along the peak of the barren hilltops I come to a cliff, and I can see down the valley. There, beaming from the middle of Chas fifty or so miles away, if I were to walk in a straight line, is the orange vortex. Though I'm still far off it almost looks like it's spinning.

Thoughts of death vanish, and hope is renewed.

Even though the distance is great, it doesn't stop me running downhill at a dangerous speed. I stumble a few times but never fall.

After running until I'm winded, I've made it past the first section of hillside. I can't keep up the pace.

I eat to try and renew my energy, but I'm still high up. I have no choice but to rest. I lay on a bank, facing toward Chas and the beautiful sight.

Caught between excitement and fatigue, my mind spins.

~~~~~~

Day log: Slept 164 times.

I'm trying to go fast. My body says stop, and I rest. Every couple miles now. I'm close though. The orange vortex beams high into the sky. Nearing the base of the hills, I'm coming up on the farmland around Chas. The journey has been long. Five cities, and half a continent. The vortex seems like it's the farthest, even though it's so close. It has to be what's keeping time frozen. Why does it exist? Maybe the Shadow Goblin was right. Maybe I can break free.

It hasn't appeared again, the Shadow Goblin. What should I think now? It warned me not to move forward. Makes me think it had foreknowledge. Though it wasn't a hallucination, I still don't know its real intentions.

The problem will be what to do if I can get time unfrozen. I guess I'll have to wait and find out.

Packing my bag, I stand and start the final leg of my trek.

Because I'm entering the farmland, being on my last couple bottles of water and my last pan of food doesn't make me anxious. My pace is quick as I head toward the unknown future.

I wonder how I'll fit here. Maybe because of the extra knowledge I have, I might be able to adapt easily.

Throughout this region they are growing three main crops: corn, cabbage, and beans. The rows of plants are laid out neatly. Large trenches filled with water follow the road. Pipes lead up from them into machinery, and the machines spray water out over the produce.

Refocusing my attention, I gaze at the sparkling city of Chas, rebuilt and immaculate. The buildings' materials have been replaced with ones similar to Gowar, but they're still just as crowded together as ever. I locate the orange light beaming above it, and it's definitely still swirling.

What is there, keeping it open?

My pace stays the same, but I'm still several miles outside the city limits before I'm stopped in my tracks by the sudden appearance of the Shadow Goblin blocking my path.

Walk through it.

I step forward and it speaks.

"Stop. We have not found a solution to the problem. You cannot continue."

"What problem? What do you want?" I ask exasperatedly.

"There is a massive buildup of solar radiation above the thermosphere of the planet, caught there in the temporal stasis you are experiencing. This hemisphere has been facing your sun and gathering solar radiation for two years."

"Is that why the sky is nearly unbearable to look at?"

"Potentially. If you enter the vortex, your time differential and its time differential will reinitialize everything. At current levels, the solar radiation will be lethal to millions of people on this hemisphere. We are looking for solutions."

"What am I supposed to do?" I become irate. "I was heading home to die, and then I find the orange vortex is still open! Are you telling me I have no hope?"

"You must not enter."

"WHO ARE YOU?"

"We are the Quvites. Have you not understood our other messages?"

"The Quvites? As in Quva the Vraditi? You should have said so!"

"We did. The interference must have been too great for the full message to make it. We have been trying to reach you for a long time. Quva has made it his priority to stop this cataclysm from befalling your planet."

"Quva? He's still alive?"

"Yes."

Knowing the Vraditi physiology, he should be long dead. Still, a more pressing question pushes forward.

"How bad will the destruction be?" I ask solemnly.

"We are estimating an eighty-five to ninety percent loss of life in this hemisphere. Civilization here will come to an end."

If I wait for them to fix it, how long before I die?

Can they even fix it?

That level of destruction. Everything will die.

Everything is already dead.

What?

Everything is already dead. These people. They're dead. Think!

The Cataclysm. Eve's wasteland.

My thoughts haunt me. My soul is rent.

"It's already happened," I mutter.

"Excuse me?"

"I did it. It happens. This area becomes a desert wasteland, and the inhabitants who survive or migrate here become scavengers." I'm discouraged by this revelation. "This is the cataclysm from the sky."

"You know for certain?"

"I've been there."

"Our efforts will be useless?" it responds.

"I don't know if it can be stopped," I think out loud. "I've affected history previously on a small scale, but this would change it for the entire world.

"We have two options. The first, I stay alive while you attempt to come up with a solution; the second is I head to the vortex and restart time to ensure the integrity of the timeline."

"If you say it has already happened, can it really be changed?" The shadow tilts its head.

"Maybe. Our efforts to stop it might somehow cause it anyway. A paradox. What is the option you're working on?"

I'm a little surprised I'm able to recall any sort of scientific knowledge at this point of fatigue and madness.

"There are several ideas currently being explored, but we have no solid timeline or projected success rate."

"What ideas?"

"The most promising is a design in process to manufacture a deflector to push the solar radiation away."

"How long?"

"Three more cycles around the sun."

"I'm not sure I can last, and I don't know what will happen if I die before you finish it. If I die, time might restart regardless."

"There is a contingency plan. Because this is a migration ship, we have an artificial atmosphere ready to be inserted in the event of the solar radiation reaching the surface. It will be erected to filter excess radiation, and protect inhabitants on the other hemisphere. However it cannot be activated without the dissipation or removal of the current buildup."

"Is there nothing you can do to construct the deflector faster?"

"In order to make it we will have to leave orbit and find a nearby source to mine enough material."

I'm conflicted and speak more to myself than to the Vraditi, "If we don't allow this to happen, we make a significant timeline alteration. It would undermine a large number of things. There's no telling the consequences."

"Then we will leave the decision to you."

"I'll go to the vortex and let you know."

"We will continue to track you." The figure flickers out and I'm alone.

"Great. I get to decide between creating a paradox where uncountable people cease to exist after the cataclysm, or ensuring the timeline stays intact and killing millions of people."

No longer enthusiastic at the sight of the vortex, I spend my time looking at it spiraling into the sky. I walk slowly toward the cityscape. The final leg of my quest has become the worst as I am forced to weigh the unknown and known consequences. My feet scuff the pavement while I trudge along.

I reach the edge of Chas and cross the paved barrier separating the city from the farmland around it.

Traversing the streets while heading toward the park, I weigh everything while eating the last of my food and drinking the last of my water. Despite my body and mind running on fumes, a moment of clarity strikes.

If I don't let it happen, it's possible we won't ever meet Eve, as she is a product of the desolation. I owe Eve my life, and it's likely I'd be dead without the help she provided. If I had died then, nothing else I've done will have happened. If I choose to create a paradox, it will create serious, but unknown issues. Would I die at the hands of the Tarak without Eve?

On the other hand if I stop this from happening I could potentially save millions upon millions of lives, both now, and those who wouldn't have to endure the desert wasteland. Why does time have to be so complicated? If I prevent the cataclysm, what happens? I don't know, but I must.

Trying to wrap my mind around the cause and effect of temporal mechanics with my clarity slipping away gives me a headache.

Chas's angular arrangement feels familiar, and I have no difficulty navigating. I find a street heading directly toward the center and follow it, walking in the middle of the road between flying MVs and people.

I reach the border street surrounding the park. Dead in the center of the park is the orange tornado, swirling. Inside it is something that brings me to a new crossroad. The house is there. My heart flutters because *they* might be there, waiting for me. I leave the cart and run toward the vortex, toward my home.

Half way into the park I discover something wrong: Inside the vortex, things are moving at an incredible pace. Movement is blurred. Even closer, more comes into view. It's the Forest of Hunger, except I'm clearly in a time where it doesn't exist. I back away and move to the side. The city is there, and yet the forest exists inside the vortex. Circling all around, I can see the old Chas. But it's not as I left it either. It's growing at a fast pace. I watch the construction of buildings in a matter of minutes. I'm confused.

As I approach, the Vraditi shadowy figure reappears. It stands there, and though its face is darkened, I know it's staring at me, waiting for my answer.

I wish there was another way; a way to save the people who are already dead.
They're dead. It doesn't matter.
It does matter. Their lives are in my hands.
You must maintain the timeline.

What if it's the wrong decision?

You've already made the decision. Otherwise Eve wouldn't exist. None of this would have happened.

Despite my desire to save people, I see no other option. To maintain the integrity of the timeline is to allow millions to die, but allow an uncountable number to be born.

Sitting on the grass with my legs crossed, I watch the Chas of the past speed past me.

"You have made a decision?" the Vraditi asks.

"Can't you evacuate the planet onto the migration ship? Teleport them?"

"There is no way to penetrate the stasis without being caught by it. Our knowledge of the manipulation of temporal mechanics is still weak at best."

I sigh.

"Then this is it. It isn't an easy decision, but there's no choice – our fates have been woven too far into the timeline. To change this event is to change the whole history of the world. I have to let The Cataclysm happen."

"We understand the decision. Can we assist you?"

"Yes. Rebuild Salvoa. Put the artificial atmosphere up after the destruction, but do not start restoration until after I've appeared in the desert. It will be my past, and your future. The house will appear right here in the desert. Upon the house's departure then you can start. You must strictly adhere to this or you'll disrupt the timeline."

"Understood."

"Make sure Quva receives that message. Stress it to him." My eyes are heavy. "Now, I'd appreciate it if I was left alone. I have to come to terms with what has to happen."

Without further communication the shadow disappears. I am alone for the last time before I step into the vortex. My stomach grumbles, but I have no food left. Everything aches from lack of sleep, but I cannot rest. I stand, brushing my pants off.

Knowing this has already happened doesn't make it easier. Following through with what I know has to occur doesn't negate the impact I'm about to make. Millions of people are about to die because of me.

It was my fault because I insisted on breaking the cycle.

I froze time and I have to unfreeze it.

Their souls will weigh heavily on me.

If I had died, none of this would have happened.

So many lives affected because I lived.

Why am I so important?

Why did it have to be me?

Stop pitying yourself! Make up for it by saving people in the future!

I pace, circling the orange vortex. My resolve slowly builds while I conflict with myself.

I stroke my long beard nervously while I make my way to the apple tree. Stopping and facing it, I hold my hand up. I reach to the orange wall. There's resistance when I rest my hand on it, like pushing through a thick liquid akin to the gel in the purification chamber.

"I'm sorry. I'm so sorry."

When I breech the barrier I'm not immediately in the yard. There's an empty space between the two times, in between the orange and blue vortexes. I look back and watch in horror as the world restarts. It's slow at first, but as time resumes an intensely bright light descends on Chas.

Turning to the house, I move closer to the yard. In the grass, inside our boundary, I'm safe from the effects in the time behind me. Curiosity forces me to look. On this side of the vortex of blue, Chas is incinerated and I know all of the places I had seen on my journey are burning.

I retch, knowing what I've done. My knees give way and I hit the grass. The despair within me becomes active once more. Misery screams inside of me. They build and feed off one another, and I realize the collective is born now, because of my meddling with time. The loss of their lives all at once created the legions inside of me. Millions dead in a tragic moment of hopelessness. They scream in my head, in my soul, and they blame me.

"What is this?" There's a distant voice.

"Your fault! Your fault! It's all your fault!"

"You killed us! You had the ability to change it, but you didn't!"

"You imprisoned us here! We exist here because of you! Bring us into the light!"

"I didn't have any other choice! You were already dead!" I cry and mumble.

They scream over and over, *"Murderer!"*

"Why is this happening now?" Another voice.

The sight beyond the blue vortex changes to a lush landscape, and the winds die down. The blue is gone. It's a new time with no sign of destruction.

My mind is shattered by the accusations of the millions of souls inside me. I scream and grip my head. They are consuming me, crying for retribution. I can feel them crawling out from my chest, through my arms, up to my face.

"Is that Rain?"

"You killed us! This is your fault! Why did you kill us? Murderer!"

"LEAVE ME ALONE!" I yell at the voices but it does no good.

It breaks me, and I wail, "It *is* my fault! I did it! I killed them!"

Misery seeps into every corner of my body, coursing through my veins. It explodes outward in a storm of darkness. It covers my skin until it blackens. Shadowy tendrils flail about in the air, killing the grass and plants near me.

"How did this happen?" a man asks.

"Rain? Rain it's us! Are you okay?" The voice is familiar, but it does nothing to console my tortured psyche.

"No, stay back!" someone else warns.

"He needs help!" I can distinguish this one. It's Emma.

"Look at the area around him!" Eve yells. "That darkness will kill you!"

"We have to do *something*. He's going to self-destruct!" Ami yells at Eve.

I can't even look at them, ashamed of my actions. I'm devastated. My mind can't take the agony and shuts down. My vision goes black, and all sound fades away.

It's not long. I regain consciousness standing in the yard. Hatred and anger spews out like a burst dam. The shadowy tentacles flow from me seeking to destroy everything, destroy the world as punishment for my actions. Turning to face the house, my body acts on its own, or perhaps Misery has control. In front of me stand Ami, Emma, Eve, Agatha, and James.

A primal force deep within urges me to vent on everything. Inside, I can feel Misery reaching for them, to take their lives in revenge. But I exert some control over the black mass, and hold the horde of souls at bay, mere inches from killing all five of them.

With my teeth clenched, I feel a deep hate for myself. The line separating me from Tiberius grows weaker, and our thoughts are closer now than ever.

Don't let the darkness reach them. Fight!

Spare them the torture of knowing what you are.

Maybe death will stop them. If you die in despair, maybe they'll be taken back to the void with you. A shockwave to your skull.

"Can you hear me?" Ami yells.

"I...don't...deserve...to...live..." My jaw clenches and I yell, "Kill me!"

"Stop it! You can't leave us again!" Tears are streaming down Emma's face.

A ringing in my ears drowns out everything. My vision goes black. The force within me is too much to contain, and I am losing control. It's going to win. Misery is going to destroy the world out of spite. My ability to keep *them* contained within me is failing.

"Bring us into the light!"

"OKAY!"

~~~~~~

3 PROVOCATION

Awakened with a start, I'm staring straight up into a blue and white sky. *Where am I? Who am...I...?*

Three familiar faces are huddled over me. My head rests on Ami's knees, while Emma and Eve sit to my sides.

I jump to my feet and scream incoherently. Agatha's coming toward me with a bowl of water and a rag, but I don't want it. I back away.

"Rain, it's okay."

That's right. I'm Rain...aren't I?

"Ugh!" Words elude me. I want to tell them what has happened, but the words won't come out.

Retrieving the towel, Ami wrings it out. "It's okay. Let me put this on your head. You're burning up."

Why do I feel like...I'm...Tiberius? Tiberius? I am who I've always been, aren't I? I'm King Tiberius...

I shake my head and move away from her. I can't look at her knowing what I've just done.

Ami steps forward, then the others stand to approach me. Turning, I run. I can't face them. Unfortunately, my body won't cooperate. Weakened muscles and dizziness stop me from traveling far and I collapse.

Something's wrong. Who am I?

They catch up, and Ami turns me over. She places the rag on my forehead, and the cool sensation causes me to realize how warm I am. It feels good, and I feel guilty for it: I want to be left in agony.

"Will he be okay?" I hear James ask.

"He's strong, but he's not indestructible. They'll help him recover." Agatha's voice is low, I assume to keep me from hearing, but I can hear her clearly. She and James head inside.

I am who I am.

Through tears I see the three of them. They are different, much older than when I had left them. The picture in my bag is true. I'm caught between the deep sorrow of what I had to do, and wanting to be relieved because I'm with them. But the price was too high.

The image of Chas burning plays on a loop in my mind's eye. The event has seared itself into my memory, and I wish I could forget.

"You're safe now." Ami leans down and rests her forehead on mine for a moment.

Time exists. I'm free. But they aren't. I've dragged them back.

Each of them has changed, even from the picture. Evaluating them I note the changes. Ami's hair is straight and significantly longer. She's wearing a light dress with a denim overcoat...it looks like she's dressed up for something. Eve's change is dramatic. Her hair is cut high, right below her ears. She has on modest clothing: a striped long sleeve shirt and tight jeans. Emma's is somewhat subtle, but I can tell she's grown as a woman, though she hides it under her normal overalls.

"What happened?" Ami asks. "Where have you been?"

I grunt. Words still elude me.

"Why can't he speak?" Emma looks at Ami with worry.

"He suffered a trauma. It's those junk-souls inside of him." Eve holds up my arm.

Looking frantically at my arms, my veins have blackened; half way up my arms the skin is as dark as the night sky. Looking down into my shirt, my chest is black too. Misery has become a virus, infecting every nook and cranny. Panicked, I try to sit up, but Ami stops me and strokes my hair.

"It's okay. It's not dangerous right now. See?" She touches my blackened skin.

I grunt and struggle for words. My voice returns. *"I'm...responsible...for so much death."*

"Shh. Whatever happened, we're here for you."

"How...long?" I change the subject.

"Eight years," Eve replies.

I stare in disbelief.

The Vraditi said I was stuck for two years. Eight...?

Emma has tears in her eyes. She's fidgety. "We missed you."

Ami helps me to a sitting position. I hold out my arms for Emma. She leans in, and I hug her. They all take their turn, and after all of my time in solitude it feels weird touching anyone again.

They huddle, trying to shield me from the terrible act they don't know about. Their presence quells the anguished voices for the moment. After sitting in silence, one by one they stand. Eve extends her arm to hoist me up. Gripping tightly, I'm lifted to my feet with ease. I open my bag and rummage. I pull out the picture, unfold it, and show them.

"Where did you get this?" Ami's surprised.

"We have..." I choke up. "We have much to discuss."

"Such as the vortex reappearing suddenly?" Eve frowns.

"Let's go inside," Emma suggests. "The grass is making me itch."

Ami grabs my hand, but I'm reluctant to let her hold it. Pulling away, I drop my hands to my sides. She shows concern, but she doesn't push me, and just leads us in. The house has minor differences. There are new pictures on the wall, a new leather chair sits next to the couch, the wall's paint is a little more faded.

I sit on the couch, and there's no fighting over who sits where. Ami to my left, Emma to my right, and Eve on the table across from me.

Ami touches my arm. "We never stopped looking for you."

"The vortex was gone for eight years. No time traveling. After we realized we weren't going to be pulled back we searched every city we could," Eve adds.

The swinging door opens, and Agatha brings me a steaming cup, the smell of chicken broth making my stomach gurgle.

I remember eating, but I don't know how long ago it actually was in frozen time. I want to smile at her, but I can't. I nod instead. It's apparent she wants to ask something, but she stays quiet and returns to the kitchen. Sipping the hot drink carefully, I savor it.

Emma rests her hand on my leg. "I'm glad you're home."

"So, it worked?" I question them. "The vortex was gone?"

"Yeah. When the orange and blue met you were gone, and we were still there." Ami moves her hand closer to mine.

"I'm sorry...I dragged you back into it."

I wish I hadn't. I want to go back there and die.

"Don't be sorry. It's okay because we're together again." Emma tries to reassure me.

My mind is wracked with guilt. Over the lives I've taken, and over my family's lost freedom.

Eight years. They should have had more. They should have lived the rest of their lives there.

"It was hard without you there to keep me out of trouble." Eve stretches her feet out onto my legs, and props her arms on the table to hold herself up. "It was a hollow victory."

"You were better off. I was frozen in a single moment in time."

I tell them the story starting from the moment I was trapped between the two vortexes. They're quiet as I tell my tale, and it's apparent they don't know what to say or how to react. In grueling detail, I explain the problematic world I encountered, and the effects I had to deal with. The hardest part comes when I have to tell them Eve probably only exists because of my decision to kill millions. I fight back a sob.

I try to look at Eve in her eyes, but I can't hold it for long. "Everything you endured in your life...it's my fault."

I'm overcome by shame.

Eve climbs from the table and takes my cup, handing it off to Ami. She sits sideways on my lap, wraps her arms around me, and kisses me. I'm shocked there is no uproar. When the kiss persists for a moment too long, Ami clears her throat, loudly.

"That's your free one," Ami laughs.

Breaking away, Eve smiles and stands. "You did what you had to, as you always have. I didn't have the easiest life, but if the alternative is possibly not existing, I'm glad you did what you did. And I'm sure millions of others who exist now because of your action would appreciate it too, if they knew."

Agatha pokes her head into the living room. "Rain, dear, are you hungry?"

"Something light, thank you."

She returns momentarily with a plate of apple slices and fresh bread.

When she passes it to me, she smiles. I give it to Ami and stand to hug Agatha. I pull her in tightly.

"I missed you, Aggy," I tell her. "I'm sorry our reunion is because you were forced to time travel again."

"I'm okay. It wasn't the same without you and I'm glad you're home." Agatha pulls away, crying softly.

"I'm glad too. You're like my mother, and it was lonely without your smile...and your amazing cooking." I wipe a tear from her wrinkled face. She laughs.

"If she's *like* your mother, that must make me *like* your aunt," Evalyn says, but her voice doesn't come from Agatha.

She's there by the stairs, visible and hovering. She laughs and holds her arms out as if to say 'ta-da' before coming down the stairs the rest of the way.

"I've had that very thought, *Aunt* Evalyn. How are you visible?" I ask.

"Eww, stop. Don't actually use that word. You make me sound old." She makes a disgusted face. "It happened after the orange vortex incident. When I didn't disappear, I knew it was only a matter of time before the blue returned."

"She's been such a nuisance too!" Eve pipes up playfully. "I can't get any privacy!"

"You mean I won't let you lounge all day? Lazy sloth!" Evalyn retorts, but her tone is also jovial, not spiteful.

"Old hag!" Eve laughs.

Things have changed.

Returning to the couch, Ami hands me the plate, and I eat slowly.

"If I had a physical form I'd box your ears right now," Evalyn waggles her finger and grins mischievously. "Not to mention that I'd beat both of you at winning his affection."

"Evalyn!" Agatha proclaims and swats at her sister's apparition.

I choke on an apple piece, and my face turns bright red. Coughing and sputtering, I attempt to catch my breath.

The room dissolves into an uproar. Though I'm embarrassed, I have missed their antics.

"Auntie, that's gross!" Ami scowls and sticks her tongue out.

"Over my dead body!" Eve yells at her.

"Don't worry, Rain, I'll protect you from them." Emma sticks her tongue out at Evalyn. "There's no way he'd go for a woman as old as you!"

Ami snatches an apple piece from the platter, and puts it to my mouth, waiting for me to take a bite. Eve sees what Ami's doing, and immediately tries to do the same thing.

I ignore their attempts, and pick up the broth for a drink. Their love overshadows my grief and keeps Misery contained, for now.

James enters, and I try to calm everyone.

"James, I'm glad to see you are doing well. You look healthier," I comment.

Cleaned up, he appears years younger, despite the eight year gap. His gray hair is significantly shorter, and his beard is neatly trimmed. His facial features have filled out and I can see Ami's resemblance to him.

"Thanks. I'm doing well because Agatha keeps putting full plates in front of me, and I keep eating." He smiles. "Which I'm wondering how we'll do that now. We don't have much in storage."

"There's the garden, right? And I can go hunting on Maximus." I suggest.

"We found a farm for Max to live on," Ami says.

"That's not a euphemism for him dying is it?" I look at her.

"No!" She laughs. "We actually found a farm, and he lived a good life. It had lots of space for him to run. He did pass about a year ago though."

Agatha walks to the window and makes an observation. "The plants beyond our boundary…their color is wrong. We should conserve what we can, in case they're not edible."

Emma follows to the window. "Why are they blue and pinkish?"

We crowd around and take in the sight. I step outside for a better look. Beyond the dead patch Misery created is a bright blue plain. Patches of trees colored pink, purple, and red litter the land as far as the eye can see.

In all directions there are sporadic mountains, but none of them create a range. Around the other side of the house, out past the apple tree there is a lone cloud clinging to a mountain, far in the distance.

"We've seen these plants before." I turn and tell them. "This is Quva's work. They revived the land after the cataclysm."

"What does it mean for us?" Eve steps next to me.

"There doesn't appear to be any civilization here. Perhaps after planting they moved everyone to the other hemisphere so this side could be reborn." I explain. "I still have Vraditi knowledge in my head. I'll be able to find edible plants."

This area appears to be ours for the taking. With exploration in our near future, a shower and a full night's sleep are what I need right now.

I head into the house, but am stopped by Emma calling after me. "Where are you going?"

"Shower and a shave," I tell her while tugging on my ratty beard.

"Oh! Okay!" She smiles.

They continue to discuss the situation, and their voices fade when I enter the house. I crave hot water. I grab a towel from the closet under the stairs and hurry to the bathroom. Inside, I look in the mirror.

As I have done in the past, I examine who I am. Again, I cannot recognize myself because I look so different. My hair reaches past my shoulders, my beard reaching my chest. My pitch black eyes have heavy bags under them, making me look ghastly. Closing the door, I shed my clothes to have a better look. The pitch black which was previously contained has now engulfed my body. The dark within is taking hold. In the center of my torso, a few inches above my scar, is a solid mass with tendrils of black flowing throughout my veins.

You're quiet now: where have you gone? Where is the condemnation for my acts? You will try to consume me, I know. I can feel it.

Grabbing scissors from a drawer, I cut away the dirty and matted facial hair. I lather my face with soap, and finish with a razor, leaving a rather large mess all over the counter and sink.

I start the shower and turn it up as hot as my skin will allow. In the stall, I lean against the wall, the showerhead pointed at my neck. My moment of peace is interrupted by a quick opening and closing of the hall door. Cool air drifts in and I yelp.

A shadow moves through the room. My time being stalked by the 'Shadow Goblin' Vraditi, and Misery's outburst has made me jumpy.

"Who's there?" I ask abruptly, louder than I had intended.

"Shh!" Ami scolds in a whisper. "When you're done, come to my room through the adjoining door."

What?

The hall door opens and closes again, and though I'm curious, I'm in no rush to leave the warmth of the water. My knotted muscles begin to soften in the heat, and I want to relax, but the guilt of my actions hangs on me. It builds, and Misery condemns me. Scrubbing at the black does no good. I hide tears of anguish in the water.

By the time I'm done torturing myself, the water has run cold and I'm shivering. I'm weary and want to sleep. It takes considerable strength to step out and not fall on my face, and drying off is a chore. Looking in the mirror, I search my soul for answers.

Who am I now? Rain or Tiberius?

I'm me. A king and a vagabond. I am both.

A light knock comes from Ami's adjoining door and breaks me from my trance, causing me to jump. The latch clicks, and she opens the door a crack.

"I made these for you," she whispers handing me a bundle of clothes. "They've been waiting for you."

"*Thank you,*" I whisper back.

She closes the door, but leaves a crack. Ami is spying on me, but I don't give any indication that I see her. Laying the clothes out, they're a little more formal than my normal clothes. A sleeveless top, underwear, pants and shirt. They're all black, and I laugh in my head about the coincidence of the clothes, and the appearance of the collective. The pants are soft cotton with firm creases. The shirt is a button up with a rigid collar. In the mirror I note how they fit, her handiwork never ceasing to amaze me.

"Rain." Ami enters, having seen that I'm finished. "It's been eight years without you. Eight years of missing you."

"*I missed you too.*"

She shakes her head and smiles, tears starting to run down her face.

"I kicked myself every day for holding back. I got angry at Eve every time she tried to make a move on you, because I was too scared to be like that. I thought we had more time."

"*We have it now.*" I step forward to where she's hovering in her doorway.

"I vowed if we ever found you, I'd tell you how I feel: I love you."

"*Ami.*" I caress her cheek with the palm of my hand. "*I love you too. I have for a long time.*"

"I've loved you longer." She laughs and cries at the same time.

Leaning forward, I press my lips to hers and it quickly turns passionate.

We embrace each other, our bodies pressed to her doorframe. Her hands grip my back, my hands slip to her waist. The passion carries us, our tongues twisting with and against each other. I pull her in closer. She wraps her arms around my neck, and puts her fingers in my hair.

Ami. I missed you.
How could I have been so stupid?
Why didn't I do this before?

A heavy thump in the house startles us out of the intimate moment. We wait, listening to see if we've been caught. There's no indication anyone is aware.

She smiles coyly.

I lean forward and rest my forehead on hers, staring into her eyes. *"We should tell Eve. I'm not going to hide anymore."* I kiss her neck.

"She already knows. I've had eight years with her, and she spent that time agonizing *with* me over your loss."

Ami retreats into her room, smiling uncontrollably, and closes her door. I head to the mirror. I grimace as I pull a brush through my knotted hair.

There's a knock at the hall door and when I open it, Ami is there with a chair and a long piece of cloth. I smile at her, and she bats her eyelashes innocently.

"It sounded like you were done. Would you like a haircut?" she says a little louder than normal in an attempt to be heard.

Before she can start, we hear a strange hum. We look at each other, puzzled.

Emma heads to the kitchen, looking for the source of the noise.

Ami and I follow, and the hum becomes louder once we're in the living room.

"Rain!" Emma yells.

I race through the kitchen, cutting James and Agatha off, and out into the yard.

Too good. It was too perfect.

"What is that?" she looks at me and points.

Coming from the large, white fluffy cloud above the mountain, miles in the distance, are a type of flying vehicle unlike the MVs in the past. A dozen or more rectangular ships fly toward our location descending at great speed. Four engines, one attached to each corner, twist and turn to direct the massive vehicles.

Fearing the worst, I anticipate that whatever's coming isn't a greeting party, simply because of their numbers. The others join me and Emma. I point at Eve.

"Get my sword!" My command is forceful and she reacts.

She's gone, and I look back to the vehicles. Though still several miles away, their rapid approach tells me they will be here within moments.

They're hostile.

Hurry and come closer. If you attack, I will show you who I am.

A tap on my shoulder with the hilt of my sword brings me little comfort. Grabbing it, and buckling it to my waist, I keep my eyes focused. Sword drawn, I turn and start pushing them inside.

The retained Vraditi information rattling around in my head connects implanted images to similarities in these vehicles. I yell over the whining of the engines. "They're drop ships! Get inside!"

Ami, Emma, and Agatha run into the house while James, Eve, and Evalyn stay.

Not wanting casualties, I turn on them. "Inside! Now!"

The ships reach our perimeter and encircle us, hovering.

I point to the door, forcing the rest to comply. I turn my attention back to the drop ships as doors slide open. I raise my sword and channel a shockwave through it. It fires like a bolt, and flies across one of their bows as a warning shot. They ignore it.

Men and women dressed in pitch black uniforms, dark helmets, and goggles rappel down as the vehicles come to a stop outside our perimeter. Four of them from each craft carry down large, round, reflective metal orbs, planting them beyond the edge of the property line. They enclose the house with them.

Yelling can be heard from the people now surrounding us, but I can't understand what they're saying. They seem focused on the orbs they're placing. An opening appears on the top of each orb, and long collapsible poles extend upward. The air fills with an immense amount of pressure, and electricity shoots from one rod to another all the way around the house. A red hued wall of energy distorts the space between each pole.

I run to the barrier, watching the troops line up. My eardrums are assaulted by a screeching noise. An image appears on the red wall.

Disoriented, I stumble away.

A bald man with burn scars across his face appears. He pushes up his glasses on his large nose, his voice ringing out. I wince.

"You are in violation of Planetary Code, Section One, Paragraph Two. No humanoid can inhabit or build on the planet until the ecosystem has been declared restored to a normal status," he states before turning away to talk to an unseen person. "I want a full analysis of their biology."

A voice off screen speaks, "There are massive amounts of de-synced *Chron* particles dissipating in that location."

"I–" I start, but he cuts me off.

"You are also in violation of Temporal Code, Section One, Paragraph One, Subsection 1 Alpha. No humanoids are allowed to participate in or conduct temporal displacement. You will be detained until further notice."

Openings appear in the energy barrier. More soldiers drop down to accompany the ones already on the ground. Each of them reaches to their belt as they cross the boundary. Pulling small, strange looking devices from their hips, they hold what look like curved door handles and close in.

"Whatever you think this is, it's a misunderstanding!" I yell at the energy projection. "We'll move voluntarily in a month!"

"That is unacceptable," he responds sternly.

The soldiers move in, and the urge to fight kicks in.

"Leave or die." I warn the soldiers moving in on me.

"Non-lethal force is authorized," the projection commands. "Subdue and detain."

One of them points her device at me, and I take it as a hostile gesture. Pointing my sword at her feet I unleash a shockwave to trip her. She falls on her face.

"Confirmed! He has *alkos*!" another yells out and I recognize the Vraditi word.

"Initialize anti-alkos measures," the projection replies.

They each fiddle with their gloves, and almost immediately the same type of energy barrier surrounding the house covers their body in a type of suit. They return to an attack stance and hold their handle-like weapons up.

I place both hands on my sword, and swing while releasing a shockwave. As the arc reaches them they steady themselves for the impact. Their shields absorb some of the energy, but they're not immune to the pressure created by the shockwave. It pushes them back, and they move to flank me. My best option right now is close quarter combat.

I want to attack all out, but do I kill or just maim?

"Take him alive. He may be the cause of the temporal anomaly."

As they come upon me, I charge in with my sword at the ready. Electricity arcs across two end points of their weapons. Taking turns getting close, they attack me. I defend and swing my sword, but they're quick enough to move out of the way, or deflect my swings.

I jump back. They rush forward. I swing hard and release an arcing shockwave at their feet to distract. A small divide forms, sending the clotheslines to the ground.

My attackers are unhindered. Leaping into the air with a shockwave-jump, I launch an aerial attack of shockwaves to scatter them. They're pushed back, but only a little.

I land, and distressed screams from inside the house divert my attention. Eve grunts aggressively, and I hear the clang of metal pots being thrown. Running into the kitchen, I can see that some of the troop has entered from the other side and flooded the kitchen.

Eve and James do their best to oppose the armored soldiers, swinging fists in an attempt to fight off a couple attackers. They are overwhelmed by additional forces, the devices in their hands shocking my family. They fall, thudding heavily and convulsing, causing an outcry.

"James!" Agatha cries out.

"Daddy!"

My efforts are futile in keeping them from harm. I'm useless in defending them. Holding my sword up in surrender, I lay it to rest on the island counter.

Soldiers enter the door behind me, and before I can raise my hands, they shock me too. The sensation is incredibly painful. My muscles spasm, and I hit the floor.

More screams follow. We are outnumbered and, thanks to their technology, outdone. Troops reach the others, and though my mind cries out, nothing escapes my lips. They're surrounded, and I fear they too are being shocked.

I am thankful when Ami, Emma, and Agatha appear unharmed, but enraged at their arms being bound behind their backs and paraded by. It takes two soldiers each to lift me, Eve, and James.

Carried sideways, my field of vision becomes the world at an angle. Though I don't know where they're taking us, I anticipate it's to one of the drop ships coming lower. When we near the energy field, a section of the wall opens up.

"Operation complete. Team One returning to base with offending parties," I hear a soldier report.

"Confirmed. Team Two, sweep the house for additional persons and return to base," the man in charge dictates.

Ami, Emma, and Agatha are forced to board a low flying drop ship while Eve, James, and I are tossed in like cargo and secured with straps to the deck. I can't see all the way down the length of the hull, but the echoes tell me it's large.

I'm facing Agatha, and there's a subtle shift in her demeanor. I can tell she's housing Evalyn, but there's no way for me to signal her that I know. Evalyn allows Agatha to take over, and she looks at James, worried.

Idiot. Stupid. I should have stayed in the stopped time.

These people will pay with their lives for attacking my family.

The door shuts, and the ship lifts off. A sense of motion sweeps over me as its engines roar, and turns us nearly sideways. My weight shifts, and if it were not for the straps holding me in place, I'd be thrown into the metal siding.

Other than the loud whirring created by the drop ship, there is no sound. Neither the women nor the soldiers speak.

After a few minutes of flying, a loud voice comes from a speaker near the corner. "Team One, V-Three on approach vector. Requesting de-cloak of the island docking bay, and permission to land."

Island? Is there water near here?

There's no audible response to the request, but they speak again. "Understood. Touchdown in three minutes."

The ship accelerates. The straps are once again my friend as it turns nose down, and my center of gravity shifts toward Agatha's feet.

The numbness starts to fade. Sensation starts to return to my toes and fingers. I attempt to wiggle a hand free, risking a second electric shock.

Watching each soldier carefully, I wait for a moment. Turbulence provides cover for me as we're all briefly lifted from the deck and dropped.

Emma shrieks, and while everyone's attention is on her, I seize the opportunity to rotate and pull my arm out. I keep it near my side to avoid alerting them.

If you think you can kidnap my family...

Counting them, we're surrounded by seven soldiers: five on one side of the craft, two on the other. Assessing my chances of overtaking them, I don't like the odds, especially with my power rendered nearly useless.

Is the ship vulnerable from the inside? Can I blow it open and save them one at a time?

"Docking procedure initiated," the voice announces from the speaker.

My time runs out. Because I don't want to risk their lives unnecessarily, I take no action. For now. The ships engines slow before leveling out and landing us softly.

The best option now is to gather information on where we are, what we're up against, and hope I can rationalize with whoever is in charge.

The door slides open, and the soldiers unstrap us. While our wrists are bound with metal cuffs, soldiers stand at the ready, weapons drawn. They eye me, anticipating a fight.

Led out onto the deck of a massive hangar, the few ships which surrounded the house were but a small portion of the armada docked here.

Surveying the large, immaculate metal room, the flotilla of various sized vessels leaves me dumbfounded. Numerous walkways create a network to the crafts. Their advanced technology surpasses what I had seen pre-cataclysm.

"Hey," I assert myself with a soldier. "How about you lead me to the person in charge."

The man with the scarred face appears around the side of the ship. He's short and stout, wearing a white coat as long as he is, the white offsetting his dark skin. Behind his glasses, a callous stare meets me, and I wait for him to speak.

"You are being detained for violating directives set in place for the safety and rehabilitation of the planet. I hereby charge you—"

I cut him off, "*Stop there. There's no possible way for us to have known or avoided this. We had no control over occupying that space. The anomaly is random.*"

"Ignorance of the law is not an excuse," he states while crossing his arms, clearly not listening to me. He turns his head to someone out of my vision on the other side of the craft. "Is he contagious?"

"The scan shows no viral, bacterial, or parasitic agents," a woman tells him.

"What is wrong with your skin?" He looks at me again while adjusting his glasses. "Are you contagious?"

What's wrong with yours?

I refrain from saying it. Looking at my group, I lock eyes with Agatha, and I can't tell if it is her or Evalyn right now. She does however nod slightly and I turn back to him.

"*I will answer in exchange for concessions.*"

"You're in no place to demand—"

"*As a matter of fact, I am. You may have neutralized one power, but I am beyond your comprehension.*" I'm feeling bolder. "*I guarantee you've never seen it. If you want to know more, you can release us and we'll discuss matters in a more civil manner.*"

He appears to contemplate my offer, stroking his chin. Shaking his head, he looks to his side and beckons the unseen person over. A woman appears and leans so he can whisper in her ear. She whispers back, and he keeps his attention trained on me.

"Why should we trust you, a blatant alkos user?" he asks in a snarky manner.

"*Why not?*" I respond with my own question.

"It's dangerous, and should not be given the opportunity to spread its seed. You are an affront to mankind."

"*It's not a virus. I can't spread my power to you.*"

"Nevertheless, it's dangerous. If one is allowed, more will reveal themselves, and soon mankind will be overtaken by your kind."

"Kind? You speak as though we're not human. There are powers that aren't dangerous. There was a girl I knew whose ability was rapid healing. We can talk more, if you'd like, and I'll tell you about it."

He is obstinate, glaring at me with uncaring eyes, as he continues to rub his face. Sighing, he gives a curt nod.

"You shall have an opportunity. Our interrogation room has a dampening field, and there will be soldiers on hand…in case you get any ideas."

I nod in understanding. He turns, walking away, and the woman nods. I'm shoved forward and nearly trip. Looking over my shoulder at the soldier, I glare. He responds with another shove to keep me moving. The others submit and follow silently. All attention is on me.

The stout man in the white coat walks us through the fleet. At the far end of the hangar is an elevator. The doors open and we are herded in, with him entering last. He presses an unlabeled green button set apart from the labeled ones, and a red beam scans his face. The elevator whirs to life and it ascends rapidly.

We come to a halt and the doors open to a bland hallway. The leader exits first, and we're shoved out. Doors line the hall, each numbered and without windows.

At an intersection the man in the white coat turns around. "I'll interrogate him first. Take the others to the holding cells. Keep them separated, and make sure the dampening fields are engaged," he directs harshly.

Not a word is heard from the soldiers as they follow his commands, but my group fails to cooperate willingly.

"Where he goes, I go!" Eve snaps.

"Please don't separate us!" Emma pleads.

He waves his hand dismissively at them.

Catching Ami's concerned look, I nod to indicate it's okay, for now.

Abruptly grabbed by the cuffs binding my hands, I'm led down one hall, while they are taken down another at the intersection.

Thoughts of escape enter my mind, but I have no way of gauging the possibilities of success, or where we would go if we managed to succeed for that matter.

I'll just bide my time. We'll find a way back before the vortex returns.

We reach a door marked 'Fifty-two'. The leader's face is scanned by another red beam, and the room opens.

Inside, the room is also white and bland. There are a couple chairs and a table, bolted in place. Soldiers lead me in, and below the chair is a chain and ring attached to the floor. They shove me into the chair. One of the soldiers bends down. The chain clinks as they wrap it up over my cuffs and attach it back to the floor. I'm locked in place.

"Is this necessary?" I ask.

"You are a criminal. Does that answer the question?" The man sits in the chair across from me. "If you haven't understood by now, your alkos is useless."

"Your countermeasures will do nothing to stop my other power," I threaten. "I'm complying with you because I believe we can come to understand one another."

A soldier's fist hit's the back of my head, and my ears ring.

The leader holds his hand up and waves them off. They leave, and I am left alone with my captor. He studies me carefully from behind his large glasses for a few minutes.

I stare directly in his eyes to intimidate him. Though my eyes are blacker than night, I know he sees me staring.

"I'm Colonel Ashton Tigby. You can however address me by 'Colonel'," he tells me.

"Ah. An introduction. Does that make you feel better for abducting us?" I'm impertinent.

"Tell me about the temporal anomaly." He ignores my contempt.

"It's an anomaly with temporal properties." I grin.

"The more cooperative you are, the better I will treat you. *I* am not normally a man of violence, but if you are unwilling to yield information, I'll employ less than savory interrogation measures," he threatens casually. Leaning forward, he rests his forearms on the tabletop.

"What do you *really* want to know?" I ask.

"What do you use to create the anomaly?"

"Nothing. It just exists. Our house got caught up in its whirlwind and taken along for the ride."

A half-truth.

"Temporal anomalies don't *just* exist. What caused it?"

A man of his position would seek to abuse it, no doubt.

I play dumb. "I found the house in the woods one day," I reply sharply.

"Keep going."

Editing my story a great deal, I tell him fragments of what transpired. My time, the ambush, near death, survival in different environments. Nothing truly informative or pertinent to the use of powers, or my involvement in timeline meddling. He leans back in his seat and watches me while I explain.

When I'm finished I lean back to copy him. "I might be more cooperative if there was a shared exchange of information."

"That's not how an interrogation works." He scratches his face, unamused.

"True, but if you share information, I might have more to say." I grin and lean forward. My chain clanks against the uncomfortable metal chair.

"I suppose I could humor you. Go ahead, ask." I finally get a reaction: he smirks.

"What is this place? You have a big fleet out there."

"We are in the New Asta Immigration and Flight Ops building. It was used to facilitate the migrations of people from the ground to our city," he answers quickly. "My turn. What is wrong with your skin?"

"New Asta?" I'm shocked. "Who named this city?"

"Answer my question and then you can re-ask yours."

Something's very wrong.

"Fine. It's hard to explain and will take blind faith to believe what I tell you is true. In our travels we reached what I would call the 'end of time'. There we encountered a disembodied entity: a collection of souls which took on an abstract physical form."

"Describe it for me."

"Black, shadowy, moved like a liquid. If I'd have let it go unchecked, it would have followed us through time and done terrible things. I couldn't let them run rampant, so I allowed them to inhabit my body."

"I'm not sure I buy it, but if it's true, that would be foolish."

"It was that or allow it to destroy the world. There were no other choices. Now answer my question. New Asta, why was that name chosen?"

"Our knowledge of time prior to the 'Great Cataclysm' is quite limited. However our High Chancellor had located ancient volumes, and named the city after this location's previous name."

A lie. Whether he knows it or not. There couldn't be any ancient volumes.

"Ancient is the most accurate word for it. Asta was my city, in my kingdom of Astid, ruled by five generations of my family."

This piques his interest, and he leans forward to study me. I grin wildly because I feel the flow of information may have turned slightly in my favor.

If I wasn't chained...

"At what point before the Great Cataclysm did your kingdom exist?"

"Is the 'Great Cataclysm' the burst of solar radiation which scorched this hemisphere?"

"Correct. You're well versed in technical terminology for someone supposedly from such an...'ancient time'."

Good. At least I have confirmation of when.

"I don't know when it existed at this point. Several thousand years maybe? With random time travel we never knew when we were going to end up. I've seen things as far back before man, to whenever this is now."

"Because time displacement is strictly forbidden we will do what's necessary to counter the anomaly."

"If you can, I'd be more than happy not to time travel anymore, but good luck. We haven't been successful in stopping it, and it's on a timer."

"We've acquired some resources recently. We'll succeed," he boasts with a grin of perfect teeth. "In fact, if you've been bouncing around time that long, I'm willing to bet the Quvites have data on you."

"You're familiar with the Vraditi? Makes sense, you using their word 'alkos'."

"You know their species?" He looks at me, lost.

"I've had contact with them on two occasions, but they weren't always known as the Quvites."

"We're aware. Quva and his race have become a thorn in our side," his tone turns sour. He's annoyed, and strokes his scars. "We've been in a state of disagreement for three decades over their desire to cohabitate on the planet."

"He's still alive?"

"They're an extremely resilient race with cloning technology." He huffs.

"He was here before we were, cultivating the land." I omit the information of their transplanting the Tarak. "Technically they have at least an equal amount of claim to Salvoa as us."

"You best not profess support for the Quvites. You're in a bad situation because of the laws you've already broken. But to be a Quvite supporter in *this* city means execution for treason."

"Really? The Vraditi restore Salvoa, and the best our species can do is ostracize them and murder people who support peace?"

"It's long been speculated that their meddling caused the cataclysm to begin with. They of course won't admit it, but we have obtained files covertly, confirming they were influencing and interfering," he raises his voice a little.

I sigh.

They must have hidden my involvement and any information on the temporal anomaly. He doesn't have the full story.

With his threat of execution looming over my head, it seems wise not to tell him it was my fault.

"If you're thinking of aligning with the Quvites, reconsider. During their interference, Salvoa suffered immense losses. Millions dead. An entire society obliterated. It's impossible it's a coincidence."

I've unintentionally hit a nerve.

"As survivors of the wasteland we had to scavenge, to fight over miniscule resources. If there's even a remote possibility the Quvites were involved, I think they should all die for it."

Misery convicts me of my involvement, urging me to turn myself in. I grind my teeth against the guilt. Millions of voices calling me a murderer.

I start yelling at Colonel Tigby. "Don't talk to me about that society and the millions dead, because you weren't there! And I know precisely how bad the wasteland was, because I was there also!" I bark at him. He's taken by surprise and leans back in his seat. "I also know the Vraditi preserve life, not destroy it. They tried to fix it, but were unable."

We sit, staring at each other in silence, and it becomes awkward because

I can't leave. Shifting several times on the hard metal chair, I attempt to get comfortable, but it hurts the more I move. The cuffs feel like they're cutting in.

"It seems you're very well ingrained in our timeline," he states calmly. A nagging fear that I've overshared pesters me. "We must do what we can to ensure it stays intact by stopping the anomaly."

"If you succeed, you'll make us all very happy. You have approximately thirty days to figure it out because the vortex happens regardless," I tell him. "If you fail, you'll need to let us go because it will pull us back no matter where we are."

"Intriguing."

"It would be best if you keep the vortex's existence only known to a few people."

"I agree." He stands and paces. "The High Chancellor will commit team resources for this project."

"You'll need my help. Despite not knowing how it works, I'm your best resource to understand it. While I wait for you to call on me, what's going to happen to us?" I work to steer his decisions to my advantage.

"As a user of alkos, you must be isolated. Normally that would mean prison."

"I think I've been cooperative enough to warrant a bit of leniency. And I'll continue to be cooperative if you treat us with dignity, rather than as criminals."

"But you *are* criminals," he argues with me, pushing his glasses up.

"If you believe my explanation, it was impossible to avoid," I reply, raising my voice again.

He circles the room, before stopping in front of me and leaning on the table with both hands. "I will arrange for you and your family to be put in quarantine apartments. They were designed to make sure people immigrating to New Asta weren't contagious with deadly diseases. They're now used for the occasional group migrating from one city to another."

"Apartments? That's not a euphemism for prison cells, is it?"

"No. Though I could throw you in prison for what you are, because of your familiarity with the anomaly and others with alkos...you may yet be of use to me."

"I want to be cooperative, Colonel. The better you treat us, the more I will be," I smile, covering the lie. "Our first priority should be the anomaly. If you succeed in stopping it, there will be plenty of time to make use of me."

"Indeed"

Maybe with his resources he can do what I couldn't.
But he's not trustworthy - he wants to exterminate the Vraditi.

Colonel Tigby moves to the door. I watch the panel scan his face. The door clicks, and he pulls the knob. A soldier enters.

Pointing at me, Colonel Tigby speaks to the man. Though I don't think he intends for me to overhear, I can hear their conversation.

"Captain Pit," he addresses a muscular man with a round face, "I need to confer with the High Chancellor before we interrogate the rest of them. You'll command the escort of this group to Tower Zero. Take Specialists Jackie and Lyle, as they have the most alkos experience. Ensure dampening fields are at maximum, and set them up for level one requisitioning. I want them totally segregated from the public."

"Yes sir!" he replies.

A female soldier, who I assume is Specialist Jackie, enters and secures me by the shoulders while Captain Pit unlocks my chains. My cuffs remain locked. When Captain Pit has the chain free, Jackie removes her hands from my shoulders. I stand and they lead me out.

Colonel Tigby and I exchange glances, his scars making him difficult to read. I keep my face expressionless.

They lead me to where my group was separated. They aren't here, although the lines of uniformed personnel stretching on each side of the hallway tell me they're in the rooms on either side.

"Attention!" Captain Pit bellows out. "We are moving the detainees to Tower Zero. Keep them handcuffed until we arrive."

"Specialist Lyle!" Captain Pit barks.

"Yes sir?" A rugged man steps forward.

"You are on special duty with me as of this moment. The rest of you, prepare to transport detainees to Tower Zero! No public exposure!"

"Yes sir!" they reply unanimously.

In a flurry of movement, the soldiers proceed to unlock the doors of the holding rooms. One by one my family emerges.

Eve is riled up: the moment she's in the hallway she kicks and yells. She swings her leg out and trips one of them. Several rush to subdue her, weapons at the ready. She shoves them away.

"Hey! Hold on! Calm down!" I yell.

Their attention is on her, but Eve's is on me.

"Eve, calm down! It's all right."

"All right? All right?! I've had to pee this whole time! But would they let me go to the bathroom? Nope!" She kicks another one away while three struggle to hold her. Her clasped hands hammer faces.

Eve is hit with a stun weapon. She goes rigid under the shock, and collapses. What happens next makes me want to laugh and cringe, but I control my face. Eve's pants become soaked with her urine.

Emma screams. "Gross, Eve!" she yells, emerging into the hallway.

She's going to lose her mind when the paralysis wears off.

Captain Pit calms the commotion. "You all have jobs to do! Go!" he yells.

My family, minus Eve who can't move, looks to me. I nod to show my cooperation.

Specialists Lyle and Jackie turn me around to the elevator. Captain Pit is scanned, and the doors open. Piled into the elevator, Captain Pit starts the elevator moving. Instead of descending, we ascend again.

There's little elbowroom, and I'm right next to Eve. The smell is overpowering, but no one says anything.

The elevator comes to a stop. The doors slide open to a large, almost empty lobby with clear dividers leading toward a bank of glass doors. At the end of each divider, a uniformed person stands in a door-less black frame. Each of us is led to one, then stopped.

"Requisition a level two vehicle, darkened windows," Captain Pit instructs the attending soldier.

"Yes sir," she replies and taps on a screen hanging from the ceiling.

Letting go of my arms, Lyle and Jackie move past the black frame. The soldier at the station beckons me forward with a wave of the hand, and points to an illustration of feet on the floor. Doing as requested, I plant my feet on the image of feet.

"Don't move," she instructs.

The frame on either side of me comes to life, and red beams of light shine from them. It startles me as it begins to rotate around my body. It beeps loudly, and more beeping comes from other stations.

"Sir, four of these people have alkos," they state with hesitation while looking at Captain Pit.

Four? Me and who else?

I glance around to work it out, but I've no idea who they are.

"Stand down. Colonel Tigby instructed us to take them to Tower Zero for isolation," Captain Pit barks at them.

The machines become quiet, and Captain Pit motions for me to step forward. A vehicle, much smaller than the ones in the hangar, comes to hover directly in front of the doors. It's sleek: the front is rounded with a blunt nose, and toward the rear it's taller and wider.

Captain Pit exits the building, and pulls open two doors at the back of the vehicle.

We are led outside and crammed into the enclosed space with almost no opportunity to observe our surroundings. I catch a glimpse of New Asta in the distance; it's immaculate.

Inside the vehicle are two benches. We're split across them, and Captain Pit, and Specialists Lyle and Jackie file in. They sit at the ready, hands on their weapons.

The vehicle lifts off and accelerates.

It takes several minutes to get wherever the vehicle is taking us, but it finally slows and comes to a halt. Thoughts of breaking free still linger within my mind, but with nowhere to go, it seems futile. Specialist Lyle opens the doors, and we're herded out.

The sun overhead causes the pointed towers to sparkle like jewels. My view is cut short when Specialist Jackie pushes me toward a massive building. Looking off to the side, I catch a strange sight. Floating in the air is a small isle with a massive chain leading down to the ground we're on. In the dead center of it is a familiar purplish-pink crystal jutting out from both top and bottom.

Vraditi technology. The 'island'...it's a floating city?

The entrance of Tower Zero is similar to the last location, large with a bank of glass doors. Inside is about the same, with minimal people. Instead of scanning stations, there are rows of desks, two of which are staffed.

Captain Pit leads us in, while Jackie and Lyle silently follow carrying Eve who is beginning to regain some control. Inside the immaculate, half circle lobby are at least a dozen hallways sprouting off in all directions.

Captain Pit speaks quietly to one of the clerks. They nod and hand him something. He returns to the group, pointing to the right.

The fourth hallway on the arc stretches a great distance. The number of doors indicate this place was probably packed at one time.

At an elevator, Captain Pit swipes a coin-like object against a black panel on the wall. The elevator dings, and the doors slide open. Inside, he hits the number thirteen. The trip is brief as the elevator climbs at an extreme speed.

Into another hall, Captain Pit walks to the end. There's a window there, and while he fiddles with the door I look out.

It appears we're at the center of New Asta. I suppose this means if we do escape, we have to cover at least half of it to reach the edge. Then what? We're obviously too high up to climb down.

I'm sure Tigby won't be releasing us anytime soon. He'll probably avoid doing that at all costs.

The door swings open, and the room's farthest wall, made completely of windows, follows the contour of the building in a wide arc. It's a lavish room fit for a king.

"You'll be assigned two persons to an apartment. No more. You will not be allowed to leave unless cleared by Colonel Tigby. You will have level one requisitioning from the attendant robot," he tells us sternly.

"Can we all stay here for now and split up later?" I ask.

"That is acceptable."

There are two extravagant beds with big pillows and heavy blankets near the windows. In the corner, near another doorway I recognize an attendant robot as Vraditi in origin.

"Your accommodations are sufficient for basic needs," Captain Pit explains. "Level one requisitioning will get you—"

"I'm aware of what level one is. What I really want to know is if there is a purification chamber behind that door." I'm excited by the prospect.

"There is. Now if I may continue," he answers irritated. "You'll have no contact with the outside world, so don't bother asking."

He continues. "The three of us are more than enough to subdue a dozen alkos users. But we'll have a whole team ready for you," he warns.

"I'm not going to have any problems when I remove the cuffs, am I?"

"No. Eve will be irritated, but she'll calm down." I turn to her and wink. She's begun to regain motor control.

Captain Pit eyes me, but proceeds to turn me and unlatch the cuffs.

With my hands free, I rub my wrists and stretch my arms.

He unshackles everyone else while I head to the window. Scanning the horizon, I notice most of the city was created with a significant amount of glass and crystal. I examine the closest building to ours, a few blocks away. Its walls are murky with a purple hue.

I am joined by everyone but Eve and the soldiers. When I look around, Captain Pit is readying to hit her with his weapon as she grunts and moves her arms sharply.

I intervene. "Eve, stop! Don't make them stun you again."

"Yoush...no...I am..." she attempts to speak but her efforts are labored.

I put my hands on her shoulders.

"Pants," she mutters and glares at Captain Pit.

"She'll be fine," I tell him and then look at her. "Right, Eve?"

"If she swings at me, I'll zap her again," he warns, and points his finger at me. "And then I'll zap you for not keeping her in line."

Looking at Eve, I wait for her response. When she nods to indicate her compliance, Specialist Jackie removes her cuffs, and places her in my care. Putting her arm around my neck, I lift and hold her weight as the three soldiers head out.

"This and the next two rooms over are yours," Captain Pit says before shutting the door.

Moving to the robot, it whirs to life and hovers near us.

"Can you stand on your own?"

"I think so," Eve grumbles.

"Okay, I'm going to let you go."

I move away and stand out of the robot's vision. She wobbles but manages to stay upright.

"Attendant, scan. Determine size and replicate new clothing."

"Command confirmed. Scanning, please wait," it replies in a monotone speech pattern.

It fabricates a new set of clothes at her feet, identical to the ones she is currently wearing.

Eve picks them up hastily and heads into the adjoined purifier room. Before closing the door, she looks back at me, smirks, then motions for me to follow her with her index finger. I shake my head. She shrugs and closes the door.

Emma and Ami have already made themselves comfortable lying on one of the beds and staring out the window. Agatha and James are sitting on the edge of the other, and are waiting patiently while looking at me. I put my hands in my pockets and stand next to them.

"What do we do?" James looks to me.

"Err on the side of caution," I say. "These are a barbaric people who have their hands on Vraditi technology."

"What's 'Vraditi'?" he asks.

"They're here?" Ami looks confused.

"It's an alien race," I tell him. "They're calling themselves 'Quvites' now. I encountered them again, when I was frozen in time. They may have been here all along, since we first met them."

"After I caused the destruction of this hemisphere, they stepped in and revitalized the planet per my request. My instruction for them was to do it after we picked up Eve so they wouldn't interrupt the timeline."

"Wait," Eve says from behind me. "My people may still be alive?"

"It's possible. Humans have apparently been in disagreement with the Quvites for three decades over sharing the land they helped revitalize."

"If there's a chance my people are still alive, I want to find out," she states. "I may have been a harsh leader, but there were people I cared for. No doubt Kohan assumed command of an army somewhere."

Waving them all closer, I fear we may be under surveillance. Everyone edges in, and we huddle.

"I'll cooperate for now and do my best to gather information, but I don't trust Colonel Tigby. He said he might be able to use me. I anticipate it's for something terrible," I whisper.

"Are you going to help him?" Ami asks.

"Only enough to keep us out of prison. The four of us who have alkos need to be on guard." I pause to look around for any sign we're being watched.

"We have two objectives to accomplish. The first is stopping the vortex. The Colonel believes he can accomplish this task. We'll work with him for our own goals."

"Second. We need to work for a diplomatic solution between humans and the Vraditi."

"Do you think the Colonel will try using an artifact or another person with power to stop the vortex?" Agatha asks.

"I doubt it. He is seriously against alkos, and it sounds like this society follows suit. It's more likely he'll try to use technology."

If we're successful I'll have to assume power and change the rules. If I don't, it will be prison or a life on the run with the Qavites.

"I have a bad feeling deep in my bones," James starts. "Something isn't right."

"I agree. Colonel Tigby gave me information, but I don't know if I should share until I've collected more."

New Asta...

"But there's not much we can do." I turn to Agatha. "She's in there, isn't she?"

"Yes." Agatha nods and smiles.

"Evalyn, since circumstances have changed, can you exit Agatha and roam freely?"

"No." Agatha changes to Evalyn. "Being in a body is my only option here. If I leave, I will be pulled back to the house."

"But you could possess someone else. Like you had with me," I offer.

"We could try it again. I don't know how big of a gap I'm able to jump before the pull is too great to overcome." She shrugs.

"I want you to try possessing each of us soon. We need an agent who can roam freely, and if you are able to jump bodies we can infiltrate the government."

"What are you thinking?" Emma asks.

"Forced diplomatic relations. Control them, control the vote, control the cities. Once we control the cities, we can reform everything as we see fit."

"That's dirty, even by my standards," Eve adds in and giggles evilly. "I *love* it!"

"This is different. You're different." Ami reaches over and touches my hand. "Are you...you?"

How do I answer her? Tiberius was the opposite of who I became as Rain, but there's no more conflict in my thoughts. Our thoughts are in sync. But am I still Rain with parts of Tiberius? Or am I Tiberius with parts of Rain?

"I'm me. You wanted me to pursue non-violent conflict resolution. This is an opportunity." I smile. "The Quvites are not favored. Despite a right to be here, it sounds like they're being blocked from Salvoa."

"Let's eat and rest," Evalyn suggests. "It seems we have another adventure on our hands."

Commanding the robot, we individualize our own meals. I opt for simplicity; potatoes and sausage. We all stare out the window while eating. Though the past and the future weigh heavily on my mind, to be back with those I care about lends me the strength to carry the burdens.

With the sun sinking below the floating island's horizon, the sky above darkens, and the stars appear. The lights of the city compete with the stars, giving the island the appearance of floating in space.

Finished with my meal, I lie down on the bed and yawn.

"Hey babe." Eve sits next to me. "Think I could sleep here? I've been awful lonely."

"In your dreams. You're bunking with Emma," Ami says, laughing.

Eve laughs, "You're staying then?"

"No, I'll be with Mother. Father will stay."

They're not fighting. What spurred the change? Did they actually become friends?

"I'm tired," I tell them. "We need to rest."

Without argument or warning, the women make their way out. It's a strange sight, seeing them go willingly. When they're gone, I close the door and return to the window to stare at the brilliant city lights and the glimmering stars.

"I won't pretend to understand what you've been through…" James sits on the edge of his bed and looks at me. "But I've spent the better part of the last eight years with her because of your sacrifice."

I shrug.

"Ami thinks the world of you. She searched for you, followed any lead she thought might lead to your whereabouts."

"And I think the same of her. I'd do anything for Ami."

"Would you?" he asks while crossing his arms with a serious expression.

"*Without a doubt.*" I sigh. "*With the vortex active again it's extremely complicated. But I love your daughter. In due time, I'll ask for your blessing.*"

He's silent for a moment.

"*Don't mention that to anyone. We have a situation to get through first.*"

"I understand." He pauses for a moment. "She agonized over you every day for the first year. She was inconsolable at times."

"*If I knew what was going to happen, I wouldn't have tampered with the vortex. I wouldn't have left her.*"

"You and I haven't had much time to get to know one another, but you seem to be a good man."

'A good man'...if he knew what I've done, who I really am... I am a monster, and I will continue to be one in the eyes of some. I will gain control of this city and mold it to a better society.

I keep that to myself, letting him believe what he likes.

An awkward silence fills the room. I want to be honest with him, but I can't. The darkness within is too dreadful for someone as innocent as he is to understand. In silence, we watch lights flicker and move through New Asta.

"Good night."

"*Good night.*"

He lies down and turns away.

The quiet is my enemy. For too long I fought against it in the frozen time. For too long silence haunted me, and I felt like I was slowly losing my sanity. Remembering it forces me to think about the souls who lost their lives because of me, and the pain returns.

Short of heading to one of the other apartments for companionship, my only recourse to alleviate the silence is the purification chamber. My muscles are stiff, and I think of how relaxing the jets will be.

In the purifier room a light turns on automatically. In addition to the familiar tube, there are also typical amenities for a regular bathroom.

Standing in front of a mirror by the sink, I look at the effect the collective of despair has wrought on me. Taking my nice clothing off, and draping them on an empty towel rack, I examine myself.

"Misery, when will you attempt to take over? Do I have the strength to keep your anger at me contained, or am I destined to fall to your power?"

They don't answer, but I can feel their rage burning within me.

I approach the chamber and hit the button to start the process. The cylinder's door slides open and I step inside, anticipating the feeling. The door closes behind me and the tube fills.

I remember the sense of dread as the gelatinous substance climbed my skin the first few times. The dread is a sliver now of what it once was. It reaches my mouth, and I let it flow into my body. Closing my eyes, I lean on the wall, and the tension in my muscles melts.

All too soon the jets stop, and the tube drains. I cough out the goo and air blows around me to get the rest. I shake my head like a mutt coming in from the rain. My muscles are weak with fatigue.

The door slides to let me out, and when I open my eyes I'm greeted by a terrifying sight. My first thought is that I'm hallucinating, but when a scaly Tarak hand reaches to shock me with one of their stunners, I know it's real.

He stops me falling with one lengthy, rough arm. "When Colonel Tigby brought report to me, I couldn't believe it," it hisses. "But, here you are!"

I'm forced to look into his eyes, and my worst nightmare has become reality. In my peripheral vision, I see what I had hoped to never see again. It's the dagger.

"Hello, Tiberius," Drake's voice is raspy coming from the Tarak's throat. His thin lips and scaly mouth draws back in an evil grin.

Paralyzed, I am helpless.

No...this can't be real. How cruel is fate? How can this be? The sinkhole...it went all the way to the Tarak habitat under the earth? How is he possessing one?

"You should have accepted my offer. But I'm grateful you didn't, because I am able to rule anew. New Asta is my city and you are my prisoner, to do with as I please." The toothy grin fades and I can tell he's become angry. "You left me."

You left me! You betrayed me!

Looking to Specialists Lyle and Jackie who have entered, Drake waves them over. They grab my underarms and calves, and lift. Carrying me out into the room, I see James being held hostage. He's not stunned, likely on purpose so I can see the fear in his face.

In the open hallway, a breeze chills my naked body. The women have been hauled out and are watching me as I'm carried past.

"Rain!" Ami cries out. She's sobbing.

The soldiers are pinning them to the wall, forcing them to watch. I'm humiliated, mortified, and scared. Eve is stunned again, likely due to noncompliance.

I'll save you Ami. I'll save all of you. I swear it!

Calling out with my mind, I attempt to use Misery as my weapon. *"Come on!"*

They are defiant. They will not lend me their power.

"You think I'm a monster for doing what had to be done? At least I'm remorseful! Drake has no remorse! You exist as much because of me as because of him!"

They still refuse to aid me.

"Take him to the alkos prison," Drake tells them. "I need to make preparations for an execution of this public menace and traitor."

"Yes, sir," Lyle and Jackie reply.

"What of his companions?" Captain Pit asks.

"Tell Tigby they're at his disposal, but to keep them alive while I find a use for them." He sizes Eve up and snorts through his large nostrils.

"Yes High Chancellor," Captain Pit replies.

Stupid! Why didn't I destroy it? Prison? Execution? High Chancellor?!

As much as I want to rip the dagger off of his belt and stab him in the skull, I have no control over my body. I have fallen into my brother's clutches.

"I'll see you at your execution." Drake hits me in the head with the handle of his weapon.

~~~~~~

Jostled, I wake with a start and grunt incoherently. It's mostly dark, and paired with a swaying movement, it's disorienting.

A small beam of light allows me to examine my surroundings, and it appears I'm crammed inside a moving box maybe twice the size of a coffin. There's not much to examine. My hands are shackled above my head, but my legs are free. There's soft cloth on my legs. It strikes me as a little odd that as a prisoner they've given me a shred of dignity by putting a pair of pants on me, but I'm grateful.

The paralysis has worn off. I have little room to move, but I crane my neck to the light source. It's a small, barred window. Specialists Lyle and Jackie are on the other side of it, Lyle driving the vehicle.

Watching lights pass, I conclude we are still in transit to the prison.

It's not too late.

To break free is my hope, but I anticipate a dampening field will negate my attempt.

Try or die.

Grabbing each chain, I pull myself up and reposition my legs so they're under me.

Focus. Build it up.

Closing my eyes, I bring the energy to my hands. With my grip tight on the chains, I stop holding back and force it out. To my surprise there isn't any countermeasure to stop me.

Deafening myself with the powerful shockwave, I shred the chains and tear a gaping hole in the roof of the transport vehicle. It swerves violently. Specialist Lyle tries not to hit other flying vehicles passing at high speeds.

They forgot to turn it on?! They must have thought I'd be out the whole way.

Specialist Jackie pulls the window open. Electricity crackles through the air as she attempts to stun me, but with the chains severed from my shackles, I'm unaffected. It's a triumph, even if it's temporary. Pointing my hands at the side of the vehicle, I tear another hole in it. The force rips the paneling off, and I have a view of our surroundings: we're above many buildings by a large distance.

Don't hesitate now. Jump.

Specialist Lyle loses control. The vehicle spirals out of the sky, plummeting toward the floating island.

Nearing the roof of a building, I calculate when to jump to avoid serious injury. The window of opportunity closes fast.

Running at the opening, I catch my foot on metal. It shreds the soft tissue in the arch of my foot. I stumble, and my legs buckle. Using shockwaves against the plummeting vehicle, I dive out.

I've missed the roof, and am now heading for a bank of windows. To avoid death on impact, I use a small shockwave to break the surface tension of the glass. Plowing through it, I land in someone's living room.

The tenants scream in panic as I land feet from their dinner table.

I hear the vehicle crash below. Looking out, I see a smoldering wreck on the street.

Unfortunate collateral damage.

"He's landed inside Building Four-Alpha of the East Side Apartment block!" Specialist Lyle yells from above.

They're alive.

A glow is emitted from his and Specialist Jackie's suits, floating in the air and they descend slowly. They don't appear to be in control, but upon landing, I have no doubt they will be on their way to find me.

Frantic, I turn to the family of four with hands raised to show them I'm not going to harm them. Bending down, I grab onto the fabric of my pants and pull at the seam. It stretches, refusing to tear. I look up at the man.

"I need something to cut these pants with."

"Get out of my house! Go!" the man yells at me.

"Now!"

"Honey, just give him the scissors!" the woman's voice shakes.

He retrieves them from a drawer and rather than handing them to me he tosses them at my feet. I nod and snatch them up, cutting quickly.

With a long strip and a few smaller ones, I create padding and a dressing to keep it all in place on my foot. Leaving the scissors on the floor, I move to the door.

Though the pain is intense, I forge ahead down a white hallway, leaving a trail of blood. At the end of the hall is an exit. When I open it, it seems I didn't land too terribly as there's an exterior staircase I can use. The pointed grates of the staircase dig into my feet. Loud horns and sirens surround the area. With several flights to go before I reach ground level, I conclude they'll beat me to the bottom of the staircase.

I vault the side railing, padding my fall with a couple shockwave bursts, alerting them to where I am, I'm sure. My foot screams in pain when I land, but I don't have the luxury of babying it. Yelling soldiers are coming around the building. I run down an alley and duck into a small niche.

Eluding capture for the moment, I look for somewhere dark to hide. But all of the areas are well lit. Sirens scream above my head. My hope is to keep running, but at the end of my current alley there's more yelling. I turn around to the sound of feet running toward me.

The loss of blood is making me dizzy, but I push hard to try and outrun them.

My advantage is lost and they overtake me. I'm struck in the back of the head, and then shocked…twice.

~~~~~~

Lingering in a state between asleep and awake, I become aware I'm lying on hard metal.

Screams and wails echo from all directions; the noise quickly rankles. The annoyed feeling disappears when my nerves scream in pain, both up my leg and through my forearms. My hands, arms, legs, and foot have been bandaged. My wrists are shackled, and I'm chained to the wall.

I'm in a small prison cell. There are three solid walls, a set of bars for the fourth wall, a single cot, an open air toilet, and absolutely nothing to use as a weapon.

It appears that death by my brother is inevitable.

Outside of my cell is an open area. A single soldier sits with his back to me at a desk a few feet away. He's watching several screens, each of a different cell, except for one which doesn't appear to have anything to do with the prison. It's moving images of me, recapping the mayhem caused by my escape attempt.

My limbs are heavy, my body reluctant to do what I want. Trying to sit upright, I let out a moan of my own. The aftereffects of my escape have taken a great toll, and I fail. I fall back to the hard metal, but I'm disoriented and lose my balance, falling to the floor instead. Everything hurts.

I labor to climb up onto my cot. It takes me a minute, but I succeed. The soldier has kept his eyes glued to the screens, not seeming to notice me, or perhaps doesn't care.

I attempt to gain his attention. "Hey!" I yell at him.

Turning, he glances at me, but his gaze returns to the screen. Crossing his arms, he does his best to ignore me.

"*Hey. I want to ask you a question.*"

"Shut it, newbie!" He whips around in his chair.

"*I want answers.*"

"Too bad." He spins back.

"*Then give me some water. I'm parched.*"

"You'll get some at meal time."

"*Fine, then give me a meal.*"

He laughs callously. "Sure. Tomorrow."

Footsteps approach from the right of my cell, getting louder. Coming into view is a bronzed woman, wearing a white overcoat like the Colonel's. She's accompanied by two soldiers. Dirty blonde hair curtains to her face, covering most of the frames of her glasses.

She stops at my cell and her face is scanned. The lock clicks open, and she has to push hard to make the door swing because of her petite frame. The three of them enter, and the soldier at the desk turns to watch, crossing his arms and legs.

The woman turns to the man at the desk and lays into him. "This patient requested water, didn't he?" she asks angrily.

"And?" he replies defiantly. "He's a prisoner."

"He's injured and dehydrated. Next time think before you flap your lips," she scolds him.

"What am I? A doctor? That's your job! Besides, why do you care? He's an alkos user, and his injuries are his own fault." The soldier rests his hands behind his head and slouches further.

"Get this man a glass of water," she commands one of the soldiers who followed her into the cell. She's flustered, fuming at the insubordination.

The soldier she addressed exits, leaving her and the other soldier, who holds his stunner ready. He sees me gauging the situation and shakes his head to dissuade me from making any moves.

The woman looks at her electronic tablet and taps it a couple times. "I'm your attending physician. I need to look at your wounds. If you attempt to harm me or run, extreme force will be used to secure you. The chains holding you will be retracted into the wall, the bed will go away, and you'll hang by your arms," she warns.

"I'm a little worse for wear. Perhaps I'll fight you another time." I shrug.

She smiles gently. "I guess we'll take it one day at a time then."

"Not that it matters one way or the other, right? I'm to be executed."

She doesn't respond. Entering my range, she kneels and starts to remove the bandages on my legs and foot. I try to make it easier for her by holding my wounded foot up, but I don't have the strength. She props my toes up on her knee and continues.

"So you imprison people with alkos?"

"I don't. I'm a doctor. But if you mean New Asta, then yes. Alkos is dangerous. Everyone who exhibits a power is housed in this prison so they cannot harm themselves and others, much like you tried to do yesterday."

"Abducting someone who is stronger and expecting no retaliation is foolish at best." Despite my imprisonment, I'm as brazen as when I was ruling Asta.

Pulling off a small satchel, the doctor digs into it and produces a round can, and new bandaging. She sprays my foot and legs. The mist cools the sharp pain, and then dries. She wraps my feet and legs with fresh bandages. I want to wince, but I hold it in.

Show no signs of weakness.

Moving to my arms, she handles them one at a time, following the same pattern. The cuts on my arms range from light to moderate. Smashing through the glass wasn't the smartest, but I had no other choice. The wounds itch, but I resist scratching and making them worse.

"You attempted to kill two soldiers with your alkos for a chance to get away?"

"My intention was not to kill them. It was to escape."

"Your actions prove the case for why normal people need protection from people with alkos," she says solemnly, but smiles. "Imprisonment is the only answer."

"You don't seem too happy about saying that though." I raise an eyebrow, a little disarmed.

"As a doctor, my oath is to help people, but the people in here will be in agony until they die," she says while finishing with my arms and frowning. "I can only mitigate the pain."

The first soldier returns and hands me a glass. As I guzzle it, a deep agony within and around me gains my attention. The souls of Misery are restless, weighing heavy with raw emotion. It's the people of this time, in this place. I shudder. My heart beats faster as I feel the people's anguish surround me. I feel their pain.

"Are you all right?" she asks, taking the glass.

"Sure."

"Because you just arrived, you haven't had a meal on the rotation. I'll send a tray for you shortly." She and her companions exit.

"That's out of protocol, *doctor*," the soldier at the desk protests.

She shoots him a glare and he shuts up.

The lock on my cell door clicks back into place and I'm left with the disgruntled soldier. He scoffs loudly while they leave.

Getting as comfortable as I can on my metal bed, he stares at me. I stare back for a few minutes before he finally breaks the silence.

"Shouldn't get special treatment…" he mutters.

"Eating is a special treatment?" I egg him on.

"It is if it's outside the scheduled rotation!" he barks and spins to face the screens.

I'm satisfied I've got under his skin, and try to rest. The crying of the other prisoners keeps me from achieving a peaceful state of mind.

More footsteps, and my door clicks open.

With one eye, I watch a soldier set a tray on the floor and kick it at me. Some of the food flies off. The door slams shut and locks.

I climb down and move to the tray. Bland scrambled eggs and a small plastic jug of milk seem paltry, but I'm hungry. It doesn't take me long to devour it.

On the bed, I lie facing the wall. I attempt to sleep off the fatigued feeling left by being shocked or being frozen in time, or both. With despair creeping in, I do my best to shut it out along with the echoes ringing through the long corridor.

If I can harness and control Misery as a weapon I could escape. The hope of deliverance lies with the Qavites at this point. But with Qava's people being ostracized, how will I contact them?

Misery has destructive power, but how much? With them watching, and my time short, I don't know if I'll have an opportunity to hone control. But what if they lent me the power?

It's not alkos. These people would be unprepared.

I feel the dark world within tugging at me. Despite my best efforts to stifle them, they finally get to me and I probe to see if I can pull useful information from nearby prisoners. As I listen, I feel myself edging closer to the dark world, teetering on the edge outside of it. The thoughts flood my mind, and what I find disturbs me.

"Why do I have to be in here? What did I do?"

"Please mommy, come back! Mommy, why did you leave me?"

"Sleep. Eat. Sleep. Eat. Please, kill me. Kill me. Kill me."

"Six hundred forty-eight thousand, two hundred and one. Six hundred forty-eight thousand, two hundred and two. Six hundred forty-eight thousand, two hundred and three."

"I'm going to kill every single person when I get out. I'm superior!"

Feeling the anguish of the other captives overwhelming me, I sit up and press my foot into the floor, making my own pain drown them out. Shaken to the core, I sense a large number of people being held.

Drake, you're a monster. This is insane. This can't continue.

With my own throbbing foot keeping me from focusing on the other people's problems, I focus on my brother.

How did he possess a Tarak? I should have destroyed that stupid thing. If I can reach him, he can't be allowed to live. I won't make the same mistake twice.

His goal in life has been to hurt me. I'll raise an army. These people and the Quvites. This must end.

The doctor. Can I use her as a pawn? She seemed sympathetic. Maybe I can manipulate her and get a message to Evalyn to start possessing up his ranks.

Time passes slowly; with my neighbors howling, I anticipate they won't be very good conversationalists. I watch the screens over the soldier's shoulder: they change images every once in a while. He sits silently, arms crossed, his head moving from one screen to another.

"Hey. Why are the other prisoners being so loud?" I ask, raising my voice to be heard over the noises they're making.

He ignores me and continues to stare at his screens.

I try again, now yelling, "Hey! Why are the other prisoners being so loud?"

He spins in his chair, shooting me an annoyed glare. I have his attention. "Pipe down."

"Hey!" I get louder. "If you want to be rude, I can start wailing and moaning loudly. It might become annoying since you're only a few feet away."

"It'd be no worse than those two." He points to either side of my cell, provoking a response from the inmates in the form of grunting and snorting.

He sighs rather loudly, and gives in. "You people can't exert your power because of the dampening tech invented by the Quvites. Just like those two, your energy will slowly degrade your mind and body. Eventually it's fatal."

"What right does society have to treat people this way?" I'm outraged.

He laughs. "We're keeping people *safe* from the likes of you Alkosians and your destructive powers."

"'Alkosians'?"

"I coined that term. You like it?" He snorts.

"Not all alkos is bad. I've come across one that couldn't be used to harm anyone," I argue angrily.

"You are a danger simply by existing. You spread your Alkosian seed and infect others. Imagine if these people were allowed to run amok on the streets. They might try and form their own governments, or overthrow this one," he retorts.

"Your indoctrination is solid. That logic is based on hypothetical situations."

"Are you trying to lie and say you never hurt anyone?"

"I've done what I had to in order to keep myself and my family safe from bad people and situations. As for overthrowing governments, it's not a terrible idea. You people are alienating the race who helped ours come back from destruction."

"Alienating...good choice of word."

Huffing angrily, I glare at the back of his head while he fidgets with the screens. A line crosses the screen and he spins to face me, rolling his chair over to my cell. He looks at me with less hostility and whispers, "Are you a supporter of the Quvites?" He eyes me nervously.

"Why?"

"Answer the question. The video is on loop, but I can't leave it for long or they'll notice. We don't have much time, maybe a couple minutes," he speaks hurriedly. "Do you support the Quvites?"

"Yes." I squint and furrow my eyebrows. "Because the Vraditi helped rebuild Salvoa, they have as much a right to it as anyone else, Alkosians included. What's happening now is wrong."

"Look, I don't really hate Alkosians. Y'all scare me, sure, but I don't agree with this treatment. I have to put up a big front because it's my job: if they thought I was a sympathizer of either group they'd kill me. I'd be hung in public."

"Barbaric. Alkosian, Quvite supporter, and my dear brother Drake is having me executed as a traitor. I'm un-savable it seems."

"High Chancellor Drake?

"Yes."

"How is he your brother? He's Tarak."

"He's human, or was. He has alkos: the ability to possess other people. Our rivalry goes way back, and I'm not here because I have alkos. I'm here because he's in a position of authority and is using it to punish me."

"I never would have thought. How have you avoided him?" he asks eagerly.

"It's an extremely long story. Needless to say I'm new to New Asta. I was taken from Salvoa's surface by Colonel Tigby."

"The supporters of the Quvites, and their right to Salvoa, are in the minority…"

The sound of a door closing echoes and his eyes widen. He spins back to the desk and fiddles with something again. Everything returns to normal on the screens. Footsteps approach, and the soldier casually looks from one screen to another.

A new soldier appears and heads to the desk. He makes no attempt to hide his disdain as he addresses my guard. "Any of these freaks gettin' out of line?" He chuckles. "My stunnin' finger is itchin'."

"Nah. Put one down for a nap and there will still be hundreds moaning and wailing," the soldier replies.

"It's ridiculous these people are kept here, eating our food. They should be killed and be done with it," he snorts.

"You're inhuman," I snap at him. "Do you have no regard for life?"

"Who asked you?" he replies, annoyed I spoke to him. "If it were up to me, parents would be screened to see if they were going to produce a kid with alkos."

My guard nods and smirks at the soldier, I assume to fit in and conceal his true allegiance.

"You think if they did, they might be able to fix this problem in a few generations," the soldier continues his line of abominable reasoning.

"We have as much right to exist as you do!" I yell. "We have the right to live, and no government should be able to imprison people because they're different."

"Hey." He grins and taps the holster on his hip, threatening to shock me. "Calm down there buddy or Imma come in there."

"Do it!" I taunt him. "Are your morals so eroded you'd abuse a prisoner for fun?"

"Morals? As far as I'm concerned you're a dangerous freak of nature that needs to be stomped out." The soldier moves toward the bars of my cell.

"Hey, Danny, chill. Don't let the newbie get under your skin." The soldier from the desk stands up next to him. "You know they usually have a bit of fire when they first arrive."

"Yeah, and my favorite part is gettin' to break them," he replies, trying to be the alpha male.

"The doctor won't like that with this one. Wait until he's healed and then we can have some fun," the soldier offers, trying to deter him.

Huffing loudly and waving his arm in a swift motion, the soldier shakes his head and turns away. They look over the screens silently for a moment.

"They're gonna come take one for tests soon. And Cap says you need to report in more, Gregory," the soldier says with a smirk and turns to leave.

"Sure," Gregory says sitting and acting nonchalant.

The soldier is gone, and several minutes later the sound of a door opening and closing comes from far away. A man screams, and I can barely understand him, but a few words of anguish are clear.

"No! No more!"

There's a struggle, and in a few moments it's quiet. Footsteps approach and the man I assume was screaming is hauled past my cell by Danny. He's incapacitated. A 'White Coat' supervisor follows, and then they're gone, through another door. I'm angered and saddened, but I can't help him.

"*Psst.*" I attempt to get Gregory's attention, but he ignores me.
I guess I have to wait for him to initiate conversation.

~~~~~~

Several hours pass with nothing to do. It's agonizing. With all of the noise and the uncomfortable cot, I find it extremely difficult to rest.

Bored of sitting and watching Gregory, I speak up, if nothing more than to hear sounds other than moaning and wailing. I badger Gregory simply for the contact. "*I'm bored,*" I yell. "*Could I have some reading material?*"

"Pipe down!" he yells.

"*I'm bored!*" I continue.

Over his shoulder, he glares at me. "Regulations say that prisoners can't have personal items."

"*Look, all I want are books!*"

"Shut up!"

Were it not for a slight wink, his act would be convincing. I cross my arms and glare. He spins back to the screens.

"*Then knock me out. I can't take much more of the noise.*"

"That I can do," he replies.

He fidgets at the desk, and within a few minutes a White Coat and two soldiers show up at my cell. Not a word is said as they enter and stab my arm with a needle.

The effects overcome me before they've left my cage. I drift off. The full force of whatever they injected hits me.

~~~~~~

I stir at different noises. Several people, White Coats and soldiers, are milling about.

Gregory is gone, another soldier having taken his spot at the desk. The doctor who attended to me is talking with another White Coat, a man, in whispers. She looks at me, and continues in a tone lower than I can hear.

Motioning to my door, the doctor instructs her attending company to stand guard while she opens it. The four of them move to my cell, and the lock clicks.

Pushing in, the soldiers stand at each side of my cell, their hands on their weapons, while she enters and tends to my wounds.

She smiles sadly at me while changing the bandages. "I had to argue with my superior to get in to tend to you." She looks at the man in the white coat. "The High Chancellor thinks my tending to you is unnecessary because of your pending execution."

"I'm certainly not surprised," I reply. "But you're here - you must have been convincing."

"I'm sorry it has to be this way, but execution is the better option. You don't want to stay imprisoned for the rest of your life." She frowns and works to clean me up. "Are you not surprised?"

"High Chancellor Drake has been trying to kill me for an extraordinarily long time. This is the opportunity my brother has been waiting for."

She looks at me, confused. "Who's your brother?" She glances at her superior. He shakes his head but she defies him and returns her gaze to me. They're clearly unaware of his abilities, or who he really is.

"Drake is my brother." I spell it out for her. "He's not Tarak, but an Alkosian pretending to be one. He can possess others through the blade he carries."

I frown and stare at the wall for a moment. "When am I due to be executed?"

"Tomorrow. I'm scheduled to change your bandages one more time." She shakes her head slightly. "Our High Chancellor having alkos…that's a heavy accusation with no proof."

"I can prove it. But even if I did, he'll still have me killed."

"What do you want for your last meal?" the scruffy man in the white coat asks.

"A fat juicy steak, medium. A baked potato with butter, and bacon chopped up. And a big glass of wine," I say facetiously, not expecting any of it.

But he takes me seriously and nods. The doctor, the White Coat, and a soldier leave. My cell is closed by the remaining soldier, and she stands with her hand at the ready on her weapon.

A few minutes later, the other soldier returns. He brings a tray with exactly what I wanted, though there are no utensils, and my steak is pre-cut into bites. He sets it on the floor inside the door.

When I hear the click, I slide off of the cot and retrieve my meal.

Eating it slowly, I savor the warm meat and potatoes, and drink the wine that compliments it nicely. I try to keep from eating it too fast, but even so it's gone too soon.

When I set the tray on the floor, the plate shifts to reveal the corner of a piece of paper.

Looking up, the two soldiers are still there, standing near the new soldier, their attention on the screens while they talk quietly.

Casually, I reach over and move the plate. There's a tightly folded piece of paper. I tuck it away in my pants; with it successfully hidden, I move the tray to the door.

Lying with my back facing the bars, I pull it out, taking care to keep it out of their sight.

There is a faction who supports unity for all races. Through Gregory, I learned you are a Quvite supporter. I overheard my superior talking with Colonel Tigby, and your attack is going to be tied to the Quvites as terrorism to incite the outrage of the public. You're a scapegoat.

The faction feels a shared planet and cooperation can be achieved, however it is up to a High Chancellor vote. The goal has been to sway the vote to peace, but High Chancellor Drake is a cunning opponent and has recently caught onto the efforts. A few High Chancellors of other cities "mysteriously" disappeared; now those cities are undecided.

If there is any truth to what you said about High Chancellor Drake having alkos, you might be the best opportunity to oppose his grasp for power by exposing him. If I help you escape and get you to the Quvites, are you willing to help the faction?

Have your response ready by the next time I return. And eat this note. No one must know.

I do as instructed and bit by bit, the paper disappears. I dispose of the note completely without being detected. The soldiers leave the area, and the new guard of the cell block is left alone.

Okay. But how? And how do I get my family? I can't leave them behind.

It takes time to quiet my mind. But even when my own thoughts aren't keeping me awake, Misery is. The echoes torture my soul, and instead of reaching a restful state I am sucked into *their* dark world.

In the darkness I'm alone. The quiet is soothing, but it doesn't last long. A barrage of feelings and voices from my cellmates crash over me in waves. They cry out and wail in agony, their hopelessness apparent. Sorrows and agonies slam me, flooding me with images of different cells from their various perspectives. The misery of being unable to release any of their power is destroying them, tearing their minds apart.

On top of that, they are victims of malnourishment, mistreatment, and torture. The millions dead by my actions try to barge in, but my proximity to these people in agony keeps them at bay.

The Alkosians cry out in my mind and I try to console them. *"Calm yourselves!"* I reach out to them.

"My body is on fire!"

"Don't let them take me! I don't want to be part of the tests!"

"Hungry…tired…"

"Calm yourselves!" I try again. *"I will rescue you!"*

"You can't! We'll die here!"

"Others have tried and failed! It brings more problems!"

"You need to be patient with me. I can rescue you and bring you to safety!"

"You won't succeed!"

"Let me die!"

There's no arguing with the people's despair. I've hit the impassable tenacity of a man who wants nothing but death to come. The rest echo him. They want help, but they don't want to be freed. They call for death. I refuse to let them persuade me, setting my mind on saving them. Instead of focusing on them, I focus on the power they're generating by their despair.

Misery is able to manifest physically from me. Why can't I harness them?

"Lend me your power!" I implore them.

"So you can kill more?" the millions accuse me over the Alkosians.

"So I can stop those things! Look into the past and see what Drake will do! See his evil!"

"You have put us here — will you bring us into the light, like you promised?"

"Yes! I will change your fate!"

They become silent for so long it feels like they've forgotten I'm here. They don't reply so I can hear them, but tension builds in my body. It's familiar, like every time Misery has spewed forth. The pain in my soul is crippling, and I succumb. It builds to the level after I emerged from the vortex into this time: millions screaming at me, trying to rip my soul into tiny pieces. The Alkosians lend their powers to Misery, and push me into another level of anguish. I sob under the weight, but when it feels as though I'll be crushed, light appears to grant me an exit. With their full force consuming me, I drag them to the light.

Snapping back to reality, I sit up.

There are many soldiers several feet outside my cell, pointing actual firearms at me. A blaring siren drowns the normal noises in the cell block, but I can still feel each and every one of the prisoners longing for relief. My face is wet with tears for them.

"Fire!"

The sounds of shots ring over the siren. The dark tendrils, acting as extensions of my body, whip around to defend me. Dozens of shots are fired, but not a single bullet reaches me.

Anger overtakes all other emotions, and the darkness reaches out to consume them. Every place the darkness touches them begins to turn black. Like a virus, Misery spreads through them, and they scream in agony, touched by the pain they inflict on the prisoners. They scratch at themselves trying to dig it out.

The few soldiers not touched by the dark appendages retreat to the others side of the desk. One smashes some buttons on the desk, and my chains retract into the wall.

It doesn't stop me. Misery hardens and shatters the shackles.

Standing, I move to the bars of the cell. An evil grin emerges as I terrorize them by slowly extending Misery's fingers toward them.

A soldier scrambles away, but another stands paralyzed. It touches him and he becomes afflicted.

"*You will suffer for causing us pain!*" Misery cries from my mouth.

The lingering pain in my foot doesn't hinder me as I step up to the bars and swing the tendrils at the door. The metal buckles and, with a second impact, it collapses.

Stepping out of my cell, I pass stairs leading up to another level. I can finally see the magnitude of the prison.

Cells on top of cells are filled with people simply because they're different. The stairs near me are only one set of many leading up and around the building's interior to all of the individual units.

The Alkosian cries echo, and I soak in their pain in to strengthen Misery.

"How?" The doctor's voice reaches my ears.

A dark mass flies at her in response, but I halt it before it hits her between the eyes. She stands there, filled with fear.

Misery calls to me inside the darkness.

"*You are our conduit into the light. Bring us into the light like you promised!*"

"*Our power is yours! Bring us into the light!*"

"*Salvation!*"

I revel in the power being lent to me. Where once I would have rebuked myself for this, I now embrace the chaos. I want to save these people at any cost, and I'm going to do it with force. The soldiers still standing fall under the effects of my terrible power.

...Miserable Rain. I'll make sure these people understand what they've done. The agony. The hurt.

I casually walk to the doctor, and the fear in her face delights me. A dozen more soldiers burst into the cell block several hundred feet away. Rifles come up and are aimed at me. The guns fire, and Misery manifests, spinning out from me. It crests like a wave of black between us stopping the bullets in midair.

"How are you able to use alkos?" she asks.

"Colonel Tigby didn't believe me. You will though. They all will." I yell and laugh maniacally. "This is the embodiment of the suffering you have wrought on these people."

"There's no escape. You're in a secured facility. Give up now!"

She is unaware of my intent to go through with her plan.

I'm able to control the dark form just by thought, and it does as I please. I circle the shadow wall around both of us, closing it in the back. We're shielded from gunfire – I can talk to her without raising suspicion.

I whisper, "Whatever you had planned for my escape, this is it. Right now."

"What?" she's confused.

"Escape. Now. What's your plan?"

"I...uh...the roof. If we get there we can steal a vehicle," she tells me hurriedly.

"I'm going to make them think you're my hostage. That way if this power fails me, you won't be implicated as an accomplice," I tell her. "Can we release the prisoners?"

"We can't take everyone. They won't all fit on one ship. How many people can you protect in here?"

"I haven't tested the limitations."

"Then we'll come back for them when we can keep them safe. I don't want them harmed." She grabs my shoulder and nods. "If we get you to Quva, you can plan a prison break."

The Alkosians cry out in the darkness.

"You said you'd help us! Don't leave! Help us escape!"

"I don't have a choice. I have to come back with an army to make sure you're all safe!" I tell them.

Wrapping the shadow wall into a cocoon over us, no light seeps in. I grab her by the hand to lead, opening an eyehole in the black wall.

Pulling her along, I stop in front of the soldiers blocking our path, who continue to fire. I give them one chance.

"I'm leaving now, and I'm taking the doctor with me as a hostage. Any attempt to apprehend me will result in your death and hers. Now move!" I command.

"Don't hurt them," she whispers. "They're just doing their job."

Colonel Tigby bursts in, and behind him in the hallway is another troop unit. Pushing his glasses up, he stares at the black oddity in front of him.

"Come now, we can reach an agreement, can't we?" he calls.

"Kill me now rather than at my public execution? Thanks, but no thanks. I'm leaving, and the doctor is my insurance," I reply harshly.

"Where will you go?"

"Quva will provide me asylum," I reply

"How do you expect to get there?" he asks calmly.

"I'm resourceful, as you can see. I won't be murdered by my brother, and I won't be a prisoner. If you try and stop me, I'll attack, and everyone here dies." I play my part well.

Colonel Tigby stands aside, and waves for his unit to do the same. As they make a path for us, I edge forward. Bringing the bubble inward, I hug the doctor closer to me, making sure the dark mass injures neither her, nor the soldiers. She moves ahead of me, taking control of the eyehole, and pulls me along. Blindly, I follow her lead. We turn several times and finally stop. She moves, and we are at a closed gate with another dozen soldiers beyond it.

"Open the gate or I'll tear it down and kill you all!"

They hesitate until Colonel Tigby calls from behind me. "Do as he says." Tigby stands immediately outside the bubble.

The door's latch clicks, and it swings open, but there's still the blockade formed by men and women attempting to stop our escape. They refuse to budge.

"Move!" I yell.

They stay still and no further word comes from the Colonel. My patience tried, I walk forward and the doctor protests.

"Please don't!" The doctor cries out for them to hear. "Don't hurt them!"

"Unless you want to die too, doctor, I suggest you tell them to stand down. When Misery touches them, it will infect them and kill them." Power and hatred consume me.

"I'm a doctor, I won't allow you to hurt them!"

"They aren't my concern, and you have no leverage! You are *my* prisoner." I try to make her understand. "If they move they won't be harmed."

Still no movement, so I walk forward. The black touches the first soldier, and I feel his soul as the darkness overtakes him. His pain becomes a part of me as it spreads across his body. He collapses. As he writhes, I step over to continue on. The others hustle to move and allow our passage.

"What is this power?" Colonel Tigby asks. "Are there more like you?"

Ignoring him, I push the doctor forward and she leads to the end of the hallway where elevator doors lie.

"I need to press the call button," she whispers.

I concentrate to keep the bubble up, defending our backs while opening the front for her. The shield is taking more effort to project. She presses the button, giving me time to think while we wait.

"It's weakening," I whisper in her ear. "I may lose the ability to generate a wall."

The elevator dings, and the doors open to reveal an empty ride. We step in, and I pull the black shield to the doorway, shrinking it so I'm not wasting energy. She presses fifty-five, and we ascend.

A minute later we reach our stop. When the doors slide open, I shield us with Misery again, with the same small hole to see. The ramp up looks clear. I form a new bubble, but I'm having difficulty keeping it solid.

"Please tell me it's not far," I say as the elevator whirs to life behind us.

"There's a large landing pad at the top here."

We run up the ramp. In the daylight our black bubble emerges, and waiting for us is a battalion ready to attack. But they fire no shots. They wait, watching us while the doctor finds the nearest vehicle, a large drop ship.

A voice from behind startles me, my shield fluctuates. I'm losing control.

Is it my distance from the Alkosians?

"Let Dr. Oreda go," Colonel Tigby tries to convince me.

"I'm a dead man if I do," I reply as we get into our escape vehicle. "At least with her as hostage I have a chance."

I keep us protected while we enter the ship. Dr. Oreda slides the door shut with a slam. Misery creeps back to me, but I force dark roots out through the cracks and crevices to hold the soldiers and Colonel Tigby at bay.

Dr. Oreda enters the cockpit. The engines whir to life and I drop into the chair next to her.

"I'm sorry in advance. I won't harm you, but I can't ensure your safety either."

"I'll be fine." She fiddles with several switches, not looking at me. "Let's get you to the Quvites."

With her hand on a panel in front of her which illustrates the four engines on the ship, she slides her fingers upward, and the ship lifts. We hover above the roof, and Colonel Tigby's voice projects into the cockpit.

"Authorization of lethal force has been given. Dr. Beth Oreda is now considered an acceptable loss. Shoot that vessel out of the sky," Colonel Tigby orders.

A barrage of projectiles begin hitting the sides of the ship. I deflect some, but when she takes us higher Misery recedes into me without warning. We're vulnerable.

Engines of other vehicles spring to life to pursue. We pull away, the city shrinking behind us. Dr. Oreda heads toward the edge of the floating island. I shake my head and try and redirect her.

"We need to go to Tower Zero."

"There's no way."

"My family is there. Unlike leaving the prisoners, I can't leave my family behind," I tell her. "Drake will kill them."

"If they're at Tower Zero, it's too late," she tells me while managing her attention between the control screen and the large window in front of us. "The High Chancellor won't kill them. He'll use them as leverage to make you turn yourself in."

"You don't know my brother. He's a monster," I plead.

She glares at me. Lashing out, she replies, "I just risked my life to save you! And you want to throw it away? We're going to have our hands full in a few moments. We can't afford a detour!"

A rapid beeping gains my attention, and Dr. Oreda points at a screen in front of me. On the circular screen I note a central triangle, and behind it several other triangles trailing. As they close in on us, a sense of dread falls over me.

"What is it?"

"They're pursuing in attack ships."

"I'll buy some time, but you *need* to head toward Tower Zero. We're saving my family!" I insist.

We stare at each other, locked in a moment of anger.

"What floor are they on?" she says resigned.

"Thirteen." I stand and move to leave the cockpit. "Toward the side with a large window."

"That's not helpful. Have you *seen* it from the outside?"

We change direction. While she pilots, I move to the hold, shutting the cockpit door behind me. Hung on the wall are ropes, harnesses, and eye protection similar to what the soldiers used when dropping to the ground at the house.

I fumble with the full body harness, making sure it's clipped under my arms and groin. Pulling goggles over my eyes and clipping the harness to the wall, I'm not sure what I expect to do.

I open both side sliding doors, a deafening wind roaring into the compartment, its freezing bite sending shivers up my back.

An explosion rocks us in the air, detonating off the side of the ship. Fire and hot smoke relieve some of the cold, but only for a moment.

My heart races. I breathe deeply to ready myself, but no amount of preparation can ease my nerves as I lean out. Wrapping the rope around the handle of the door makes it my anchor. I shift my weight to lean from the vehicle. My heels planted against the deck, I'm hanging above New Asta.

The doctor takes evasive maneuvers to avoid being hit while the pursuers attempt to knock us from the sky. I raise my hand toward the rear of the ship, aiming inaccurately at the attackers, firing a wide arced shockwave.

They can absorb my alkos, but can they fight the turbulence caused by the shockwave? Or the sheer force?

They veer to avoid being hit, and I try again. As it nearly misses tearing one of our own engines off, I feel the need to take more drastic measures.

A projectile slams into the back of the ship and explodes. The turbulence shakes us hard. Metal buckles inward, but the hull is still secure.

I return to the cockpit, yelling over the noise. "I need you to bank as close to completely on the ship's right side as possible for ten to fifteen seconds. Can you do it without crashing?"

"I think so," she yells back. "Now?"

"Give me five seconds then do it!"

I slam the cockpit door shut, and remove my rope-anchor from the handle on the sliding door. The ship begins to tilt, and gravity tries to pull me out the opposite side. Straddling the door keeps me from being sent into free-fall.

When we're mostly turned, I lift myself up and out and run across the hull toward the tail engine. We descend in a wide spiral, and she starts to level out before I've reached my destination.

Struggling to keep my footing, I make it to the short, thick wing holding the engine. I grab the far edge of it as she's forced to straighten.

Standing on the edge of the drop ship triumphantly, I put my arms out and let huge blasts sail unimpeded through the air.

The ripple effect grows, and the first wave impacts two ships. The large current of air being carried along causes them to lose control and slam into each other. The resulting explosion scatters the others, who move into new attack vectors.

Two swing around hard: one from the left, the other from the right. The last pair seek to overtake us from behind. They fire three projectiles. I unleash a wide shockwave to knock them away. Two are diverted, and one reaches our tail section.

The explosion knocks me off my footing, and the resulting fireball singes me. Dropping my guard, I'm forced to kneel to avoid falling.

Our vehicle slows dramatically, nearly throwing me off my perch, and the aft pair of ships pass overhead. Taking the opportunity I unleash large shockwaves at them.

The resulting impact rips the tail off of one. With the loss of engines, it drops, barely missing us as it plummets. The other retreats to a safe distance.

I launch more shockwaves in front of them, leading them, before firing one right at them. Another explosion knocks me off the wing.

My heart stops for a moment while I fall toward the city below. The harness catches me, and I exhale violently. I swing back and forth, feeling ill at both the height and thought of hanging by a rope only an inch thick.

Trying to grab it and climb up, I'm delighted when it retracts into the ship on its own, pulling me back to the deck of our heavily damaged ship.

Only two craft still pursue. The third, which I don't know if I hit, has disappeared. Off to the left, a vessel turns straight toward us, intent on a collision with our side. It launches a long skinny missile from its underbelly, and it closes fast.

I send the weapon off course with a shockwave blast, and it explodes underneath us. With both palms extended, I expel energy at the oncoming vehicle. The sheer force shreds panels away, and it disintegrates into flying shrapnel. I leap out of the way to avoid being impaled.

Dr. Oreda continues to fly defensively as the last ship dogs us. I remove the rope and return to the cockpit, closing the door to kill the wind noise. She's furiously tapping on screens. Our blip on the radar is being chased by their last vessel. She banks hard left and right to avoid being hit.

"Does this ship have weapons?"

"It does. But I'm not prepared to shoot them down!"

"Then show me, and I'll do it. You'll be absolved of any guilt," I persuade.

She glares at me and points to a display screen and button panel on my right with several large red buttons. The screen shows a crosshair in the middle, and the image is directly in front of us.

"Can you drop behind them?"

"I'm barely keeping us in the sky! I can't do much else," she barks in protest.

"Let them overtake us like you did with the others."

"I'll see what I can do." She doesn't even look at me.

Suddenly we dive directly at the buildings below us. The radar indicates they're following, confirmed as she veers left and a detonation occurs off our starboard side.

As the city fast approaches, she puts everything in full reverse stopping us several hundred feet from a building. The other ship avoids a collision by swerving.

She pulls the ship around leading them into the crosshairs, and I hit the first two red buttons marked with the images of missiles.

The enemy craft evades our missiles, but the double explosion causes them to veer too close to a building. They pull up, but it's not enough: an engine clips the tower and their craft careens out of control.

Dr. Oreda gives no warning, accelerating again, and arcing toward the center of New Asta.

Scanning the city, I find Tower Zero, and see we're closing fast on it. She circles along the arced, glass face, and I jump up to exit.

"Hurry. Reinforcements are coming," she warns. "If you can't get them out in the next couple minutes, we will have no choice but to retreat and return with the Quvites."

I shake my head. *I have to save them, no matter the cost.*

In the hold, I reattach the rope to my harness, standing at the open door facing the windows.

The ship levels out as the doctor circles the tower. My heart sinks as she brings the craft to hover yards away from the glass wall.

Drake, in his Tarak body, stands beside my family who are all down on their knees, their hands pressed on the glass in surrender. His evil sharp toothed smirk can be seen as he gloats at his victory. Soldiers stand over my family with rifles pointed at their heads.

I scream in rage, and launch shockwaves at the windows above and below. They shatter and glass falls.

Drake puts his long claws to the window and scratches downward, leaving three distinct marks. A swift swing of his tail causes it to shatter outward. He points his dagger at me and yells.

"If you give up now, Tiberius, I'll make your death swift and spare these people you care so much about." His heavy, rumbling voice cuts through the noise of the engines.

"I'll trade my life for theirs! You can have me when they're safely in the hands of the Vraditi!" I yell, seething.

"You would willingly come back for execution? You're a fool if you think I'd believe that!" Drake waves for someone, and a soldier pulls James to where he is. "You are an enemy of the state. A Quvite supporter and an alkos user. Surrender now, or they too will be counted as insurgents subject to the death penalty."

"Father!"

He'll do it anyway. The moment I turn myself in, we're all dead. I don't want to leave, but Dr. Oreda is right: he'll be forced to hold them as leverage until I turn myself in.

He forces James to his knees, the dagger at his neck, posing in victory like a hunter over prey. Ami and Agatha cry out.

Shaking my head and gritting my teeth, I stare angrily. *"Don't do it!"* I yell. *I have to put on a show for them. They need to believe there is hope. To believe that I'm doing everything I can.*

"Comply and I won't have to!"

"I'll kill you!" I threaten. *"I will tear you limb from limb!"*

"We have to go!" Dr. Oreda yells at me from the pilot's seat. "We have more ships incoming fast! If you want to live and save the people with alkos, we have to go now!"

"Do not fly away!" I turn and yell at her.

"Brother!" he yells, "What's it going to be?"

I turn it back on him. *"Let me take them to the Vraditi and I will return!"*

"No deal!"

Drake begins to draw the blade across James's neck, and blood trickles down. I let my shoulders relax, and my mind gives in.

Maybe I'll have a fighting chance if I leap over there now. An opportunity to push him out the window, maybe? Or buy them enough time to escape? I have to try. I can't let him murder James.

Unexpectedly, Eve leaps to her feet and shoves a soldier. When she hits him, it sends him flying hard enough to break the wall. Other soldiers attempt to grab her, but she grabs them before they can shock her, throwing them out of her way with inhuman strength. She gets a running start, and barrels right into Drake, shoving his massive Tarak form away from James.

This must be her Alkos.

"Don't turn yourself in!" Eve yells. "You know he'll kill us anyway!"

He's only stunned for a moment. My horror intensifies as he picks her up by the head.

She kicks and swings, one hand trying to pry the claws off of her face, the other aiming for his head. A hook lands square on his scaly jaw and knocks a tooth out. It doesn't faze him for long. He walks to the broken window and dangles her outside the building.

"This one first then!"

He drops her.

I imagine screaming is happening, but if there is I can't hear it. Wind rushes past my ears because I've leapt from the ship. There was no conscious thought behind my legs shoving me out an instant before his claws released.

Angling my body downward, I stretch my arms out, knowing the harness will buckle when I reach the end of the coil. Eve reaches for me and I grab her. We pull together as the rope snaps taut. I nearly lose my grip, but she climbs up me.

"Don't let me go!" she yells.

The spool automatically retracts.

Drake peers over the edge of the building. Before we're inside, an explosion rocks the other side of the ship. Drake orders a soldier to the window.

"Death is coming for you, brother!" he roars. "Remember this moment: I gave you the chance to save them!"

The soldier takes aim. There's protest and struggle from my people, but they're subdued with force. Eve's back is to them. I swing my legs, trying to spin us so I can take the bullet. A shot is fired, but I'm not fast enough. Eve's eyes widen. She coughs and spits blood on me. Finding the wound, I scramble to put pressure on it.

Inside the cargo hold, I scream in rage. I pull my hand from her back while laying her down, sticky with her blood.

Misery is returning, but now *I'm* fueling *them*. I unleash the dark tendrils to strangle Drake. An explosion hammers us, buckling the rear paneling. Dr. Oreda pulls away from the building, and he's out of reach.

She banks hard. I'm forced to retract the tendrils and grab Eve, pinning her so she's not thrown from the craft. The side doors start closing on their own but the closest one jams on my rope; it's still open a crack. Even with the wind no longer at a deafening level, I scream at the doctor.

"Go back! I have to save them!"

She ignores me.

"Rain." Eve touches her hand to my cheek. She coughs up more blood. "Rain, I love you."

"Shut up. Don't talk. The pilot is a doctor." I stare into her dark green eyes. Tears stream steadily down my nose and onto her face.

"No. I'm not going to make it."

"I said shut up!"

More explosions threaten to send us plummeting to the ground in a ball of fire, but by some grace, and a lot of luck, we're just barely managing to stay in the air.

This can't be happening!

"...please. I want to die...in peace. Tell me you love me too." She coughs violently.

"Eve, I..."

"I...know you chose Ami. I don't care...never did."

"Eve, I do love you! I do! Please, hang on."

I wipe the blood from her mouth and kiss her as though it would keep her alive a little bit longer. Long enough for us to get her to safety, and get her medical attention.

I cradle her head with one hand and stroke her cheek with the other. I break away when she stops responding to my kiss. She's smiling, but her eyes have become unfocused. Her breathing has stopped. It's too late.

I want to be strong. I want to scream in rage. I want to go back for the others. I want to kill Drake. My mouth runs away from me, confessing feelings I had repressed.

"Eve, please. Eve? I love you! I need you!"

Dr. Oreda pushes the heavy-duty ship to its maximum, the engines reaching a high pitch whine, and the entire craft shudders. An explosion tears the tail section open, and I see New Asta in the distance. We're out over Salvoa.

I hold hard onto Eve, bracing myself against the nearby seats. When there's a moment of calm, I struggle and lift her into a seat to secure her. Disconnecting my tether, I return to the cockpit.

If I can survive being stabbed, she can survive this. Right? What artifact did Evalyn use to heal me? Maybe I can find it!

"Eve needs medical attention!" I yell at her, in denial that she is dead. "Head for the house on the ground!"

She ignores me and focuses on trying to save us.

I feel her lack of attention to my request is unwarranted. "Are you listening to me?!"

Our tail is hammered by three consecutive blows, and she loses control. We plummet toward the ground, spinning. Dr. Oreda flails at the controls, trying to fix it and regain altitude, but her efforts are useless.

"Is your friend secure?" she yells. "We're going to crash!"

I slam the cockpit door shut and sit. My stomach is in knots, a vomitus feeling creeping up my throat. I don't know if it's because of Eve or the spinning. The ground is coming.

The impact will kill us.

We're still alive, for now. In a moment of clarity, I blow out the front window with a shockwave. Grabbing her hands, I toss her onto my shoulder.

"What are you doing?" she yells and pounds my back with her fists.

"Saving your life!"

"What about your friend?"

I climb onto the console, teetering precariously at the edge of the craft. We're at terminal velocity, hesitating will ensure our death.

Several hundred feet from impact, I leap out.

Dr. Oreda hangs onto me for her life. Trying to dive away is fruitless, but a couple shockwaves puts distance between us and the metal husk.

When we approach the bluish grass, I put both palms in front of me and release a broad, padding shockwave. We're launched back upward. Though the initial impact is averted, the shockwave has only altered our course and sent us flying a few hundred feet. I shockwave again to slow our impending collision, but we still hit hard.

Skidding on my back, I absorb the brunt of the force. Dr. Oreda is safe, cradled in my arms. But not for long. Our capture is near.

It was all for nothing. Her death was for nothing!

A dozen ships in pursuit now hover above us. Rappelling down, soldiers surround us and point rifles.

I throw the doctor off of me, and prepare to die before being recaptured. I'm startled when the ground starts exploding around us, grazing the troops.

Larger and faster craft swoop in, a firefight ensuing between the ships from New Asta and oblong black discs. Our would-be captors are distracted, firing their weapons in the air at the black discs.

I seize the opportunity, and send shockwaves at the ground to distract them. There's a thud on the ground, a hum of energy filling the air.

"Rain! You must hurry!" a voice calls me.

When I turn, one of the taller, gold armored Vraditi is waving at me from a teleportation device. I grab Dr. Oreda and haul her toward the glowing interior of the metal cylinder.

He steps aside as we enter. I feel the familiar upward rushing sensation for a moment before being deposited on the bridge of an alien vessel. Pulling the doctor from the cylinder to make way, the Vraditi who rescued us teleports in.

"Shoot them down!" I order.

"We are not here under orders to take lives," he responds. "We are here to save yours."

"Then disable them! I have a friend on the crashed ship!"

"There are no life signs in that vehicle sir," another Vraditi speaks.

"Then retrieve her body!" I yell. "You have to bring her back!"

Several of them, big and small, look from their stations at me, and then to the one who saved us. He shakes his head. The vehicles which were pursuing break off and land, no longer engaging in fighting the Vraditi. And the Vraditi ship ceases firing on them.

"We do not have the ability to bring someone back from the dead."

"Then leaving her there will open her up to being defiled by *them*!" I point at the screen and then to him, pressing my finger into his chest.

"There is a military presence on the ground. I will not engage them for a body. When the area has cleared we can return for her." He shoves my arm away.

"Then I have *living* people who need saving." I shove back. "At Tower Zero in New Asta. If we go now we can kill Drake and save them!"

He puts his large palm on my chest, pushes, and easily sends me to the floor.

"Return to base," he orders.

I launch a shockwave at the tall brute, and he stumbles. The crack of the wave startles everyone, and ignites chatter. A dozen crewmembers jump from their seats, but no one advances. The large one grabs me by the arm and lifts me up, bringing me to his eye level.

"I will not start an inter-species war without permission!"

He throws me into a console like a doll, knocking the wind out of me. I cough and heave, lost in an overwhelming barrage of emotions. Anger, hate, sadness…despair. I lie there.

"Return to base," our savior Vraditi commands again.

"Course laid in," another responds.

Dr. Oreda helps me to my feet, and I watch on the screen as land becomes distant. The lead Vraditi takes a seat in a command chair on a raised platform while the others continue about their business in the three tiered bridge. He fiddles with something, examining a tablet attached to his armrest.

"How did you find me?" I ask harshly.

"We have infiltrated communication and personnel networks. We have been monitoring the situation as it has developed. Our initial attempt to reach you was thwarted as Colonel Tigby intercepted you first."

"Maybe you should have been a bit faster…" I mutter.

"Don't make an enemy of them," Dr. Oreda scolds me. "You're going to need their help."

The lead Vraditi stands back up, and waves for us to follow. A platform descends from the third tier. My family's wellbeing hangs in the balance, but I'm powerless to do anything. I stand up and step on the platform.

With Dr. Oreda, the commander of this ship takes us to the second level and down a hallway. In a minute we're at a conference room at the edge of the ship. There's only a window, a table, and chairs. He motions for us to sit, taking a spot across the table.

"I am Yaqta, the *Onsuer* of this vessel. It is the equivalent of a Captain of one of your ships."

"Some command," I spit. "Can't even save half a dozen people."

"I command this ship and crew," he replies loudly. "But I report to Quva!"

"Then contact him and let him know I have people there!"

"He will know, the same as he will know how insufferable you are being! You should be thankful we saved your life at all! We have risked a diplomatic firestorm coming to your aid!"

"I've got news for you! High Chancellor Drake wants you dead anyway! He wants all of his opposition dead!" I stand and slam my open palms on the table. "He won't give you concessions or mercy!"

"What will happen to me?" Dr. Oreda shifts nervously in her seat, trying to steer the conversation.

"As of now, you are likely regarded as a traitor. You will be offered safe haven with us, as have others who have defected," Yaqta replies.

Slumping into a seat, my mind replays Eve's death over: holding her in my arms, the shot, her blood. Tears well up and I want her back.

Terrible thoughts of everyone else's deaths flood my mind. Images in my head of Drake doing horrible things to them agitates me. I try to convince myself the others are safe.

He can't kill the rest of them now. They're leverage to bring me back. The moment I return, he will kill them to torture me...unless I bring an army to stop him.

I need to stay on Quva's good side, if I'm not already. I can use them to wage war against him. He will die again, and I'll make sure it's permanent.

"You've mastered our language?" I try to distract myself.

"In terms of total population, only a small fraction of Quvites can speak it," Yaqta replies.

"Tell me how all of this started." I cross my arms and stare at the darkened face guard on his helmet.

"I will leave the discussion of diplomatic relations to Quva." He copies my mannerisms.

Dr. Oreda has become pale. She's staring blankly past Yaqta. Though my life has been overturned, hers has been too, and I seek to offer her solace.

"Dr. Oreda, you okay?"

She nods slightly, blinking slowly, but refuses to look at me.

She will need to toughen up; this is the first of the causalities. War is coming.

I compliment her. "You did well to keep us alive. You're an exceptional pilot."

A brief upturn in her lips indicates to me she's not in a complete emotional coma.

Standing, I move to the window. Above us, there's no starlight where it would normally be. Instead, the dark circle of the main ship hovers there with lights glowing all across its exterior. A larger light appears on the underbelly as its doors open for us to enter. Our vessel is but a speck entering the massive entryway to a multi-tier hangar.

I wonder if this is the original migration ship.

Dr. Oreda joins me at the window. We fly over several hundred other vessels similar to this one, and thousands more which are different, parked on the numerous tiers of floating walkways. She's quiet, and I'm unsure if she's marveling at the sight, or in shock. It's a brief reprieve from the oncoming storm.

I turn back to the table. Yaqta hasn't moved. When we dock, he stands and waves me along.

"*Doctor,*" I call, motioning for her to follow.

We step onto the flying platform, and Yaqta pilots us back to the first tier of the bridge and into a new hallway. At the end of the corridor is the exit, and a ramp to a walkway.

A gathering of Vraditi, both large and small, is waiting. A few of them are dressed extravagantly, but despite all of their alien similarities I recognize Quva right away. He brings both arms up to chest level, palms faced toward his body.

I extend my hand and he shakes it firmly.

"There is much to be discussed," Quva says, frowning.

"*You're right, but we won't forget manners.*" I wave my arm to my emancipator. "*This is Dr. Beth Oreda. She helped me to get here, and I owe her my life. She's a defector.*"

"It was fortunate you came across her," he replies and then addresses her. "Are you one of our underground operatives?"

"No," she replies, shaking her head. "But I've had contact with them. Because of my position, I've been quiet about Quvite support, waiting for an opportunity to leave the prison."

"Good, well, let us head to my conference room and we can debrief each other." He turns and waves for us to follow.

"*Why don't you set the doctor up in a room while you and I talk,*" I suggest.

"This is agreeable," he states. "Welcome aboard, Dr. Beth Oreda. I hope your stay is comfortable."

He speaks in his own language to one of the taller members of his party, and they nod, then motions her to follow. She looks at me questioningly and I wave her along to indicate it's safe. She's led across one branch of the massive floating walkway, while Quva and I head in a different direction. A few more glances backward tells me she's nervous.

Quva, and the others with him, step onto a flying platform. I'm the last on before we lift off. We're flown to another set of large doors.

They open to the living quarters of the hive-like ship. The rooms are full, and every walkway is filled. There's almost no space for anything.

Changed since my previous contact with the Vraditi, I can tell their normally emotionless but productive demeanor has been replaced with a depressing lack of energy. The population as a whole feels deflated.

"Is this the same ship I was on before?"

"Yes," he responds.

The platform veers off, and turns into a corridor. In the well-lit, crowded hallway, Quva is forced to slow our speed while everyone moves to the sides. Every one of them we pass looks at me, and though I can't feel them through Misery, it's clear they're desperate.

We enter another open area, the bridge. Its enormous structure enthralls me. An attack vessel could fit in here with room to spare. There are many stations, screens, and personnel keeping the ship running. Though the interior is large, there are only two levels; in the center is a chamber surrounded by a cylinder of crystal. There are at least a hundred chairs surrounding the table inside.

Quva and his entourage move off the platform, and I follow. Inside the conference room, his people settle on one side of the table.

When I try to sit next to them, he directs me to sit on the opposite side by pointing. I hesitate, but make my way over there. With at least a hundred feet in between us, I wonder how we are to talk. However, when Quva speaks, it's like he's next to me.

"It is good to see you are alive."

"Why can I hear you so clearly?"

"The walls were designed to carry vibrations, distributing them evenly through the natural resonance of our home world crystals."

"Fascinating."

"Please, let us begin."

"Do you want to go first or shall I?"

"Tell me what has been happening."

Recounting the near past, I bring him up to current. I make sure I hit the important points: we want to stop the vortex; the Alkosians are being held prisoner simply for existing; one of my own has been killed and the rest are in mortal danger. His eyes widen with shock when I explain Drake is my brother, and that he isn't actually Tarak. After I finish, he waits a few moments.

"We are sad for your situation. We too are in a precarious diplomatic situation. Perhaps we can help one another." He looks down. "How long has High Chancellor Drake been Tarak?"

"His dagger allows him his ability to possess others. At this point, I'm guessing thousands of years. Why he chose to stay a Tarak rather than assume a human identity is unknown, but my guess is that it's a power thing."

"The Tarak's emergence from underground came when we put the artificial atmosphere in, and began reviving the planet. High Chancellor Drake's rise to power is unprecedented, and we were shocked that the Tarak could speak your language. If he has had thousands of years, then their development as a sentient species may not have been their own."

"The Vraditi have been instrumental in reviving Salvoa, whether anyone wants to acknowledge it," I start. "I intend to do everything possible to help you achieve your goal of cohabitation, but my goals must come first due to the lives in danger. We need to start a war to get what we both want."

"It is humorous you should say we have been instrumental. After we planted the Tarak here, we had to transport Humans from Earth." His throat vibrates rapidly in a laugh. "You are the result of our migration program."

"So you stuck around to watch?"

"No. We had left. Our sun went supernova in a deliberate attack." He looks pained as he talks about it. "Our solar system was destroyed. A handful of our vessels survived the destruction, and I led the remnants to this sector of the galaxy."

"I'm sorry about your planet. How long *have* you been here?"

"Over fifteen thousand years, excluding the first visit," he tells me. "When you instructed us from the temporal stasis anomaly not to restore until you reappeared, we had no idea it would be a thousand years later before your past-self would appear."

"Fifteen thousand? So you've seen everything I've been doing?"

"Correct. We have also identified that the temporal anomaly at this point is destabilizing. You are making much larger jumps each time, and we are afraid you will come to a time in which you cannot survive. Potentially to a time before or after the existence of this solar system."

"We've been experimenting with stopping it, and have failed."

"We can assist. We will loan you the technology to cancel the effect."

"You have something like that available?" I give him a perplexed look.

"We have had a significant amount of time to study the effect and initiate a solution, especially after the temporal stasis anomaly."

"If it works, we'll be able to stay, and we can both call this our home. I understand the human underground was attempting to replace the High Chancellors who opposed cohabitation."

"Correct. However there are High Chancellors who cannot be convinced, subverted, or controlled. High Chancellor Drake, for example."

"Even death couldn't stop my brother. It doesn't stop you either."

"We had to bend our ethical standards. Cloning and consciousness transfer were banned prior to the supernova, but empowering new leaders while trying to survive as a species was not a viable option."

Quva lets the conversation, and his attention, stall for a moment while a few Vraditi bustle around outside of the conference chamber.

"Is there no option to remove him peacefully?" Quva returns his attention to me and asks. "He does not appear to see or understand reason."

"No. It's going to come to bloodshed, plain and simple. Even if you choose to take no aggressive actions, I will. Drake will die by my hands for his actions."

A voice resounds, louder than our conversation: "There is an incoming message from the underground of New Asta."

"Thank you, Xera. Connect it to the holographic display," Quva instructs.

"Confirmed. Patching through," she replies.

A three dimensional hologram appears of a man standing on the table at the far end. It's Gregory.

Quva stands and greets him formally, and Gregory responds with his arm to his chest diagonally.

When Quva sits, Gregory makes eye contact with me and nods. "I'm glad you made it. Taking Dr. Oreda as a hostage was the perfect opportunity. Did she make it?"

"She did." I nod back.

"Status report?" Quva interjects.

"Many people died in the escape. Whatever power he yields…" he pauses to point at me. "…is beyond what they are able to control. The tide has shifted in our favor with him as a weapon."

"What is High Chancellor Drake's movement?" Quva taps his fingers on the table.

"He has returned to his personal dwelling with captives in tow, but it is a fortress."

"What was their condition?" I demand.

"The report identifies one of them as wounded. The other three appear to have minimal or no injuries."

My heart sinks and my stomach wrenches inside, but they're okay, as I hoped. *There's still hope.*

I hesitate to ask but my mind insists. "Man or woman?"

"Man, sir."

"How bad is he?" While I'm not happy James is hurt, I am relieved it's not one of the others.

"Unknown. Our operatives haven't been able to infiltrate the High Chancellor's trusted advisors and employees. Best info we have is from a man stationed outside." Gregory shakes his head. "I'm sorry."

With Eve dead, and James wounded, my rage has more than enough fuel, boiling under my skin. I fight Misery's desire to unleash destruction, struggling to keep them under control.

"I want as much intelligence as possible on the fortress," I seethe, gritting my teeth.

"I'll send everything we have. It's heavily fortified. Anti-air artillery, thick perimeter walls, and a legion of men and women ready to defend it." Gregory says.

"Thank you. Once we have received the data we will form a plan," Quva instructs. "I want to do this with minimal casualties."

"Also, send any information on the Alkosians you can," I tell him. "I'll supplement our army with the thing Drake sought to stamp out."

"Understood." Gregory salutes again and his image fades.

Quva sits silently, rubbing his chin and appearing deep in thought.

My patience is in short supply while the others are in danger, but I wait for him to identify our next move.

A beep comes from his tablet and he looks at it. He taps and swipes, and then addresses me. "It looks as though there is a point in the outer perimeter which may be a good insertion point for a ground crew to enter," he tells me.

"Is the fortress large enough to stage a distraction from the air on the opposite side, to pull their resources to one area?"

"Possibly."

"I will lead the mission on the ground," I assert myself.

"Will you be able to operate without letting emotion interfere?" He looks up at me.

"Not likely, but I'm counting on chaos to get me through. I want those Alkosians by my side because they're how I'll boost my power."

He stands and turns to look upon the bridge.

"A small insertion team will not leave much room for Alkosians."

"Then I'll take the most unstable. But we still need to free all of them."

"I also feel it would be better to have someone more objective leading. It would be easier for them to make the call to fall back, should the invasion become impossible," he says without looking at me.

"Understood," I concede unhappily.

Knowing they'll be putting their people at risk too, I appreciate the caution he wants to exert. Even so, I resolve to do everything I can to save my family and kill Drake in retribution for every evil he has done – even if they retreat.

"Let us adjourn for now. You should change your clothes and get some rest." He turns to me. "We will discuss our strategy for the prison later."

"Thank you. Dr. Oreda may be of help with her familiarity of the prison's layout."

Quva pulls one of the taller Vraditi aside and speaks softly while I exit the conference room. I wait, observing the movements of the crew, and listening to a gentle humming ambient noise. The one who was speaking to Quva approaches and motions for me to step onto the platform. Looking back, Quva is deep in discussion with the members of his entourage. I'm whisked away, to the living quarters.

The remnants of a civilization all stuck in here. I can see why they need part of the land they helped revive. They're surviving in this ship, as prisoners.

Up a few levels we come to a stop. The platform docks and the Vraditi guard leads me through the pedestrian traffic to my accommodation.

I'm surprised to find Dr. Oreda is lying on the one bed in the room. Jumping to her feet, she's startled by our entrance, and I look at the guard questioningly.

"What's going on?" she asks, frazzled.

"*I have no idea,*" I tell her while keeping my eyes on the guard. "*Why am I in this room?*"

He holds up a finger to indicate he wants me to wait, and hands me a Trauna translator.

Taking it hastily, I put it in my ear and try again. "*Why am I in Dr. Oreda's room?*"

"Apologies. Space is limited. We must share two or three to a room. You also must share quarters," he replies.

I shake my head to indicate my displeasure.

Turning to Dr. Oreda I explain. "*Space is limited. We have to share.*"

"We can make this space more accommodating, if that is your choice."

"*I need a second bed, and a wall dividing the room between the two beds,*" I instruct.

"As you wish."

The guard motions for Dr. Oreda to stand, and when she does he moves her bed to the far side of the room. He commands the requisition robot tucked in the corner, and initiates my requests.

As it comes to life and starts its process, I think I can feel air being sucked away while it creates. In a few movements, both the wall and another bed are created. Its task done, it retreats to the corner on her side.

The small sense of privacy should put us a little at ease.

"If there is nothing else, I have duties to attend to." The guard stands there, waiting for me.

"We are okay now. Thank you."

I nod, and he takes his leave.

Lying on my bed I stare at the ceiling. I'm exhausted. I know there won't be much reprieve with our attack on New Asta imminent. I toss and turn on the comforter.

I need rest. If we settle here, I'll go away after this is over. Maybe the blood on the hands of my lineage can be forgotten.

This is my fault, and I have to fix it. I have to take responsibility for what I've done, and what I've allowed to happen. I have to take responsibility for my brother because if I had executed him instead of employing him all those years ago, none of this would have happened.

Slamming my fists on the bed, I grunt and grind my teeth. I get even more frustrated when the cushiony blanket and bed absorb the impact.

For what feels like hours I lie there and seethe about being powerless to help the ones I love right now. Reaching a point where the mind is completely overloaded, I stare blankly at the ceiling. My pillow is soaked with tears.

I sense movement as Dr. Oreda peeks around the wall. Not wanting to take my frustration out on her, I shut my eyes to avoid a conversation.

~~~~~~

Nightmares of Eve dying in my arms haunt me.

Her sticky blood. That iron smell. Her lips pressed to mine as I tried to will her to live. Our reunion was brief, and now our separation is forever. The sick feeling in the pit of my stomach is compounded knowing what Drake will eventually do to the rest of them to get at me.

Sensing pressure on the bed, I start awake.

Dr. Oreda is looking after my wounds. She takes her time redoing my bandages, smiling sympathetically when she sees I'm awake.

"Sorry, I didn't mean to wake you," she says softly.

"It's fine. I was having nightmares." My voice is hoarse and I cough. "How's it looking?"

"It'll be healed within another day," she tells me.

"It was deep, wasn't it?" I sit up and rub my head.

"Yes, but thanks to Quvite technology, we have the capability to rapidly heal *non-fatal* wounds."

She emphasized that on purpose. She must have seen the blood and known back on the ship that Eve was as good as dead.

"Good to know. I'll make sure every wound I inflict on him is fatal," I retort. "Does it heal limbs torn from the body?"

She looks away, disturbed at my morbid question. Regardless of her reaction, my determination to obliterate Drake stays the same. My heart aches, wishing I had even one of my family members to mourn with. Spinning my legs off the bed, I sit up.

Dr. Oreda looks at me again and breaks the silence.

"Quva is sending an escort to take us to a dining hall. Apparently they're holding a ship wide banquet because of your safe arrival."

"A waste of effort, but I suppose it would be rude if I skip it."

"You might want to clean up, and make new clothes," she points at my lack of a shirt, and my torn pants.

"Attendant," I call.

I hear the robot whir to life on the other side of the room. It floats to my area, and hovers next to my bed, waiting for my command.

"Identify me and replicate the same clothing I had last time I was here."

"Confirmed," it acknowledges.

Materializing in front of me is a familiar set of clothing; Ami's designs replicated down to the orange chrysanthemum embroidered on the right shoulder. I smile sadly while looking at it.

Taking the clothes into the purifier room, I disrobe and hop into the chamber for a cycle. When it's finished I dress in the new clothes and shoes, no longer feeling like a wild animal.

Just as I step out into the main room, a tall Vraditi enters. "Come," he beckons.

I wave for Dr. Oreda to follow me out. A platform is waiting for us. He pilots to the bowels of the ship, dropping dozens of levels to the bottom floor.

Looking at the massive interior reminds me how small I really am. Dr. Oreda also admires the immense view and I find a reason to break the silence.

"I once stayed with the Vraditi. Humans didn't exist on the planet then."

"What?" she asks, looking severely perplexed.

"Were you informed of the temporal anomaly on the ground?"

"The department heads heard of your capture, and the laws you've been charged with violating."

"When I first met the Vraditi, I'm guessing it was a few hundred thousand years ago. Large scaly beasts roamed the land."

She appears to ponder this for a moment before changing the subject. "What is the plan for people with alkos?" she asks.

"My plans or theirs?"

"Aren't they the same?"

"Not necessarily. I'm going to free the Alkosians and rally them to save my family and kill Drake."

We veer left, entering a wide corridor near the edge of the living quarters and speed up. Following the curve of the hull around, we reach an opening and emerge into an enormous stadium-like dining hall, which looks as though it could seat the entire population of the ship. A flood of Vraditi flows steadily in from all directions, and take seats. The chatter is low, but still fills the room with a noisy hum.

At the far end of the room, on the second floor, are a couple long tables on raised platforms to overlook the whole dining hall. Both large and small Vraditi gather there, distinguished by their extravagant robes and cloth hoods shimmering in the light. Gold tassels dangle freely from the shoulders and back of the hoods as they move and collect themselves at their seats. Next to Quva are two spots which have been left open.

Our escort docks near them. Dr. Oreda and I make our way to the seats and sit. I nod in respect to our host, and he responds in the same way.

"Quva, may I requisition a Trauna for Dr. Oreda?" I ask quietly.

Reaching into his robe, he produces one. I hand it to the doctor, and she places it in her ear.

Quva stands and raises his long, thin arm with his hand open. The murmuring ceases, and complete silence falls over the hall. He waits for a moment while picking up a glass with clear liquid in it, and speaks with enthusiasm.

"The day is coming, my people, where we will be liberated and not confined to this vessel any longer. You will be able to freely bask in sunlight once more, to taste the fresh air of a planet, to feel the soft grass under your feet, to play in the waves of an ocean." He pauses for breath and continues with just as much energy. "But in order for us to achieve this, you may be called to stand against those whom we lent our technology, but refuse to honor the commitment to share Salvoa!

"We are not naturally a race of violence, but we offered a fair trade to the inhabitants of Salvoa, and have been denied our rightful inheritance. We must stand up for ourselves, and there are those who would help honor the original agreement.

"You have heard his story. You have watched the adventure of his life. He has had his struggles, and made tough decisions to help better this world and protect the integrity of the timeline. Today *he* is here! Rain the Time Warden! And he will help us defeat High Chancellor Drake and free us!"

The entire assembly bursts into a deafening cheer. They stand and wave their arms back in forth in excitement.

The moment overwhelms me. Quva grabs my arm. I'm surprised when he pulls me to my feet. Holding my hand up, I wave nervously while they continue to cheer.

They're counting on me. An entire race. No pressure. But I suppose they need the morale boost.

Is this Asta all over again? My brother does evil, I'm put in a position of power, I kill leaders who won't conform. It's who I am, isn't it? Can I resist my urge to control it all?

"Rain is our mediator of choice between *our* people and *his*, as elected by the hierarchy, and with the support of the underground movement!" he bellows, then turns to me and returns his voice to its normal level. "Please, give them a few words of encouragement."

I let out half a laugh anxiously as they quiet and wait for me to speak. My mind races with the things I might say to comfort or encourage them. I speak with authority, as I've done as King in the past. It's familiar and intoxicating.

"*A great error has occurred between our two people. While there are those who want to grant you the right to cohabitate on Salvoa as it was agreed, they are being repressed by an evil so great he has transcended time itself. I'm here to tell* you I'll right that wrong!" I slam my fist on the table, causing silverware to clatter. "High Chancellor Drake, and those who support his treacherous regime, will fall! I swear my life on it! You showed kindness to our people, and I'll make sure the kindness is repaid! We will be victorious!"

The crowd returns my enthusiasm, and roars to life once more, cheering and stomping. Turning, I see even the Vraditi council members have erupted in applause and shouting – all but Quva who nods at me smiling.

He raises his arm up to quiet them. When they've become silent, he speaks. "For now, eat, be joyful and know that we are not alone in this struggle!"

He returns to his seat and I, too, sit down. Carts are wheeled in from the side of the room, stopping shy of the two dignitary tables.

Quva points at them. "Though our attendant robots take care of the daily needs, there is a group of my people who continue to perfect recipes. This food has not been replicated, but taken from animals and plants of various planets, and bred onboard."

Observing the servers coming down the line, they arrange each plate with food. When the first cart approaches I recognize the teardrop leaves of the Io plant. The next cart has a steaming pile of steaks, but they smell nothing like any meat I've ever eaten. By the time the procession of carts passes, I have been given a little of everything.

With my large plate filled, I start with the meat, cutting into its tender flesh. When I put it to my tongue I'm stunned by its spicy taste and soft texture. The flavor rolls around my mouth and it's so delicious I shovel more in.

Dr. Oreda looks disgusted, a minimalist plate in front of her. She has opted not to eat the meat.

"Did you not want any meat?" I smile.

"No. I try to avoid meat under most circumstances," she replies politely.

"Quva, what is this?"

"*Ralu*, an amphibious reptile found in the oceans of a planet we encountered long ago. They have been specially bred for millennia."

"It's delicious!" I shove a couple bites in my mouth.

I taste everything, and have my likes and dislikes. I'm torn between the spicy, savory Ralu meat, and the Io as my favorite. A hard bread, which tastes the way grass smells, comes in as my least-favored. Though I eat as much on my plate as possible, there's too much.

"Will they be upset if I don't finish?" I look to Quva, hoping I won't offend.

"No, they are delighted for their food to be eaten. It is enough for them."

Sitting back, I relax. As the food settles in my stomach, I listen to the clinking and shuffling of dishes. The murmuring of conversation has returned. I look and find Quva resting his eyes.

"Do you think I could schedule time on the observation deck? I need a peaceful place to think. I'm sure Dr. Oreda would appreciate the view also."

"I will arrange it with your escort." He opens his eyes, taps a few times on his tablet, and returns to resting.

"Thank you."

I'm tapped on my shoulder and see our escort has returned. I stand and Dr. Oreda follows. He takes us back to the living section, and ascends to a port in the ceiling. The doors open and allow us entry to the garden.

The magnificent, glowing garden comes into view. She gasps in wonder.

Looking straight up, I am in awe of the view of our planet. From this perspective, I'm looking up and down at the same time. I trace the clouds with my eyes while stepping off the platform. The Vraditi stops me while Dr. Oreda wanders off.

"I have duties to attend to. There are panels along the wall you can use to contact me. When it asks for input, tell it to 'retrieve Perat'. It will notify me, and I will return at my earliest convenience," he tells me.

"Thank you, Perat."

I turn back to the garden. Others have come up here after the banquet also, and I've lost sight of Dr. Oreda in their midst. I let her be, and make my way around slowly.

Nodding at passing Vraditi, I find that they can't help but stare at me with anticipation and hope in their eyes. I put on a good front and smile, despite the exhilaration of dinner wearing off, and the dark reality setting back in.

Eve, I wish I could tell you how sorry I am. We didn't have enough time. I chose Ami, but I loved you too. It hurts...so much.

I want them to be okay. My family. After all the time alone, I was glad to have them back. I can't fail them.

If Drake thinks he can hurt them and get away with it, I'll show him the error of his ways. But no matter how much I hurt him, no matter how painful I make his death, the damage he's already done cannot be undone. We can only move forward.

At the far side I come to the grassy spot I'd visited with the girls before. I hope to meditate on the situation and how to defeat Drake. But the spot is already taken by a male and female Vraditi.

Hearing, or perhaps sensing me, they turn and look. The male holds his arm out to the open grassy area next to them as an invitation.

"I'm not imposing, am I?"

"No. We welcome you," the female replies cheerfully.

"Thanks." I sit next to them and stare into space at the multitude of stars. "I've only been here once, but this is my favorite spot."

"When you were here last, you had several companions, did you not?" he asks.

"Yes, I did." Hiding my sadness is impossible.

"Are they not here?"

His probing hits home and my heart aches. "High Chancellor Drake is keeping them captive until I turn myself in."

"Are you considering that as an option?" the female enquires.

"I almost did, or rather I almost fought him, but we were attacked mid-air, and the person who came with me saved my life. But I will not abandon you."

"We thank you." He puts his hand on my shoulder and then lets it drop back to his lap.

Lying in the grass, I place my arms behind my head for support and gaze at the deceptively peaceful world below. As I look upon the surface, the sun is disappearing around the other side, as we maintain a synchronous orbit above my continent. Night falls across the planet.

~~~~~~

I nap and wake with a start.

Dr. Oreda is staring out the window. Looking at me, she smiles weakly, and returns her gaze upward. "The odds are stacked against you," she says. "They'll be ready for you."

"I have no choice. People I love are in danger. All because I couldn't deal with my brother in the past. Even if they were safe, I still have an obligation to clean up my bloodline's mess." I sigh.

"I admire the dedication and strength you have in helping the Alkosians and Quvites while your family is at risk," she says softly.

Is that supposed to be comforting?

"Honestly, if you hadn't pulled away, I would have jumped into the building and either killed Drake or died there. It may have been better if it was both."

I stand and hold out my hand. When she takes it, I pull her to her feet and we walk the garden. Passing glowing trees and bushes to where the window meets the metal wall, I locate one of the panels Perat mentioned. When it springs to life I call for him.

We head back to the platform entrance, and he is just arriving. We board the disk, and Perat drops into the living quarters. A few minutes of travel brings us to our room. Before disappearing, I turn to him.

"Thank you for your assistance, Perat."

"You are welcome."

Inside, Dr. Oreda has already retreated behind her wall. I knock on it and wait for her to reply.

"Yes?"

"I didn't want to barge through. I'm going to use the purification chamber," I announce.

"Thank you for knocking. Go ahead."

In the purifier room I remove my clothes, and climb into the chamber. Gel fills it and anxiety overcomes me. Visions of my brother haunt me, and I fear what he's doing to them.

James. I can't imagine how Agatha and Ami are feeling right now. I hope he will be okay. Drake has probably been aggressive with them because I didn't comply. But his life is probably not in danger yet. I haven't angered Drake enough.

But Eve. They saw her shot, but they don't know she's dead. They've likely assumed the worst though.

Why does it ache this much? Eve was a friend, so why do I love her? I chose Ami

*and I want to be with her. I want to marry her. Why does Eve's death make me feel
I lost the love of my life?*

*I'm sure they aren't taking it well, but poor Emma. Even having grown up, she's
still innocent - she's the most innocent of us all.*

I have to get them back safely. I have to fix this.

The cleansing cycle is finished too soon, and I contemplate starting it
again for the relaxing massage the jets provide. But I'm dwelling too much,
and I decide against it.

Dressed again, I return to the main room. The lights are dim, and Dr.
Oreda's asleep.

I collapse onto my bed, my face smashed in the pillow.

~~~~~~

My muscles spasm, and I'm awake.

There's little light. A sense of dread falls on me and I stand in haste as
if it would give me a better view.

Peeking around the corner, the doctor is still asleep. Outside our room,
the ship circulates with life, as it has been. Nothing is standing out.

I curse myself for getting worked up over nothing and return to the
bed. I'm irritated because I'm awake. I'm not hungry, I don't need to use
the bathroom, and my temperature feels fine.

Still, something woke me. I'm tense.

Is my imagination playing tricks on me, or is there's something amiss?

Desperately trying to go back to sleep, my mind pummels me with
unpleasant thoughts.

*Will I be able to kill Drake? The Tarak were difficult in numbers, but they
weren't developed. His inhabiting one grants him the strength of the body and the
cunning of his mind.*

*When I confront him, I expect he'll keep them front and center. He'll make me
watch anything he has planned for them. He's sadistic.*

How do I deal with him even if he harms them?

*I wonder, do the Vraditi have a method to block my memories so I can act
unhindered? Can I forget about them long enough for me to kill him? Can I forget
Eve?*

I laugh to myself at the irony of such thoughts, of wanting to give up my memories. My laughter turns to tears, and I bury my head under my pillow.

Why is my life complicated?

Why couldn't I keep them from harm?

Why couldn't I have died in the woods that day?

Who am I that I'd get a second chance to destroy people's lives?

~~~~~~

A knocking sound wakes me, and I pull my head from underneath the pillow. The room is bright and I squint.

Xera's there. My body aches and I'm slow to respond.

"I apologize for the intrusion." She smiles at me while adjusting her silver robe.

"I'm sure I've been sleeping too long anyway."

"Sixteen hours," she states.

"I could sleep a hundred more." I run my hand through my long hair, trying to comb it so it won't be as wild.

"I was sent by Quva to tell you there is a meeting in a half hour, and to bring you there personally."

"What about Dr. Oreda?"

"She is being given a tour. She will assist in non-essential medical functions," she replies.

"She won't be at the meeting though?"

"Negative. Though she assisted you in escaping, she was not part of our network. We are taking precautions to ensure the success of the missions."

"You suspect her of being a spy."

"We are trusting to a fault, as you are aware. Because she aided you, she has some credibility, but we would rather she help in capacities other than primary functions," she states as a matter of fact. "Shall we go?"

Standing, I slip my shoes on and move to the doorway. Outside my door and docked at the edge of the walkway, my 'chariot' awaits.

"I've noticed most everyone else walks, but I've been carted around on these platforms. Why?"

"The lifts are reserved for several uses. Emergencies, key personnel, special dignitaries. You fall under the categories of 'key personnel' and 'special dignitary'."

We head down several levels, and into the large corridor leading to the command center. She takes her time because we're early; we're the first ones to the conference room.

"Sit anywhere." She sits where Quva had sat before.

My stomach grumbles.

"Could I have something to eat? I haven't eaten since the banquet."

"What would you like?"

"A sweet pastry. Surprise me." I smile and sit next to her.

"I have just the thing."

She taps on her tablet and a round flaky and glazed pastry materializes in front of me.

It doesn't take me long to devour it, and I lick my fingers for the remaining sugar.

About fifteen minutes pass and Quva, with an entourage of other well-dressed Vraditi of all sizes, enters and takes a seat next to Xera. The seats fill quickly and more enter than there is seating for. Personal conversations continue for a few moments before the group quiets and Quva takes the reins.

"Welcome, my fellow Quvites and our comrade Rain. We have, in the immediate future, three separate objectives which will lead to one overall victory. These campaigns require a large amount of coordination, and preparations will begin as soon as we conclude here." He taps on his tablet.

"The first mission is to deploy our temporal negation module."

A holographic image of the house appears in the center of the table, showing it as it currently sits now with the energy barrier set up by Colonel Tigby.

"We will infiltrate the perimeter under the cloak of night with a single stealth ship, and a small team led by Mazaq. The angle of attack will be hidden from the sight of New Asta."

As he talks, a projected image appears depicting the stealth ship. Sleek and compact, it appears to be smaller than the size of the house, enough for a pilot and a few troops. It lands, and several holographic figures depart to break through the barrier.

"We will keep operatives to a minimum for this particular incursion, however, any and all human troops found within and near the house shall be taken into custody for the time being. They will be released when High Chancellor Drake has been usurped."

"Time will be limited. Expect attention from New Asta when their soldiers do not check in. Rain, you will designate an area for the module within your home: somewhere obscure if possible. Mazaq will arm it and the anomaly will be nullified."

He pauses for a few moments. The image of the house disappears, and a new hologram is displayed. I recognize it as the prison. Though part of the structure is above ground, the cells are all under the base of the floating city, dug deep into the rock.

"The second incursion will be to free those with alkos, or otherwise known as Alkosians. High Chancellor Drake has abused our technology and sought to oppress and exterminate them, because they may have the ability to threaten his regime. That which was created to identify and negate abilities while aboard our ship for safety is now being employed to imprison them unjustly."

"This mission will be difficult. We need to break into the prison, release the inmates, and escape. Gregory will be exposed in the process, and will escape with one of our teams. Expect heavy resistance from New Astan soldiers, and it would not be a surprise if Colonel Tigby or High Chancellor Drake join the skirmish. Because of the degradation of the Alkosians mental conditions, we will employ dampening technology to ensure everyone's safety."

The image plays the scenario with several larger vessels flying in. A few dock on the landing area, and Vraditi jump out and fight with soldiers on the deck.

"Gregory will make sure he is deployed topside to give us access via the service elevator, but he will not be part of the first fight. His cover and safety must be ensured until the first wave is dealt with. One group will enter the complex and release prisoners while the rest stay to defend."

The holographic forces are victorious, and a group moves into the hallway where the elevator is.

"We are unsure exactly what resistance to expect inside, so we must stay alert. Volunteers are requested for this mission, with the exception of Mazaq as the appointed lead, as there may be casualties. It is our intent to free the unjustly imprisoned people. We hope some may be willing to assist in the attack on High Chancellor Drake."

"Mazaq's team will carry a mobile teleportation device to send the prisoners directly to vessels still in flight. When they are aboard, we will assess their health, mental status, and alkos to ensure the safety of everyone. Reinforcements will be sent as needed to combat any air mounted defense."

Once again he pauses, and the images change from the prison to the layout of a massive structure. It's not a skyscraper like the other buildings in New Asta, but it is long and wide, surrounded by guard towers placed uniformly on a massive outer wall. The fortress itself looks to be three or four stories tall, with watch towers attached.

You built a castle. This is exactly what I expected of you, brother.

"The final mission is to remove High Chancellor Drake from his seat of power. With his removal, we can move forward with peaceful cohabitation of Vraditi, Humans, and Tarak. We have never wanted to take the offensive to enforce the agreement, but the oppression is worsening. Given enough time, there is a high percentage of High Chancellor Drake drafting the entire planet against all who would oppose him."

"Our attack on his fortress will be unlike the others. Based on the first two attacks, the fortress will be readied in anticipation of our assault. We will attack in broad daylight and employ a distraction."

New animations appear. At the east wall, five large attack vessels and five drop ship vehicles approach and engage with an estimated number of New Asta's own. Violating the airspace above the fortress, the carrier ships unload, and forces fight in air and on the ground. Anti-aircraft cannons fire from several locations on the estate, and are subsequently targeted. The hologram spins to the opposite wall and a team approaches.

"The goal is to avoid lethal force as much as possible. The mission of the attack team is simply to distract and disable in order to reach High Chancellor Drake. But as you can see, the distraction will be full scale. During the distraction, a small ground team should be able to breech and invade nearly unhindered. Mazaq will have Mission First Command of the ground forces, with Rain in Mission Second Command. Their team will be given a Harmonic Resonance Crystal Explosive, devised after Rain's own ability to vibrate his alkos through our crystals. It will tear a hole into the wall at the weak point designated by Gregory. Once inside the goal is to locate and eliminate the High Chancellor."

Quva turns to me for a moment. "Would you share your thoughts?"

After being put on the spot the other day in the dining hall, I'm not surprised or unprepared. "Sure."

I stand to address them, and place my arms behind my back like I've seen commanders do. It always directed attention to them, and I seek to have all eyes on me.

"Drake is cunning, and his will to survive knows no bounds. He's died, possessed an artifact, and came back from the dead to possess a Tarak. He is not to be underestimated, ever. Expect that if you come into contact with him, you'll be fighting for your life. He'll be ready, despite the distraction."

I continue. "As long as I draw breath, I must be the one to strike the killing blow: he is my brother and it falls to me to right his wrongs. What I need is protection getting to wherever he is. I don't know his true power, but he *is* an Alkosian so we need to be prepared. With other Alkosians under our direction, I hope we can mitigate losses."

"I want the freedom of the Vraditi and Alkosians, but it cannot be achieved without sacrifice. I'll be putting my life on the line same as anyone out there, because I am committed to the cause. If I fall in battle he must still die, and the dagger he keeps must be destroyed."

I return to my seat and look to Quva. He nods at me with a thin, solemn smile, before continuing with the battle plans.

"We have mapped the interior as best we can with scans, however sections of the complex are similar in size, shape, and layout. There are four rooms we have identified as potential places High Chancellor Drake is likely to be."

The image changes. The walls become transparent, and four rooms around the five story castle illuminate, flashing red. Two are on the third level, one on the second, and another on the first are highlighted.

The one on the bottom, which I anticipate is the throne room, is where

I would expect to find him. The second floor room is directly above the first, but is not easily accessed through the hallways. The third and fourth are at opposite ends of the building lengthwise, and sit centerline with rooms and hallways around them.

"With limited information coming in about this location, we are forced to assume he could be anywhere in the complex. But these four will be the first objectives to clear. If the first level is clear, the team inside will proceed up the staircase in the grand hall to the next, and repeat the same steps until all four rooms have been cleared, or High Chancellor Drake is found. If he is not found at all—"

I cut him off. "I apologize for interrupting, but he'll be there. Once he realizes what's happening, he won't miss the opportunity to finally kill me. He won't hide from me." My confidence resounds.

"Then it is settled. Our first mission launch is in four hours. Preparations are to begin now. Dismissed," Quva commands.

Everyone files out hurriedly. In a minute's time four people are left. Quva, Xera, myself, and one of the taller Vraditi. The taller one doesn't have a helmet on, and I finally see what they look like. His head is blockier than the shorter members of his race: his wide chin juts out a little, his four eyes closer together. He's covered with tattoos which remind me of war paint. Spirals of red and orange symmetrically wrap his eyes, and around the back of his head.

"This is Mazaq, your Mission First Command," Xera introduces him. "You will follow him. You will be given leeway on the mission, but remember that the Quvites are under his direction."

"It's a pleasure to meet you."

"The pleasure will be mine if we succeed. Be ready to die for the betterment of the Quvites," he says brashly, but I can tell he isn't trying to be rude.

"I will follow your lead and do my part to ensure success is exactly what happens," I return, leaning back in my chair.

He nods at me and stands up. "I will meet you in the docking bay in two hours."

He stands and leaves. The three of us sit in silence: me with nothing to do, and the other two busy working on their tablets. I have too much time to think. My thoughts turn against me.

Were it not for my brother's actions, I would not have been out there that day, but the opposite can be applied. If it weren't for my actions bringing him back from banishment, I would not have been there.

Under either circumstance I wouldn't have met Agatha and Ami - or be time traveling. And this wouldn't have happened. Drake might still exist though, if he were to possess the dagger.

"So, 'Quvites'?"

"We are still 'Vraditi' as a species, but because of Quva's leadership over the survivors, it was voted that our group would be called 'Quvites'," Xera responds.

"Rain, I have things to attend to. Whenever you are ready, Xera will take you to the docking bay. I am going to head to the second level of command and begin coordinating." Quva stands and rests a hand on my shoulder comfortingly.

"*You will have a world to call home soon. This I promise.*"

"Thank you for your dedication and friendship." He takes his leave.

Xera stays next to me, working diligently.

Crossing my arms, I simply sit and observe the movements of the crew outside the conference room as they go about their duties. They move efficiently, and I hope it leads to smooth missions.

I hate letting them sit in Drake's clutches while I take care of other things, but this is logical, I guess, with the exception of stopping the time travel.

~~~~~~

"Would you like to head to the docking bay now? We are nearing the two hour mark Mazaq allotted," Xera asks.

"*Already?*" I rub my face.

"You appeared to be deep in thought for a significant amount of time." She stands and moves to leave.

"*I suppose.*" I stand and follow her out.

We find our platform has been taken. Without missing a step, Xera continues into the long hallway leading away from the command center. Because of the crowd, it takes much more time to cover the distance on foot. On reaching the living quarters, I can barely make out the docking bay doorway.

With the distance, there's no way we'll make it on time.

Xera is unconcerned, her attention still on her tablet. I want to speak up, but I follow. A platform descends to our level, and the pilot relinquishes control of it to her without a word. She turns to me and smiles, while stepping backward onto it. The platform whisks us away toward the far end of the chamber.

The bay door opens moments before we reach it, revealing the fleet. Xera flies to a grouping of small ships, which have a single door at the aft ends of their egg shaped bodies. Two engines attached to the aft end of each craft rotate up and down, with support staff checking their movement.

Mazaq is there with one other taller Vraditi, and a few shorter.

A heavy looking device sits on the deck. Cylindrical in nature, as has been the theme with other Vraditi designs, it appears to be solid metal with a small keypad on the top, and handles on opposite sides.

Mazaq appears to be in mid-briefing already. When he sees me, he glares. "*You* were supposed to be here two minutes ago," he states, angrily. "If you cannot be more efficient I suggest you stay behind and let us accomplish the mission."

"Mazaq, dear, relax. His lateness is not his fault. Our lift was removed from the bridge, and we had to wait for a new one," Xera explains in a cheery tone, touching his arm softly.

He looks at her, then back to me, unsatisfied with her response.

I keep silent so as to not intrude, standing at attention with the others already in a half circle formation.

Xera pilots the lift away, and he picks up where I assume he left off. "Our mission is to drop to the surface, infiltrate the location, subdue and apprehend combatants, and plant the module. This is in and out in as little time as possible. For security, the module will be secured to its setting, and a field erected to avoid detection. Quva has instructed the use of non-lethal measures unless absolutely necessary."

"Your suits are inside. I want everyone geared up in five," he commands.

Following the line, there's one suit hanging on the wall not sized for either a tall or short Vraditi – it's clearly mine. Pulling it down, it's heavy, but it moves freely. Its outside is soft, but woven in is a layer of material with the consistency of flexed muscles.

The Vraditi have the advantage getting into their suits over me, as the majority of them are already bare-skinned. Those that aren't strip down right on deck to change, dumping their clothes into a trunk. While it may be normal for them, I'm unaccustomed to undressing in front of others. Turning to face a wall, I hastily strip down to my underwear and jump into the one-piece.

One of the crew closes up the back for me. Though the collar comes up and over my neck to the base of my skull, it feels loose while everyone else's is form-fitting. I tug on it in the loose areas wondering why mine doesn't fit right. The problem is remedied when he touches my shoulder and the whole suit contracts around me. I cough as it squeezes around my neck.

When it no longer feels like I'm choking, I copy the others by dumping my clothes and grabbing a helmet. Though the visor looks restricting from the outside, I can see well out of it, with unhindered visibility.

Mazaq and his tall counterpart haul the temporal negation module onto the ship. Metal clanks against metal when they set it down, and they take their seats. Everyone else, including me, straps themselves in, and the final Vraditi boards and heads to the pilot's chair. She takes control, the door closes, and we lift off.

My attention is fixed on the window. The pilot takes us toward the hangar doors and my anxiety builds. We enter the blackness of space and into the shadow of the ship as the doors close behind us.

Orbiting in place while night falls on the continent below, I realize everything will be over in a relatively short time.

This is it, where the end begins. It won't be long. I'll save the surviving members of my family. We'll lay Eve to rest, and finally be able to move on from the house, time traveling, and my feud with my brother.

The world has suffered enough because of my family, and finally it will be able to move on from our legacy of destruction.

The longer we sit in space, the more my anxiety level rises. An urgency to get going nags at me until the thrusters kick to life and I see the planet moving beyond the window.

My heart beats faster and harder. Our side of the planet, now cloaked in darkness, has reached the conditions needed to complete the first mission. We drop into the atmosphere.

Here we go...

~~~~~~

4 CULMINATION

Plummeting, gravity takes hold of the ship and our bodies. I slide forward in my seat an inch, but the harness holds me.

The ship nears the ground and I fear for a brief moment the pilot won't pull up. Moments before impact, the ship levels out. The window shows a technical display, outlining everything outside.

Off in the distance, flying above the enormous mountain, sits New Asta; hopefully unaware we have made our way planetside. A small dot on the screen pops up, outlining a structure on the ground. The house becomes visible through yellow highlighting on screen, along with the energy barrier highlighted in red. On approach, the pilot maneuvers to ensure we are flying low, and that the house blocks us from New Asta's line of sight.

Coming up on it, I flex my hands and stretch my arms. We're not on the ground yet and the door is opening. Our landing is swift as the ship spins around, and our team jumps up to disembark. Their stealth is commendable as they file out. Mazaq and his counterpart follow after me. There's a blip on my visor, and a tone in my helmet.

"New Asta communication frequencies blocked," says a voice inside my helmet.

"Confirmed," Mazaq replies.

The first Vraditi to the wall puts his hand on one of the spheres. Electricity arcs and there's a low hum. Smoke rises, and two sections of the barrier fall, allowing entry into the yard. The soldiers inside are alerted and the eight of us quickly engage the four of them. A fifth joins from the living room door.

Each of them has a firearm leveled at us.

As I leap aside to dodge, the team jumps forward head first, apparently not worried in the slightest as the guns fire. Running around to the side while the soldiers are engaged, I flank one. My legs carry me at an inhuman speed – by the time he notices me it's too late to do anything.

I tackle him and, because my strength is enhanced thanks to the suit, we're launched into another of his unit. The three of us collapse in a heap. With swift and minimal motions, the others are subdued. I stand, and the New Astan soldiers are hit with stunners, incapacitating them. The five men lie there in a pile while I move to Mazaq's position.

He appears displeased with my efforts. "Move them onto the ship, now. Make sure they are properly restrained," he commands the others. "Rain, with me – we need a secure place to mount this."

"The basement."

I wave for him to follow me into the house. Inside, I'm struck by emotion I had hoped to avoid. I can imagine life in the house, the banter, the company. I had been home for less than a day, and then was ripped away again. But it's empty. Devoid of the people I want to be with.

I hesitate inside for a moment. Looking back, the two tall Vraditi struggle to push the module through the small doorway without damaging it. It jams and they have no choice. The doorframe cracks as they shove. The floorboards creak under their feet.

"Can I help?"

"No. Move on and show us to the basement."

In the kitchen, I hold the swinging door open for them. It's no use. Mazaq reaches up and rips the door from its hinges, and slams it down. In the silence of the house, the cracking echoes. While trying to keep the module from hitting the floor, he over corrects and stumbles backward into the table. It buckles under his weight, and the leg gives out.

He stands back up with no remorse.

I flip the light switch on in the stairwell and head down. The wood creaks and cracks under their weight, and I fear the steps will collapse. The boards bow, but somehow they remain intact. Mazaq grumbles, and I pull open the final door.

"Last one."

I lead them in, and they set the module down. Mazaq fiddles with the buttons on top, and the other leaves. I watch as he works.

"Get out and back to the ship. We do not have much time before they realize their men have gone silent," he commands.

"Will this be safe here?"

A mechanical humming comes from within the module, there's grinding into the foundation underneath it. I step back and look at Mazaq for answers while he presses a few more buttons. A blue illuminated field appears, and the module becomes invisible to the naked eye. Where it sits, there appears to be nothing – I can see the shelves through it. I bend to examine closer and there's no trace it was ever there.

"I said go!" he yells.

It startles me enough to get me moving. At the top of the stairs, I hear him coming. In the kitchen, a gleam on the island counter catches my eye. Grabbing for it, my palm grasps the hilt of my sword, and I smile. With the extra strength provided by the suit, it feels like a toy. Malicious thoughts of dismembering Drake with it come to mind.

Outside, the craft is barely visible against the blackness. On my approach, I hear a buzzing. Our team and captives are already strapped in. The pilot appears to be preparing for lift off, as several blips appear on her radar. New Astan ships are on their way.

"Hurry and sit," she commands me.

I sit and strap in, holding the flat of my sword between my knees.

"Where is Mazaq?" she asks.

"He told me to go. He was supposed to be right behind me," I respond.

There's a loud crash inside the house, and I fear he's caught. But the blips on the radar, four of them, haven't reached us. Because our ship is small, I expect we'll get away unimpeded. The pilot barely lifts off, ready to go the moment Mazaq is on board.

He tears out of the house and thuds across the yard. The enemy appears over the top of the house, and fires on his position.

He leaps and dodges to avoid being hit, and continues on a steady course toward the ship's opening. A missile blast shakes us. He climbs aboard and the pilot lifts off.

We start a high-speed exit while Mazaq closes the door and straps in.

Darting through the air, we skim the foliage. Missiles appear on the radar, and she executes evasive maneuvers. She's extraordinary, and we're undamaged. The four ships pursue. No matter how fast we go they keep pace.

The ship angles straight up. We speed toward the higher levels of the atmosphere. A rear view image comes up on the left side of the window to show they are still following. The ship veers hard right, and another explosion detonates off the side of the ship. The hum of the engine on that side dies, sending us into a free falling spiral.

"Mayday, mayday! Stealth-One is hit," the pilot reports. "We are descending back to Salvoa."

"Understood. Do you have control of your vehicle?" the voice over the communications channel responds.

"Negative. I am attempting to regain control, but we will not be able to evade. Requesting evacuation measures."

"Understood. We are showing a range of hills nearby. If you can regain control, attempt to steer there and land. Avoid capture, and we will send a rescue crew at first light."

"Appreciated. Stealth-One out."

Gripping my sword tightly, I hope to prevent it from impaling someone when we crash. My stomach is in knots, but despite imminent death, the pilot remains calm and collected. Her lengthy arms fly about, moving her hands across the screens, and maneuvering the controllers on her chair. The stalled engine starts, and our corkscrew descent is halted. We level out, and she races toward the hills in the distance. The four combatant ships are still in pursuit.

Her maneuvering is enough to avoid another impact from incoming missiles, but the left engine threatens to quit again. It sputters, and our speed drops.

When the engine finally quits for good, we're above the hill range. It's much larger and wider than I anticipated. Plummeting, this time from a much more survivable fall, we spin like a coin and crash. My body is thrown forward, but the harness does its job.

The door to the ship pushes the aft end up, and the Vraditi troops unlatch and jump free. Throwing my harness off, I move to pull our captives free, but Mazaq stops me.

"Evacuate now! Set the ship to self-destruct on a one minute timer! Go!" he orders everyone.

"These men will die!" I argue.

"This is not a debate! Stay and die *with* them, or come with us! Everyone else, evacuate! That is an order!"

"This is wrong!"

Mazaq has already turned his back on me. A timer appears on the screen counting down sixty seconds in their language. He and the crew leap out and disappear into the dark, leaving me with five men whose lives I'm forfeiting by inaction.

Can I leave them? Am I doing wrong again at the cost of my survival? How much more before I lose my soul? How many more lives?

Sounds of the incoming attack ships become louder. With my sword in hand, I run. Their deaths will be added to my tally.

If I'm apprehended now, the Alkosians will suffer until they die. I'll be tortured; Ami and the others will likely be killed.

Pushing hard to find the fleeing Vraditi, the directions I can go are limited because the New Astan craft are now overhead. I lunge into a dip a hundred feet away as the enemy gets close. Spotlights search the area, and I stay hidden. I steal a look after it passes: they're in a close and low formation to our vessel, unaware of the imminent danger.

Their ignorance is remedied when it explodes in a ball of fire and shrapnel. Instinctively, I duck.

Distressed engines garner my attention, and I look up in time to watch two of them crash. One slams hard into the side of a hill, while the other simply falls from the sky. Soldiers rush out of them and scour the area, weapons drawn. Under the cloak of a dark sky, and with the hills covering me, I set out across the small valley.

The New Astan soldiers are shouting, but I'm too far now to understand them fully. The other vessels fly overhead in a search pattern.

When they come near, I hide amongst plants and trees. There is a thicket ahead, nestled in between a couple large hills.

I try to avoid detection by ducking into hiding spots while running away, but I fail. A ship flies above and the searchlight finds me. I am forced to do what's necessary to keep from being caught.

Holding my sword with both hands, I release the power I've had pent up.

A nearly invisible beam fires off the tip of the sword. The air cracks like thunder, the ship unable to deal with the brute force. It tailspins into a hill on my left. Knowing I've given my position away, I run, putting as much distance between myself and the wreckage as possible.

Up and down several hills, I try to avoid climbing the tallest ones. But I corner myself in an alcove, and there's no choice. Digging my hand, sword and feet into the steep grassy hillside, I climb. Half way to the top, I glance around and see the last ship is still looking, but in the wrong direction.

At the top of the hill, I sprint while looking for another depression to get below their line of sight. The terrain is treacherous with little light to guide me. What I'm looking for finds me. I misstep on a downward slope and, as my foot gives, I throw my sword away to avoid killing myself. Tumbling, bushes and rocks batter me until I reach what I hope is the base of the hill. Even with the armor absorbing some blows, I'm going to feel the aches tomorrow. But there's nothing broken.

It's a literal shot in the dark as I fumble around to find where my blade landed. Checking nearby bushes in the direction I threw it reveals foliage unnaturally weighed down. It's there, and I'm ready for another fight. I'm patient in waiting for anyone to appear over the ridge.

A gentle breeze flowing past is the only sound. Twenty minutes later, I feel safe enough to even sigh in relief. Separated from the Vraditi, I'm desperate to look for my team, but fear moving from my location. There's no communications via my helmet, and it makes me anxious. The rescue is scheduled for after sunrise – it seems better to wait it out.

Hours pass, and there are no signs of either Vraditi or New Astan personnel. I'm thankful Colonel Tigby or Drake didn't send an armada to locate us. The sky lightens: dawn is coming, and soon I'll be able to see.

How long do I wait?

The embankment I fell from is steep. Even with the suit aiding me, I'm tired and have to muster the energy. It takes a fair amount of time to reach the top. I'm in the clear, but there's also no sign of the Vraditi.

Am I lost to them? Mazaq probably isn't looking for me. And if they leave me, I'm in trouble.

I can't return to New Asta to contact Gregory. So how do I get back to the ship?

At the top of the hill, I see plumes of smoke in the distance. Despite my better judgment telling me to avoid the area, I need to locate anything I can salvage to make contact.

Fast and low, I head back toward danger. Despite trying to keep the smoke in my view, I have to enter a gully and follow the canyons of the hilly network. Only by poking my head above the hill-line am I able to keep my bearings. It's a mistake. There are soldiers near the craft I shot down.

I drop flat out of sight. My fears of unwanted discovery are alleviated when the same model ship from my previous rescue shoots in and hovers a few thousand feet away from the smoldering ship. It drops a teleportation cylinder into a different rift.

"Rescue inbound. Converge on the cylinder. We will provide cover," comes a familiar voice through my helmet. It's Yaqta.

I'm already running, exposing myself to attack. My arms swing hard as I push to escape capture. Several New Astan attack ships lift off from a nearby canyon and rush to the scene.

Yaqta fires warning shots at them. One refuses to back off, and they launch their weapons. The missiles hit out of sight in the canyon. Fire and smoke billow up.

A drastic course of action comes to mind. Pointing my sword at the ground, I hold onto it for dear life, crouch, and jump at the defiant ship. With a shockwave to propel me, I'm flying right at them. The air is cold, but my helmet protects me.

The ship pulls up and I'm going to barely miss it.

Unwilling to accept missing, as I pass underneath it, I swing my sword and fire a shockwave. The hull gives. Both the ship and I are now heading to the ground.

Spinning while I fall, I catch a glimpse of the cylinder in a small valley. My back hits the earth, the sword flying out of my hand. I'm left breathless, choking to inhale any sort of air.

The wreckage lands a few feet from my head and I panic, both because

I can't breathe, and because I anticipate New Astan soldiers pouring out any second. The Vraditi vessel hasn't moved.

My lungs finally cooperate only after I'm crawling away from the fires in the engines of the wreck. I push to my feet. I'm unsteady. My sword is nowhere to be seen, but my escape route is – the cylinder is waiting. New Astan soldiers pursue me, but Yaqta fires on them.

Using shockwaves to supplement my natural inability to leap great bounds, I race to the cylinder while the other New Astan ships circle like vultures. The warm, white light is inviting. When I finally reach it, and enter, I'm comforted by the upward rushing feeling carrying me to safety. Deposited on the ship, I find myself amongst Mazaq's team.

"Shut down the teleporter and take us up!" Yaqta bellows.

Within the blink of an eye we're already reaching great heights. There's no further attempt by the New Astan ships to intervene. We are outside the atmosphere in less than a minute. The tension levels on the bridge drop dramatically, and there is a cheering for me.

"I thought for sure you were caught or dead!"

"That was incredible! I have heard stories of your ability but never did I think I would witness it!"

Their encouragement and praise continues. I feel flushed from embarrassment, but it ends when Mazaq speaks in a condescending tone.

"You thought I was wrong to leave the captives to die and yet, in the end, how many did you just kill? Do you hold your sense of morality above ours? Do you think yourself greater than us?"

With my body still surging, my anger flares. I teeter on the edge of sanity. Spinning around, I take my helmet off and throw it at his head. He deflects it, and throws his at me. Both of my arms take the full force, and for a moment it feels like they've shattered. We glare at one another, and I lay into him.

"A 'thank you' would be nice. I saved you, twice! I killed humans to save Vraditi! Humans who were following orders and may have been innocent. They may even have been underground resistance!" I make no attempt to restrain my volume. "I've made many life and death decisions. I have millions of souls weighing on me because of one action to protect the timeline and survival of the future."

I point aggressively at him. "I killed to ensure your survival. Don't you dare be ungrateful for my assistance, because if I hadn't helped, you would have been captured or killed last night!"

"That is enough," Yaqta addresses me.

Turning my stare to Yaqta, whom I've also had sharp words with, I huff loudly. I breathe deep, trying to calm down in the silence that has fallen over the command center.

I stew while we move into the docking bay. As angry as I am at his attitude, I'm equally mad at my own mistakes.

Feeling the need to explain myself, I try to calmly talk to him, but it's labored. "I'm trying to make up for my mistakes. I've hurt more people than I've helped." I sigh. "This world is the way it is, because I made it this way. These stubborn people, my brother included, are a product of my failures as a person and as a leader. There's nothing I wish for more than to fix it all. That's what I'm here for."

Turning to face Mazaq, he is still there, listening. His mighty hand reaches for me, and I envision him choking me to death. In a surprising move he holds his hand out for me to shake. Knowing it is not Vraditi custom to do such a thing, I wonder if this is a peace offering.

Putting my hand out slowly, I grip his enormous palm and he responds with a gentle pressure.

"I was unsure until now that you should be trusted with the fate of the Quvite people," Mazaq's tone is firm. "But standing up to those who are bigger and have more power than you shows promise."

Is he meaning him, or Drake?

"Quva bestowed on you the Mission Second Command title. I would have rather had someone who immediately followed my orders, but you were acceptable." He returns his hand to his side. "Two days from now we launch on the prison, and you will continue to hold that title unless you are killed."

Should I be comforted or offended?

Mazaq turns to the exit hallway while Yaqta's crew lands. Our team follows him, and each of them lays a hand on my shoulder as they pass by.

When the last one passes, I follow, grabbing my helmet from its resting place a few feet away. Before leaving the bridge, I nod at Yaqta in appreciation of him saving me again.

He nods, and returns to commanding his ship.

We walk in single file down the long corridor. By the time we reach the door, it's open. Quva and Xera await.

"Status report," Quva requests.

"The module has been deployed and is active," Mazaq tells him. "We will rest and prepare for the second mission."

"Understood. Dismissed." He nods at him.

Filing out, I intend to follow them to the living quarters, but Quva stops me with an outstretched arm. He beckons me to walk with him.

Putting an arm over my shoulder he leads me away from Xera, who is content to stay there typing on her tablet. Speaking softly so I have to strain to hear him over the chatter nearby, "Rain, I want to you to know we appreciate your contribution."

"*I never doubted it from you.*" I frown.

"The communication channel was open. Mazaq is—"

"*It's fine. I have too much on my mind lately and I took it out on him,*" I cut him off and break away. "*I need food and sleep, and I'll be ready to go.*"

Without a further word, he nods at me and leads me back to Xera.

Xera smiles warmly and motions for me to follow her onto a platform docked against the walkway. She is silent flying me back to my room. It's not until we are inside the glass pane does she speak.

"I will retrieve you two hours prior to mission start. Should you need anything, please contact either myself or Quva."

"*Thank you, Xera.*"

"Congratulations on the success of the mission," she says and departs.

I remove my suit and toss it on the foot of my bed. I have the attendant robot fabricate some new pants to change into. Freed from the suit, my muscles start to relax. I had grown accustomed to the compressed feeling, and now that it's gone my body hurts. I order stew and a loaf of bread. Two bowls, and half a loaf eaten, my hunger is sated.

The attendant robot recycles my leftovers while I throw myself onto the bed and curl into a ball.

~~~~~~

Sleep nowadays never seems long enough. I suppose it's because I'm actually not sleeping much. I could sleep a week and I don't think I'd feel rested.

I drag my feet as I step out to the walkway where everyone is going about their business. Despite being in preparation for the next attack, their movements are still without urgency. People watching is a poor pastime when you're waiting for military action.

Inside, I knock on the privacy wall between mine and Dr. Oreda's beds. There's no answer. Peering around the corner, her bed is empty.

Lonely, I consider calling up Quva or Xera just to talk, but settle for issuing commands to the attendant robot. I eat a hearty breakfast, and when full I lie back in the bed. I drift somewhere between sleep and awake. Though I'm aware I'm partially conscious, I dream.

I'm in the house with Ami. It's peaceful, and we're happy. Passing each other in the kitchen she moves toward the door with a load of laundry, but I catch her by her waist and pull her in close to me. I wrap my arms around her and nestle my chin into the space between her neck and her shoulder. She giggles.

She turns her head, and our lips meet briefly before she pulls away with her basket of laundry and a bigger smile. I let her return to her duties, and when she's gone Eve is scowling at me from the living room doorway. I grin and shrug, and she lets the swinging door close.

I follow her into the living room but she's gone. Drake is there, his weapon drawn. It meets me in the gut and he whispers unintelligibly. My blood pours out of the wound.

I gasp for air.

I sit up in bed. The dream state blurs with reality and I scramble to check my scar. There is no blood. The wound is long healed. It reminds me of when I was first attacked, the dark nightmares I had of waiting for my then unknown attacker to come finish me off.

Sweat drips from my forehead, and I wipe to clean it off. The unnerving thought of blood compels me to wash up. I head to the side room, disrobe, and step into the purification chamber.

I force my mind to go blank while the cycle runs. When it's finished and I'm clothed, I expect to feel better, but a feeling of dread lingers.

A knock on the door startles me. It's Xera. "The time for the second mission nears. You should put your suit on."

"What?"

"The second mission. It is two hours to start."

"Has it been two days already?"

She nods and steps aside for me to pass. Dr. Oreda's side is still empty. I turn away from her and change into my suit. I want to ask about Dr. Oreda, but I don't want to intrude on her privacy.

Xera watches intently as I ready myself, and then motions for me to follow her out. We board a platform, and I have a few moments to think.

Once, when I was corrupt, I would have reveled in being carted around as a dignitary in a foreign land. But it's sickening now. There is much at stake and many lives at risk.

I feel dread instead of joy as we prepare for war. A byproduct of the amnesia I once had, and good influences during that time. Is this why I haven't taken a more dominant role as I once would have? Is this how I should have felt all those years as King Tiberius?

It could be because I have everything to lose. I was proud of Asta, of what I built, but there was no love there except for myself. Love of others was incomprehensible.

Now I have people I'd give my life for. I have a woman I love.

The docking bay doors open, the activity and energy inside far greater than the living section. Everyone is busy preparing, even a few humans whom I don't recognize.

Amongst the vehicles being readied, there are a several of Yaqta's type. I imagine the behemoths swooping in on New Asta, covering the sky. I count four mid-sized carrier vessels, with a small army in formation outside of them. Mazaq is easily recognizable by his unique tattoos. Xera docks right next to him.

Only a moment after I've stepped off, Xera disappears from sight above the ships. Giving my attention to the masses congregating, I move to stand beside Mazaq.

"Rain, tell us about this facility."

"It's a high security prison for alkos, but I've only seen two floors: the one I was held on and the exit. I'll accompany, but don't count on my primary ability. I should be able to provide limited cover with my secondary ability, but that is also not guaranteed."

"These people will be disoriented, confused, and they may even fight you due to madness setting in. You need to be patient with them, and herd them quickly. Our enemy is essentially the whole of New Asta's fighting force. Be prepared to incapacitate *anyone* if necessary."

Mazaq leads our team onto one of the passenger ships. Two levels of seats on each side allows for a significant number of riders. In the middle of the floor is a teleportation device with four handles equally spaced, secured with straps. It's slightly larger than Mazaq; I hope it will fit in the service elevator. I'm forced to trust Gregory has thought this through.

Sitting on the bottom level on the port side, I look forward to the front of the craft. A bulkhead prevents me from monitoring our flight situation. Everyone shuffles around, finding seats, the ship nearing capacity.

The ship hums to life and starts moving, but with no visual cues I can't tell how fast we're moving. We've tilted forward, and bank left and right a few times. The noise of the large bay doors is audible over the hum throughout the hull. Within moments, we must be out in space above Salvoa.

As before, we decelerate, and it feels like we're sitting still for a long time. Mazaq is sat directly across from me on the opposite side, with empty seats next to him. In a hurry, I throw my harness off and bolt over.

"How many vessels are we expecting as backup if we lose control of the situation?" I strap into the seat on his right.

"The whole flotilla if necessary, except for the migration ship. This mission may have been voluntary, but every Quvite has volunteered to help you. It was an overwhelming consensus because of your promise to liberate us. Thankfully, we could not take everyone. A great number of them would not know which end of the suit their head went in."

I smile. "Was that a joke?"

With a straight face he turns so his four eyes are locked with mine, then grins, showing his teeth.

Still moderately confused by Vraditi expressions, I cannot tell if it's a real, sarcastic, or a wry smile. I take it as developing rapport, and chuckle.

"But in seriousness, the people we have with us are the best. Our teams, coupled with our technology, will allow us to operate without casualties."

He turns away from me.

"Good. The last thing I want is for the safety of the Alkosians at the cost of your men and women. I'll do what I must to protect them," I reassure him.

"The suits will aid us well."

Everyone becomes silent in anticipation before Salvoa's gravity asserts itself as we drop into the atmosphere. We lurch heavily to the left, and there is turbulence.

An announcement comes on in our helmets. "Attention. Engaging hostiles. Brace for impact."

Several explosions rock us, making the ride bumpier. A strange noise emanates from the roof, starting with a low hum and gradually increasing. It reaches a peak, and then disperses in rapid succession. Weapons fire. For about a minute we're entrenched in battle. More explosions. Additional firing from our ship and other nearby vessels.

It calms, and we level out, touching down. Everyone jumps up and into action. With the protective suits and helmets on, they're ready to exit. Soldiers are yelling outside the hull.

Mazaq and seven others as large as he prepare to lift the teleportation device. I step up and prepare for battle.

"Shields up! Stun as able, but lethal force is authorized!" Mazaq yells.

The exit begins to open, and gunfire rings out. Bubbles of blue energy surround the Vraditi as bullets hit; we are unhurt.

Seeing the bullets deflected, fear and hesitation are purged, and my violent side is eager to join the fray. I leap into the nearest group. They fire their guns at me, and I still flinch, but the bullets are stopped. Using my shoulders to shove through, I fight to the middle of their formation and keep them briefly distracted from our soldiers flooding onto the deck.

I'm too fast for them to hit, either with stun weapons or flying fists, thanks to the enhancements given by the suit. I'm outnumbered, and it would be safer just to keep their attention on me while our side takes them out, but the itch for combat is too great.

I grab the barrel of a rifle, draw it close, then shove it hard away. It cracks the soldier's shoulder. I rip the firearm away and swing it like a mace, clubbing men and women to incapacitate and disable.

Sheer luck allows a soldier to knock my weapon away, and I shove an open palm into his sternum. He exhales violently, but before he can fall I twist his arm behind his back and hold him in front of me.

There's an attempt to stun me, but my hostage is my shield. He's hit, and I drop him to the deck.

Blocking a second swing gives me an opening, and my knee hits his stomach. A woman attempts to overtake me, and I fling the man in my arms at her. They both collapse like ragdolls.

The Vraditi have fought to me by stunning the front lines. We overtake the New Astan soldiers, and there's nowhere for them to run. It's only a matter of minutes before the last opposing human hits the deck, with zero casualties for us.

Four ships full of Vraditi have successfully taken control of the roof of the building, but overhead there is still an ongoing battle for the airspace. The New Astans are being stopped from landing and providing reinforcements. The first part of our assault is successful.

Numbers and superior technology has given us the advantage. So why do I feel dread? Drake should have been more prepared. He had to have been expecting this. There must be more of his forces below.

Mazaq and the seven other taller Vraditi from our compliment haul the mobile teleportation device down the sloped hallway toward the elevator.

I follow, and Gregory appears from the shadows near the entrance.

"Glad you made it," Gregory says, extending his hand for a handshake.

"It's only the beginning. There's more to do." I shake his hand.

"Yes there is. There are fifty-five floors, fifty-five being the top where we're at." He leads with enthusiasm. "Floor one is where those deemed the most dangerous are held. Where *you* were held. Most of them there are in the late stages of mental breakdown due to alkos-inversion. I hope Quva has a plan to rehabilitate them."

We reach the elevator. Gregory calls it up with a scan of his face, and when it reaches us I am the first in the doors. Hugging the wall, I make sure there's room for the Vraditi with the device. They ease in, followed by as many of our troop who can fit.

Gregory reaches in and hits the first button, but holds the doors from closing. "I haven't been on duty yet today. I don't know what you'll encounter in there. Be on guard and move systematically.

"The first four floors actively house prisoners with a total of maybe a thousand people total. The remainder of the prison is awaiting new prisoners, so there's no need to search any further than that." He lets go of the door. "Good luck!"

It closes and we descend. Though it drops fast, my perception of time becomes distorted, feeling like it's taking too long to reach the bottom level.

The despairing souls within me become stronger the farther we descend, and I can feel Misery's dark power rising in me again. With it we have the advantage. But my dread is reinforced when the elevator opens and there is not a single soldier in the hallway.

My stomach turns and my throat constricts. We're walking into a trap. What it is, and where and when they'll spring it, become the immediate questions.

I swallow hard and hold my arm up for them to stay. Alarms ring in my head as I step out and move to the first intersection. Looking down empty corridors, I wave them forward. The doors separating the sections are unlocked. At each corner, my muscles get tighter.

"This is wrong. We're being set up," I blurt while entering the noisy cellblock.

"We are here, and it would be a waste to retreat so early." Mazaq grabs my shoulder. "Is it clear in there?"

I nod.

"I'm telling you, this is a mistake."

"They cannot stop us." He pushes me out of the way.

The prisoners have been left alone, to wail and suffer.

Brother, what have you planned?

Sure an ambush is imminent, I ready my borrowed power. I soak in the feelings of desperation, and they tear at my soul. The teleport device is activated while I look at the screens. The live images switch every few moments to show me the prisoners. There isn't a single soldier in the facility.

"If they are going to make it this easy, I will not complain." Mazaq laughs.

"Start breaking the cells open while I reach out to these people," I instruct the Vraditi.

Diving deep into Misery's dark world within me, I begin trying to reach those unreachable by traditional means. It takes me a few minutes to delve far enough, but the more time I spend there, the easier it becomes. I'm immersed within their woes. The darkness surrounds me, and I see the lost.

"*Be calm! Be still!*" I yell.

"*Trapped! I'm trapped forever! I'll die here!*"

"*Daddy? Mommy? Where are you? I want to go home.*"

"*This is unfair! I didn't do anything wrong!*"

"*Be at ease! I have fulfilled my promise! I have brought the Quvites to rescue you!*"

"*There is no rescue!*" I'm confronted by a hostile man whose image is distorted greatly.

"*Do not harm the Quvites. They'll get you out and to safety.*"

They fall silent; I have their attention.

He will pay, and these people can have vengeance.

I push further, to edge them forward toward retribution.

"*Even if it has been only a day, you have been oppressed for too long! This is your chance at freedom. We can destroy your oppressor! Follow me to the light!*"

Breaking my link to Misery's world, I reenter the real one. The Vraditi are leading the Alkosians in droves from their cages on the many levels. My attempt has succeeded. Nobody is fighting their rescuers.

Everything is proceeding far too smoothly for my comfort. Pacing anxiously, I stop to look at the screens. It's the same images, including the one of our level. I watch things happen in real time on the screen. After fifteen minutes, the last of this floor's prisoners enter the cylinder. Mazaq calls out.

"First level clear! Back to the elevator!"

I lead my allies, and when we reach the elevator it opens automatically.

Did Gregory override the system? Or is this Drake's doing? Would he let us take the Alkosians? Why?

We cram in, and press the button for the next level. We're lifted to level two, and follow the same cautious pattern. We're taking it slow and steady, but I hear Mazaq grumbling.

The layout is the same, making it easy to navigate. No ambushes lie around the corners. I feel like I'm going to vomit from the tension.

Another well-lit prison block. Another group of Alkosians in need of freeing. I shove the doors open and wave the team in. The wailing in this block isn't nearly as bad as the last. Coherent voices ring out, and it becomes an uproar.

"Who is there?"

"What are they?"

"Help me! Please!"

"Get us out!"

We're working against an invisible clock, but I let Mazaq run the cycle. I don't have to reach out to this group to get their cooperation, so I help opening cells. The one I've arbitrarily chosen houses a little boy who's crying in the corner.

"Hey," I say softly trying to coax him. He doesn't respond.

Without my suit I'd have to wait for help opening the cell, but the metal warps, and the lock pops when I pull. I have the boy's attention. His long auburn hair is matted to his face, wet with tears. A need to comfort him compels me to bend a knee and wave for him.

"It's going to be okay now." Forcing a smile, I try to ease the tension.

He's hesitant. He stops crying, but sniffles and hiccups. Slow to react, he stands from his metal cot. By his size, I assume he's six or seven years old.

"You're safe with us." I keep my smile going. "Do you know the Quvites?"

He shakes his head.

"The Quvites are our friends from another world. They came here to help," I tell him and point to the cylinder. "All you have to do is step into the bright light over there, and you'll be on a big ship with our friends. Okay?"

He nods while drying his tears with the sleeve of his shirt. Standing up, I put my hand out for him to take. When he does I lead him to the cylinder where the others are lined up.

"Where's…hic…where's my mommy and daddy?" he asks so quietly I nearly miss the words.

"I don't know. We will look for them after you're safe aboard the Quvites' ship."

He starts to cry and I comfort him with a pat on the shoulder. "Hey, shh. We'll find them. For now the Quvites will take good care of you. Step in this light and you'll be okay."

I let him go, crushed by his sadness. He steps in and disappears. Memories of what it was like not having parents from a young age flood in. And then came the corruption. With poor and malicious guidance, I became a monster.

The Vraditi will take care of him, and whether or not we can track his parents down, he'll have better influences than I did.

Upright, I turn and assist the others releasing the remaining prisoners. As the last of them file through, the Vraditi let their guard fall and head to the elevator out of formation. When we arrive at the elevator, the doors open with no prompting.

On the third floor we start over, the people even more reasonable. Our job is significantly easier because there's no resistance. Misery has been slowly weakening with every person sent to safety. At this point I hope the nagging in my head is all for naught, because I'm not sure if I'll be able to command Misery in its decreased state.

Drake knew we were coming. There's no other explanation for this place being deserted. And he certainly didn't pull the soldiers out to keep them from being captured or killed.

We are done far faster than expected. The number of people on the third level are a fraction compared to one and two. Success is near. The final level with prisoners waits for us.

"Mazaq…" I want to say something, to tell him that we need to cut and run. Our eyes meet but we're interrupted by the elevator doors opening.

The opposition has finally shown up in the form of Colonel Tigby and a handful of soldiers. They're concealed behind a machine. On the front of it is a large white disc with four rods coming together to make a pyramid. Inside the disc's base, well-placed crystals line it with no empty spaces. The machine's base is planted with posts driven into the floor. A whine fills the air and the disc glows.

"You've been a good scapegoat, Tiberius." Colonel Tigby is smug. "The world will see this event how we want them to. A wanted felon escaped from prison, and enlisted radical Quvites in attacking our peaceful city to break out other dangerous criminals."

I rapidly press the button to close the doors and ascend to the fifty-fifth floor, but the elevator is slow to react.

"High Chancellor Drake has a message for you." His voice is almost sing-song.

A dark purple beam of light is fired at us, and it incinerates everything in its path. Narrowly missing me, I press to the side of the elevator and grab Mazaq. He's slow, and his left arm is hit with the beam. His scream of agony resonates as the arm is consumed in fire.

The doors shut, but the beam burns through. We're helpless to do anything but watch everything be cremated or melted in a horrifying show of death. Those caught directly in the beam had no time to react, their agony ending moments after it started, but the injured howl. Amongst the few survivors there are burn wounds on all but two of us. Even though I wasn't hit, my skin feels as though I've received a severe sunburn.

We arrive topside, the threat of the weapon gone for the moment. Mazaq grunts, tries to move, and loses his balance. I catch him, and motion for everyone to stay to the sides. There's no threat on the ramp, but on the roof is a devastating scene. Flames rise from outside the hallway. There's no one standing.

"Stay behind me!" I yell at them.

The survivors help each other while I focus. Because Misery won't respond, I'm not able to form a black shield. Cautious, I edge forward, keeping an eye on our front and back. On the landing pad, my heart sinks at the destruction. Only one of the ships which our teams landed stands undamaged. The other three are towering infernos. Scorched Vraditi litter the roof, Gregory's remains amongst them.

There's still a battle overhead. Quvite vessels are protecting our escape method. They're holding steady, with no sign of any light-weapons being used on them.

"Get in!" Mazaq yells at the survivors. "We need to leave!"

"It's a trap!" The last vessel is too inviting. "It wasn't left by accident!"

"It does not matter! Everyone on!"

We rush. I try to avoid looking at the bodies, but guilt makes me. My eyes meet the dead lying on the roof. The price of saving the imprisoned Alkosians is high with significant loss of Vraditi life.

I should have done better. I should have tried harder to bring Misery up. I should have reached them.

How will I explain to Quva what did this? Light burned his people?

Everyone is aboard. The pilot struggles to get the ship airborne due to loss of fingers. Another heads in to help her, and they get us moving. Our trajectory is nearly vertical for a minute. When we level out, I unstrap and inspect Mazaq's wound.

The beam left a crescent shaped wound where his arm once connected to his shoulder. Though the damage is heavy and his arm is gone, he's in no danger of bleeding out because the weapon also cauterized the wound.

His breathing is becoming labored, and I pull at the zipper on the back of the suit to help him to remove it, at least from his torso. The smell of burnt flesh is nauseating, but I fight down the lump in my throat. Mazaq doesn't, and vomits.

Chatter from the open cockpit door catches my attention, and I leave him in the care of his crewmembers. I sit behind the pilots and watch out the window while we come to the migration ship.

"Give me access to the communication system," I command.

The main pilot looks back and nods at me. "It is active."

"Whoever can hear this, we need immediate medical attention. We have many wounded."

"Request received. Upon arrival direct your vessel to landing zone fifty-two," a voice responds through the console. "Triage units will be standing by."

What did he accomplish though? He didn't kill me. He killed Vraditi. And he let us leave with the Alkosians.

Tigby said I was a scapegoat. Was this all just to turn the world away from ideas of helping the Vraditi?

There has to be more. There always is. It's a message to Quva to stay out of it because Drake has the power to kill them.

The bay doors open, and the moment there's enough room the main pilot rushes us to our docking area. She's reckless, coming in fast and rough. The rear door drops open, and I help Mazaq to the triage unit. He's taken from me and carried away on a stretcher.

Quva's impatient as he nearly bowls me over after seeing the state of

Mazaq. "What happened?" he asks frantically.

"They have a new weapon. It can eat through and burn with the light generated by it. I'm positive they're using your world's crystals in it."

Those not in life threatening danger are tended to on site. Because Mazaq was lifted away in a hurry, I fear he won't make it.

"What did it look like?" his voice shakes.

My attention is distracted. My mind is in shock. Quva taps me while I watch the bigger vessels begin docking at the far end of the bay. The Alkosians are safe, but I feel the cost outweighs the reward.

"It was a disc mounted to a machine. Crystals were arranged in a circle around an antenna of sorts. They powered it on, and it shot a wide beam of light, burning or melting everything it touched."

"How did they figure out that technology?" The question is clearly rhetorical – he knows I don't have the answer.

"*Rekwa* is a mining tool. Never a weapon. Still the dangers of abuse were always present. This is not something we shared with them because of that. High Chancellor Drake's lust for power is insatiable." He's distressed. "Plans will have to be adapted for the final mission if they are going to use *that* against us."

As I'm about to speak, a loud noise echoes across the entire bay. Where the attack vessels docked, a few thousand feet away, great distress comes from the Alkosians inside. There's no time for me to find out why, because in a brief moment the enormous vessel starts to implode. Quva's eyes widen.

"Everyone! Get—" He's cut off as it explodes outward.

A deafening sound. And then heat. Intense heat. The explosion's shockwave sends all manner of craft directly at us. I stumble and grab Quva's scrawny arm. Hauling him into the vessel I just exited, I drag him to the cockpit. One other who had not disembarked joins us. I slam the cockpit door shut

Impacted by shrapnel, debris, and a full vessel, we're knocked from our platform. We enter a free fall past the other tiers, heading to certain destruction upon impact at the bottom of the hangar.

"Start this thing!"

They're already working on it though, trying to make us airborne.

Another stifling feeling of trouble comes from the Alkosian group on the second attack ship. The nearby souls are screaming inside me, begging for someone not to go through with *it*. Another large explosion tears across the hangar.

Our craft hums to life, and though they pull out of the fall they are forced to work hard to avoid being hit. We bank, and my hands fail to hold the chair tightly enough. I'm hurled into a console, jamming my left shoulder and slamming my head.

I'm dazed and seeing double, but I have sufficient sense and control to sit down and buckle in as we head straight up to avoid everything coming down, including an uncountable number of Vraditi falling to their deaths. At the ceiling, Quva levels out and the true damage is revealed. The fleet is mostly destroyed, either from a chain reaction of explosions, or sucked out the gaping hole in the bottom of the ship. And there's nothing we can do.

Everything not tethered or fighting the pull of the escaping atmosphere is being vented into the nothingness. The hangar lights flicker, and a blue energy barrier is erected over the hole. But it's far too late.

The death toll is no doubt in the tens of thousands. Humans and Vraditi. Every Alkosian screams inside of me, permanently in despair in the last seconds of their lives.

It was a setup; through the eyes of the dead, I can see plants by Drake within the Alkosian group, rigged with complicated devices. The ones I wanted to save are dead; my rescue the instrument of their deaths.

"Drake...you vile..." In disbelief, I can't speak a full sentence.

Quva and the co-pilot are silent as the hangar continues to crumble. When it's calmed, they bring us to a broken walkway near the door to the living quarters section. The Vraditi strewn about are either lifeless, or in disarray and shock.

"I need you to grab every Quvite who is still alive and bring them on board," Quva instructs me.

Without acknowledging him, I turn and kick the door open, furious. A large piece of metal has cut deep into the body of our vehicle. It sits at an angle, and is wedged in a way which will require me to use a shockwave to push it out.

"Turn away from the walkway. I need to dislodge debris."

He does, and I unleash my power at it. It creaks and moves, but I have to hit it a few more times to knock it loose. It falls, ripping the door off. Both clatter to the bottom of the hangar. Quva repositions the aft of the ship to the walkway, and I run out to pick up my first survivor. She's unresponsive, but she's breathing, barely. Depositing her near the front of the ship, I return to the docking bay.

Each time I leave the craft to bring a survivor on board, I look in the direction where the attack vessels were. There's nothing left of them to save.

Thinking of Colonel Tigby's comment that my brother had a message for me, I understand now that the beam-weapon was only part of it. Colonel Tigby never intended to kill me; Drake wanted me to witness the power he had over the situation – and see the devastation he would cause.

Flying in circles for a great amount of time, I tire, losing energy. My head is spinning, but I refuse to give up on finding signs of life. After a few dozen saves, the success becomes infrequent. Despite the decline in survivors, Quva circles countless times. At the bottom of the hangar he moves slowly along.

"Is there any more?" he asks from the cockpit.

"I'm not seeing any. I'm sorry."

"There has to be someone! Anyone else!" He is agitated. My heart hurts for him.

Though there is nothing, he continues to fly over the vast amount of wreckage. Finally, as we near the doors to the living quarters, I catch a slight movement. I'm unsure if it's settling scrap or something more.

"Quva! Hard to port!"

He turns, and I'm sure I saw another shift in the mess below. There's a hand sticking out from underneath a chunk of white walkway.

"Bring us down and hold location!"

I point at two Vraditi who have only mild injuries.

"You, come with me now!"

He keeps us above the debris, but he can't safely land. I evaluate a jump of a couple feet down onto hazardous terrain. When I've determined a safe trajectory, I sit on the edge of the craft and slip off of it. Hitting a sloped, broken walkway, I slide away from the arm. I struggle, but make it back up while my chosen helpers also leap out. Even with the suit granting me increased strength, because of my shoulder injury it takes the three of us to lift and move several heavy pieces.

I'm partially relieved when I see the face. "There's no way…"

It's Mazaq. He's near death, but his chest is moving. His helmet is gone, and his face has been sliced open with full loss of both eyes on his left side. Much blood has been spilled, but somehow he's holding on. We lift him carefully, but the deck is too high.

"Drop the tail. We can't climb back up."

It takes precision maneuvering not to crush us, but Quva lowers the deck enough so we can hoist Mazaq up, and follow him aboard. We reach safety, and while the ones who were helping me care for Mazaq, I return to Quva.

"Mazaq will die if we don't help him right now," I tell him. "We can come back and look for more survivors after this group is safe."

"Understood. Heading for the port," he tells me and then turns on a screen to his right. "Contact Xera."

Xera appears on the screen, and there's relief on her face.

"Quva, you are alive!"

"I have Rain to thank for that. We are bringing this ship to the living quarters. Have Medical waiting," he tells her as calmly as he can, but there is a hitch in his voice. He is about at a breaking point. "Xera…Mazaq is alive."

"He…is?! Understood! We will be ready for you!" Tears form in her eyes and the screen goes black.

He brings us up, and heads directly for the bay doors to the living quarters. They open, and he eases the ship through. He lands on the nearest teleport platform. Xera and others are already waiting there.

While I help the injured, starting with Mazaq, my anger rises. There's nothing I can do for the grievously wounded except watch them be carted away on stretchers. Those not in danger of death are tended to on site by medical staff and Dr. Oreda.

Xera sticks next to Mazaq while he's being flown off. She looks my way, but there's no condemnation. She just looks happy to be by his side.

Tears fill my eyes. *I brought this on them. What do I do now? How do I express my sorrow for what's done?*

Quva pulls me by the arm back onto the ship, and we take off again. I can only hope to find others still alive as atonement.

Barely into the hangar, my head aches, and my vision goes black.

~~~~~~

"Honey? Dinner's ready. You should come inside." Ami smiles at me from the doorway.

I toss my gloves down and pick up the basket of potatoes I've gathered. Beads of sweat roll down my face, and I wipe it away with my sleeve. The sweltering sun overhead beats down relentlessly. It's hot, and I fully intend to stand in front of the refrigerator with the door open. I know I'll be reprimanded, but it will be worth it.

"The garden will die if this summer sun doesn't let up. I'm going to have to go out tonight and water it all down again," I tell her while setting the basket on the island counter.

"Well, we can't have that, can we?" She moves to me, and grabs my waist.

We embrace and kiss. Breaking away, I brush my hand across her cheek, and then play with her hair. I never tire of staring into her blue eyes — I do it every chance I get. The look of excitement is always there, and it's intoxicating, even though nothing is happening.

"Where's Mom?" I ask.

Mom?

"She took Maximus out for a ride. She should be back soon."

"Maximus?" I'm confused. "Didn't you leave him on a farm?"

"Why would we leave him on a farm?" She looks at me, equally confused.

Why would I think she left him on a farm?

"Go wash up. I won't have you getting dirt all over the table." She winks, turns me toward the swinging door, giving me a gentle shove.

As I'm heading to the living room, I run into James. He jumps out of the way to avoid being hit.

"Sorry, Dad."

Dad?

"No problem. How was your honeymoon?"

"It was fantastic. The ocean was amazing, and the room we stayed in had this

incredible view where we could see the sun set," I reminisce.

"Good to hear it. Now you're back though, we need the extra hands at the construction site."

"Sure thing. I'll be ready to go tomorrow. But right now I better go wash before Ami scolds me for taking too long."

"I heard that!" She laughs. "Also, tell Emma she needs to come down for dinner. She's been sulking in her room all day."

I peek into the kitchen. "Yes, dear."

"Emma! Ami says you can't mope all day!" I yell upstairs playfully.

"That's not what I wanted you to do!" she scolds me. "She broke up with Denis. Be a little sensitive."

Denis? That can't...that's not right.

I grin at Ami and head to the bathroom. Rinsing my arms, face, and hair I feel much cooler. I dry off and look at myself in the mirror. My eyes are a little red from the arid weather, but a quick dab of water relieves at least the itchiness. My complexion has begun to darken due to the amount of sun I've been getting, both from working outside and the honeymoon. Pulling down the neck of my shirt reveals a clear tan line.

As I exit the bathroom, Eve is there, but she's silent. She has a sad look on her face.

"Eve? Are you okay?"

She doesn't respond.

"What's wron—"

She coughs and blood drips from her mouth. She says something, but there's no sound.

I feel sick to my stomach and when she begins to fall, I grab her.

I try to scream but it jams in my throat.

My gut wrenches. Reality snatches me back, and I can't tell which is worse. It was just a dream, but it feels as though I'm being mocked. That my mind is telling me that even if things were perfect, something would go wrong.

"Rain, can you hear me?" Dr. Oreda stands over me with Quva and Xera to the side. A rapid beeping noise fills the air.

"His eyes are open," Xera observes.

I try to speak, but my body refuses to function. My vision is locked pointing in one direction. Up.

Dr. Oreda shines a light in my eyes. "They're dilating properly, but he's been in and out. The concussion is wreaking havoc on his brain right now."

The beeping noise becomes faster. My chest rises and falls like I'm struggling to breathe.

"He's already tachycardic, and his heart rate is climbing. It's too fast. We need to put him under or his heart will fail."

"Will he be okay under sedation?" Quva asks.

"Sedation is only a start," Dr. Oreda tells them.

She sticks me with a needle, and everything becomes fuzzy.

~~~~~~

I groan. It feels like I've died and come back, something I'm familiar with.

There's movement next to me. Opening my eyes a little, the room is dark. Dr. Oreda is there.

"Can you hear me?" Her voice seems loud.

"Yes. I have a ringing headache."

"You suffered several traumas, including your head. You also went into shock. We had to keep you sedated so we could stabilize you."

Sitting up, my injured shoulder protests at the weight. I wince and shift the weight to my other arm. Tossing my legs over the side, I stand.

"Where are you going?" she asks.

"I have to help the Quvites."

"You *need* to rest up for your fight with High Chancellor Drake." She reaches behind her back.

"My...fight with Drake...?"

Why is she concerned about that?

She sticks me with a needle again. "You're going back to sleep."

"What...did...you...?"

~~~~~~

With or without her blessing, resting is out of the question.

Dr. Oreda gave the okay for me to move about the ship only after I badgered her. Unfortunately, she'd also given strict orders to Xera not to let me exert myself.

I ignore them both when they aren't watching over me, and I push myself to help search and clean up in the hangar.

There's no talk of retaliation. Days turn to weeks, and it's the same thing day after day. Search, clean, repair, and rest. A lot of scrap is reclaimed by the use of attendant robots, but the process is slow due to their small size. While some simply convert the materials to particles of air, others work at the destroyed edge, rebuilding the breached hull.

Taking a break, I watch a robot's methodical movements and ignore everything else around me. *We were lucky to find the few survivors we did.*

Quva passes through my field of vision. Every time I see him, he has the same look of sorrow and resentment in his face. It's even worse at our daily launch of the dead into space.

The deaths of the Vraditi and Alkosians weigh heavily on my mind. The child whom I tried to comfort keeps coming to the forefront of my thoughts. Guilt tortures me.

The ones in the ship. They would have died instantly. No physical pain, but they are trapped now inside Misery. Though they were rescued, they still died in hopelessness.

My actions, my insisting they be saved, killed them. All this death because I refused to die.

My break is done, and I walk alongside Quva while he directs the robots. The search for the dead is long and arduous.

I've been awake for almost a full day, but he hasn't reported me to Xera or Dr. Oreda. In fact, he's hardly said much of anything.

Pulling a Vraditi from in between two plates of metal, her lifeless body is light. A few others are standing by with a stretcher, waiting to take her to the rest waiting to be sent off.

For no particular reason, this is the one that sets me off. Sadness, rage, and frustration surface. My chest is tight. I try to catch my breath, but my chest stutters as I inhale. Tears start, and there's no controlling it. I collapse onto walkway debris, and sob. I grieve and want to take it all back. I can feel eyes on me.

I bury my face as if it would hide my shame. *I want to die! Why couldn't I just die?*

A lifetime ago I would have been unaffected by the loss of life, when I was conceited and power hungry. Haunted by everything I've ever done, and all the death I've caused, an urge to take my own life comes over me. It's poison to my soul, but I know if I did, the hurt would end. The deaths I'm sure to cause in the future will be avoided.

When a hand touches my shoulder, I don't want to look up. I do involuntarily anyway.

Quva motions for me to stand. "Go rest," he insists softly.

"I just need a few minutes and I'll be fine," I mumble hoarsely to him.

"Rain…" He's trying to be nice. I can't stand it. It sickens me.

"Don't you understand? I. AM. DEATH," I yell in his face. "If I can't even clean up the aftermath of my own destruction, what good am I? I tried desperately to be a better person than I was. But there's no end! I am who I am!"

"There is no way you—"

"I had a bad feeling throughout the mission! It was too easy - I should have called it off. The deaths of every Quvite and Alkosian are on my head!" I stand up and become louder. I won't allow him to take my guilt away. It's mine. "When I've finished cleaning up my mess, I'm going there *alone* to finish this."

My anger burns, and I act impulsively. Taking my helmet off I heave it into an unoccupied area, and let out a frustrated grunt. The suit augmenting my strength sends it farther than I intended, and it lands a few hundred feet away. Quva looks at me sympathetically.

"I won't endanger any more of your people. Consider this my official request for a small ship. I intend on turning myself over and ending this."

I've overdone it. My blood pressure is too high, and my head is swimming. My legs give, and I fall on a pile of debris.

"I am sending you back to your quarters. I will notify Dr. Oreda that you are hysterical."

He motions to a taller Vraditi nearby on a flying platform.

"Take Rain to his quarters," he instructs. "No deviations."

He's compliant with Quva and reaches his burly hand out. I smack at it like a child, a warrior disgraced by bad decisions.

"I don't want your help."

Quva stands aside, and the brute grabs me forcefully. Lifting me up with ease, he sets me on my feet. "Hold onto the rail or you will not be able to martyr yourself."

Quva doesn't reprimand him for his cold words. I can't tell if the Vraditi is being spiteful, or encouraging my willingness to die. He brings the platform up rapidly, and speeds toward the living quarters.

Though I don't know if it's true or not, it feels like everyone is staring at me. I try to avoid them, but it's impossible. Each set of eyes which meet mine make me want to apologize to them individually.

When we reach my room, he docks, and I hesitate to step onto the walkway where *they* are walking. But I don't have a choice when I'm pushed and forced to wade through them. The words 'failure' and 'disgrace' plague me. I'm unable to hide behind my privacy wall fast enough.

Dr. Oreda appears from her side of the partition.

Great. She's not what I need.

"I told you to take it easy. Sit," she insists, pulling out her medical kit.

The bed sinks under my weight. She examines me, and I avoid eye contact.

"How's the shoulder pain?"

It hurts from throwing my helmet. "It's fine."

"Your heart is beating fast and your blood pressure is high. You're confined to quarters."

I rip my arm away. *I'm not your child.*

"I'm going to get cleaned up." I head to the purifier room. "Attendant, follow."

I'll do what I please.

Disrobing and stepping into the purification chamber, I hope to relax at least a little. But the cycle runs and there's no comfort. My muscles are weak, and I prop myself up, my back against one side, my feet against the other. When it's finished, I step out and address the robot.

"Attendant, recycle old clothes, use my previous scanned parameters and fabricate new undergarments."

It does what I ask, and I put them on while pondering a way to best present myself to the anguished Vraditi, so they might see I'm mourning too.

Thoughts of the formal attire people wore at my parents funeral, gives me an idea. "Attendant, do the Quvites have attire programed for mourning?"

"Confirmed," it responds in its electronic monotonous tone.

"Fabricate a custom set for me."

Materializing at my feet, it starts with a deep purple pair of soft slippers, followed by thin silky pants, and a shirt of the same color. While I put those on, it creates gloves and a veil. I opt for the gloves, but not the veil.

"Attendant, fabricate a full length mirror on the wall."

"This does not fall within level one requisitioning."

"Request special permission from Quva."

It's silent for a moment, and then completes the task. I examine the clothing's fit. Turning left and right, I dislike how loose it is. Still wearing it, I give the robot commands to make alterations.

"Fit the shirt tighter, and add decorative padded shoulder guards of the same color."

When it's done, I'm mostly satisfied. It's my hope that they view this as a gesture of me joining them in mourning this tragedy.

Grabbing my combat suit, I head out to my bed. Dr. Oreda appears. I don't want her company, but I stay silent.

"There were many parties involved in this. The Quvites are equally at fault." What she says comes out harshly.

I snap to a sitting position. "What do you mean?"

"What I'm saying is, don't bear the burden alone."

"Don't bear the burden...? What's your problem?" I become angry at her. "The Quvites didn't use a weapon of mass destruction, or blow up ships full of *both* of our species. The two parties to blame are me and Drake, because our fight has spanned thousands of years and we both refuse to give up. The collateral damage just stacks up around us!"

"I'm sorry...I..."

"You should have never flown away from Tower Zero! I was going to surrender! If I had, I may be dead, but many more would be alive!"

I'm fuming, and can't look at her. I turn away. A needle pokes me, and before I can protest I feel the effects.

~~~~~~

"Wake up," Dr. Oreda barks at me.

I brush her off with a wave of my arm, but she's determined.

"Quva needs to speak to you immediately." She becomes insistent. "He's on the screen."

Huffing and sitting up, I swing my legs off of the bed and stand. Partially blinded by the light, I stumble to the doctor's side of the room where the screen is.

"Rain, your attire..." Quva is surprised.

"I wanted to honor your fallen. This seemed to be the best way to express it to all of the Vraditi at once."

He nods but redirects the conversation. "Xera is coming to you right now. You will be brought directly to the conference room." He speaks fast. "A situation has developed."

"What situation?" I ask, my heart sinking into my stomach.

"I cannot say until you arrive," he replies.

"Rain." Xera is already here. "Come with me."

"I'm coming too – I need to monitor his condition," Dr. Oreda says, giving no opportunity for argument.

I nod, and we follow Xera as she jogs out. Mere moments after we are on the docked platform, she is pulling away.

Xera pilots to the command center yelling for people to move as she races there. In the command, she leads me to the central chamber.

Quva and multiple delegates are already seated at the table. Two seats are left at the end of the table closest to the door, and I assume they're for Xera and myself. She sits and I sit next to her.

Everyone faces the crystal wall on the far end, and a disturbing image is displayed: Drake's scaly Tarak form appears.

My anger flares. I stand and slam my palms on the table. "Murderer! Filth! I should have destroyed you when I had the chance!"

"Brother, so Quva wasn't lying. You *are* still alive!" he hisses and grins. "I had wondered how my present had been received, but since you're still standing I assume you rejected it."

"I'll rip your insides out with your own dagger!"

"Do you even remember the people you left in my hands? They've been here much longer than I expected you to let them be!" He laughs maniacally. "If you attack, I'll kill them and make you watch. And then I'll delight in watching you self-destruct. Would you take your own life, or allow me to take it from you?"

The screen pans to show Ami, Emma, Agatha, and James chained to a wall behind him. Each of them is bound with metal shackles and chains to the floor. They've been beaten, they're malnourished, and when Ami looks up there are large bags under her eyes. She attempts to speak, but nothing comes out.

I want to scream, cry, and rage. "I will tear you limb from limb," I snarl.

"Look at you. That's the vicious little brother I've missed all this time. Have you given up pretending to be something you're not, Tiberius?"

I'm too enraged to respond.

"I tire of this." His evil smile fades. He looks in Quva's direction. "I'm going to be generous and offer an opportunity. If you convince Tiberius to surrender himself to me, your transgressions against *my planet* will be forgiven."

"And you, Tiberius." He turns to me once more. "You must have influenced this passive race, which led to the loss of life on both sides. That's on you. You are a war criminal, but if you willingly turn yourself in to be executed, I will free these four."

"Should you refuse, the consequences will be dire. I'll kill them, and then I'll shoot the Quvite ship out of the sky. You've seen the devastation from our latest weapons first hand. We pulled our punches."

Though Drake fills the screen, I'm unable to tear my eyes away from Ami for more than a moment. I want to reassure her and let her know it will be okay, but any attempt would be stopped by him. My chest hurts. My heart is beating fast. Angry tears stream down my face at what he's done to them already.

I have to give in.

"Shut this broadcast down!" Mazaq bellows from behind.

Despite the grievous injuries he sustained, he's recovered enough to make an appearance. He points accusingly at the screen and becomes heated.

"Are we going to let this filthy beast direct us?" Mazaq shouts in our language for Drake to hear. "The liar who has orchestrated the Humans against us after we helped them?"

"Quva, you have a few hours to decide," Drake says, ignoring Mazaq. "If I don't hear from you by midday of New Asta, I'll assume you've refused my offer. The consequences will be on your heads."

His image disappears, leaving my heart racing and my stomach in knots.

An eruption of voices echo through the room, arguing about the situation. Give me up, or take the ultimate drastic measure and invade with full force.

This continues until Quva speaks over them all. "Silence!"

The noise instantly stops, and Quva stands. With his arms behind his back, he paces the room slowly. In thought, he says nothing while we wait.

It isn't his decision. It's mine, and I won't let him sacrifice their whole race. I won't let my family die for my sake, because I was too stubborn to cave to his demands. Eve's dead, but I can save the rest of them.

When he's directly across from me, I won't stay silent anymore.

"Quva, agree to a mutual trade. I've already cost you too much - I don't want any more death but my own."

"I commanded silence!"

He turns and glares at me. He's angry in a way I've never seen, but my resolve is strong. Stronger than his.

"I won't be silent, nor will I let you sacrifice the Quvites for me," I reply stubbornly.

"Rain, if you cannot be quiet I will have you removed and confined to quarters!" He points at me.

Quva resumes circling the table. When he passes me, a chill runs down my spine. Back at his chair, he turns to the table and leans on it with both arms. He sighs loudly and looks around the room.

"The choice is clear," he tells the gathering. "We will take what is owed by force, starting with New Asta. Our enemies have employed *Rekwa* against us, and we will use it on them.

"We have come to an impasse with the people of Salvoa. If we are to ever move forward with what was originally agreed upon, then we will have to take it. We have come too far, risked too much, and lost too many to give up. Drake said he would forgive the transgressions, but there is no guarantee. He cannot even honor our previous agreement."

"I won't let you do this!" I raise my voice higher. "It's my choice and I *choose* to die so my family, whom I promised to protect, and your race, can survive! My brother may not be trustworthy but let him satisfy his bloodlust with me!"

"Xera, escort him to his quarters," Quva instructs her. "He is under arrest."

Xera stands next to me. Rather than apprehending me, in a surprise move she puts both arms behind her back, and raises her chin in defiance.

"While I agree we cannot trust High Chancellor Drake, we cannot assert control over Rain, who is not of our people. We have no right to force him. If he wishes to surrender we cannot stop him."

"Xera, you are teetering on the line into insubordination. You are one of my closest advisors, but that is all you are, an advisor," Quva states, asserting his authority. "I am the fleet commander, as elected by unanimous vote of the advisors and a majority vote of the Vraditi. If you refuse to follow my order, speak now."

"I refuse to remove him," Xera says adamantly.

"Understood. Mazaq, escort him to his quarters, and Xera to yours. Put them both under lockdown until we are ready to push for the assault on the fortress." He waves her off and looks directly at Mazaq.

"No," Mazaq refuses. "We cannot hold him. He is a guest, and if he wishes to leave, it is in the bylaws of our people for him to be granted safe passage."

"Mazaq! I gave you a direct order!" Quva barks, his face crumpling in disappointment. "If you refuse again, I will strip you of your rank, and you will be repurposed to another job with less responsibility!"

"Stop. I know you're angry because Drake has devastated us. You're angry about the loss of life, and I am too. But you need to let me go," I try and reason with him. "I am ready and willing. I have brought disaster on your people with my ideas of rebellion. If I can make up for it somehow by turning myself in, then I have to try."

"Rain!" He sighs, slamming his fists on the table, shaking his head. "I do not want you to do this. You have been a guide for me, helping me with the tough decisions I have been unable to make on my own. And you so casually make yet another difficult choice despite the certainty that it is a deception."

"It's what I have to do. If I don't, I'll live with the guilt that I didn't do everything I could to save lives."

Quva continues to shake his head, as if in deliberation with himself. Closing all four eyes, he breathes in and out several times, and then straightens up.

He finally breaks. "If it is what you choose, Xera and Mazaq are right, and I cannot keep you here. We will inform High Chancellor Drake, and you will be provided transportation." He returns to his chair.

"When he establishes contact again, tell him I'm surrendering and that I expect my people to go free."

"Yes, I will. Perhaps you should take some time up in the garden for reflection?" Quva makes a suggestion.

I nod, and Quva motions for Xera to take me. Dr. Oreda is shooed out after us.

When we're on the platform, I look back and find all attention is on me.

Xera flies us away in silence. There's tension from Xera, as if she wants to say something. She shifts her weight several times, but stays quiet.

The garden's door opens and we enter. This last bastion of serenity calls to me before I run to my death.

In the grass, I kick off my slippers and walk.

Still in earshot, Xera calls after me in a sorrowful tone. "I will be by the panel there." She points to the wall. "I will inform you when Quva is ready."

"Thank you." I give her a weak smile.

Is there any hope of fighting Drake after I'm in his custody? Misery lent me their power for my escape from prison. But that power came from the Alkosians, and they were still alive. They're dead because of me, and no doubt hold me accountable. Maybe if I can convince them this is all Drake's fault...

Even if I can't fight, if I don't turn myself in, I won't have done everything I can to save everyone else. I am not blameless in their suffering. I can only hope Drake will accept my sacrifice, and spare the unwilling participants of our feud.

Taking the time to savor the view of Salvoa above my head, I trace cloud patterns with my eyes. From here it all looks so peaceful. I wish I could disappear into an obscure area somewhere, and live in peace for the rest of my days.

I sit below one of the luminescent trees, and lean on its trunk. The idea of giving myself up should be causing me anxiety, but I'm forcing myself to stay in the moment, despite knowing it will end soon. Peace and acceptance of my situation comes like a revelation, at least for a few moments.

I don't sense Eve in the collective of souls. Did she truly find peace in the end? Can I?

If I had turned myself over in exchange for their safety in the first place, she might be alive. I won't allow that to happen again. I have to die in order for others to live.

I let my mind go blank while staring at nothing. I'm sure I doze off, and am startled when I hear Xera.

"Rain?" She's only a few feet away. "It is time."

"Already?"

"Yes. One of the stealth craft is waiting for our arrival in the hangar." She holds her hand out for me to take.

Grabbing her hand, she pulls me up. When I try to let go, she holds tight. It comforts me a little, knowing someone is here for me. Dr. Oreda is already on the platform waiting.

"I hope this is okay." Xera tugs on my hand. "I thought you might need comfort, and having observed your culture this seemed appropriate."

"I wish it hadn't come to this. I think our two peoples could have been good friends."

"There is still hope." She smiles.

When we reach the platform, she lets go. We drop into the living quarters and head to the hangar. The doors open. The reconstruction of the bay is well under way, with Vraditi and robots working diligently, but there's much to do.

The handful of surviving ships are clustered near the main hanger doors. Xera stops at a stealth craft where Mazaq is waiting.

I exit the platform onto the deck, and he inclines his head. Dr. Oreda follows me, but Xera stays on the platform.

"I wish you good fortune," Xera says, nodding at me.

I return her nod and give a weak smile. *Good fortune is an unattainable dream, at least for me.*

Dr. Oreda is only steps behind me as I climb into the craft.

"*What are you doing?*" I frown.

"I'm going," she tells me putting her hands on her hips.

"*You're safer if you stay up here. I'm surrendering, and I don't want you to be collateral damage.*"

"You need supervision," she says climbing aboard the vehicle and sitting.

Mazaq and I look at each other, and he shrugs his one shoulder. Joining her on the ship, Mazaq and I sit across from her while Vraditi jump in, filling all the empty seats.

The pilot presses several buttons, and the two engines spring to life, their hum filling the cabin.

I'm confused for a moment as to why there are such large numbers for my sendoff. Then it hits me: they are all wearing combat armor.

Looking back at Xera, my eyes widen in shock. She waves at me with what I believe is a mischievous smile, and the door closes.

Standing up as we lift off, I hold onto the railing between my seat and Mazaq's.

I glare at him. "*What is this?*" I demand.

We move through the newly constructed door to space. He reaches up to a compartment above him, opens it and pulls my combat suit out.

"Put this on. You will need it."

He tosses the suit at me. Each of the Vraditi salute to me with one arm straight up and down following the centerline of their chests.

Not oblivious to this rebellion against my intentions, I'm stunned.

Despite only having one arm, Mazaq does his best to salute me also. A grin crosses his face, one I've seen on battle-hardened warriors as they ready to enter the battlefield. Bloodlust.

"*You...Quva...*" I'm at a loss.

I look to Dr. Oreda to see if she knew, but I don't have to ask – she's shocked, too.

My heart beats hard. Flooded with anger, fear, betrayal, and hopelessness, everything becomes jumbled. Flustered, I manage to start putting the suit on.

What if they attack, and Drake kills Ami and the others thinking I'm not surrendering? Why are they risking their safety?

"This is not acceptable!" I yell at Mazaq.

"An order has been given, and we are tasked to follow it. Not a single Quvite will disobey," he replies.

"I thought you had my back! You agreed with my decision!"

"I still do. You will be taken to Drake to surrender yourself, but the Quvites have decided to take what's ours," he tells me, grinning wider. "We do not even have to break through the wall. That fool has given us an opportunity to walk right through the front door."

"This isn't right!" I cinch the suit up, and punch him in the chest. His armor absorbs the blow. *"You couldn't have waited until my loved ones were safe?"*

"It is out of my hands. You should sit. We are going to be entering the atmosphere."

Salvoa has entered the view in the front window. I do as he suggests, taking my seat.

We push into the upper level of the planet's atmosphere and descend rapidly. The world below becomes visible. New Asta shimmers in the light, but it's overtaken by an enormous shadow, consuming all of the land below. My transfixion is broken when a voice comes over the intercom.

"Lead stealth ship will drop inside the wall of High Chancellor Drake's fortress at the designated point. When the package has been delivered we will initiate the attack pattern. All hands at the ready. Prepare for contact," Quva rings out. "This is our chance. We live or we die today!"

An unwilling accomplice to this coup, I stay silent. There's nothing I can do but participate. Dr. Oreda on the other hand looks terrified as she clings to her handles and bites her lip. She's rightly nervous.

We drop inside New Asta's borders, our stealth craft flying over skyscrapers now shadowed by the main ship. Darting and weaving, we make our way past the tallest the city has to offer, including Tower Zero. We head toward the far edge, and Drake's fortress becomes visible.

Flying around the perimeter, the main building is a metallic dark grey color. The balconies and guard towers attached are filled with armed soldiers, but none of them fire on us. There's an open yard, and landing pad where numerous New Astan ships are parked. A whole battalion waits to greet me.

The pilot swings the ship into an open spot within the paved area. We touch down, and the aft door opens up to reveal Colonel Tigby waiting for me.

Standing, I look at Mazaq and he nods. I step slowly from the ramp, and am seized by my arms. It's Specialists Jackie and Lyle. They're rough, twisting my arms behind my back and fitting me with cuffs.

Mazaq and Dr. Oreda follow, but Colonel Tigby holds his hand up.

"You have relinquished control of the war criminal. Your duty is done," Tigby tells Mazaq. "But Dr. Oreda may accompany him."

"We were assured by High Chancellor Drake we would be allowed to escort him in," he protests.

"Due to safety concerns, that portion of the agreement has been nullified," Tigby replies.

"It is not possible for your kind to keep agreed arrangements, is it?" Mazaq isn't upset. I hear excitement in his voice.

Specialists Jackie and Lyle step forward, leading me away through the battalion standing at attention. Over my shoulder, I try to get a glimpse of Mazaq. I'm just in time to watch him plant his monstrous fist directly into the side of Colonel Tigby's face. Blood spatters and teeth fly.

A riot ensues. The remaining Vraditi exit the ship and take on the soldiers.

Specialists Jackie and Lyle speed me along, Dr. Oreda keeping pace.

An explosion rocks the yard, followed by another, and another. A wave of heat hits us, and my escorts stumble.

Gunshots ring out. Precisely aimed beams of purple light tear through the yard from above the clouds, incinerating New Astan ships before they can lift off.

Quva was serious about using his Rekwa technology.

The mass of the Vraditi migration ship descends from the sky. Its bay doors open, and the surviving vessels of the flotilla join the battle.

The New Astan craft that are able to get into the air start fighting back. Missiles fly from them and the ground in attempts to destroy the Vraditi ships. Though some are hit, most of the projectiles are intercepted by the beams and other beam weaponry mounted to the smaller craft. They have begun a full scale invasion.

Teleport cylinders rain from the starship, and power on moments after impact. A flood of Vraditi pour from the white lights to join the battle on foot. It's a full warzone.

I struggle to watch the outcome, but being forced forward toward the castle doesn't afford me much opportunity.

Drake's own wide purple beam arcs across the sky from the top of the fortress, aimed at the underside of the migration ship. There's destruction, fire, and debris, but the fate of Quva and his Quvites is left to my imagination as we enter the castle.

The sounds from the battle resound throughout the massive grand hall. Ideas of struggling enters my mind, but this is the greatest opportunity I will have to confront Drake. They're taking me right to him. Behind the grand staircase are jewel-encrusted doors, reminding me of how vain he is.

The soldiers push the doors open to a great throne room. It's mostly open with a low balcony covering one half. Gold plated pillars run from floor to ceiling in an ostentatious show of wealth.

Red carpet is laid out, leading up to a raised platform with two empty chairs at the far end. Only one is large enough for Drake's Tarak body. But the room is devoid of people, save for the four of us.

Beyond the throne are red and gold embroidered curtains concealing another door. It's not as cleverly hidden as the secret passage in my castle's bedroom though. We pass through the door to find a corridor high enough to accommodate Drake's Tarak bulk.

As we walk, I expect to see paintings or photographs of him, but to my surprise the walls are plain. Dr. Oreda fearlessly continues to follow.

Why is she still here? She can't hope to do anything for me. Maybe I can convince Drake to release Ami and the others to her, and have her escort them to safety.

Deep in the passage, there is a spiral staircase, and I have to laugh out loud at his lack of originality. Instead of going down, it curls upward.

The building rocks as something hits it with a continuous barrage. It's steady, and emits a loud hum, leading me to believe it's Quva's Rekwa beam. Audible cracking in the stonework startles Dr. Oreda.

At the top of the staircase is a short hallway and a door. When it's open, I let out another laugh at the predictable second throne room.

"You're an idiot stuck in the past!"

A unit of soldiers stands at the ready, their weapons drawn and pointed at me. Against the far wall, my brother squats on a secondary throne with his captives – my true family – chained to the wall. My anger is at a peak, but I bide my time.

Because he is Tarak, Drake sees fit to wear nothing but a spiky oversized crown. His dark scales shimmer in the light as he shifts. Tapping a claw on the crown, he grins smugly.

Drake waves the soldiers to bring me forward. They kick the back of my legs, shoving me into a kneeling position several feet in front of him.

But my attention isn't on him right now.

Ami, Agatha, Emma, and James look at me. They are sick with malnourishment and exhaustion. Desperation and worry are plastered on their faces, but none of them speak. They don't have to, though. I know what they're thinking and feeling because their torment is bleeding into Misery, cutting me to the core. Each of them is crying out silently, warning me to run, telling me I shouldn't have come. The only thing I can do to reassure them is smile, weakly.

"You've accomplished for me what I've been hoping for, little brother. With you here and the Quvites soon to be exterminated, I will be left unquestioned." He shifts in his seat and picks at his teeth. "Do you realize how hard it has been to goad the Quvites into attacking?"

"It doesn't matter." I turn my attention to him. *"You have me, now let them go."*

Heavy explosions cause the structure to shudder, and a crack splits the wall to my left. Cool and collected, Drake ignores it and stands to stretch his long, muscular arms.

"Do you think because I have you captive the Quvites might surrender?" He laughs. "Will they be as gullible as you were, and bend to my will?"

"This attack was against my wishes. You pushed them too far, and now they are taking their promised share of the land by force."

"They won't have it. This is *my* world!"

He walks past his captives, running his claws down their faces. Each of them shies away except for Emma who attempts to bite him. He draws his claw away and backhands her with a closed fist. She spits blood at him and grins like a wild beast.

"Come closer you wretched lizard," she hisses, but it's not her voice. Malice is present in her eyes.

Evalyn?

"Why do these people mean so much to you?" he asks me.

"It doesn't matter. They have no part in our quarrel. You have what you want. Me."

"This woman..." He stops at Agatha. "She is what to you, hmm?"

"She's what you see: an old woman." I know what he's getting at, and he's unlikely to believe she's not more to me.

"Come now: it's in your eyes. She is who saved you after I left you for dead in the forest, isn't she?" He grabs her by the chin, and she looks away from him.

"What do you gain by this?" I fear what is coming next. Misery is surfacing, but not fast enough.

Quval! Where are you?

"She is, isn't she?" He smiles that evil, heartless, and ruthless smile.

"She's nothing!" I get louder. I'm practically pleading for her life, and he knows it.

"You thought she could replace our mother?" He draws his dagger and smirks.

"How many people do you need to kill if you have me? Aren't I the one you really want?" I yell at him.

"Do you remember what I did to *our* mother?" He smiles, placing the edge to her throat.

Agatha whimpers. James grunts like a madman, trying to stand and break his chains.

"She saved you. Now she needs saving, Tiberius!"

"Stop!"

"Save her, Tiberius!"

I try and agitate Misery into giving me control. *"Come on! You want justice? Come out and destroy my nemesis! He is the reason I exist! You hate me for what I've done! How much more should he be hated for making me who I am?"*

"Can you save her?"

Misery is aware of the situation and their presence is weighing heavily on me, but they won't intervene.

"Why won't you act? You can help me save her!" I call to them in my mind.

"I...I can't."

I'm forced to watch in horror as Drake snaps his mouth several times, chomping his sharp teeth together. He's watching my anguish and reveling in it.

"That's right. You can't. This is your reward for doing a good job and bringing the Quvites so I can slaughter them!"

In a swift and violent move he swings his arm back, and jams the blade into her gut. Not satisfied with the initial plunge, he pushes it completely through and pulls up.

Agatha gasps, and a cry of shock escapes her throat. She coughs up blood and stares at me. Ami shrieks, and Evalyn in Emma's body wails in agony. James goes into a frenzy, cutting his wrists on the shackles trying to get at Drake.

"Agatha! Agatha!" I scream.

"She's free now, Tiberius." Drake laughs. "Just like I'd promised."

James flings his legs out trying to kick him. Drake punches him in the head, and he goes limp.

My vision blurs with tears. My chest rises and falls, but I can't catch my breath. Struck with grief, I rock on my knees and sob. The life drains from her sunken face. He waited for the right opportunity to torture me. He murdered her just to watch me suffer.

"Agatha," I whisper. *"I'm so sorry..."*

This can't be real. How could I have let this happen? Why did they save me when I should have died in the forest?

He comes over and grabs my face, lifting it up. "Ah, now see! That's how I wanted you in my presence. Distraught!"

Worse than the agony of watching her murder, is that I can feel her inside the darkness now. Dead in her hopelessness, she cries out. Her woes and accusations are toward me.

"Rain! Why didn't you save me? Why did you take so long to come and rescue us?"

"My daughter! I am dead, and my daughter is soon to follow!"

"Don't let him kill Ami!"

"Let me into the light! Please!"

She's a shadow of who she once used to be, now consumed by her despair. The weight of the souls on me is immense, but this one hurts much more than everyone else. To be accused by someone I love, and who loved me, of not doing my best is crushing.

My fury overtakes me. Grunting and straining, I pull the cuffs hoping they'll break. I grind my teeth and attempt to stand, but I'm shoved back to my knees.

Agatha's introduction to the world of the lost is enough to draw Misery to listen to me. Their voices drown out the world, and the black oozes to every corner of my body. Shadow tendrils extend outward and shoot toward Drake.

I am shocked from behind, my control lost. I'm paralyzed, and the darkness recedes. Falling to my face, my assailant walks by. It's Dr. Oreda.

"Did you have to kill the old woman?" She moves up to the throne and crosses her arms.

"Ah, Beth." He returns to his throne and pulls her onto his lap. He wraps his enormous arms around her waist. "You know as well as I do they all have to die. Him, them, the 'Alkosians', the Quvites. Anyone who doesn't pledge allegiance to *me*! I am eternal, and will have obedience from my subjects."

She gives him a scolding look, and he sighs. With a wave of a hand, he signals the soldiers to lift me. I'm placed on my knees and held there. He gives Dr. Oreda a small push, and she stands. Leading her to me, he hands her his dagger.

"Tiberius, meet your executioner."

I guess he can retain possession when not in contact with it, as long as he's in something else, like Evalyn. If it's destroyed, will he be gone forever?

"No, don't..." Ami cries out weakly.

"Do I have to?" Dr. Oreda asks. "You know this is against my oath."

"Consider it your gift to me as a wedding present." He stares into my eyes.

Everything was a farce. Caring for me, escaping to the Vraditi, pretending to be invested in my welfare. I truly was a scapegoat, from the very beginning. She told me so. I was just too blind to understand her meaning.

"What about your present to me? You promised to take a human form, and his body is superior." Dr. Oreda tries to get out of killing me.

"I did, but I'm not ready. I like the Tarak form for its brute strength and ability to instill fear. Meanwhile, I do not want to share his body. He would still exist if I did, and I want to see him utterly destroyed."

Wanting desperately to close my eyes and accept my fate, I'm forced to watch because I can't blink. Dr. Oreda hesitates, gripping the dagger tightly. Drake gives her a nudge, and she lifts it to her chest, holding it with both hands.

Agatha and Eve. Gregory and the Alkosians. The Qavites. The deaths of millions. Simply because I exist and made choices which should have never happened. This is the final result. I deserve this, don't I?

Am I ready to die?

"Hey! Over here you wrinkled hag!" Evalyn yells through Emma at the doctor. "If you're going to kill him, come kill me first!"

Drake looks back at Emma and grins.

"Yeah, that's right. You're a nasty, ugly harpy! What are you going to do about it?" she prods.

"Evalyn, shut up!" The paralysis is lifting.

"I won't until she comes and kills me first!"

He doesn't miss an opportunity to make me suffer more. He holds his hand under the point of the blade and points to Emma.

"That one first dear. Did you hear what she called you?" he snarls.

"Stop! Leave her alone!"

Dr. Oreda looks, deciding whether to react or not.

"That's right, you're a murderer aren't you? Just like he is! You're disgusting and aren't worthy of being called human!" Evalyn is relentless.

What is she doing?! Is she buying me time?

It's enough for Dr. Oreda to react.

"I won't kill you. Maybe, if you shut up, I can talk the High Chancellor into letting you go," she warns her.

"Puppet! Coward! You're brainwashed, or ethically challenged, to believe you can take Rain's life and this will be the end of it!"

"Shut up!" She slaps Emma.

Even over the battle outside, the strike is heard. Her head drops, and she cries. Dr. Oreda shakes her head and returns to me.

Evalyn failed to buy more time. I'm not recovered!

"That's no fun," Drake pouts. "I'll just have to do it later."

Once more, she stands in front of me, poised to strike. Resigning myself to the idea that the end is coming, I ready myself to let it happen and close my eyes. A hand comes to rest on me, and I feel a jolt. I wait for the blade to be plunged in.

The dark world I dread consumes me: a plane of existence where I am surrounded by every voice who's ever died in despair. I'm ready to become one of them. Consumed by my hopelessness, I'm already a part of Misery. Hanging my head in shame and agony, this is a fitting place for me to spend eternity. To suffer with them because it's all I can do to console them.

"*RAIN!*"

Evalyn appears within the dark world.

"*You shouldn't be in here! You were supposed to go somewhere else! This is my end!*" I lament.

"*Can you stop moping for a moment? You need to get control of this and fight!*" She yells at me.

"*What?!*"

"*I used that woman as a vessel to jump bodies and give you a chance. Now stop whining and fight, or Ami is going to die!*"

I'm not dead?

The light to release me appears, but not without condition. The souls bear down on me, like they've climbed onto my back. Their cries exasperate me.

"*Release us from this prison and BRING US INTO THE LIGHT!*"

It's their wish as it was when I allowed them out of the void through my body. They don't *just* want retribution, they want to be set free. They want to be allowed into the world, to overwhelm it. I know that once it's done, drawing them back to containment will be difficult.

"*Then stop fighting me and lend me your full power! Stop acting when it's convenient for you, and let me bring you into the light!"*

Everything I held back from them, every block I had keeping them in place, I release. Thrust forward, the light reappears.

Beyond it, in the real world, there's confusion and yelling.

"I will slit her throat Tiberius, I swear it!" Drake threatens.

As I'm pushed back into reality, I'm already straining the cuffs. The material of my suit is keeping me from tearing my hands off, but the force is threatening to break my wrists.

Misery is already protecting me, without my direction. Shots are fired at me, but the darkness swirls around me like a tornado, deflecting them, and infecting soldiers near me. When it feels like I'm near to pulling my arms out of their sockets, Misery solidifies on the cuffs and shatters them. Enraged, I roar.

Our eyes meet while he holds Ami captive. Instinct compels my movements and the darkness follows. With arms outstretched, dark hands manifest as extensions. They're quick to immobilize Drake, and keep Ami safe from harm. I rip the dagger from his hands with a third extension coming from my chest.

"Ami, I'm sorry. This is just who I am."

I regret having to break my promise to her. I don't want to be violent, but only for her sake. The dagger is mine now, but instead of breaking it, or killing him with it, I seek to wound him as he wounded me. With the death of a loved one.

Dr. Oreda cowers behind his throne. A fourth dark hand snatches her, dragging her screaming to me. Misery's black walls continue to spring up and protect me while soldiers in the room try to save her life. Her veins blacken as Misery starts killing her. She writhes in my grasp, screaming, suffering. The motions are too easy, too smooth. I put aside my care of holding back for Ami's sake. Staring Drake down with my teeth bared, I raise my hand and plunge the blade into Dr. Oreda without pause. She gasps. Dumping her body, the blade cuts upward to seal her fate sooner.

You wanted me to lose my mind with grief. Now it's my turn to repay the favor, you wretch.

The moment Drake's soul is crushed is visible, even with his Tarak face. But being held in place, he can't retaliate and take Ami's life in exchange. Despite being able to exert physical force on him, I wish that I could watch the same black creep through his veins like a virus, infecting and killing him as it had Dr. Oreda's. But the Tarak appear immune, same as the Vraditi.

He can't move his hands to slice Ami's throat with his claws, or snap her neck, or crush her. I wrench his arms open with my dark appendages. Ami falls to the floor.

I pick Drake up and throw his massive form over my shoulder. Before he can recover I've reached him again.

"This is your fault!" I punch him in the throat.

Misery continues to spread outward, overtaking my opponents. Each one touched is infected, and they become a part of me. The echo of their screams resonates in me, but I use them as fuel. There are some not close enough for my immediate grasp, and they try to escape through the room's few exits. I let them go.

He starts to get back up, and in the same motion tries to sweep me with his tail. The move is predictable. I leap over it, and onto him. Misery urges me. It wants me to rend his flesh and end his life for his part in their suffering. My hatred for my brother and what he's done pushes me to punish him first. I need to satisfy my lust for retribution.

"If you'd just finished the job in the woods..." I punch him while yelling. "...this wouldn't be happening! None of this!"

He's in my grasp. With supplemented strength, I twist his arm. Drake bends to alleviate the pain, and I spin him. Off the ground and into the air, I let go and fling him into the wall. Several shockwaves follow, but he rolls out of the way before impact.

"Believe me, brother. I tried!"

He runs to a bookshelf nearby, grabs an object, and vanishes.

He's collected artifacts of power.

"Coward!"

His disappearance likely leaves me only moments to attend to James, Ami, and Emma. I try to pull everything back inside, but *they* won't allow me. But I am able to retract them enough to get close. Using small shockwaves, I sever the chains and free them. James picks Agatha's body up.

"Go!" I instruct them sternly.

"Rain?" Ami's frightened.

"We don't have time to talk!" I have to be hard with her. "This isn't finished. Go! Now!"

It's hard, but they have to leave. I know Drake's regrouping.

Time is short, and if they're here, he'll use them as leverage.

My senses are heightened as I escort them. Near the door I came through, Drake reappears in our way.

He has my sword in one hand, and a doll in the other. He snarls and huffs. He's angry. Looking past me, I sense his eyes are on his beloved, Beth.

That artifact...I must take it from him.

On impulse I leap at him. He disappears. I fail to collide with him, and I assume he's teleported. A pressure in the air behind me gives him away, and I dodge the tip of my own sword. I swing my elbow back to hit him, but he's gone again. When he doesn't immediately reappear, their chance to leave opens.

"Go! Now!" I direct. "Stay low! Get to the Quvites!"

They run into the hallway, and the door closes after them.

I'm alone with the dead, waiting for his return. Not knowing when or where he'll reappear, I ready a few black shields to protect me. The walls shake, and there are crumbling sounds. A reprieve in the noise for just a moment allows me to hear it: a slight puff of air. He's returned.

Drake grunts and swings my sword down on me.

My hand comes up to take the cut, but a black mass surrounds it. Misery absorbs the impact, and I'm safe. Still, I feel his weight pressed into it. He's trying to use brute force to break it. I duck and roll. He stumbles forward. We face each other and I swing for his jaw.

Drake vanishes and reappears moments later – with Ami, Emma, and James.

"You can't leave! He needs his *loved ones* to motivate him!" Drake sneers and disappears, leaving them unharmed.

There's a slight pressure of air to my left. I turn to it, but he's used it as a distraction. Appearing on my right, I'm unable to react in time. My sword cuts the suit, and leaves me with a slash to my ribs. Swinging again, he puts effort into cutting me in half.

The dark wall blocks the blow. The blade is close enough for me to grab it.

With my hand on the metal, I send a shockwave up to the hilt. His grip loosens, but my opportunity to disarm him is thwarted by his clenched fist coming for my head. I shield with a dark wall, and restrain him with a tendril.

A purple beam cuts into the room through the three floors above, tearing diagonally through the building. Chunks of ceiling and various objects fall from above. A Rekwa weapon has reached the belly of the castle.

Hopefully Quva is sending me reinforcements.

Instead, New Astan soldiers rappel in, firing on me before they're even on the floor. The shadow solidifies into a bubble. I'm safe for now, but the continuous gunfire allows me no opportunity to retaliate. Drake beats on my shield.

Ignoring the blaring pain in my side, I concentrate and eject a bubble shockwave. He stops hitting the dark shield for a moment, and I assume I've pushed him back. My shield drops, and the black spreads and races for the soldiers. The shadows snake across the floor to grab them. They flee, and the gunfire stops for the moment.

Drake uses the opportunity to teleport. When he reappears, I reach for him, and he teleports again. He toys with me, appearing in a circle around me. I'm caught off guard. He rips my helmet off, and breaks my nose with a solid blow from his scaly fist.

I stagger backward, dazed. The room spins as my brain rattles against my skull. Blood pours from my nose and the lacerations caused by the scales.

My control on Misery is fading. They're resisting my commands, and I can't bring up any walls to block. Drake notices and becomes confident, and instead of ending it he batters me. Blow after blow, he slams me with his fists. He kicks my leg and sweeps me with his tail.

"This is the only way it could have been, brother," he says while raising my sword to end it. "You were never going to defeat me."

The collective acts of its own accord.

Underneath the fleeing soldiers, it strikes and impales them with massive spikes. The souls surround us, caging Drake, hanging his minions above our heads to die in his sight. A multitude of dark hands fly at him from the sides.

Hastily, he tries to kill me, but hands jut up underneath him. Drake can't take my life and avoid their grasp too. Dodging and lurching causes his thrust to miss.

"Grab the doll!" I yell at them.

The hands grab from all angles. In a rare moment of surprise or panic, instead of trying to teleport he tries to hold the doll from them. He fails, and they snatch the doll away. It's gone, sucked into the black, and he is at their mercy.

The hands of the dead restrain him, and I am in control of his fate. They bring him to his knees. Cocky, I hover over him. Running my fingers on the blade still in his hand, I find another chance to make him suffer. With the blade in between my palms, I unleash a shockwave. It rips his arm off. I can't stop myself now. My hatred for him reaches its peak.

I speak into the dark world and pit them against him. *"Everything I was as King Tiberius and the decisions I made as Rain, are ultimately his fault. He deserves no mercy!"*

"Brother…" I stare at him with contempt. *"You made me who I am, and this is the only way it could have ended."*

I'm falling into the same trap he did. We are both overconfident. Both arrogant. That's who we are. But taking his life without making him suffer wouldn't be justice.

Starting with his ribs, I beat him. Blow after blow he takes it, because there's nothing he can do. The darkness has him. Every punch pushes my rage farther, and I call up Eve and Agatha's images in my mind to push me through the pain of my injuries. Finally he coughs up thick, dark blood. Misery follows my lead, and starts to envelop him. It surrounds his body.

"You may be immune to the plague effect, but you can't stop their physical force!"

A swift kick powered by a shockwave through my foot breaks his sternum, and he falls over. He's pinned to the floor. I enter an uncontrollable fit, using both fists to crush his lizard face.

"How dare you take Eve and Agatha from me?!" I yell at him, continuing to crush his bones. "Everything is your fault! Your fault! Your fault!"

My rage relinquishes control to the greater entity. Misery controls my movements, and they've taken my autonomy away. It feels good to release the anger I've held in. Even better with their weight leaving me for good.

They dig deeper into him, and there's a flicker of hopelessness from within Drake. They've reached his human soul. It delights me, and I grin evilly.

As I beat the life from him, the black expands, spreading everywhere. All across the building, enveloping walls, draping down the side of the outer edge, flowing across the city at an exponential rate.

But I don't care. My adversary's neck is between my fingers. His blood covers everything.

"Rule over the dirt!" Misery forms spikes and stabs him repeatedly. "You only have yourself to blame! You should have never double crossed me. I was the king, and you were my servant!"

Disconnected from my body, I'm consumed into the collective, but it's different this time. I'm floating as a part of them, and can sense everything *we* touch. My primal rage fuels us and we overtake New Asta. People begin dying, and I feel them enter eternity with me. Their fear of death adds to the power as chaos erupts. Each new soul helps us grow. My vision blackens, and I fear losing my individuality and disappearing forever.

"Evalyn?! Help!" I call to her, sure she's here with me.

There's no response from her, but there is a voice calling out. It's very distant and faint. I try to look around me, but everything is becoming dark. I can't tell if I'm disembodied in the dark world, or if it's because the black has blocked the light.

One voice turns to a few, and they persist. I strain to find where they're coming from. There's a patch unaffected by us, a protected place because of who is in there.

Huddling in a corner are Ami, Emma, and James, screaming at the top of their lungs. It's faint, and I can't make out the words.

They're still there and alive.

Whatever control I may have had over Misery is gone. We seek to envelop everything. Time is running out to save the three surviving members of my family. My efforts to pull us back in are useless. The millions of others won't listen to my one voice. They're too enamored with being free, with being 'in the light.'

"Rain, you need to regain control!" Evalyn finds me. Her voice is panicked.

"I'm trying!"

All of the focus I can muster to draw them in is useless. The more I try, the more they resist. They don't want to be contained any longer. They have their 'light' and I can't stop them. I can't even stop myself from drooling and bleeding on Drake's lifeless body.

James and Emma scream, and their anguish cuts so deep I feel it. Ami breaks away, tearing herself from their grasp in what seems like slow motion. Running out one step at a time onto the black mass, she's coming for me.

No! Ami! Go away!

Watching in horror, Misery touches the bottom of her feet. While she runs toward me, it creeps up her bare legs, into her veins.

"No! Please! Don't take her from me!" I plead with the souls.

"She will be with you soon. Everyone will. And we will bring you into the light." They reply.

She cuts a swath across the black floor. The blackness is past her ankles. No matter how hard I try to cry out to her, nothing leaves my lips.

Despite the danger, she does not turn back. Her face twists. She's fighting it. When she reaches me, she grabs my waist, trying to pull me off of Drake. The black creeps up farther.

My hands raise to hit him once more, but she kneels on his chest, and gets in my way. Shaking me violently by the shoulders, Ami tries to snap me out of it. But I sense she's receiving a dead stare from me. She stops and caresses my face with her hands. The darkness invades her arms.

"Shh, it's okay now!" Tears are already flowing from her eyes: she's in agony.

Her lips press to mine, and she kisses deeply. I cherish the warmth of her lips. She is my hope and my love, and I want to pull it together for her. The balance of her tenderness and comfort help me dig deep for strength. Slowly, I regain control of myself, bringing mastery of Misery with it.

They scream at me as I pull them back into their cage within my body. They curse me. Light, true light, becomes visible again.

I try to reverse the effects on her. Held in my arms, I kiss her deeper. She puts her fingers into my hair. I concentrate, hard, but fail to draw the darkness out of her. The poisonous entity is killing her.

Tugging at me, she pulls me off of the Tarak corpse. We collapse to the floor, sitting cradled together. It's climbed through her neck, and into her face now, every blackened vein a highlight of my failure to keep her safe.

I shake my head, unwilling to believe it's inevitable. I cry because she's dying and it's my fault.

"It's okay, Rain." It's as if she knows I am condemning myself. "I know you didn't mean for any of this."

She smiles despite her pain.

"It's not okay! I should have died in those woods. If I was dead you would have lived. You shouldn't have saved me!"

"I have…a secret." She strains herself.

Her breathing becomes labored. As the black seeps from the veins to cover her skin, she pulls me in. I kiss her, my lips quivering. She's deeply passionate despite the pain, and a strange phenomenon hits me.

Images and thoughts flood into my head, showing me Ami's point of view, through her eyes. All of her memories and emotions allow me to literally feel how much she loves me. But there's more.

It was at the very beginning, when she and Agatha saved me. A moment comes back, and I can see it now as she's giving me her memories. It's hazy at first, but it becomes clearer as our memories merge. She kissed me on the couch after the attack, and took my memory, completely wiping it out. It was never Drake or the attack that gave me amnesia.

"Why?" I ask. "How…?"

"I wanted to give you peace in death. But you didn't die. I didn't know Evalyn would heal you with an artifact." She musters a half-laugh and weak smile. "And so you were reborn, and I fell in love."

I laugh and cry at the same time. A million questions run around in my head, like how she knew she had an ability; if she knew I was the King of

Asta before I did. After all, they'd had plenty of time to explore while I was unconscious.

But none of it matters. She had given me the gift of starting over, and I squandered it. My lungs shudder as I try to take a breath.

With Misery receded, James and Emma are able to come near. Kneeling, they're already sobbing. Ami is now nearly enveloped by the toxins overtaking her.

"*This wasn't supposed to happen,*" I mumble. "*We were supposed to be safe. You...you were supposed to be safe!*"

"Shh, I know. I know." She can no longer smile. The pain is too great.

"*Ami, I wanted to settle down. I wanted to be with you, to marry you.*"

"I know, dear."

I look up at them trying to fool myself into thinking they might be able to fix this. Though the truth is evident, it doesn't keep me from trying to argue for her to fight.

"*Fight it! Please!*" I return to staring in her now black eyes.

"I'm not like you – I'm not strong."

"This isn't fair!" James yells.

"Ami, don't leave us! Please!" Emma cries.

"I love you all. I *love* you, Rain." Her breaths are shallow and she coughs for air.

"*I love you so much,*" I choke. "*I love you!*"

Ami becomes limp in my arms, and I rock her. Kissing her forehead, I wish for a miracle, that she would spring back to life and this nightmare would be over. She's gone though. Tears fall from my face to hers. There's nothing I can do but scream and wail, the sounds echoing off the grand walls.

I've ruined everyone's lives!

Sitting there, James and Emma cling to her lifeless body too. We cry for what could be hours.

The noises from the battle fade away eventually, as do our cries. Shock sets in.

Death surrounds us, or more accurately, me. I've caused irreparable damage, and my death now would be pointless. Even suicide wouldn't be adequate penance. As thoughts of my own demise swirl in my head, it occurs to me that when I die, Misery may be released permanently.

I need to be put in a prison. Is there a prison strong enough to hold Drake, Misery, and myself? Can we be utterly destroyed? Perhaps the Vraditi will have an answer.

There comes a moment when it feels like it's time to leave. We can cry no longer. I muster the strength to open my eyes and pick her up. My companions look at me, exhausted and weary.

For now, all I want to do is take them home safely. Into the warm, inviting house. That house with the green circle of grass. With the apple tree and garden to keep us fed. Where the kitchen always smelled of delicious foods. To sit at the table where we became friends. And family. And I learned to love.

"James, I need a favor," I mumble.

"What?" He's devoid of emotion.

"Retrieve the dagger from Dr. Oreda's...that woman's chest, and stick it on top of Ami. Don't touch it with your bare hands."

He nods and moves to her crumpled heap of a body, but he hesitates. Tearing his shirt, he wraps a strip around the hilt, and pulls it free. A look of disgust is on his face, and I can't tell if Drake is penetrating his mind, or if it's because he had to pull it from a corpse. With haste, he gets rid of it by running over and tossing it onto Ami.

"Come. Let's go...home." The words are barely out and I'm fighting back another breakdown.

Emma takes me by the arm, and I carry Ami out. James walks slowly behind us. We walk down the hallway toward the spiral staircase.

At the bottom is Agatha, where Drake had apparently snatched them. James lifts her and whispers. He whimpers and fights tears again. Emma closes her eyes tightly for a moment.

We're soon back in the grand hall. Surprisingly, some soldiers were unaffected by Misery. Specialists Lyle and Jackie are there, guns pointed in our direction, but they don't fire. They understand that with my emergence, their side has lost and they lower their weapons.

Through the grand doors and outside, Vraditi and humans continue to fight overhead. The Quvites are near victory. Only their Rekwa continues, and they rip ships from the sky without hesitation.

The starship is ablaze though. Its underbelly has been torn asunder, and it's losing altitude slowly. The edge of it begins to arc toward the floating island, threatening the buildings in its path.

It's not my concern anymore. It's for them to finish now.

The fallen of both species litter the ground. Amongst an uncountable number, I recognize Mazaq's tattoos, his torso scorched from a Rekwa weapon, lifeless. A look of terror is frozen on his face, his eyes wide, but with my arms full I cannot close them.

There are few humans left alive, in the process of being captured. A triumphant walk for our victory would be in order, had the cost of this battle not been so great.

How did it come to this? Why did I let it?

Everyone stops to stare as we cross the yard. Focusing my attention on an unscathed stealth craft, we ignore both factions. Gently, I set Ami into one of the seats, buckling her in as if she were still alive. Taking the dagger in my hand, I briefly hear *his* voice. It's only in my hand long enough to secure it under her leg for transport. James follows my lead and secures Agatha with his blood soaked hands.

"Strap in," I tell them somberly.

They sit on the opposite side of the craft from Ami and Agatha. I exit the vehicle and find the nearest Vraditi. I'm barely keeping my composure, but it's enough to command him.

"Mazaq is dead. I am Mission First Command. Pilot me to Salvoa's surface, to the crash site where I was first rescued by Yaqta, and then to where the house is," I bark an order harshly.

He snaps to attention. "Shall we inform Quva?"

"On the way." I turn abruptly and enter the ship.

I sit between James and Emma. I try to hold their hands, but James refuses. Emma takes my hand weakly, and I rest my neck back against the head rest. The Vraditi moves to the pilot's chair and starts the engines while closing the door. In a few moments we are airborne, and far above the city. No shots are fired at us.

A communication line is opened, and Quva appears on the screen. The bridge of the starship is heavily damaged. The crew are working fervently to put out fires, attend to wounded, and still keep the starship running.

"Rain is leaving the fortress and heading to the planet's surface. Confirm flight plan."

"Confirmed. Status?" Quva asks.

I look at the screen. *"Drake is dead, as is half of my family. Finish without me. I'm going home."*

"We cannot allow you to go to the house because of the temporal negation module," he speaks gently.

"I'll tell you once: I'm going to that house. I'm going to lay my fallen to rest, and there is nothing you can do to stop me. I've earned that much." I'm angry. Not at him, but it gets directed at him.

He is silent. The pilot looks between the two of us and breaks the uncomfortable silence.

"Orders?" the pilot asks.

"Do as he says." Quva backs down.

"Understood." He continues on his course.

Bringing us close to the ground, he races along the bluish grass. The wreckage of my escape craft comes into view, and he lands next to its burnt hull. The rear of our ship opens. A lump in my throat forms, and I'm quick to exit. My feet hit the grass, and I vomit. I bend over, retching and heaving.

The loss...it's too great.

I finish and move to the wreck. The door is shut, and there's no power to open it. I climb in through the broken window to the cockpit. Eve's body has begun to decay, and the smell offends, but she deserves a proper burial. Her face is sunken, her beauty gone. Keeping my emotions in check, I unbuckle her and carry her out.

Nearing our stealth craft, Emma sees the body in my arms and she sobs again. James moves over and comforts her. He pulls her in, and allows her to cry. He strokes her hair and makes a shushing noise while I strap Eve into the seat beside Ami.

"Pilot, take us home."

He lifts off, and I sit away from them. A few moments pass and I see the house. On the approach, it's clear the energy barriers are still in place, and my anger flares. I plan to destroy every orb.

"Pilot, I want you to drop the door and keep the vessel hovering. We're going to

each one of the orbs at the perimeter." I instruct him while Quva continues to watch from the console.

"Understood," he replies and proceeds.

We decelerate and he arcs the vehicle to the left, pulling us right up next to the barrier. With the aft end open, I drop a few inches to the ground. The orb's mirror-like surface provides me a view of my tattered suit and now completely black face. A literal shadow of who I used to be.

It hums with electricity. I grimace, thinking about the first time I saw them, because they were an unknown herald of death. A shockwave crushes it easily.

If only I'd known that before...

Electrical arcs jump from the device for a moment and then die. The red walls connecting this orb to the next two dissipate.

Climbing on and off of the stealth craft, the pilot circles the property, and one by one I obliterate them.

When we've come full circle and the craft has settled just short of the grass, I climb aboard to retrieve my family. Quva speaks before I can depart.

"We are sorry for your loss. Is there...can we do anything for you?" He's sorrowful.

"An attendant."

"Certainly. It will be sent down shortly."

He frowns. He wants to ask more, but I ignore him.

"Pilot, please retrieve my friend from her seat and help me bring her to the grass."

He jumps up and assists by taking Eve, while I take Ami. Undoing her harness, I come face to face with her pitch black skin. My heart thumps heavily. I want to kiss her again, but she's gone.

Slinging her up into my arms, I look to James and tilt my head toward the dagger. He's quicker than the first time. Emma steps onto the grass while I wait for him. He retrieves Agatha, and we walk together, carrying mother and daughter to their final resting place. The pilot follows.

"Set her there in the grass," I say to the pilot.

He does and waits expectantly.

"Dismissed..." I pause for a moment. *"Thank you."*

He returns to the ship. The door closes, and he speeds back toward the migration ship barely keeping itself from colliding with New Asta.

The three of us cross the lonely yard. Clothes are strewn about, the garden has wilted, the grass is unkempt. Emma leads us inside, and it smells stale. There's no arguing. Agatha's gentle smile isn't there to comfort me when I need reassurance.

"Where should we lay them?" James asks.

"In Ami's room for now. We can bury them tomorrow," My voice comes out barely above a whisper.

Emma holds the swinging kitchen door open, and I head down the hall to Ami's room. Like I might if she had fallen asleep on the couch, I lay her to rest softly on the mattress. I kneel and slide my arms out from under her. James places Agatha gently on the other side.

Kneeling, I rest my face on the soft blanket, Ami's cold hand pressed to my cheek.

Why can't this be a bad dream? I want to wake up and have this be a terrible nightmare. I'd give anything for that.

Even through the multitude of dead because of my actions, I'm too self-absorbed to see past the loss of three women: my surrogate mother, the love of my life, a great friend.

Footsteps pad away, but I don't have the strength to look. Instead I kiss Ami's hand and speak to her.

"Ami, I'm sorry. I wish it was me, and not you." My lips quiver. I'm repeating an apology which will never mean anything to her. "I'm so sorry."

~~~~~~

After losing track of time grieving in Ami's room, I don't want to part from her, but I need rest. I'm utterly spent.

Standing, a sharp pain in my side reminds me that I have a wound which needs dressing to avoid infection. In the bathroom, I pull the top half of the suit off and inspect it. The material caught the brunt of the slash, and the wound isn't too deep. It's long, though, and any movement of my arms pulls at the scabbing.

After cleaning and bandaging myself, I head to the living room. They're sitting on the couch, in shock. When Emma sees me coming, she shifts to make room for me.

With Misery contained for now, it's safe to comfort her when she throws herself in my lap and cries. She hiccups and sobs, and all I can do is comb her hair with my fingers.

I doze off a couple times, but never long enough to actually rest. In the middle of the night there's a thunderous crash from the direction of the mountain. When I get up to look, the city above the clouds is aflame, and highlighted in the fire is the migration ship which finally crashed into the floating island. It's sinking to the ground and will soon collide with the mountain.

I return inside and rest my head on the back of the couch. The night drags on. Eventually I become aware that Quva's come to the house.

Despite the crash of his ship, he's left whatever remains to bring the attendant robot himself. He speaks, but the words don't register. I ignore him and he's gone soon enough.

~~~~~~

Devastating images of all the death replays in my mind's eye. I may be free from the past and Drake, but there's no rest for me, and this torture is deserved after what I've allowed to happen. Being motionless and hoping that a moment will come when I'm not conscious has become impossible.

I need to make myself busy.

Grabbing a shovel from downstairs, I head outside to dig three graves. Morning creeps up as the first hole is done, and Eve is first.

Inside, I head to retrieve Ami. James is up, staring out the window. Words of sorrow and remorse are on my tongue, but they won't come out.

His family is dead, and it's my fault. How can I say anything?

While burying Ami, I hear a door. James wanders past the well. He doesn't stop, doesn't look back. His feet carry him farther away. The bag and lantern hoisted over his shoulder gives the impression he's not returning for a while. I can't blame him for leaving, but I don't want him to be alone either. I run to him.

"Hey. Wait!" I catch him and put my hand on his shoulder.

He spins and hits my jaw with his fist. Blood fills my cheek. I spit it into the grass and respond with a plea.

"Don't leave."

"Why? So I can die because of you too?!"

I deserve that.

"It's not for me. It's for Emma."

"I…I can't stay. I can't be here. They're gone and…"

He's not wrong for wanting to run away. If she weren't there, I'd do the same.

Turning, he walks away from me, headed for the hills. A few minutes pass and I return to digging.

It's well into the day before I finish burying Ami and then Agatha. The fresh dirt mounds are too bare. Bringing the attendant out, I have it create roses to lay across the graves. I choke on a lump in my throat as I cover them with bouquets. Sitting in the yard, I pick at the grass.

Emma startles me from behind with a hug.

"I don't know what to say," I tell her.

She clutches me tightly. "Whatever comes to your mind will be the right thing."

I do my best to honor them.

"Agatha: you weren't my mother, and yet you treated me like I was your son. You cared for me, you loved me, and you encouraged me. I don't know how we're going to go on without your guiding light. I am in your debt and I'll never be able to repay it. But I will try, in your memory, to be better."

"Eve: you were a thorn in our sides, but we wouldn't have wanted it any other way. We started out rough, but in the end we were great friends, weren't we? We grew close and we had each other's backs. I wasn't in love with you, but that doesn't mean I didn't love you. You understood me, my true nature, in ways that no one else could."

"Ami…I'd do anything to bring you back. I would give anything for you to be alive right now, even my own life. I wanted nothing more than to help you and Mother break the curse so you could live normal lives. You were the reason I strived to be a better person, to help people. You were my inspiration. You were the love of my life."

A long silence falls and she tugs on my arm. We force fake half-smiles and I know she approves of my words.

"Where's James?" she asks.

"Gone…" I pause to breathe and fight back tears. "And to be honest, I want to do the same, but you're still here."

"Please, don't ever leave me." She buries her face in my arm.

"I…" I struggle to tell her I need to be imprisoned for the safety of others, but the words elude me. Not yet. I change the subject.

"I wish he'd have stayed to at least see them laid to rest."

I look to the crashed migration ship smoldering in the distance. It tore New Asta from the sky, and ripped a chunk of the mountain away, now resting on the slant of the mountain. Even after my war with Drake has finally ended, the casualties keep coming.

Emma leads me inside, and we collapse on the couch. She curls into me and I wrap my arm around her.

Misery calls to me. The souls dead in their despair weep and gnash, trying to tear me from the living world for my transgressions. They're angry that I have confined them to the prison inside me once more. They hate me. I punish myself and let them take me.

They're brutal in their attacks, even Agatha. It hurts, but it's worse from her because of who she is to me. Millions of voices torture me with the knowledge that they exist in this state because of my misguided actions. Hands grab and pull me to the point that it feels like my soul is being torn into ribbons.

~~~~~~

"Destroy it!"

Amongst the millions of accusations, one voice stands out. Turning in circles, I'm beaten by those who want to be released back into the world.

"Destroy it!" It comes again, as a whisper in my ear.

"Who's there?" I reply.

"Destroy it!" A dark figure appears, cutting through the multitude to get to me.

"What?!"

"The house!" it pleads as it comes closer, reaching out a dark arm.

"Why?"

"You must destroy the house!" It's insistent, and it reaches to grab me.

Turning to run does no good. The endless hands grasping me keep me in place. I'm grabbed by the shoulder and spun. It's Evalyn.

"Rain, wake up!" she instructs me, and distant light appears as my exit from this world. *"You need to get out now! I can't hold them back anymore!"*

"You can't hold them back...anymore? What do you mean?"

The souls become more violent, seeking to rend my soul from my body and make me a permanent addition so they can escape. Grasping harder, they try to tear me into pieces. I shove them away and run. Evalyn clings to me, attaching her soul to mine as I carry us into the light. She helps me push through, shoving souls out of the way. At the threshold, we return to the world.

When I snap awake from *their* existence, she's standing in the living room. I wiggle free of Emma, who has passed out. In my excitement to see Evalyn, I stretch out my arms to hug her, forgetting for a brief moment she has no physical form. I drop my arms, but she reaches for me anyway.

"You can't feel this, but I can," she says, touching my hand.

"I'm sorry." She's the only one left to apologize to. *"I tried to save them."*

"I know, dear. It's okay though."

"How is it okay?" I whisper harshly, trying not to disturb Emma.

"Come," she beckons, and heads for the stairs.

Following, I look back to make sure she's still asleep, and then creep up the stairs. She leads me to her room and disappears through the door. Inside, she's waiting. She motions for me to close the door.

"What are you doing?" I ask while doing as instructed.

"We have a chance." She smiles broadly.

"Is this a joke?" I become angry.

"Shut up," she snaps, suddenly irritated. "We have an opportunity to change things."

"What do you mean?" My eyes sting with the onset of tears.

"We can fix this so none of them are dead. They won't have died in the first place."

"My heart hurts already without you putting strange thoughts into my head."

"Inside of you I sensed...there is something different in you that wasn't there before. It's a good thing though."

"Stop being cryptic."

"*You* are out of sync with time. Or rather, your soul is out of sync with time. My experience being tethered to a temporal anomaly led me to find that you are too. A new one, created by the blue and orange vortexes," she states excitedly. "I think you can undo what's happened. All of it!"

I'm not sure if I should believe her or not. Tampering with time is what caused this chain of events in the first place. Should I indulge her? Is there a chance?

"How?"

"Our anomaly exists because I exist, and I'm tethered to the house. If you destroy it I won't just unhinge, but it will destroy me *and* the temporal anomaly." She uses her hands to make an explosion gesture.

"How do you know?"

"I told you. When I didn't disappear, I knew the blue vortex would appear again. I wanted to be ready, and I researched. Played with different artifacts. Experimented with their destruction.

"If you destroy the house the blue vortex will try to cease to exist now and everywhere it's ever existed. But it can't, because nothing will have changed yet. I believe we'll reset to the moments our fates were intertwined with time traveling!"

I fail to understand how this is helpful. "But then you time travel, you die, and bind yourself to the house. Everything happens again."

"You're not listening. You are a new anomaly. Out of sync, you can be the event in which there's no origin!" She puts her hands on her hips. "Everything will reset, but I'm positive your soul and memories will stay intact."

"What if you're wrong? We've tampered with time too much already."

"What if I'm right? Isn't it our responsibility to try?"

The answer is yes. To save them all, the answer is definitely yes.

"How do I fix it?"

"You know how."

I do. I just needed confirmation, I guess.

I nod.

"I'll gladly die so they can live."

"With your death, everything will change. All you have to do is not let them take you in."

The thought of not being with Ami hurts me as much as her death, but it's the better alternative.

"What happens to Eve? Her time is a direct result of my actions. Will she exist?"

"I wish I knew. I'd like to think we're all destined to be born at some point, regardless of conditions, but that's probably a childish notion." She shakes her head.

I'm ready to go forward with her plan. The look on her face is almost giddy, and I'm not sure how she's managed to be in a mood other than distraught or depressed.

"Emma isn't going to like this."

She nods at me and I turn to leave, but when I grab the doorknob I hear a pattering of feet out in the hallway. Pulling it open, I see Emma trying to sneak away. I wave her back, and she returns with her head down.

"Rain?" She looks at me in fear. "I don't want to not know you."

Holding my arms out, Emma steps into my hug. I pull her in tightly.

"We have two choices. It's this, or I have Quva create a prison to hold me until the end of time. I'm sorry, but I'm too dangerous for us to stay together."

I let her go.

"How do we do it?"

"The house must be completely destroyed," Evalyn replies. "You might even be able to do it with your shockwaves."

Taking Emma's hand, I lead her out and downstairs.

"I won't remember you?" she asks.

"You'll never have even known me. But I'll hope for your sake there's an afterlife other than Misery, so I can find a way to keep Denis away from you."

She laughs, but her eyes are watering.

"I love you, brother."

I lean in and kiss her forehead.

"Head as far away from the house as possible, in case it doesn't work as planned. I don't want you hurt."

At the door in the living room, she's reluctant to step outside. I nudge her. She's slow to exit and walk out into the yard.

Turning back a few feet away, her once bright eyes are sunken and dull. I want her innocence back, for her sake.

I wave her on and she moves farther away, past the boundary.

"So..." I turn to Evalyn.

"So, indeed," she replies.

"*Will you stay with me until the end?*" My chest tightens.

"As long as *you* stay with me."

"*Quva and I planted a device in the basement to counter the vortex. The plan probably won't work if it's still active. I need to be down there to destroy it and the house at the same time.*"

She nods. Before we head to the basement, I return to my room to pick up the Vraditi crystal necklace hung on the wall, given to me by the tribal boy.

Without my sword to augment my ability, this is the next best thing.

In the basement's storage area, I look at where I know the device sits, invisible to the naked eye.

Moving to it, I hesitate when reaching out to touch it, expecting an energy field to deflect me. Instead, it reacts with my suit and becomes visible. I sit and cross my legs, staring at the device.

I put my hand on it with the crystal trapped between my palm and the metal. I hesitate.

"Rain, there's hope for me. If I can change in this timeline, I can change in another. It will take someone as stubborn and thick-headed as you to start it, but I can be better," she reassures me. "Despite the outcome, you've tried hard to help Ami and Agatha, and I appreciate that you made them happy."

I nod and close my eyes. Concentrating, I build energy. My alkos begins to cover every inch of my body. My extremities tingle like they've all fallen asleep. The power engulfs me. Giving my whole self, it threatens to overwhelm me. I make every effort to center the energy, but I'm on the advent of seizing. I keep pushing and exhaust the power from every inch of myself. It's there, all of it. In a single moment I expel everything. The shockwave is pushed through my arm, into my hand, then the crystal pressed against the machine.

The explosion is unreal. There's no feeling for a few moments. I can neither see nor hear. But I'm still alive. When sensation returns I feel heat. I don't know if it's fire or the sun overhead.

Vision and hearing return, and I'm lying face up on something hard.

Debris rains on me, but I'm pinned, impaled by a large piece of metal shrapnel. I go to reach for it, but my arm is gone. It doesn't hurt though.

High in the sky, I spot the blue vortex swirling above me. The air around the perimeter starts picking up small debris. It increases in velocity. It changes from its normal pattern. It spins harder and more violently than I've ever seen. It bubbles and bows.

The sound of the wind can't drown out Emma's scream of terror, and Evalyn's cry of agony. Evalyn's form begins to dissipate, and her eyes become empty. It's unnerving. Deep down I question whether she was right about it all – about the reset. Her form is ripped into ribbons, and she's torn apart by the tornado raging on top of us.

The glue which held our family together is dissolving. Memories which won't be remembered, because they won't have happened. Except by me. And I'm going to die.

Wood, metal, and even concrete are lifted. As the pieces pass the outer wall of the storm, they vanish. They cease to exist. The chunk of shrapnel pinning me pulls free, and so am I.

As the air current lifts me, I see Emma struggling to hold onto the well, but it too breaks apart. She's pulled beyond the blue, and is gone. Vanished into time.

It's just me now.

As I spin through the air, I embrace this fate, this moment as the time of my redemption. I will reset, and refuse Ami's help in order to stop these dark times ever happening. I enter the violent whirlwind, the beautiful marble blue of the vortex. Out of control, the world fades around me. My heart aches as everything I've come to know and love is gone. My body fades, dissipating like Evalyn.

A strange sensation overtakes me as my spirit is hurled through time. I'm moving, and yet there's no wind or sound. There's a snap from my soul, like a tether breaking, and time is undone. Pressure expands all around, and when I reenter reality, horror hits me like a wave.

I'm in the forest before it was the Forest of Hunger. There are trees and an open field in front of me. I look down.

Drake's dagger is being pulled from my abdomen. My pale hands are on the wound, and they're turning crimson. I'm stabbed and soon to die. Looking over my shoulder, he is there behind me, grinning malevolently.

I chuckle.

It couldn't have been a moment sooner? I guess this is how it has to be.

Evalyn's idea was right, my soul has been sent back from the now unrealized timeline.

As Drake turns his back on me and leaves, I'm relieved. The peace of this place is nice. I stumble forward.

The pain is sharp, and I collapse. Hands and knees hit the dirt, and I cough up blood. I don't have the strength to hold myself up. Turning onto my side I remember this moment, watching my blood flowing onto the forest floor. Death is coming for me.

But the ground is my comforter, congratulating me on a job well done. Tears fill my eyes because I'm happy. A familiar noise calls my attention. The dirt becomes mud as a heavy rain starts falling. It feels good washing over me. It's washing me away, pushing me to just let go. There's no agony anymore, and there's no Misery here.

Another familiar sound reminds me my job is not yet done – the beautiful blue vortex is bringing the house to the field.

A door opens. A girl's scream cuts the air.

When I strain to see *her*, a smile crosses my lips. She's alive. It's Ami. *My Ami*. But as much as I want to feel her gentle hands on me, as much as I want Evalyn to heal me and Agatha to nurse me, I must finish this. It can't be allowed to start again.

The two of them run toward me, but I refuse to let them reach me.

As I lie dying, it hurts deeply when I yell out. "Get away Ami! Go! You shouldn't be here!"

Ami hesitates and looks at me bewildered. An unexpected result of my meddling happens: she, Agatha, and the house vanish. As if they were never there. In the blink of an eye they're gone, no longer existing in this time.

I'm confused, but I hope wherever they are, they're better off without ever having known me. I weep openly in happiness and sadness at once.

Now, finally, death has come. My life, like my final mission, is complete. Blood flows freely from my wound, and with it all of the events that didn't and now won't happen. All of the death and destruction undone.

I close my eyes and embrace my death, the death a very long time coming.

I know who I am, who I'm not, and who I could've been.

I know what the world is, what it's not, and what it may have been.

I know what did, what did not, and what would have happened.

I'm satisfied. This is what's right.

Everything is heavy. My breaths are shallow. Weariness overtakes me. It's time to let go.

My journey is over, and the heavy *rain* is washing me away.

~~~~~~

EPILOGUE: ELATION

I admire my work, and plant my hand shovel in the dirt. A whole new row of strawberry plants will now start to thrive in Mother's garden.

The sun is out in full force today. I'm parched to the point that I can't take another minute of the heat without something cool to drink.

I wish I'd planned ahead and brought a pitcher of juice out. But it would have gotten warm anyway. Or watered down with ice. Yuck.

I sigh and stand up. After I dust my overalls off, I toss my gloves next to the shovel. My drenched sleeve is no help for wiping the sweat from my forehead. On my way to the kitchen, I dream of a more exciting life.

One of these days I'm going to leave Chas. Maybe I'll travel the world. I've never been to the ocean. That will be my first stop.

I hate doing the yard work alone, but Auntie Evalyn has been insufferable lately, ranting about how 'something isn't right' and 'it should be time'. Whatever that means.

She's so weird – the complete opposite of Mother, despite being twins.

Cool air hits my face when I enter the kitchen, and it's refreshing. I barely have the door shut, and there's a knock. I feel unsettled, like they snuck up on me while I was coming inside.

I wasn't expecting anyone. Who is it?

I peek out the window and there's a handsome young man smiling at me. His hair is chocolate brown, trimmed and spiked. He's assertive, staring with his green eyes right into mine.

My cheeks flush.

Clean-shaven, and carrying himself professionally, he almost seems like a business man from the deep city. But he is dressed in plain clothes, and has a brown satchel hanging at his side. He's almost familiar, but I can't place where I'd know him from.

I crack the door open a few inches and put my foot behind it, remembering that Chas isn't the safest. Raised to be smart about people, good looking or not, I make sure my feet are planted and my shoulder is pressed hard into the wood.

"Yes? Can I help you?" I ask, keeping my tone steady.

"I've come to visit old friends, and wondered if they might be around." His voice is smooth, the tone disarming.

He looks and sounds like what I imagine one of the men of my romance novels would! He's so...

"I'm sorry but my parents aren't home right now. You'll have to come back later."

Idiot! You basically just told him you're alone!

"Who said I'm here to see your parents, Ami?" He grins.

"How...do you know my name?" My heart skips a beat. "What do you want?"

"It's a long story. May I come in and talk?"

"I'm sorry, you need to leave." My pulse increases.

"Ami..." He's soothing. "You don't remember me yet, but you will."

I can't help it. My life is boring, and yes, I'm intrigued. I want to know. But I'm not going to throw caution to the wind and let him in.

I'm not here alone! I'll get Auntie. She needs to come out sometime today anyway.

"Can you wait here a moment?" I ask him, and push the door closed, flipping the latch to lock it.

"Sure," he replies from behind the glass.

There's no attempt to stop me from locking him out, no move to break in. I back away, watching for any sudden movements. He's in my sight all the way to the swinging door.

When he turns away I bolt up the stairs, taking them two at a time. My feet thump against the wood as I run for Auntie Evalyn's room. With the light off, I barrel down the dark hall and nearly trip myself.

Auntie! Stop turning off the light! I'm going to break my neck one of these days!

At the end of the hall I bang on her door.

"Auntie, there's someone at the door!" I'm a little scared, and my voice is giving it away.

"Answer it then! Why are you bothering me?"

"I'm a little freaked out right now: it's a man who says he's here to visit old friends. He knows my name!" I bang a few more times. "He's really suspicious!" *And good looking!*

Auntie's door swings open abruptly. It slams into the wall, and her eyes are wide. Despite looking disheveled, she still somehow manages to make sweatpants and a tank top look good.

"Who is he? Did you ask his name?" she asks hastily.

"No, I…" I start to respond but she shoves past me before I finish.

Auntie races down the stairs faster than I came up. Though I'm following her, she's reached the kitchen long before me. She's already let the man in, and greeted him without hesitation, speaking in excited tones.

Thanks, Auntie. So much for discretion, and strength in numbers.

At the bottom of the stairs, I can hear them through the walls, but not what they're saying. Near the door, their voices become clear.

"You're late!" she accuses him.

"How long since the last time?"

"Ten years."

"Then I'm right on time." He's grinning, I can hear it in his voice.

"You're insufferable!" A slapping sound resounds. Knowing how feisty she is, it was she who hit him, and not the other way around.

"I know. But you know why I didn't stay. Why I couldn't," he replies.

Ten years? He's close to my age. He would have been what, twelve? Why would she call him insufferable for leaving?

"Hold on, I'll grab Ami," Auntie says quickly.

I have little time. Jumping back, I try to make myself semi-presentable by tugging the hair tie from my ponytail. Brushing my hair with my fingers a few times, and wiping any remaining dirt off my face is the best I can do.

Auntie pops into the living room, waiving her hand like a maniac to get me to follow her. She holds the door open for me, and he is there, sitting at the head of the table.

Auntie puts her hands on my shoulders, and pushes me toward the table. I sit two chairs away. She leaves me there, with him, to get the pitcher of juice I originally came in for. Bringing it and three glasses, she pours some for all of us. I do what I can to avoid eye contact with him, but every time I look, he's smiling at me.

What's their secret? Are they going to make me wait for some grand revelation?

"So…you're friends with my Auntie," I say, making conversation while taking a sip from my glass.

"I am," he replies. His knowing grin tests my patience.

"And you say you know me."

"I do." He picks up his glass and drinks.

"Where from?" I squint and purse my lips at him.

"You wouldn't believe me if I told you."

"Why wouldn't I?"

"Well, I've been here several times over a few decades. The last time was ten years ago, like Evalyn said."

A few decades? How old is he?

"I was nine then. Is that why you seem familiar?" I put my glass down and run my finger over the rim.

"Probably. At least for this timeline."

He's crazy like Auntie. He has to be.

Having told me just a few minutes ago he wanted to tell me how he knows me, I'm aggravated that now he's being coy. And yet, he still has my interest.

"What is your name? Maybe I'll remember you if I actually knew who I was talking to," I say trying to get more out of him.

"Rain."

"Rain? Why'd your parents name you that?"

"My parents didn't. My birth name was Tiberius."

"No wonder you changed it. It sounds like a name for a grandpa."

"I didn't change it. You did." His grin widens, and I feel like I'm playing cat and mouse.

"I'm sorry, I think you have the wrong girl."

He looks at Auntie, and she smirks at him. He lifts his hand and waves for me to lean over the table.

Should I?

Almost as if I anticipate hearing an amazing secret, my body responds before I think it through. I lean over.

I'm glad I'm wearing a regular shirt instead of a tank top. Otherwise I'd be giving him a show.

He puts a purple, polished, gem on the table. It glows, and he motions for me to take it. It's pretty, and not like any other stone I've ever seen.

What is he doing?

I reach for it. My hand touches it, and I feel tingly all over.

"You're gonna get slapped," Auntie tells him with a smug look on her face.

"Yep," he replies, grinning.

"Why is he about to…?"

He leans forward, grabs my hand with the gem, and presses his lips to mine.

I'm shocked both at the kiss, and the strange sensation overwhelming me. My mind is flooded with images, thoughts, places, people, and strange creatures; things that are bizarre to me, things I never thought imaginable.

They are images of me and Mother: this house, finding him in the woods almost dead, nursing him back to health. There is so much information it hurts.

I pull away and strike his cheek as hard as I can. The slap echoes off the walls and he yelps. Slipping back to his chair, he nurses the red handprint.

"I told you," Auntie gloats.

"Yep." He's still smiling. "The crystal and her power will complete the process."

My what…?

We're not touching anymore, but the images continue. Memories unfold, things that never happened, and finally it hits me. All at once, I know who he is. All of my other self's memories are there, including the greatest one: that I love him.

Rain! My Rain! I named him that because I found him in the rain as he was dying! I helped save his life! We had adventures, and I fell in love with him! I gave my life to save him…

"Rain? Rain?!" I'm elated. "How?!"

I leap from my chair and jump into his lap. Leaning in, I kiss him deeply, and he matches me. As our lips and tongues intertwine, it occurs to me how strange it is having been totally oblivious.

How am I alive? What did he do?

The love I had for him in another time, in another place, swells through my heart and mind. I can't understand how I didn't know he was missing.

It dawns on me: I hit him. A man who I didn't think I knew, yet the one person who I wanted most to be with when I died in my other life. In an alternate timeline.

"Oh, Rain! I'm sorry I hit you!" I laugh and caress his cheek. "Are you okay?"

"I am now." He smiles and gazes lovingly at me.

"How is this possible?"

"Does it matter how?" he says, grinning.

"It does! But it doesn't because we're together!" I proclaim.

He laughs. I remember how much I loved his laugh, his gentle chuckle. I laugh with him. My heart is beating so hard it feels like it'll jump out of my chest. I examine him closely before I kiss him again.

My Rain is home.

"I love you so much, Rain."

"I love you too, Ami. You have no idea how much my heart has ached for you."

"Is that why you came before? To see me?"

"The first time was to meet Evalyn – I nearly gave her a heart attack when I snuck up on her rifling through the artifacts at the castle. I convinced her to not use her power...too much." He reaches over and pats Auntie's hand.

"That was before I was born. Wait...you didn't get into a relationship with my Auntie, did you?" I protest.

"No!" he laughs, turning red.

"I tried, but he wouldn't have it. He said his heart belonged to someone in the future," Auntie replies.

I make a disgusted face at her.

"It took him a while to convince me what was going to happen. He stalked me through time, and then we adventured a bit."

"How is any of this possible?"

"It's quite the story, but suffice to say Evalyn and I – the other Evalyn that is – reset the timeline. I had to fix my mistakes."

"How did you survive, though?" I frantically pull up his shirt as if he were dying now. The scar where Drake stabbed him is there. "What about Emma and Eve? And the Vraditi?"

"We have plenty of time to talk about all of that."

"What do you mean? Did you go find them?" I feel a twinge of sadness, longing to see the women I regarded as sisters in the alternate timeline.

"I'll tell you after we run away together: we can go wherever you want."

"Really? As long as it's just you and me!" I exclaim and glare at Auntie. "And *no* time traveling!"

"Only you and me, I promise. And no time traveling. The only thing I want is right here, right now," He says, squeezing my hand.

"But, what will I tell Mother?"

"Why tell her anything? Your alkos is active now. You can share your memories with her, and she'll understand."

"You're right! I'm going to go get ready!"

Just us. It will be weird, but nice. We can finally be together and have a life!

I leap up and head toward the living room door. Looking back at him, he's there, real and alive.

And he came for me.

I'm ready to start our new adventure, together.

Our love is timeless.

~~~~~~

~~~~~~~~~~End~~~~~~~~~~

ABOUT THE AUTHOR

Thomas W. Everson loves spending time with his wife, Brandi, whom he adores, and their amazing son, Thomas (Bubby). They indulge in the fantastic and stretch their imaginations with books, shows, movies, LEGOs, and video games. Thomas is inspired by much, and loves to test the boundaries of fiction.

Like what you read? A review on Amazon would be appreciated!